LAHAINA NOON

MODERN LEGENDS OF DRAGONS & SHADOWS
BOOK ONE

TRISTA RICKETTS

Warning: *Here there be Dragons!*

Join forces with the Dragons and Wielders!

T HE MODERN LEGENDS ARE all about the ongoing battle for ancient magical creatures working to defeat their enemies while facing the challenges of modern society mixed in with the whims of a few old Gods along the way. If you love Vaughn and Bridget's story and want to see what happens with the rest of the clan, then sign up for my newsletter! You'll be the first to know about the launch of the next books in the series, get sneak peeks at other series coming out, deleted scenes, short stories, and more.

Sign up for my newsletter at
www.tristaricketts.com

Want to send me your feedback? You can do that through my site as well. Just beware, the snark dragon sometimes visits my house so if you snark me, it may just snark back.

Acknowledgments

That's my story and I'm sticking to it!

Actually, the following pages contain the story, but it's sentimental to me because it's a lifelong dream finally come to fruition. There are a few people that helped me make this a reality and they need to be thanked. In truth, they should be put on a pedestal and lauded as heroes, alas, they might be afraid of heights.

So, if you have read this far, perhaps you'll be kind enough to read the rest of this page so you too can know the amazing folks that are so dear to me and helped me get this far.

My darling husband who supported this crazy idea of mine and encouraged me to pursue my dreams. Who listened to me giggling to myself at one in the morning about snarky dialogue I was writing. Who let me read the book to him and gave me inspiration, often without realizing it. Thank you, Joel, you are my mate.

My two best friends who were my biggest cheerleaders, editors, and were not afraid to tell me if something I said was stupid. Jana Mabry and Laurie Black, you two are the best bitches anyone could ask for. Thank you for being there for me, for your love and support, and for inspiring your character.

Lastly, to my mother Karen, the best mother in the world who has always been there for me no matter what. No matter how crazy and out there I got, she always pushed me towards my dreams. I love you, and I hope you're proud of me.

Contents

1. Chapter 1 — 1

2. Chapter 2 — 6

3. Chapter 3 — 13

4. Chapter 4 — 18

5. Chapter 5 — 28

6. Chapter 6 — 37

7. Chapter 7 — 45

8. Chapter 8 — 54

9. Chapter 9 — 58

10. Chapter 10 — 66

11. Chapter 11 — 75

12. Chapter 12 — 86

13. Chapter 13 — 92

14. Chapter 14 — 101

15. Chapter 15 — 109

16. Chapter 16 — 116

17. Chapter 17   123

18. Chapter 18   130

19. Chapter 19   137

20. Chapter 20   144

21. Chapter 21   154

22. Chapter 22   165

23. Chapter 23   173

24. Chapter 24   181

25. Chapter 25   189

26. Chapter 26   199

27. Chapter 27   207

28. Chapter 28   215

29. Chapter 29   223

30. Chapter 30   232

31. Chapter 31   236

32. Chapter 32   243

33. Chapter 33   252

34. Chapter 34   258

35. Chapter 35   268

36. Chapter 36   274

37. Chapter 37   284

38. Chapter 38   292

39. Chapter 39   301

40. Chapter 40   310

41. Chapter 41   321

42. Chapter 42   332

43. Chapter 43   341

44. Chapter 44   347

45. Chapter 45   358

46. Chapter 46   365

47. Chapter 47   373

48. Chapter 48   380

CHAPTER 1

SO THAT'S THE KIND of day it's going to be, Bridget thought. She stared at the two halves of her hairbrush, which, incredibly, had snapped while she was getting ready after her shower. The handle still in her hand while the other half lay in the sink staring at her accusingly, as if she'd done it on purpose.

"Guess it's going to be a ponytail kinda day," she muttered to her reflection in the steamy mirror. She glared at her bleary-eyed image; the dark circles under her normally bright green eyes were going to need some extra concealer today. Digging through the vanity drawer, she came up with a backup comb. She held it gingerly between her thumb and forefinger, suspicious about how it had become covered in a sticky substance.

"Gabriel!" she yelled. "Have you been using my comb again?"

Her son poked his head around the doorway, taking in his mother's thunderous expression, the comb, and the broken brush. He put on his best angelic face, widening his eyes, batting his eyelashes, and replied, "No, Mom, that was the cat!" He held up their cat Poe, who, while known for pilfering odd things around the house and drowning them in the toilet, was not necessarily known for using copious amounts of hair gel.

She sighed, tapping her toes on the cold tile floor. "Poe doesn't use hair gel. If you *insist* on using my things, at least have the courtesy to clean them up when you return them!" she said sternly, trying not to smile at him. He was pretty cute, with his innocent eyes and bright smile. She knew he was trying to style his hair after his favorite YouTuber of the month, thus the hair gel.

"Bruh," he said with a grin, "At least I put it back this time!" before dashing off to his room to watch more videos before going to school.

"That's *Mom* to you, *Bruh!*" she shouted half-heartedly after him, laughing because she knew he only did it to drive her nuts.

Washing the goop off the comb, she attacked her damp hair, trying to wrestle it into compliance. As she continued getting ready to face the day, she thought, m*aybe I should get a haircut.* Her deep coppery red hair fell just past her shoulders, and never wanted to stay in place; frizz, was her look, apparently. She loved the color of her hair; her late husband had always compared it to burnished pennies. It was the texture and its unmanageability that drove her crazy. *Something short and manageable like a bob or a pixie,* she thought.

Right, she rolled her eyes. Like she would manage that any better, she knew it would be cute for exactly as long as it took for her to walk out of the salon and have a few cute pictures taken. The minute it was up to her to maintain it, it would be out of control and make her look like an electrified alpaca. She checked in the mirror again, ensuring she had all the defiant strands in place.

"Mom, bruh!" shouted Gabriel, interrupting her reverie. "We gotta go! It's almost time for school to start, and Ms. Jenkins said I'm getting detention if I'm late again this month! I can't stay after today; there's a CW tournament tonight!"

Oh great, she groused, *another gamer tournament!* His online tournaments meant a lot of yelling, both joyous and angry if things didn't go the way he expected.

She'd given up asking him why he bothered to play if he was going to get that mad, because there was always a new and more inventive reason why this time would be different.

Oh well, at least he was using his creativity for good in the world and not just evil. His teachers praised his academic abilities but said he needed to be challenged more. She smiled; he was challenging, alright.

"*Mom!*" came the shout again.

"Okay, okay, I'm coming! Keep your pants on!" she called back, walking into the kitchen to grab her purse and keys.

"I can't help but keep them on," he replied with a cheeky grin, "You told me it wasn't appropriate to run around naked in public. I'm also not allowed to twerk in public anymore." he laughed, breaking into a booty shaking dance which was hilarious but also really embarrassing when he did it in the middle of the bread aisle.

"Get in the car you delinquent," she muttered, trying not to laugh at his antics as she locked the door behind them.

"So, Mom," Gabriel started innocently as they were backing out of the driveway. "Can we run to Starbucks for breakfast? You forgot to feed me." He batted his eyelashes at her again, doing his best pout. He knew the way to get her to cave in. He held up her phone and said,

"See, I've already put the order in. I even got you something! All you have to do is check out, drive through, grab it. Easy!" he grinned.

Ever suffering, she sighed, approved the order, and turned right towards Starbucks. She didn't even bother asking how he cracked her phone's password. She was sure she didn't want to know anyway. She made a mental note to change the password when she got to work.

This kid—, she loved him so much she would do just about anything for him, and he knew it. Fortunately, he didn't take advantage of it. At least not too much. It was just him and her against the world, and he was worth it.

She pulled up to the school, let him out and watched him walk away. He was already talking to his friends and being a typical teenager. She was going to enjoy these last few moments with him. He was about to get his driver's license. Afterwards, she was sure she wouldn't see him as much unless he needed gas money. She hoped her work bonus came through as promised; she wanted to use it to put down a payment on a car for him rather than dipping into her savings.

Today's schedule came rushing back into her mind. "Oh crap!" she shouted, remembering the meeting with her director at 10:00 a.m. She needed to finish up a few slides for the presentation of her proposal. The outcome of which would determine how good that bonus would be. She merged on the highway determined not to let today's crop of idiots bring down her day. The power of positivity would get her through this. No one was going to take away from it!

"Put the phone down and drive, you absolute moron!" she shouted at the person who came into her lane without looking. Okay, so no one *else* would bring down her—

"What are you doing? Signaling the mother ship? Why does no one know how to use their blinkers the *right* way." she grumbled. Fine, it really was going to be one of those days, after all.

CHAPTER 2

No time for a quick pep talk in the parking garage. Once again, the only spots were on the very top floor or in the creepy lowest level, or as Bridget liked to call it, the seventh circle of Hell. Given that it looked like it was going to be yet another scorching day in Texas, and she didn't relish burning the skin off the back of her legs when she got back in the car, she opted for the seventh circle.

Both locations were a way from the entrance to her building, and she needed to get moving if she wanted to be on time. The creepy dark corners where she was sure something lurked, waiting to grab her, were something else she wanted to avoid. Laughing at herself, Bridget thought, *at least I know where Gabe gets it.* Ponytail swishing as she jogged across the lot she made it to the stairs in record time.

For once, the elevator was open and waiting for her. *Yes! I might make it up to the ground level without breaking a sweat!* She leapt through the yawning doors that made her think the ancient elevator might be as sleepy as she was and spun around in triumph only to see something in the nearest shadow shift towards her. It seemed to elongate as if the sun had shifted by hours instead of seconds; the shadow stretched out like a bony finger pointing at her.

She gasped and jumped, the hairs on her arms and neck rising with her panic, frantically jabbing the 'G' for ground level and then the Door Close button. In her panic, she made the same mistake every well-intentioned person makes when trying to hold the door for someone. She punched the wrong button and hit 'Door Open' instead.

"Ugh!" she groaned at the panel as she glanced up to see the shadow was almost to the door. Fortunately, the elevator seemed to understand, and the doors creaked as they slowly trundled shut.

Shaken and breathing heavily, she leaned against the rear wall and grabbed the handrail. "Shit!" she yelled when it shocked her. *Not my day*, she shook her head.

She really needed to stop reading horror stories at bedtime. Surely, she just imagined it. *Shadows don't really reach out and grab people, right? I've got to cut back on horror movies, too.*

"Miss?"

She looked up and saw the valet standing at the door, holding it open for her. "Sorry." She smiled at him, "Lost in thought today."

He smiled back at her and replied, "It happens."

Just today? She questioned herself as, apparently, she was losing it. Shadows chasing her! Shaking it off as her overactive imagination, Bridget made her way into the building and up to her suite.

"Good morning, team!" Bridget called as she walked in. She made it a personal mission to greet each staff member every morning, making sure she 'saw' them. She had a good rapport with the team and knew if she missed anyone, they wouldn't let her hear the end of it. She stuffed down her anxiety about what had happened and put on her office smile; it was just another day.

Finally. Some peace. Bridget could whip out those last few slides and be ready for the presentation in a couple of hours. As she powered on her laptop, she received another painful shock on her fingertips.

"Ow, crap!" she said under her breath, mindful of staff near her office. *Again?* She thought, remembering the elevator. Images of the shadows were creeping into her mind, chills raising bumps on her arms at the way the pointing finger nearly crept into the elevator with her, when she heard a light tap on the door frame.

"Problems?" inquired a velvety voice. She looked up and froze, suddenly conscious of how washed out she probably looked. Her hands flew involuntarily to her hair, patting down the stray strands and trying to corral the ponytail frizz into a smooth column. She straightened in her chair, pulling her shoulders back and putting on a bright smile, hoping she'd remembered to put mascara on both eyes this morning.

There are good-looking guys, and then there's Vaughn Drake. He's the guy you would expect to model for the covers of romance novels, with his shirt ripped open and his hair falling in his face. The kind that had rock-hard abs, piercing sexy eyes, and bulging muscles. Vaughn was indeed a gorgeous man although he was seemingly unaware and humble about it.

Tall, well-built and muscular, perfectly groomed, with long shiny black hair, gorgeous crystal blue eyes, and a voice that oozed masculinity. He had full lips made for kissing and a perfectly straight nose. It really wasn't fair. She wanted to bite that chiseled jaw of his. He made her keenly aware of her appearance, and the past six months they'd been working together had stressed to her how heartachingly single she was.

Checking her chin for drool, she watched him adjust his glasses, good grief, even those were sexy, and tried to gather herself into something less gaping idiot and more smooth professional.

"Uh," she replied intelligently. *PULL YOURSELF TOGETHER,* she shouted at herself, "Yeah, sorry, just seem to be getting zapped by static electricity today." She managed to get the words out while wondering how red her rapidly blushing face was getting. "Guess it's just my electrifying personality," she followed up.

Oh my god, you did NOT just say that out loud, you idiot, she thought furiously and, if it was even possible, blushed harder.

He smiled broadly, showing perfect teeth, and gave a little laugh. "I'm sure that's what it was."

She decided he was just humoring her because he needed her company for a joint venture. "You here for the meeting?" she asked, knowing full well he was. What on earth was wrong with her? She was a smart, educated woman in a position of leadership, a single mom with a kick-ass kid, plus a wicked sense of humor, and here she was, acting like a moron in front of Mr. Hotness.

"Mr. who?" he asked, looking confused.

Oh, dear no, please tell me I didn't say that out loud, she thought frantically. "It's going to be a hot one today, Mr. Drake." *Get it together, girl.* "Are you only here for our meeting, or did you want to take me to lunch as well?"

What? What? What had just happened? Had she really just asked him out? What was the meaning of it all? Why was the world ending, because obviously that's what was happening. She was melting into the carpet. Right here in the middle of downtown, Dallas, Texas, in the United States of America.

She might as well have been in the Land of Oz because she was pretty sure that she was turning green like the Wicked Witch. She might be sick. Could she get past him to the bathroom to throw up without making a further fool of herself? Bridget took a tentative step to the doorway when he replied.

"Well, both, actually, if you're available."

"Yeah, no," she said dumbly. *Did he say both?*

He laughed. "Well, which is it? Yes, or no?"

Bridget took a deep breath and looked him in the eye. "Oh, I was kidding. Do you actually want to go to lunch? I'm sure we can get some of the other team members to agree on a place to go and hopefully celebrate a successful partnership," she managed to squeak.

He studied her for a moment then replied slowly, "No, Ms. Ridgeway, I don't want to go with the others, only you."

That's it, I'm asleep! She thought triumphantly. *This is obviously just a dream. First the shadows, now Vaughn asking me out. I didn't really wake up yet. No, this is a prank! Someone put him up to this!*

"Ha, ha!" she said, hitting him lightly on the shoulder. "Good one, who put you up to this? Was it Jack? He's such a joker!"

He stepped closer, "It's not a joke, Bridget. I'd planned on asking you anyway, but you beat me to it. There's something I'd like to discuss with you. Something," he paused, "Personal."

He leaned into her ear, his breath warm on her skin, and whispered, "Besides, I don't want to share you with anyone else." He winked and lightly caressed her ponytail before strolling off to the conference room.

Bridget stood there, staring at his perfect behind in his navy blue slacks and tried to remember where she was.

"Okay, was it just me, or did you and Mr. Hotness have an *intimate* conversation?" her best friend Jorrie hissed in her ear.

"Jorrie!" Bridget gasped and grabbed her friend by the shoulders, dragged her into the office before shutting the door. She was fortunate to have Jorrie in her life and even more blessed to be working in the same office. Jorrie's curly blonde hair bounced and jiggled on her shoulders as she stumbled into the room and plopped into the guest chair.

Jorrie watched her friend with her warm brown eyes and started to smile. "Someone has the hots for Mr. Hotness!" she laughed in a sing-song voice. "I saw you two talking; it looked like he was saying something that had you worked up. I could feel the heat from your blush all the way down the hall! What did you..."

She studied her friend's face. "Oh no, you didn't say one of your dorky puns, did you?" she gasped in mock horror. "Please tell me you didn't! Girl! How many times?" She draped her hand over her eyes leaning back in exasperation. Today, her perfectly manicured nails were a bright purple with gold glitter that Bridget wished she could pull off.

Bridget dropped her head in her hands. "I don't know!" she wailed. "Why am I like this? I keep shocking myself, and he heard me complaining about it, and I said, I said."

"Bridge! Please tell me you didn't say something about your 'electric personality'?"

Bridget kept her head down; Jorrie knew her too well. "I did," she confessed, mortified.

Jorrie shook her head, "Well, what did he say?"

She squinted at her, "Actually, he laughed and then asked me to lunch after our meeting."

"*What*?" squealed Jorrie.

"Shh!" Bridget said fiercely. "Don't get the busybodies nosing into our business. You know, even the slightest hint of something juicy, and they start poking their heads over their cubicles like meerkats! I'm surprised they aren't already lurking outside." She peered out the window by her door.

Jorrie leaned in, lowering her voice, "Start from the beginning, what did he say, what did you say? Bridge, I need all the tea right now, ma'am. You've only been drooling after that man for the last six months."

Bridget leaned back in her chair and shared most of the conversation with Jorrie, leaving out the incidents with the shadows. She didn't need anyone knowing she was *that* crazy.

Chapter 3

Bridget nervously wiped her palms on her skirt. She'd somehow managed to finish up her presentation in time and needed to go to the conference room to set up. But *he* was in there, so of course, she was dawdling and finding reasons not to leave the safety of her office. She didn't have a clue how she was going to get through this presentation with him in the room, knowing he would be looking at her, listening to her. "Reason 8,335 why I can't have nice things," she mumbled, "I don't know how to adult."

"Talking to ourselves again, are we?" she heard an oily hiss.

It was what she imagined Cinderella's evil stepsisters would sound like. No mistaking that voice. It was her arch nemesis, the bane of her existence, and the person who was about to make or break her year. Her Director, Melissa Payne.

No joke, that was really her name. She really lived up to it, too, making sure to take every opportunity to make people's lives miserable. Everyone who worked with her wondered how she'd ever made it into management in the first place, considering how disagreeable she was.

Realizing she was waiting for an answer, Bridget smiled at her boss. "Just running through my list of everything for the presentation, making sure I'm prepared. You know me, super organized!"

She received a stony stare for an answer before Payne in the Butt walked off without another word, heading towards the conference room.

Bridget sighed. *Great.* One more reason to not want to go in there, although it would surely be held against her for not already being set up. *No-win situation here! At least Jack will be—*

"EEEKK!" she screamed as she was picked up from behind and swung around. "Put me down, you crazy fiend!" she shrieked as Jack burst out laughing. She heard giggling from her team and hoped Payne didn't hear it; she would come to destroy the cheerful mood.

"Saw Major Payne come in here and thought you'd need a confidence boost before facing the beast," her brother-in-law said.

She chuckled. "Don't let her hear you call her that; neither of us will ever hear the end of it."

Jack was one of her favorite people on the planet. He was responsible for her being part of the project. More importantly, since the death of his brother, her husband, eight years earlier, he had been the one to pull her from the abyss and get her on her feet again.

"My beautiful Bridget, love of my life and reason for my existence, why won't you just give in and run away with me?" His baby blue eyes widened dramatically, and he raked a neatly manicured hand through his immaculate golden hair without disturbing a single strand. Jerk, no one should be allowed to be that put together. Not a wrinkle on his shirt or his face.

She sighed lovingly and patted his cheek, "I would, Jack, but Darren, you remember your fiancé, right? He might not agree with that."

Jack laughed again, a genuine honest-to-goodness twinkle in his eyes. "I hear tell you had a run-in with Hotness earlier," he said in a singsong voice.

"I'm gonna kill Jorrie!" Bridget replied with mock fierceness. She never kept anything from Jack.

He smirked and spread his hands out in an innocent pose. "So, are you going out with him? You better, the way you two have been circling each other these last few months, it's about time! I have to say, that is one delicious piece of man!" He sighed, a lusty sound.

"That's your boss!" she reminded him.

He laughed. "If I wasn't solidly in love with Darren or if I didn't believe he only had eyes for one particular redhead, I would go after him myself. Alas, I'll just have to live vicariously through you. But first!" He held a hand over her mouth as she tried to protest, and his face took on a serious expression. "*You* have to get in there and deliver a stellar presentation. You know Major Payne is going to pick you apart and be a pain in your ass like always, but I heard she's really got a bug up her butt about this particular project. I don't know why, my sources weren't able to ferret out the actual reason, but she really seems to be gunning for you on this. I wasn't going to tell you at first, but I want you to be prepared."

She stared at him for a moment and whispered, "Thank you Jack, I love you. I'm going to go in there and kill it!"

Jack smiled again, although it didn't quite reach his eyes. "That's my girl. Go show them why you came with a warning label." He pulled her ponytail in an affectionate tug like he had since the day they met.

The gesture warmed her heart and her face as she remembered Vaughn doing a similar thing, although she was starting to wonder, hope, that it was for a different type of affection.

Bridget strode into the conference room with a confidence she didn't feel. Her insides were wobbly like Jell-O. She proceeded to set up her laptop and turned on the projector. When she reached for the switch to lower the blinds, she noticed a strange shadow wavering just above it. Her stomach clenched and her skin prickled. Her mouth went dry as the long, thin shadow crept closer. She saw nothing that could cause it.

She was about to ask Jack if he saw it too, when she was shocked again; this time before she touched the switch, a bright arc leapt from the metal plate to her fingers. The accompanying loud crack made everyone jump in their seats.

"Oh, my goodness, are you okay, Bridget?" asked a worried-looking Jack.

"Yeah, I'm fine." she was shaking out her hand. "That's the third time today, though. I'm starting to wonder if there's a storm coming, or maybe I should have read my horoscope today; you know, Libra, stay away from all things metal and electrical." She trailed off as she realized the room was full of people staring at her.

In addition to Jack, she was also receiving concerned looks from those gathered for the presentation. Major Payne just gave her usual eye roll. Her eyes were drawn to one specific person in the room, Vaughn. What was that look? Like he knew something she didn't?

He caught her eye again, grinned, then winked.

WINKED.

What is going on here? She thought. She stared at her fingers, still smarting from the shock.

Mentally, Bridget shook herself. *Right. Back to it, then.* She smiled and waved lightly at everyone. "No harm done, let's get started, shall we?" She walked to the table to grab the remote for the projector, eyeing it warily. If this thing grew teeth and bit her, she would go home and back to bed. She picked it up tentatively and, when nothing happened, gripped it firmly, letting her corporate smile slide over her face.

She knew it was going well when Jack gave her a small thumbs up. She was sure she had everyone hooked by the way they leaned into the presentation and were nodding along. She could see Vaughn leaning back and smiling at her from the corner of her eye. This was exciting; after six months of work, they were going to make this deal, which would benefit both companies tremendously.

"So, as you can see, by partnering with Chesapeake Industries, we can not only improve our efficiency, but we'll also reduce our overhead and in the end, make a better profit for both companies. This is a win-win!" she finished triumphantly, noting the grin on Jack's face letting her know she killed it.

Now to see what Payne was thinking, surely even *she* couldn't find a way to ruin this.

CHAPTER 4

"**WELL, THAT WAS CERTAINLY** entertaining, to say the least," started Payne, "Do you really feel this was the best use of your time? Is this what we pay you for?"

Bridget stood rooted to the spot. Confusion washed over her body like a cold wave as she furrowed her brow, trying to understand what had happened. What was going on here? Surely even Major Payne could see the benefit of the partnership.

Payne narrowed her eyes, "I'm so sorry, Mr. Drake, for wasting your time and if you were led to believe this was going to be a finalized deal but collaborating with your company is not what is best for us. In fact, I propose we adjourn. I have a full proposal from Jensen Controls that fully underbids this one here, which I think will be a much better fit for us." Payne sat back in her chair with a smug smile on her face.

Jack looked on in shock, his jaw hanging open.

Bridget dared a quick glance at Vaughn. How could this have gone so wrong so quickly? How had Payne put together a counterproposal at such short notice? What was going on here?

Vaughn was still leaning back in his chair, seemingly as relaxed as before, but she could see the strain in his body, like he was holding himself rigid. His eyes were smoldering, and his jaw was clenched tightly. If not for the small muscle ticking in his jaw and the smoke from his nostrils, she would have thought he was a statue.

Wait. Smoke? She shook her head and looked again. Nothing; it must have been her overactive imagination again, still reeling from this blow she had been dealt.

She spoke up, "Now Melissa, I'm sure Jensen Controls would love an opportunity to counter, but we evaluated them a few months ago and found their offering... somewhat, lacking. Besides, they couldn't possibly undercut Chesapeake; they don't know the details of our proposal. Mr. Drake and I have kept this information extremely confidential, so there was no possibility of a leak to investors!" She struggled to keep her tone light so as not to seem accusatory, but somehow, that villain of a woman must have snooped the files and shared them with someone at Jensen.

Bridget was beginning to panic, her palms sweating, and her heart pounding. *This is not happening.*

Payne smiled and stood. "Thank you, everyone, for your time, let's go ahead and adjourn. Bridget, I'd like to see you in your office, please." She started to walk out.

Vaughn stood suddenly. "Ms. Payne," he began, "I'm not sure how you managed to get a copy of our proposal in advance of this meeting, but rest assured I will find out." His voice was stern.

Bridget tried to reason with her, "Please Melissa, let us at least do a side-by-side comparison of the integration specs, I'm sure we can all agree that would be in our best-"

"Quiet!" shouted Payne, interrupting Bridget's plea. She turned her steely glare towards Vaughn. "And you sir, I resent your implications. As my *co-worker,*" she sneered, "Has so kindly pointed out, we've evaluated Jensen Controls' offerings before. They were given an opportunity to make updates, and they are by far the better option for us, irregardless of your opinion." She stated it triumphantly; as if she'd won the battle.

"Irregardless isn't a word," Bridget said. Her eyes widened, and she slapped her hand over her mouth, instant regret setting in that she apparently lost her filter. She heard a quiet snort of laughter and glanced at Vaughn to see him grinning at her again.

"What. Did. You. Say?" Payne gritted through her teeth.

"I, um." Bridget stammered. "Well, it's just that you said irregardless, and that's not actually a word. You see regardless means the same thing no matter which way you are trying to use it, positive or negative or anything in between. Regardless of how you mean it." She laughed nervously, trying to lighten the mood.

She could see Jack and Vaughn's shoulders shaking with quiet laughter. *Well good. At least someone is getting some enjoyment out of this. If she didn't hate me before, she REALLY hates me now.* Bridget watched as Payne's narrowed eyes got even more squinty, which she didn't think was possible.

"Well," Payne drawled, "I was going to give you the courtesy of doing this in private but since you seem to enjoy spectacles, I think we can just dispense with that and go forward with our chat now. You," she drew out the last vowel, "are fired. You've wasted enough of this company's time and resources. You are disrespectful, unreliable, and, quite frankly, a blot on our reputation. Your attitude needs some serious adjustments. Badge, keys, laptop." She finished triumphantly, holding out her hand.

Bridget stood rooted to the spot. Fired? What did that even mean? She just had a second to think, *oh crap*, before it all came spewing out like a bad case of verbal diarrhea.

"Fired? Really Melissa? You're firing me? Fine. You know what? Fan-freaking-tastic. I can't stand working for you for another second, you witch. You are, quite frankly, the most emotionally unavailable and unstable person I've ever met. You have zero business acumen, no one can stand you, and it really amazes me that you don't realize it. You know we all call you Major Payne, Payne in the Ass. Do you ever stop to wonder why? Doesn't matter. You are just a dried-up, bitter old hag, and you aren't worth another minute of my time. You want to run this company into the ground? Fine."

Jack walked over to her and put his hand on her shoulder, whispering in her ear, "Come on, babe, you are better than this. Don't let her drag you down with her. Let's go."

She snatched her badge off her collar, slammed the cover of the laptop, only wincing a little at the sharp crack she heard but hoping no one else noticed, and whipped out her keys to the building, slapping them on the table.

"Here!" she snapped. "I hope you get everything you deserve. I'm going to get my personal belongings; Jorrie will watch me to make sure

I don't steal anything. Then I'll leave, but I'm going out the back door, so I don't cause any more disruption than I already have. I know you want a scene, so you can call security, but not today, Satan." She seethed the last words and spun on her heel, marching out of the conference room to her office.

Correction, her former office.

She walked in and slowly shut the door quietly behind her, leaning against the cool wood surface before letting out a shaky breath. What had just happened? Fired? She'd never been fired in her life! She'd worked here for fourteen years as a loyal employee. Starting as a secretary, and when she'd shown some aptitude for project management, she was given a shot at moving up to the development team. From there she progressed until she became regional manager over the entire southern US. What was she going to do now? Oh God, what was she going to tell her son?

A light tap at the door interrupted her thoughts, and she turned. It was Jack with Jorrie in tow. She opened the door and gave them a weak smile. "Hey, so I guess you heard the news?" she laughed lightly in response to Jorrie's shocked face.

"Did you really call her Satan?" whispered Jorrie.

"Uh, yeah, I guess I did."

Jorrie looked at her with devotion in her eyes, "I love you. You are my hero. I want to be just like you when I grow up!"

Bridget laughed, wiping her suddenly damp eyes. She would *not* cry here in the office. "Well, I'm glad someone appreciates me. It's so weird. I can't believe no one tried to stop her. She just railroaded the whole thing. Jack, you saw it too, didn't you?" She turned towards him with a silent plea in her eyes. She needed him to reassure her she wasn't crazy, wasn't imagining things, because after the incidents with the shadows, she felt off balance.

Jack looked at her, pausing in packing up her pictures of Gabriel and the cats. "Honey, I'm not sure what that was. It was certifiably weird, though." He looked at Jorrie, "You had to be there, but Bridget's right; it's like they weren't even paying attention." He shook his head.

Bridget was relieved although still perplexed. She couldn't believe she hadn't seen this coming. She would have updated her resume and left on her own terms. She squeezed her palms together tightly, worrying about how this would look to future employers.

Jack interrupted her thoughts by asking "Hey, anything else that's yours we need to grab?"

She looked around and saw that, sadly, all of her belongings fit in the one box, and there was nothing left of her in the office. "Just this." She picked up the mousepad her son had given her for her birthday last year. She smiled, putting it in the box. "I guess that's it. Amazing how little of me there was to pack up, considering how much of my life I've lived here." She looked around at the bare walls and the clean shelves with their neatly organized binders and reference books. What was the point of it all? Just words and numbers that really didn't mean that much in the grand scheme of things. "Time to sneak out the back like a coward now."

She tried to take the box from Jack, but he held on tightly, saying, "No babe, I've got this. You walk out with your head high and know you did a damn good job. Nothing that old bitch said changes that! Let's go to lunch. I'll buy!"

"Sorry, I believe I have already claimed that honor." Came a rumbly voice from her doorway.

They all turned to see Vaughn leaning against her door. Oh no, how had she forgotten Vaughn? Mr. Sex on Legs himself was there to see the most embarrassing moment of her life, and now here he was, looking ready to commit all the sins.

Jorrie cleared her throat, "Mr. Drake, I'm not sure if you're aware, but Bridget has had a rough day, and she really needs to be with her friends now." She moved between Vaughn and Bridget, tilting her head up at him, her curls bouncing and eyes flashing.

Jorrie was a tough lady. Many people mistook her petiteness for weakness but Jorrie disabused people of that notion quickly. She was a spitfire and fiercely loyal. She knew Vaughn had been in the conference room during the 'Event', so obviously, he was complicit in the scheme. Bless sweet Jorrie and her friendship. Bridget wasn't sure what she had done to deserve it, but she appreciated it all that much more.

"It's okay, Jorrie, no," she said, holding up a hand when she could see Jorrie was going to interrupt. "Mr. Drake was just as blindsided by this as me." Bridget turned towards him and squared her shoulders, meeting his eyes. "I'm sorry you were dragged into this and witnessed that scene. I must apologize for my unprofessionalism. I assure you it is not my normal nature to speak like that to a superior."

"Superior Payne in the ass," muttered Jack while Jorrie snorted a quiet laugh.

"Yes, no matter how nasty she was, I shouldn't have sunk to her level. I'm so sorry that the deal fell through. I was really looking forward to working with you. With your company, I mean. I know it would have been beneficial for all of us. I don't know how she got ahead of us like that, but again, my sincerest apologies for how that played out. I wish I could make it right somehow, but I'm no longer employed."

Turning to her friends, she continued, "I need to go home and sort out what's next in my life if you all don't mind." she sighed, looking around the office one more time. She heard a little grumble that seemed to have come from Vaughn. *Did he just growl,* she thought as she turned, studying him closely.

His eyes flashed, and his mouth turned up in a sinful smile. "Okay, Ms. Ridgeway, if you truly want to make it up to me, I must insist you join me this evening. You want to skip lunch? That's fine; I understand this has come as a shock to you. I'll pick you up for dinner at 7:00 p.m. and we can go from there. See where the evening takes us? I think I can help you out, and I know you can help me." He reached over her shoulder and ran his hand slowly down her ponytail as she nodded, without fully understanding what she was agreeing to. "Yes," he continued, "You have just the amount of fire I need; see you tonight?" He winked and turned around, walking down the hall.

Bridget let out her breath in a whoosh. *What. The. Actual. Hell?* She turned towards Jack and Jorrie, a dumbfounded expression contorting her features.

"Did he just, did I just, did he just ask me out? Like, out, out? On a date out?" she sputtered. The disbelief in her tone made her voice rise a full octave.

Jorrie's wide eyes told her she wasn't wrong. "Holy shit Bridge! Hotness finally asked you out! And he one hundred million percent wants you, the way he touched your hair?" Jorrie squealed, jumping up and down, her curls flying everywhere.

"Slow down there, Jumping Jack Flash!" said Jack, putting his hand on top of Jorrie's head to calm her before she head-butted him in her excitement. Confusion briefly clouded his eyes before they cleared and lit up.

"*Girl!* He so totally asked you out, hot damn, it's about time! What are you going to wear? Please tell me you still have those killer red do-me pumps." He mimicked, showing off a little leg. "Those things scream sex appeal. They would be perfect with that red and black dress you have in the back of the rack. You're so getting laid!"

Jorrie looked at Jack, "How do you know about that?" she laughed.

"Brother privileges," he said airily.

Bridget laughed, "Okay, y'all are crazy, and I love you, but I need to get out of here now before the Major calls security." She glanced down the hall and saw the witch staring at her, tapping the toe of her leather pumps in irritation.

"Yeah, she's out there. I'm going home; I have to figure out what to do with my life. Maybe I'll just wallow in self-pity and become a bog witch. It's always been my heart's desire. Anyway, I love you both; get out of here before she comes after you, too." She kissed them on the cheeks, smiling.

"She's got nothing on me." Jorrie sniffed. "Let her try. I'll show her what's up."

Jack laughed. "Okay, fine, but I'm coming over after work. We are going to go through that closet and find something amazing for you to wear."

A look of confusion suddenly moved across Bridget's face. "Wait, he said he would pick me up at seven? He didn't ask me where I live!"

Chapter 5

Bridget was comfortably ensconced in her favorite ratty t-shirt and shorts, a glass of wine in hand, watching TV when Gabriel walked in the door. "Honey, I'm home!" she called out in anticipation of his confusion. She heard the thump of his backpack and the slap of his oversized feet on the tile as he ran to the living room.

"Mom?" he asked slowly and quietly, as if she was some figment of his imagination. He looked like he was afraid she would disappear if he breathed too hard. "Why are you home? Are you okay? Are you sick? Are you hurt? Do I need to call Uncle Jack? Or Aunt Jorrie? Mom!"

He rushed over, flinging out his words rapid fire. He patted her shoulders to reassure himself she was in one piece.

"Calm down, baby," she laughed softly, touched by his concern, "I'm fine, absolutely fine, never better, in fact." She saluted him with her wine glass.

"But why are you home before six and already into the wine?" he asked suspiciously.

Pfft, already, she thought as if she did it so often. Okay, so maybe she did have a glass after a hard day at work. Maybe two. And yeah, most days were 'hard' if she really thought about it. Okay every day was hard when working for Major Payne. Speaking of, "Well baby, I'm not working anymore." She watched his face for signs of alarm or concern, maybe even a little panic. She had been trying to decide how to break the news since she finished her crying jag in the driveway.

He completely surprised her, breaking into a giant grin and shouting, "Hell yeah! It's about time you dumped those jackasses!"

She sat up quickly, "Gabriel Patrick Ridgeway!" she snapped. Nothing said you mean business like using a full name. "Language, young man!"

He laughed at her fury. "Sorry, Mom, but you know you hated working for Major Payne in the Ass!" He danced backwards out of her reach.

"Where did you hear that name?" she demanded, then smacked her forehead "Uncle Jack. I should have known. He's behind this, isn't he? Well, regardless, I didn't dump their asses, they dumped mine. Major Payne surprised me today at my presentation and made a fool out of me. She did it in front of an audience because that's how she rolls." Bridget watched her son's face darken with anger.

"That bitch!" he grumbled. "Sorry, Mom, I know *language*, but come on! You know I'm right! Where was Uncle Jack? Why didn't he do anything?" he demanded with the injustice of a teenager who knew life had been more than a little unfair to him. Losing his father at a young age was certainly a battle his peers had not fought.

What a sweet boy being so outraged on her behalf. "Uncle Jack was there, honey, but there wasn't much he could do. He doesn't work there. If it makes you feel better, I did have to talk him and Aunt Jorrie out of slashing her tires in the parking lot." She ruffled his hair in the way she knew he hated, but she had done since he was little. It was a sign of how upset he was that he didn't lean away.

"Honey, you know we are going to be okay. We still have plenty of money left over from the settlement fund. I really don't need to work right away, but you know I hate being in the house all day," she reminded him.

"I know, Mom. I just hate they were so mean to you. You worked so hard for them; you didn't deserve it! Besides, I know you shouldn't be left unsupervised for too long." Gabe eyed her craft room door with unease.

"Hey!" she slapped him playfully on the arm. "I'll have you know those blankets were super comfy once you got past the lumps!" She grinned at him and was relieved to see he grinned back at her.

"I'm pretty sure Aunt Jorrie and Uncle Jack are coming over after work to commiserate with me, so you'll have plenty of opportunities to talk about the 'bitch'." She got up and started towards the kitchen, calling over her shoulder, "Tacos, okay?" knowing the answer was never no.

Bridget was in the kitchen shredding the last of the cheese for dinner when she heard voices at the door before the bell heralded the arrival of her squad.

"Gabe! Get the door, would you?" she called out. No reply. "Gabriel!" she called again, using her mom voice. Still no answer. Rolling her eyes, she set the grater down and walked to the door to let Jorrie and Jack in. "Sorry for the delay. Gabe must have his headphones on again. Playing in a tournament, I'm sure!"

She was enveloped in a cloud of blonde hair and squeezed within an inch of her life. "Air. Breathing. Not. Overrated!" she gasped, patting Jorrie on the back.

"Sorry, sorry!" Jorrie let her go and jumped back.

Bridget laughed; Jorrie was certainly an enthusiastic hugger.

Jack chuckled behind her and slid past, calling over his shoulder, "If you're done assaulting the love of my life, let's get in the kitchen. I have margaritas!"

"I thought Darren was the love of your life!" Jorrie challenged him.

"Only when he's around!" Jack trilled as he pranced down the hall.

Bridget and Jorrie giggled and followed him back to the kitchen, where they found him bent over in the fridge.

Jorrie sighed. "You know Jack, I've always said that fine ass was wasted on you. Dump Darren and run away with me instead!" she reached over, pinched his butt, and ran around the island.

He squealed and gave chase, making Bridget howl with laughter.

These two truly were her best friends. She had loved Jack from the moment Brian had introduced her to his older brother. Jack had grabbed her, thrown her into a dramatic dip, and begged her to leave his brother and be with him instead. He'd kissed her soundly on the mouth before winking roguishly and giving her back to her then-boyfriend. She'd been in her junior year of high school, and this was well before he'd come out. She had laughed then as she laughed now and knew Jack was doing his best to fill up the hole in her heart left when Brian died. She really had gotten the better end of the family deal in the marriage. Jack was the brother she'd always wanted and never had.

They had met Jorrie in college and the four had quickly become inseparable. They studied hard, partied harder, and had memorable trips together. They had all been each other's shoulders to cry on. Jorrie had been her maid-of-honor at her wedding, although Jack had campaigned hard for the honor. He had resigned himself to being best man for his brother instead. Jorrie had been her other rock when Brian had passed.

Jorrie walked out of the kitchen, calling out, "Gonna let the Rutabaga know dinner is ready," as she walked to Gabe's room. There were a few blissful seconds of quiet then shouting as Jorrie no doubt pounced him, probably tickling him mercilessly. Thank goodness her best friend and the love of her life got along so well. They had a special bond and were always trying to get one over on the other.

"Aunt Jorrie's trying to kill me!" he shrieked from his room.

"Okay, as long as there's no forensics to prove it. Dinner's ready!" she called back.

"Rutabaga." Jack mused. "I've never understood why she calls him that."

"To annoy him." She turned to Jack to ask him to set the table when she saw his face had lit up with alarm.

He looked at the clock, then back at her. "Girl! It's almost seven!" he said in a panic. "You don't have your face made up, your hair is still in a pony, and I'm sure you haven't dusted off anything to wear!" He ran to her bedroom like his ass was on fire.

She followed slowly. "Aren't you forgetting something? Vaughn doesn't know where I live; how is he supposed to pick me up? I'm sure it was just a pity ask. He probably got outside and thought, thank goodness I don't have to deal with her anymore," she said ruefully.

Jack stared at her as if she'd suddenly started speaking in tongues. "Honey," he started slowly. "That man most certainly wants a piece of you. He asked me all kinds of questions about you during the project. Things that weren't related to work. He's interested in more than a business deal. Also, he absolutely has your address. He sweet-talked me into giving it to him two weeks ago. Even if he didn't, he's Vaughn Drake! He knows everything about everyone! He's got a lot of information easily at his fingertips. He knew where you lived. I didn't tell you before because I didn't want you to get in your own head. Now, I'm telling you this because I love you, but go get your perky butt in the shower and do something with that hair! I'm going to pick out your outfit."

He turned towards the closet, then back, reaching over and gently pushing her mouth closed. "Shower. Now!" he clapped, shaking her out of her stupor.

She turned and rushed to the bathroom without even thinking it through.

"Squee!" Jorrie squeaked in an octave that shouldn't be heard by humans.

Bridget removed her hands from her ears, sure she could hear the neighbor's dog barking. *Then again*, she thought, *that doofus barks if the wind blows too hard.*

"You look ah-mazing!" her friend sighed. "That man is going to swallow his tongue when he sees you. Who knew you were hiding such a hottie under those baggy clothes!"

Bridget wasn't so sure about that. "Are you sure about this outfit? It seems a little... revealing," she muttered, trying to pull up the neckline and then had to pull down the hemline. "What if he just wants to go to Chili's? I feel really overdressed." she fretted.

Jorrie rolled her eyes and spritzed some Chanel on her neck. "Seriously, Bridge, Vaughn Drake? Some chain restaurant? No way, that man is going to wine and dine you and then hopefully have a little Bridget Ridgeway for dessert!"

"Jorrie!" Bridget said with a horrified expression. "I am *not* a first-date kinda girl! In fact, I'm not an any-date kinda girl!"

Jorrie looked at her with a serious face. "No one since Brian?" she asked quietly.

Bridget shook her head. "No," she whispered.

"Honey, you used to be the life of the party. We used to have to peel you two apart all the time because you and Brian went at it like rabbits every chance you got. I understand why you took some time off, but it's been so long. You're a beautiful woman and you don't even remember it. Quit second guessing and get back to that fiery red-headed siren you used to be. No wonder you have so much tension built up! You and Vaughn have been circling each other nonstop for the last six months. You want him. He wants you. You're both consenting adults. Time to be a bad girl and let that inner slut loose, don't you think? Brian would understand and want you to move on. Live a little. Get you some." Jorrie smiled wickedly.

Bridget gave her some serious side-eye then her face softened. Jorrie was right. Ever since Brian had passed, she had certainly turned into a shell of her former self. She knew that Brian would encourage her to move on as well, but it had been hard. No one had piqued her interest that way until now. She gave a soft sigh that made Jorrie grin.

Whenever she saw Vaughn, or thought about him, her insides were full of butterflies, and she grew warm in places she'd thought long dormant. She was about to respond, when she heard the doorbell. She grabbed Jorrie's hands and squeezed hard, "OHMYGOD. He's here!"

Something large and smelling faintly like gym socks came flying into her bedroom. Gabe stared at her in confusion. "Mom," he said softly, "You look beautiful! But Uncle Jack said you're going on a date? With a man?" his eyebrows quirked up.

"Well, yeah, a man, Rutabaga," Jorrie retorted, "Who do you think she dates, Bigfoot?"

Gabe snorted at her, then looked at his mom again, "Yeah, Mom doesn't *date*. That's the issue. And it's about dang time!" He wrapped his arms around her. "You're the best mom ever in the whole world, and you deserve someone who can make you happy," he whispered.

Bridget felt her eyes tearing up as she squeezed him tightly and laid her cheek on his. He was so tall now! "Thank you, baby," she whispered back. "You're the best son ever."

Jorrie leaned over and pried Gabe out of her arms. "As much as I hate to break up this Kodak moment, there is a *very* hot man waiting to take your momma out for the evening, and I don't think we should keep him waiting. Also, if you mess up her makeup, I'll kill you both," she threatened laughingly.

Gabe stepped back, crossing his arms. "Just who is this guy anyway?" he demanded.

Jack leaned into the room, "The guy is standing in your front hall-way waiting for your mom to come out and join him in the very nice Rolls Royce out front."

Jorrie turned to look at Gabe, and they looked at Bridget. "Ooh, a Rolls!" they said in unison, then snickered at her pained expression.

Gabe gathered himself. "Well, as the man of the house, I need to meet this guy!"

CHAPTER 6

BRIDGET HAD A SECOND bout of panic before Jack shoved her evening bag into her hand and nudged her towards the previously discussed sexy red shoes.

"Relax," he cooed reassuringly. "He's fine. It's not like Vaughn's going to bite the poor kid's head off."

"Besides," Jorrie added, "It's cute that he puffed up like that, going to protect his mama; it's really sweet."

Bridget knew they were right. She'd been fantasizing about this man for months while they worked together on that project. She knew him to be kind and laid back. She was just super nervous and needed something besides her own weirdness to focus on. As if she'd summoned it by thinking of it, the shadow on the wall behind Jack and Jorrie started to grow. It curled like a bony finger, pointing at her accusingly. It thinned further, reaching again as if trying to separate itself from the rest of the shadow cast by the floor lamp in the corner. She hated that lamp; it resembled some metal monstrosity from the Art Deco period that Brian had loved and she had merely tolerated. He'd kept the lamp from his bachelor days, and now she couldn't bear to part with it. Although if it kept making creepy wall crawling shadows, that thing was going on the curb next bulk trash day.

"Bridge!" Fingers snapped in her face, and she saw a concerned look on Jack's face.

"Earth to Bridget," said Jorrie, "Where were you just now?"

Completely losing my mind. "Uh," she stuttered. "Just trying not to throw up from being nervous I guess," she finished weakly.

"Well, get out there before he thinks you're standing him up in your own home!" Jack grabbed her and pushed her out of the room.

Bridget walked into the foyer and saw Vaughn in an immaculately tailored suit, having what seemed to be an animated conversation with Gabriel. He looked devastatingly handsome in a three-piece suit and tie. The soft waves of his raven-black hair blended into the collar of his jacket.

When her heels clicked on the tile, his eyes lifted to her, and she could swear she saw flames in them before he cleared his throat and straightened his tie. She saw his gaze roam over her figure from head to toe, lingering on the shoes before moving back up to her face. Jack had been right about them. They did wonders for her legs.

"Bridget." He breathed in. His purely male voice made her already weak knees even weaker.

Gabriel turned to look at her with a face of sheer delight. "*Mom!*" he shouted, "You didn't tell me you were going out with Vaughn Freaking Drake!"

Bridget had a moment of bemusement. "Well, I didn't have a chance to and even if I did, I didn't know you would know who Vaughn 'Freaking' Drake was." She smiled at Vaughn and mouthed 'Sorry' before looking back at her spawn, which was currently jumping around like a puppy.

"Vaughn Drake!" he said again. "THE Vaughn Drake!" he laughed.

Bridget looked around the room, confused, before Jorrie finally came to her rescue.

"I think what the Rutabaga is trying to say—"

"Aunt Jorrie!" groaned Gabe, hearing her call him their private nickname in front of his apparent idol.

Jorrie grinned and continued, "Is that Vaughn Freaking Drake is not only the esteemed leader of Chesapeake Industries and Jack's boss, but the brains behind the Cloud Warrior gaming franchise that Gabe is so addicted to."

Gabriel nodded enthusiastically, "Mr. Drake was just telling me that the next part of the story is coming out in two months. All the forums have been speculating it would be another six months at least! Oh man, wait til the guys hear I just met Vaughn Freaking Drake! He's standing here in *my home*."

Bridget noted that Gabe was staring at her date with something akin to hero worship and lightly patted his arm. "Slow down, buddy. I'm sure Mr. Drake would like to keep the game information secret for trade purposes. He also probably doesn't want a bunch of teenage heathens pouring out of the woodwork. We are just going to dinner."

She heard Vaughn give a low chuckle, "On the contrary, Ms. Ridgeway, I'd be happy to meet Gabe's friends. After all, they are my target audience. It's always good to get a fresh perspective from end users, right?"

He gave her an amused glance before turning back to Gabe. "Tell you what, if it's okay with your mom, why don't you and let's say, five or six of your friends, join me on Saturday at headquarters, 1:30ish, and I'll let you guys play the final version on our testing screen? You can meet some of my developers, and we can see what you think?"

Bridget stammered, "Oh no Mr. Drake, you don't need to—"

Seriously?" Gabriel shouted over her protest. "Dude!" he said in a quieter voice. He looked like he was about to pass out.

Jack walked over. "Wait, he gets to play Cloud Warrior-4, and I don't? You wound me, man!"

Vaughn laughed. "Of course, Jack. You know you're always welcome. You still owe me a beer after that last Ranger's game, remember? You too, Jorrie, if you don't have anything going on."

"*In!*" Jorrie replied, before he even finished.

Gabe glared at Jack, "Uncle Jack, we gotta talk. You didn't tell me you worked for CW!"

Jack held up his hands, "Gabe, I don't work for CW. I work at Chesapeake, two different companies. I didn't know you knew who he was either!"

Gabe appeared slightly mollified.

Bridget looked around at her family. "I guess I'm the one in the dark here. I had no idea," she confessed.

"Oh no," Vaughn said smoothly, "You are the one in the amazing dress, looking incredibly beautiful, and I think it's time we depart so we don't miss our reservation." He moved closer to her, and she could feel the heat from his stare on her skin.

Bridget's knees gave a little wobble. "Reservation, huh? I guess that means we aren't going to Chili's?" She could feel Jorrie starting at her back, willing her to shut her mouth.

To her surprise, Vaughn threw his head back and laughed, "Chili's? Not with you looking good enough to eat. I'm afraid we are going to have to go somewhere a little more upscale and dark so no one tries to steal you away from me." He placed a warm hand lightly on the small of her back.

Jorrie waggled her eyebrows suggestively before Vaughn escorted her outside to the waiting car.

Bridget was still trying to process the compliments and the flurries of goodbyes, as well as the reassurances from Jorrie that she would look after Gabriel for her while she had a *good* time. Jorrie had even offered to stay overnight just in case they wanted to have a *really* good time. Bridget's mind froze on that, and she could wring Jorrie's neck now for insinuating such a thing. Warmth crept up her neck, and she wished she wasn't so overwhelmed as she walked out the door.

Jack had whistled and blown kisses at her loud enough to draw attention from her neighbors. She'd thought of a dozen great witty comebacks for her friends, but now they were going to waste.

Vaughn helped her into the backseat before he walked around to get in next to her.

She gently stroked the soft leather of the seat and tried to discreetly brush her fingers across the beautifully worked metal insets on the door. ZAP! "Shit!" she yelped, shaking her fingers before realizing that was indeed out loud. "Sorry!" she called to the driver, meeting his eyes in the mirror. "I'm so sorry!"

"It's no trouble Miss," he replied, "Are you alright, though?" His kind green eyes searched her face.

"I'm fine, really," she said, "Just got a little static shock, and it caught me by surprise." She looked over at Vaughn and saw a frown on his face. Great. She'd embarrassed herself enough to last a lifetime in front of him already today. She hoped he kept up his offer to Gabe even though Gabe's mother was obviously a lunatic with a potty mouth. "I'm sorry," she repeated quietly, looking at his very full, very sexy mouth, wishing it wasn't set in that frown.

Vaughn glanced up, and his frown melted into a small smile. "Please don't apologize. I'm just concerned that you've been hurt. I know it wasn't your fault. Except, well, you did tell me you have; what did you call it? An electrifying personality?"

She groaned, shaking her head. "I can't believe you remember that."

"Of course, I remember, it was funny, and it describes you very well. You have a wonderful personality, and it electrifies me when you walk into a room."

Bridget stared at him, where was all of this when they were working on their proposal and testing the past six months? Had he been flirting with her the whole time, and she just never noticed? Or was this a new development now that the deal was over? She resolved she was going to pay close attention to everything he said going forward, so she didn't miss a thing. Which was no hardship, of course. His voice was like a warm sip of whisky on a cold night. It reverberated deep in her bones. *Wait, what did he just say? Crap, crap, crap, there goes paying attention.*

"Sorry, what?" she said sheepishly as she realized he had said something else while she was fantasizing about his voice.

He gave that silky laugh again, which made her shiver deep inside. "I said, Ms. Ridgeway, that I was concerned about you shocking yourself again. That happened this morning in the conference room, didn't it? Before that, in your office. And you said it had also happened earlier as well? Does this kind of thing occur to you frequently?"

Bridget thought about it. "No, not really. I mean, yeah, if I'm walking across the carpet in fuzzy socks and touch a switch, sometimes it happens, but not this hard and this often. It's really weird, now that I think about it. Lots of weird things today, if I'm being honest."

"Are you?" he said quietly. "Are you being honest? What other weird things are happening?" He was looking at her like he knew something she didn't.

Does he know about the shadows? she wondered. He couldn't possibly, and she certainly wasn't going to tell him now. Not when he still considered her somewhat sane. "Oh, you know, getting fired and shouting obscenities at my former boss," she joked, hoping he believed that.

He leaned back into the seat, smiling. "Indeed." He turned towards the driver and said, "Liam, let's get going! You can see the lady is unharmed; stow your fire, and let's move on."

Liam nodded and pulled away from the curb, heading off towards the highway.

"Stow your fire," Bridget repeated.

"Hmm?"

"You told Liam to 'stow your fire'. That's an odd thing to say, just thinking out loud," she admitted.

Vaughn seemed thoughtful, "Well, Liam is of Irish descent and has a bit of a fiery protective streak about him, especially towards women."

Bridget thought about it, and it made a sort of sense. "So where are we going?" she asked.

"Oh, just a little place I know," he replied easily.

Bridget studied him, sensing she wasn't going to get anything else out of him on it. "Well, in that case, you can educate me about something. Tell me more about this Cloud Warrior thing that has my son so worked up."

"Thing?" He arched his eyebrow at her. "Sure, I'll tell you about my... thing."

CHAPTER 7

Bridget was amazed and, frankly, dumbfounded. Here was a side to Vaughn she didn't know existed. How in the world had she missed this? She'd gotten to know him, she thought, from the Chesapeake project, but now she had learned he also owned a gaming enterprise. She recalled him mentioning some holdings in other industries as well, but nothing about video games.

Not just any video game, the one her son and millions of others world-wide were absolutely addicted to. It was an online multiplayer role-playing game. It even had its own E-sports league that Vaughn sponsored. She sincerely hoped that Gabriel didn't try to talk her into joining one of those, she already had a hard time watching him play football each fall.

She glanced around as the car came to a stop. She'd been so engrossed in learning more about Vaughn that she hadn't paid attention to where they were. She recognized they were close to the area in downtown Dallas known as Deep Ellum. There was quite a nightlife lounge scene here, but she wasn't sure it was the kind of place Vaughn had hinted at.

He gently grasped her hand and laid the smallest kiss on the back of it before rubbing small circles there with his thumb.

Her breath caught in her throat and warmth pooled low. Could this man get any sexier?

Vaughn seemed to understand the effect he was having on her and smiled a wolfish grin that made Bridget think Jorrie was right about his choice of dessert.

But surely, she was overanalyzing this situation. What could he possibly want from her? She was a widowed single mom from the suburbs who, oh yeah, was not only unemployed but had been fired most humiliatingly right in front of him.

"Hey," he murmured, "Quit thinking so hard. It will ruin your appetite. You're going to need it here."

Liam opened her door. "Miss." He held out a hand to assist her from the car.

Standing next to him, she realized Liam was exceptionally tall and quite handsome in his own right, with bright green eyes and reddish gold wavy hair that almost reached his shoulders. Not your typical chauffeur.

"Thank you, Liam," she said with a small smile. "I appreciate your willingness to overlook my brashness earlier. I usually wait until a second date to let the swears fly."

Liam looked startled at first, then laughed. "You are just as delightful as he said. You'll be perfect!"

Vaughn snapped a quick, "Liam." He walked around the car and joined them on the sidewalk.

The young man took a second to look admonished, then winked at her before getting back in the car and pulling away from the curb. No doubt, parking it somewhere until called.

Vaughn talked about her to Liam? She glanced curiously at him, about to inquire what Liam had done to irritate him when she saw a wavering in the shadows around the building. She stilled and looked hard at the corner, trying to see what was moving around. She couldn't see any person or animal but had a distinct feeling something was there. Waiting. Watching. She wasn't sure what it was waiting for, but it was decidedly evil, oozing menace. Her mind started shouting, '*DANGER WILL ROBINSON!*' Which she decided was fairly stupid and not at all helpful.

She was about to suggest they start walking when Vaughn leaned close and whispered, "You see it, don't you?" He held up a hand when she started to protest. "Don't deny it. I saw the way you tensed up, and I felt it staring at us. Come, you must be starving by now. I hope you don't eat like a bird. I'll be very disappointed, and it will break my heart if we don't get dessert." He took her by the elbow, which was a new, strangely thrilling sensation for her, leading her up the small set of stairs to the door.

She glanced around but didn't see any signage indicating what this restaurant was. She looked at Vaughn and said, "Where are—" when the door opened, and an honest-to-goodness textbook image of a snooty maître d'e stood there, looking them up and down.

"*Oui?*" he inquired, looking down his nose at them.

Wow, Bridget thought, *I've read about that, but I've never actually seen it happen. Who knew?*

Vaughn looked amused. "Really Derrick? French this time?"

The man relaxed his haughty posture and laughed. "Hey, I was trying to impress the lady here." His accent was more South Jersey than South France. He turned a smile on Bridget and opened the door wider, "Ma'am, welcome to Shandrick's. My name is Derrick, and I would be happy to escort you to your table. I won't even ask you the password since you've come with this riffraff. I swear, they let anyone in this joint." The now personable host held out an arm to escort her inside.

Bridget smiled and took his arm, following him, her head on a swivel. She'd heard of Shandrick's, but it was one of those exclusive places that you couldn't just walk in off the street. Reservations were required months in advance, so the rumors said, and you had to *know* someone. She couldn't believe it; her friends were going to be so jealous. She turned to Vaughn, intending to ask how he'd managed this, when she caught his expression.

He was looking at her again as if he wanted her as the main course. His eyes were flickering as if there were flames in them.

I had way too much Sauvignon Blanc earlier, she thought, swallowing to move her suddenly dry throat. *It must be this weird shadow thing that has me imagining that. It's a reflection of the candlelight. That's it.* There were sconces lining the dark wood paneling that surrounded the intimate seating area where a handful of diners, dressed to impress, were quietly having their meals. The décor was understated yet rich and comforting. It wasn't overly gaudy like you expected a high-end restaurant to be.

At least, that's what Bridget expected. She didn't really eat at too many fancy places while raising a teenage bottomless pit. Gabe could regularly eat his own body weight *and* hers, yet still look for more snacks. She'd spend a month's salary trying to feed him at a place like this. Or when she had a salary to speak of. *Don't think of that right now,* she warned herself. *It's time to focus on figuring out what's going on with the shadows around here.*

She let Derrick pull out her chair and place her napkin, finally handing her the wine list and advising them who would be their server for the evening. Bridget sent him a quick smile of thanks and received a bigger grin in return. He certainly was friendly.

"I see you've charmed the incorrigible Derrick," Vaughn chuckled.

"Incorrigible?" she asked. "Who says incorrigible these days? Anyway, enough talk about Derrick. What did you mean about what I could see? Tell me what is going on here!"

Before Vaughn could open his mouth, a young woman with a sleek bob of bright auburn hair glided up to their table, introducing herself as their server. Bridget admired her hair, so straight and shiny. She was absolutely going to ask her how she managed it if she privately got the chance.

The server quietly welcomed them to Shandrick's, advising them of a delicious-sounding salmon special and offering them a cocktail or glass of wine to start their evening.

Bridget took a brief glance at the wine list before handing it over to Vaughn. "You pick," she told him, "I'm sure you would know better than I would what's best."

He smiled and handed the wine list off. "How about we start with water, and then let's have a bottle of eighty-seven, please."

Bridget was glad to see that he didn't mind. The woman walked away to retrieve their wine, and Bridget asked him, "So, eighty-seven. Was that your college basketball number or something? What so special about that one?"

He reached across the table and took her hand in his, "My dear Bridget, I didn't play basketball in college. Number eighty-seven is just my personal favorite, a very robust and spicy Malbec that I think you will enjoy. It reminds me of you."

She stared at him, unsure of what to say next. She had fully intended to ask about the shadows, but her mouth betrayed her. "Why me?" she blurted out. *So not where I was going with that,* she cringed internally. *Oh well, I already stuck one foot in my mouth; I might as well see if the other foot fits.*

"I mean, we've been working together for six months, and just boom, out of nowhere, on the second worst day of my life, you ask me out despite everything that happened today. I mean, I'm me, and you are you. I mean, when you are so incredibly handsome and smart and funny and wow, I'm going to shut up now and let you talk."

She took her hand back and picked up her water, gulping half of it down in an unlady like fashion. She did not give one damn about that either. She was burning up with embarrassment. "I'm usually a lot better at words even though Jorrie thinks my puns are terrible, and oh my god. I'm still talking, aren't I?" She mimicked zipping her mouth shut and leaned back in her chair, gesturing for him to go ahead.

Vaughn stared at her open-mouthed for a second and leaned back in his chair, laughing so hard others in the room stared at him.

She didn't blame them; his laugh was mesmerizing.

He leaned back towards her. "Bridget," he started, "You gorgeous woman. Do you have any idea how truly incredible you are? No, I can see you don't, and I'm very sorry for that." He lifted her hand again, kissing the back of it.

"I think that's part of your charm. Let me see if I can answer all of that coherently for you. First, why you? Why not you? You are smart, witty, as I said charming, you are a natural leader and fierce when you need to be. You have the love of your family, which tells me you are a good person, and you love them just as much, which tells me you have a good heart. It doesn't hurt that you are incredibly beautiful as well. As far as why now, well, that is a bit of a longer story. Mostly, let's just leave it that the project was closing. I thought I could make a move without it seeming like I was trying to get your attention to better my prospects of closing the deal. I wanted the brilliance of the work to be focused on your actions, your talent and not give anyone a reason to suspect there was anything, shall we say untoward with it?"

She leaned further back, stunned, her heart pounding and her breath quickening.

"Bridget." he rumbled, the sound coming from deep in his chest. "Do you have any idea of how amazing and delicious you look tonight? You are stunning. And those shoes, well, I'm glad you never wore those to the office, or I wouldn't have been able to get any work done. I had a hard enough time keeping my hands to myself when you were around."

She swallowed heavily, her desire for him building even higher. She crossed her legs tightly to contain the throbbing feeling there.

He smiled and continued, "As for the rest, for the record, I think your puns are wonderful and an example of what a sharp wit you have. I think that about covers it. Unless you want me to answer whether or not you were still talking?" He finished with a smolder on his face that threatened to light her on fire.

Bridget was overwhelmed, unsure of what to say. He really thought that? He was as attracted to her as she was to him. She didn't know how to feel, but she knew she wanted him badly. Things with Brian weren't drastically romantic, although they were very passionate. High school sweethearts, he was comfortable, just a gentle falling in love with each other and knowing they were a great team. Even after all these years, thinking of him brought a sad smile to her face. He had been so kind and sweet. A little goofy like her, he loved their son, their life, and their home. The accident that had taken him from their lives was something she'd never forget.

"And now I've made you sad somehow," Vaughn murmured gently.

Bridget looked up into the eyes of this man who could burn her alive and smiled, shaking her head, "No. Not sad, just remembering."

He looked deep into her eyes and said softly, "The first worst day of your life?"

She nodded, wondering how he knew.

He seemed to understand because he offered, "Jack shared some of the details with me one night. Your husband sounded like an amazing man and a fantastic father. I'm sorry for your loss, Bridget; please know I'm not trying to take away from that. But I understand it has been a

while now, and you are not a woman who should remain unappreci-
ated. I've been intrigued by you from the day we met. I hope you'll let
me try." He smiled gently at her.

Warmth flooded her body at his kind words. She nodded and cleared
her throat. "So, what's good here?"

CHAPTER 8

THE MEAL WAS ABSOLUTELY delicious, each bite as amazing as the first. She wondered if she should be embarrassed by how much she ate, but Vaughn had encouraged her, and she didn't know when she would get to enjoy something like this again. She lifted her glass and pointed it at him, "You were right about this Malbec! I'm not sure where this has been all of my life, but I do believe in number eighty-seven now."

He chuckled, lifted his glass, "To number eighty-seven!" and tapped it to hers. He leaned back from his empty plate. "I'm glad to see you actually eat real food and don't just pick at a salad while staring at my steak." He smirked at some of the women at the next table over doing just that.

Bridget looked at the remains of her salmon and back at him, grinning about the way she devoured it. The server glided up then and swept away their plates, handing her a dessert menu.

"Oh no, I couldn't possibly eat another thing." she protested.

Vaughn took the menu from her and pointed at something, asking for two forks.

Bridget tried to protest, but it was feeble. She was sure whatever it was, it would be divine, and somehow, some way, she was going to find room for it in her stomach. "So, Vaughn," she started, "About the shadows."

"Shh," he cautioned, "Not here. I want to talk to you about them, but this is not the place. They are closer now, and I don't want to risk being overheard."

She sat back, puzzled about what he meant by 'they are closer'. They who? The shadows? The men in black? *Oh crap*, she thought, *have I been taken in by a Don Juan? Is he crazy? Like when Johnny Depp got all piratey and guy-linery.* She looked closely at Vaughn to see if she could spot any crazy or any makeup.

He looked at her quizzically. "Do I have something on my face?" he asked.

"Guy-Liner," she replied. He looked stunned, so she laughed and said "I was looking to see if you are wearing eyeliner. You have the most beautiful eyes; I was wondering if you are just naturally that hot."

His eyes widened, and he grinned. "Oh, you think I'm hot, do you? I'm happy to hear that. What is it you and Jorrie call me? Mr. Hotness? I must say that was an inventive name. It was a new one for me."

She was going to die. Again. Just absolutely croak right here on the spot. She could see the headlines now. 'Local Woman Dies Instantly in Restaurant of Extreme Embarrassment.' "Jack cannot be trusted!" she said, trying to brave her way through it. *Jack will die. A slow, painful death by a thousand cuts from a rusty tin can lid. Or I'll sick Jorrie on him.* She smiled sweetly at Vaughn.

He smirked at her, knowing she was dying inside. "You are adorable when you blush like that. And you're right. Jack cannot be trusted with tequila."

Just then, a plate of what looked like an absolute masterpiece of chocolate appeared between them.

Saved by the dessert bell, Bridget thought before sizing up the decadence in front of her, deciding where to attack first.

Vaughn picked up his fork, scooped up some chocolate and held it out to her.

Oh, he wanted to play that game? She was all for it. She leaned in, placed her lips around the bite and closed her eyes in delight. "Mm," she moaned, "That is better than sex." She was almost purring. She heard a growling sound coming from Vaughn's direction and opened her eyes to see him staring at her like he wanted to lick her entire body from head to toe. She could swear she saw smoke coming from his nostrils, and she could smell something faintly like a campfire. What was going on here?

Vaughn leaned back and waved their server over. "We're going to need this to go and please run this." handing her his credit card without taking his eyes off Bridget. After she walked away, Vaughn traced a finger across Bridget's bottom lip. "You are playing with fire, little one. That's a dangerous thing to do."

Bridget swallowed heavily and became aware of parts of her body tingling in a way they hadn't in a long time. Here she was, trying to decide if she was crazy or not, seeing moving shadows, imagining a man had fire in his eyes, breathing smoke without a cigarette, and all she could think about was dragging him across the table and getting naked with him here and now. She kept her gaze locked on his, figuring if she was going to burn, at least he wanted to burn with her.

CHAPTER 9

BRIDGET TOOK IN A deep breath of the close night air that indicated summer was soon approaching. She was painfully aware of the man next to her, desire seeping from every pore of her body.

Vaughn slid his phone into his pocket after calling Liam to pick them up. He took the container holding their dessert and set it on top of the pedestal next to them. He slowly brought his hands to her face and caressed her cheeks.

"I've a mind to kiss you, Bridget, to see if you taste as good as I think you will," he breathed quietly.

She leaned in, thinking, *yes, yes, please, finally,* and her thoughts became an incoherent jumble when she experienced the warmth from his lips close to hers. Just then, she heard a scuff on the sidewalk behind her before she was pressed painfully against the pedestal with Vaughn standing in front of her.

He was shouting in what seemed to be half growls, half threats. "You can't have her!" she heard.

Who is he talking to? What the hell is going on here? Her mind couldn't catch up to what was happening. She froze as she heard a low hissing sound, and her body began tingling like an electric current was running through her.

"No!" Vaughn shouted, and suddenly, he was gone like the wind had blown him away.

Bridget looked around wildly, not understanding how he had moved that fast and where he had gone. She heard growling and what sounded like fighting coming from around the corner. She started towards the noises; worried Vaughn was being attacked, when powerful headlights washed over her. She raised a trembling hand to cover her eyes.

Liam pulled to the curb and jumped from the driver's seat. "Where?" he demanded, grabbing her shoulders.

She shakily pointed towards the area where she'd been heading.

Ignoring her pleas, he pulled her to the car and shoved her into the back seat, slamming the door as he shouted "*Stay!*" at her.

He ran towards the darkened area, then skidded to a stop as Vaughn came strolling around the corner, jacket slung over his arm and adjusting his cuffs as if he didn't have a care in the world.

Bridget let out a deep, relieved breath. She pressed a palm to her chest to calm her pounding heart.

He glanced at Liam, frowning, then over to the car. He saw Bridget was safe and visibly relaxed. He clapped Liam on the shoulder, saying something Bridget couldn't hear, then grabbed the forgotten dessert from the pedestal before getting in the backseat next to her.

"Sorry about that," he said pleasantly. "These vagrants picked the wrong pocket to try to pick."

Liam got back in the car and pulled away from the curb.

"No!" shouted Bridget. "Stop!" she tapped Liam on the shoulder rapidly.

He ignored her and picked up speed, quickly making his way back to the interstate. "I'm sorry too," he mumbled.

Bridget turned towards Vaughn, fire in her own eyes now. "What. The. HELL. Was that?" she said angrily, through gritted teeth. "Don't tell me that was just some random pickpocket. You were there one minute and gone the next. It sounded like an all-out brawl. Who was that really? How did you move that fast? What did it want?" she rapid-fired at him. She sat there, chest heaving, fixing him with her sternest mom gaze. The one that never failed to make Gabriel come clean when she knew he was hiding something from her.

"Okay," he said, putting his hands up like he was defending himself. "I understand. You deserve some answers."

Score one for mom face. "Okay so spill. Now," she demanded, poking him in the shoulder and arching her eyebrow for an extra, secret extracting effect.

Vaughn grinned and grabbed her hand. Bringing her palm to his lips, he gently kissed it. "Oh yes, you are a spitfire. I will tell you everything, but not here. Liam," he turned to their driver, "My place, we need some privacy for this discussion."

Liam nodded and changed lanes to exit the highway.

"Your place?" Bridget inquired sharply. "You think I want to go somewhere 'private' with you when you can't give me a straight answer? I think I'd rather just go home instead." She pulled her hand from his. This was just getting too weird. *Why do the hot ones have to be crazy?* She thought wistfully.

Vaughn leaned towards her. "The electrical shocks, the shadows, the forces in the street, I thought you wanted answers?" He stared into her eyes and held them locked onto his gaze.

"Beam me up, Scotty," she whispered, then winced. *Nerd alert!*

He grinned and gently brushed his lips across her cheek.

She could swear her face was on fire where he had touched it; she imagined being consumed by that heat and shivered despite the warm night.

"You heard the lady, Scotty," he said to Liam. "Beam us to my place," Vaughn instructed.

She heard him chuckle as he said, "Aye, aye, Captain!"

He pulled the car into the garage of a swanky development in the heart of downtown Dallas. She glanced at the entrance to the tower before the gates obscured her view. *Of course, there's a doorman and a red carpet,* she mused.

Liam parked the extravagant car in a spot marked 'reserved' and opened her door, taking her hand to assist her before he handed her off to her date with a grin and wink.

Vaughn took her hand and smiled warmly. "Please," he implored, "Join me inside, where I will explain everything."

Here goes nothing, she thought and followed him into a posh lobby.

He pressed the down button for the elevator.

"What," she inquired, "Not the penthouse?"

He grinned at her. "Only for work, my darling. For private matters, I prefer something more... intimate." his voice dropping on the last word sent another shiver through her.

They rode the elevator in silence, her hand still held in his. She kept her eyes firmly on the button for S3, not wanting to get caught staring at him like some foolish schoolgirl. *And why not?* She argued with herself. *You've already made it plain that you are pathetic and want to jump him. He knows you think he's hot. Thank you, Jack. Mental note: strangle adorable brother-in-law next time you see him. So why not be a brazen hussy and lap that man up like...*

"You're thinking too hard again."

Bridget blushed and settled her shoulders.

"I'd love to know what was going on in that pretty head of yours that's making you blush like that." He brushed his mouth against her ear.

"Stop that!" She turned her face towards him and found his lips next to hers as he grinned at her. She involuntarily leaned into him, succumbing to the pull of his mouth.

DING. The elevator doors opened into a small foyer with a single door.

She moaned to herself, *Every. Time.* She faced forward and looked around. "Just one door?" she asked him.

"Yes, I have the only space down here. For some reason, most people don't want to live underground. I don't mind. I find it quite cozy."

Bridget shook her head. Cozy was not a word she thought of in relation to Vaughn. He seemed too full of life and energy to ever do something like sit and snuggle up reading a book or cuddle up and watch a movie in front of a crackling fire on a cold night.

She watched as he swiped an electronic keycard through the device next to the door and heard the lock release. "Fancy," she said nervously, then stepped through the door as he held it open for her. Whatever she was expecting Vaughn Drake's private living space to look like, it wasn't this. It was the exact definition of cozy. A huge fireplace was the focal point of the living room. Large couches and armchairs that looked perfect for sinking into, a chaise lounge that looked too divine to resist, all done in rich, warm colors. It wasn't as stark and cold as she'd been expecting for someone who had enough money to hire a designer.

But everywhere she looked, cozy was exactly the word that came to mind. She realized it reflected what she had come to learn about Vaughn. He was a man who exuded warmth and fire, so why wouldn't it extend to his home?

He had led her to a well-equipped kitchen, where she was pleased to see a gas range. "Huh," she said, "I'm surprised you don't have one of those glass cooktops that are all the rage."

"Well, I prefer an open flame for cooking," he replied with a smirk as he unbuttoned his cuffs and rolled his shirt sleeves up, displaying forearms that were toned and muscular.

"Do you do that a lot? Cook?"

"Oh yes, when Liam lets me." He opened a drawer and selected two forks.

"Lets you?" she raised her eyebrow.

"Yes, Liam fancies himself the next Top Chef, so he's always experimenting when he's here. But I gave him the rest of the night off." He grabbed a pair of sparkling crystal wine glasses, then reached for a bottle from the wine rack at his feet and opened it with a flourish.

"Our favorite, number eighty-seven." he smiled while pouring the dark wine.

Bridget laughed, "So Liam is a man of many talents," she stated, taking the glass he offered to her. Taking a sip, she rolled the rich wine across her tongue and studied the man in front of her. She wondered if he was trying to distract her from the promised conversation. She reached for a fork and decided to turn the tables. She opened the dessert container and scooped up some of the chocolatey goodness there. She held up the fork and lifted it to his lips with a smile. As he leaned forward to take the bite from her, she quickly pulled the fork away and put it between her own lips instead. "Mm," she moaned, licking her lips in what she hoped was a seductive manner. She watched his eyes as they seemed to darken, his shoulders tensed, and his fingers went white around the stem of his glass.

"A dangerous game indeed, Bridget," he murmured. He took the fork from her suddenly limp fingers and the wine glass from her other hand. Setting them on the counter, he reached out and buried his fingers in her hair. He slowly pulled her towards him and angled his mouth to hers.

Every inch of her body was on fire. She wrapped her arms around him automatically, knowing she was going to regret this next move. Just as his lips brushed hers, she tilted her head away and whispered, "Shadows."

Vaughn reacted as if she had deflated him like a balloon. He lowered his hands to her shoulders and ran them down her arms to her wrists. He looked at her squarely and nodded his head. "Yes, I promised you an explanation. You are just too tempting. Very well."

He grabbed the chocolate cake and forks, gesturing to her to get the wine and made his way to the living room. He set them on a low table next to the chaise and moved to the fireplace. He knelt and went about lighting it.

Bridget decided she was absolutely going to make use of that chaise lounge and was rewarded by sinking into the most luxurious softness she could imagine. When she looked back at Vaughn, a fire was already roaring, and he was strolling towards her.

He picked up a remote and clicked it towards some curtains she thought were for show.

To her surprise, they opened to reveal what looked like a view of the city. Almost as if they were in a penthouse instead of underground. "How?" she asked as he sank down on the floor next to her seat.

"Digital windows. The cameras are up on the top of the building; they show me what's going on outside in case I feel like looking. I just thought you might enjoy the view."

Bridget stood and walked towards the wall, marveling at how realistic it looked. "This is amazing." She turned back to him. "No wonder you don't mind living down here. This whole space is beautiful."

"Why, I wonder, do you sound so surprised," he mused. "Come, join me. Let's talk about the Shadow Claw." He patted the cushion.

Bridget immediately came back and sat down. "The what?"

CHAPTER 10

"Shadow Claw, is the official name for what you've been seeing, what has been following you around. They've been watching you for some time, I imagine. Waiting for just the right moment." He handed her a wine glass and fork. "Please, you'll need it," he continued.

"The Shadow Claw was originally an ancient tribe thousands of years ago when the first of them could travel through shadows and manipulate them. This was a dark power they gained by trading their souls to a demon. Bridget, tell me, have you ever noticed a shadow seeming somehow fuller than usual? Or that it seems to be moving without any light source to alter it? Maybe you've felt like someone was there even though you couldn't see them?" He searched her face as if trying to gauge her reaction.

Bridget slowly nodded. He was speaking about magic, which was bonkers, of course, but still. "Yes, I've always been a little leery of shadows. I thought it was my imagination. But just this morning in the parking garage, I..." she trailed off.

He nodded in encouragement, "Please, tell me what you saw."

She shook her head, "No, it seems so silly now; I must be hallucinating."

He rested his warm hands on her knees, "Please, Bridget, you weren't seeing things. The Shadow Claw is real. They want you, and I will do everything in my power to protect you and stop them. Please tell me what you saw." His eyes begged her.

Bridget wished she had one of her cats with her. They always seemed to know when she was upset and would curl up in her lap. She loved to dig her fingers into their silky fur and stroke their little ears, scratching their chins in a way that would make them seem to smile. She needed that right now. She grabbed a throw pillow and began kneading it with her fingers. Although it didn't purr, it seemed to give her some measure of comfort, and she was able to continue.

"This morning, at the office, I had to park in the seventh circle," she started.

Noticing his confused look, she clarified, "That's what I call the lowest level of the parking garage. I hate how dark and creepy it is, and it reminds me of 'Inferno'."

"Dante." He nodded, comprehending her reference. "How apt."

"Anyway," she continued, "I sensed something was in the corners, in the dark areas and I had an urge to run for safety. When I got to the elevator, there was another shadow. It was normal looking at first, but then..." she paused.

Vaughn squeezed her hand in reassurance.

"It grew. It seemed as if it was getting longer and skinnier. Like it was reaching for me. I backed up into the elevator, trying to get the door to close, and it started growing faster. I thought for sure it was going to grab me. It just oozed evil. The doors shut just in time, and when I grabbed the rail in the elevator, it shocked me. Hard. Just like you've seen today." Her voice shook and she searched his face for confirmation.

He nodded encouragingly at her.

"Then in the conference room, when I got shocked, I saw it again. It was trying to reach for me. And tonight, in my bedroom." She was sure her hands were trembling in his now. Could this be real? Shadow creatures? Surely, this was nuts, but on some level, she believed him. What else could explain this?

Vaughn tightened his grip on her hands briefly and said, "I know, Bridget, I saw them too. I was trying to get them to leave without revealing too much. I didn't want their owners to know what I was doing. I'm so sorry you got hurt." He rubbed her fingertips absently.

"Their owners?" she said with confusion, "What do you mean, oh my goodness. It's Melissa, isn't it? Melissa Payne? I've always thought she was some sort of evil witch. Damn it." Bridget dug her nails into Vaughn's grip, and he flinched. "Sorry!" she said suddenly, releasing his hands. "I'm so sorry. I just get so fired up thinking about that sorry ass good for nothing knuckle-dragging swamp bitch." Bridget's eyes widened, and she put a hand over her mouth. Seeing that Vaughn was struggling not to laugh, she burst out giggling, relieved when his rich, warm laughter joined hers.

"Well, Bridget, that is quite the mouth you have," he chuckled. "But no, Payne is not a member of the Shadow Claw. She's just an awful person."

"Why did you let her shut down our deal?"

"I had to protect you," Vaughn answered nonchalantly. "I couldn't risk her knowing who I am and that I was there to watch over you. I don't care about the deal anymore. Yes, it would have been beneficial for both of our companies, but I only cared about it as long as it benefited you. Now that you are no longer with them, I can easily find another business partner."

Something Vaughn said registered with Bridget suddenly. "Who you are," she repeated. She leaned back from Vaughn. "You aren't, you're not," she stammered uneasily. *If he's one of those shadow things...*

Vaughn took her chin in his hand, forcing her to look at him. "Bridget, sweet Bridget," he gently whispered, "I mean you absolutely no harm. I swear it. I am not a Shadow Claw; my soul is my own, and I wouldn't sell it for anything. I would never hurt you."

Bridget relaxed under the warmth of his gaze. She believed him. She wasn't sure why, but he seemed trustworthy and had been so genuine with Gabe earlier.

"Gabriel!" she said suddenly, reaching for her purse to get her phone.

"Relax," he said, understanding the reason for her panic. "He's safe. I've got your home under patrol. My men won't let anything happen to your son or your friend. The only place they could be safer would be here with us, but I assure you, they are fine." He leaned away from her, "Go ahead and call. I'm sure you will be more at ease hearing from them yourself."

Bridget stared at him, a little pissed he'd put a protective detail around her family without telling her, but also grateful he'd taken that extra step to protect what was hers. She nodded, hoping to convey all of that. She pulled out her phone and quickly found Jorrie's number.

After three rings, Jorrie finally answered. "Why are you calling me? You should be halfway through jumping Mr. Hotty by now. We are fine, we don't need you, don't want to talk to you. Rutabaga is going down!"

"No, I'm not! And stop calling me Rutabaga!" Gabe shouted in the background.

Bridget laughed and put her hand on her heart to stop it from racing right out of her body. "Thanks, Jorr. I just wanted to see if I could take you up on that offer to stay the night?"

"YES!" Jorrie shouted. "Get it, girl! Brown-chicken-brown-cow." she sang, doing her worst impression of risqué music.

Bridget could imagine her crazy friend dancing around the living room, shaking her butt. She glanced over at Vaughn to see he could clearly hear Jorrie and her face heated. "Not what you think, Jorrie." She kept her eyes on Vaughn so he got her meaning, too. "Vaughn and I have a lot to discuss, and I'm not sure how long this is going to take."

Jorrie sighed, "Boo! Whatever. It's not like you just met him tonight. How long have you been drooling after that gorgeous man? Let go Bridget. It's beyond time you found yourself again. Sleep with him, or I am never speaking to you again."

"Eww!" Bridget heard Gabriel yell before Jorrie disconnected the call.

Bridget held her blank phone for a moment before slowly returning it to her purse. She turned back towards Vaughn and took in his bemused expression. Not knowing quite what to say, she mentally added Jorrie to her 'those who must be harmed' list.

"Well, are you?" he asked with a devastating smile.

"Am I what?" she said nervously.

"Going to ensure your friendship remains intact. I quite like that friend of yours. She's a smart woman," he teased.

Bridget took a moment to catch his meaning and with a blush said, "Maybe later. For now, tell me more about these Shadow Claws. Why me?"

Vaughn's smile grew bigger, "I'll take later as long as you mean it." He pulled her close and softly murmured, "First though, I just have to." He crushed his mouth to hers in the kiss that had been interrupted too many times tonight.

Bridget could swear her eyes rolled back in her head. She heard angels singing and then blissfully, nothing. Her mind came to a complete halt, allowing her to enjoy the moment.

Vaughn put one hand behind her head so he could deepen the kiss and held her body tightly against his.

Oh god, it wasn't fair how hard and soft his body was at the same time. She could feel his abs beneath her hands as she ran them up to his sculpted chest. Just not fair at all. Their lips danced with each other, and she felt his tongue alongside hers as she struggled to keep her hands from yanking his shirt open like in those steamy romance novels Jorrie was fond of reading. *This can't be real. This can't be real*, her brain chanted.

He gentled the kiss and slowly pulled away from her. "Sweet Bridget, you taste even better than I could imagine. Now that we've gotten that out of the way, I believe you asked about why the Shadow Claw wants you." He sat back on the floor.

Bridget was still for a moment, trying to wrap her brain around what happened. She gently touched her lips and marveled at how deliciously swollen they were. She cleared her throat and reached for her wine, taking a large fortifying gulp. She was beyond caring about seeming lady like. Besides, he was a man who apparently appreciated a healthy appetite. Setting her glass down, she focused on his now serious expression. "This is all starting to sound like a fantasy novel or some sci-fi show," Bridget started.

Vaughn laughed, "I get what you mean. I hope you can hold on to how you felt a minute ago because I don't want you to forget that I'm here to protect you, and I think it's obvious how I feel about you. How I've been feeling about you." His expression returned to serious. "The Shadows, they want you because long ago," he paused, as if he was searching for the right words.

"In a galaxy far, far, away?" she supplied helpfully.

He narrowed his eyes at her for a second, then smirked. "No, you aren't Princess Leia if that's what you're thinking, but close. Long ago, as in thousands of years ago, there was a group of magic practitioners. Most were peaceful, but some insisted they should rule. They weren't content with the status quo, so they began looking for ways to become more powerful. As I said earlier, many of them turned dark and sold their souls to demons to become masters of the shadows. They began to use this power to take out leaders of the other tribes and other magic users. Planning to wipe them out and be the only ones who could wield power." He paused for a sip of wine, glancing at her over the rim to see if she was following along.

She nodded encouragingly for him to continue.

"One tribe, calling themselves Wielders, were not about to go quietly and knew there was only one way to combat the Shadows. They joined forces with…" he hesitated, "Another species to eradicate the Shadow Claw menace. There was a war of which you can only imagine the magnitude. The proverbial battle of good and evil, right versus wrong, etc. Good did triumph, of course, but at great cost. The damage done to the land and the people was horrendous. The Wielders prayed to their God, Taranis of Light and Thunder, to help heal the land. He agreed, but he was displeased at the way they had used their power and their allies; he had created those allies.

"He said in exchange, he would take away their powers for two thousand years so they could learn to use them responsibly again. Two thousand years seemed a long time to the people but a mere blink of an eye to a God. The people agreed, though, so he stripped away the powers, healed the land and removed the memory of it from all that remained." He stopped for a moment to see how Bridget was handling this.

"Well, that's quite a story," she said slowly, "Sounds like something straight from Celtic folklore."

He nodded, "There's usually some basis of truth in many of those stories."

She tilted her head, "You said these, Wielders, joined forces with another species. Like what? Unicorns? Pegasus?" She smiled, joking with him.

Vaughn looked at her seriously and took a deep breath. "Dragons."

Bridget sat there for a moment. "Dragons?"

He nodded gravely as if it was the most serious thing he'd ever been asked.

"Dragons," she repeated, then burst into laughter. "Oh, Vaughn, you had me for a minute. Dragons. I could almost believe in magical powers because I've seen the shadows myself, but come on. Dragons were never real. Is this some sort of joke? Look, I liked you for you. I'm not sure why the elaborate story." She wiped under her eyes and picked up her wine glass. "Dragons." She snorted and took a sip.

Vaughn stood suddenly, and she saw flames in his eyes. "I assure you, Bridget, it's no joke. I need you to believe me. For your own safety." He growled as smoke began to pour from his nostrils, and his fingers began to elongate into claws.

Bridget jumped up, terrified, wondering how to get away.

The sound of fabric tearing and a flapping noise drew her eyes to his shoulders where a pair of enormous black scaley wings with golden webbing were spreading from his back.

Her hands trembled, and she looked at his face again.

He had a wicked smile, which caused her to drop the glass, hearing it shatter as it bounced from the table to the floor. She could feel the blood drain from her face, and the room began to lose all color. Her world and vision narrowed down to the flames in his eyes before everything started turning black.

She saw his eyes return to their normal color, and concern filled them before the darkness took her under, and she collapsed.

She was out cold.

Chapter 11

Bridget stirred on something soft and silky. She was either lying in a nest of angel feathers, or this was the world's most comfortable mattress. She didn't remember buying this, but good lord, she might never get out of it.

Suddenly, she remembered this was not her mattress and the last thing she saw was, "Wings!" She shouted and sat bolt upright in the bed. She looked around the very masculine space and realized she must be in Vaughn's bedroom. She checked herself and was relieved to see she was still wearing her clothes, although her shoes were sitting neatly by a nearby dresser.

She noticed the cozy feeling of the rest of the house had been carried into the bedroom. There was another comfy looking chair in the corner by some bookshelves filled floor to ceiling. It looked very inviting and certainly more appropriate than lying in a strange man's bed. She started to get up when Vaughn walked into the room.

His black wavy hair was slicked back, dripping wet, his upper body bare, and a towel hitched low around his hips. Reality was much better than her imagination.

Wow, she thought, *I could just bite that hip bone and lick;* she looked up at his face, mortified to be caught staring at him while thinking what she was thinking. Her face heated and the desire she'd felt earlier swamped her again.

His gaze was steady on hers, his face unreadable as he stood in the doorway.

She looked down and realized he was barefoot and trailing water behind him. "Uh, shower?" she asked feebly.

He glanced down at the puddle. "Pool. I went for a swim to uh, cool off while you uh, recovered and um." He shifted his feet nervously.

She started at this version of Vaughn. He seemed unsure of himself for the first time, and she wasn't sure what to make of it. He was unsure? She had just laughed at a dragon, and he didn't eat her.

She gasped and scooted back across the bed in alarm. Trying to get off the other side to put space between them. "Dragon," she whispered.

"Relax," he tried to assure her, holding up his hands, "I'm not going to hurt you, remember? I promised you."

Had he? Had he promised that, or did he just say it to confuse her? She continued to back away.

"Bridget," he groaned, "Please, my sweet Bridget, if I was going to hurt you, I could have done it a dozen times before now."

That's true, she thought, *maybe I was just imagining things, and he didn't really change right in front of me.* She gave him a small, tentative smile. "So," she cleared her throat, "Is it. True?" She hated that her voice wavered. "Are you really a," she paused.

"Dragon." He nodded. "It's okay, you can say it. And despite the legends, we don't devour virgins or demand sacrifices anymore." He winked at her.

She took a deep breath and tried to settle her pounding heart that hadn't let up since he said the D word. "Okay. Dragon. Draaaagon. Dragonnnnn," she said it a few times, drawing the word out, testing how it fell from her lips.

Vaughn was watching her face as she took it all in and seemed to be waiting patiently for her to become comfortable with it.

"Can I, um. Can you show me your... wings again?" she winced as if he was going to recoil from her crazy request.

He nodded slowly and shook his shoulders, unfurling his wings. He stood there, slowly waving them behind his back.

She sat up on her knees and stared. "It's true," she whispered. Her gaze flew to his. "You're a dragon!" Her voice quaked in awe.

He blew smoke from his mouth in a small ring towards her and nodded. He seemed to be one giant ball of tension and fear.

She could see that her acceptance meant the world to him. Suddenly, her brain and heart caught up with each other, and she realized that regardless of it all, he was still a man, an amazingly gorgeous one, who was enamored of her and desperately wanted her approval. She thought about all she knew about him from their months of collaboration. "Vaughn," she began slowly. "All that about being a dragon, about Shadow Claws, protecting me and whatnot, does that affect how you feel about me?"

He stood still and looked at her speculatively for a moment. "Not at all," he finally replied. "Whatever else happens from here, wherever we may be, I still believe you are the most beautiful woman in this world or any other, and there is nothing I wouldn't do to be by your side. From the moment we met, I knew I wanted you. It's been so hard to hold back, and this morning, you looked so adorable, grumbling at your computer. I couldn't wait anymore. It's why I asked you out. I— I want you, Bridget, so much it hurts, so much more than you could know."

He gazed at her with such obvious desire she had no choice but to believe him. She trusted him. She sat up on her knees and dropped the straps of her dress down her shoulders, letting it fall to show a little more cleavage. "Then I suggest, my dear dragon," she said smoothly, "You ditch that towel and let's be sure we don't disappoint my friend."

He hesitated for a second.

"Vaughn, I want you too."

He smiled shyly, dropped the towel, and walked slowly, cautiously towards her.

Bridget had a moment to savor that the man was absolutely stunning, head to toe. Apparently, he liked swimming in the nude, as he wasn't wearing anything under the towel.

He climbed onto the bed with her like a lion stalking prey.

Make that a dragon stalking its prey, she thought as she began to wonder if that's what she was.

"Little one," he growled, "You're thinking too hard again. I need to give you something else to think about." He stopped before her and rose up on his knees to match her pose. He gently laid his hands on her shoulders and began to caress her collarbones.

Bridget felt her breath catch in her throat at the softness of his touch and raised her own hands to his chest. She kept repeating in her head to not look down as she didn't want to seem like a total wanton hussy, but it was hard not to take a peek. She couldn't stop her eyes from sliding down the man like there was a magnet drawing her gaze to a specific point. She bit her lip at the size of that point. She snapped her eyes back up to his, and he laughed softly.

"Don't worry, my sweet; I'll make sure you're ready for it."

She sure hoped he meant that.

He leaned forward and began to trail kisses over her neck and up to her ears.

She could feel the warmth of his breath on her, and it sent a thrill coursing through her body. Everything was on fire. "I, uh, I haven't done this in a while," she admitted, "I may be a little rusty." She laughed lightly. She was nervous. She hadn't been with anyone since Brian. She knew she needed to move on, but it was terrifying to trust her body to another person this way.

Vaughn leaned back to take her face gently in his hands. "You will be amazing, Bridget. Relax, and let me take care of you." He took the straps of her dress and slowly lowered them down over her breasts, and she thanked the gods on high that she let Jorrie talk her into the sexy underwear. He seemed to rumble in his chest, which she took as a sign of approval. "Let's see what else is under there." He let go of the dress and watched it pool around her knees. He picked her up, lifting her entire body so she could kick the dress off from around her feet. "Beautiful," he rumbled again.

"Holy crap," she said, amazed at his show of strength.

He chuckled as he set her back down. "I think you will find, my sweet Bridget, there are many benefits to having a dragon as a lover." He put his hand on her hips and pulled her to his body. He wrapped his arms around her and began to kiss her in earnest.

Bridget was so lost in his kisses that she didn't realize at first that he had removed her bra until she noticed the cool air brush against her nipples. Good grief, this man could make her lose her mind. It had never been like this with Brian. *That's not fair!* Her mind protested; *he wasn't a freaking dragon!* "Shut up, brain," she whispered against his mouth.

His head fell back, and he laughed. "So, you can still think? I'll have to do something about that." He grabbed her by the hips, lifted her up and threw her down on the bed. Before she could even gasp, he was stretched out above her. He looked deep into her eyes as he slowly lowered his body to hers.

She watched the flex of muscles as he kept himself up just enough to avoid crushing her under his amazing frame. "Show off," she said with an impish grin. Her earlier nervousness was fading with his playful attitude and obvious appreciation of her body.

He shut her up in the best way possible, melding his mouth with hers. He lifted one hand and began to knead her breast, making her arch her body into his. This of course had the side benefit of helping her feel his hard length pressing into her hip.

She moaned into his mouth, which made him deepen the kiss further.

He broke away from her lips, and while she panted, he made his way down her neck, kissing, licking, and biting lightly until he reached her breasts. He lightly circled his tongue around one nipple before sucking it into his mouth and putting pressure on it.

She cried out and buried her hands in his silky hair, arching her back again in a way that he knew meant she wanted more. He flicked his tongue back and forth over her nipple while gently sucking before letting a little of his fire warm his mouth and blowing the heat over her.

She bucked underneath him, gasping at the sensation. "What was that?" she asked breathlessly.

"Just a little perk." He winked and switched to the other breast.

She laid back against the soft pillow and slid her hands from his hair to his broad shoulders. Reveling in the sensation, she let go and began to lose herself in the moment.

Vaughn shifted his weight and kissed her stomach as he lowered himself further, gripping her thighs with his hands and pulling them wider.

Bridget's eyes flew open. Was he about to do what she thought he was about to do? *Oh, my sweet baby Jesus and all ten toes!* She began to tense. This was moving too fast!

He sensed her body move, and he growled low in his throat.

She stilled as his eyes came up to meet hers, and she could see the flames dancing behind them again. His desire was so obvious, she was able to relax again.

He draped an arm across her stomach, effectively pinning her down and lifted the other hand to her field of vision.

She watched as one finger developed a sharp, wicked-looking talon. She frantically looked back at him, and he smiled the most devilish smile she had seen yet.

"I hope you weren't too attached to these." he rumbled in a gravelly voice. With a quick flash, he ripped through her panties and flung them over his shoulder.

"Hey!" she tried to protest, but he chose that moment to blow his extra heated breath between her parted thighs, and all words clogged her throat. She let out a strangled groan, and he loosened his grip as he dipped his head to her legs and pressed a kiss on the inside of her thigh.

He ran the claw from the inside of her knee, up her leg to the junction of her thighs and then higher to circle her belly button.

She squirmed, and he blew another heated breath across her. She understood the instruction and stilled.

He retracted the claw and gently pushed her thighs wider, watching the trembling of her body. "Don't worry, my sweet, I just need to know how good you taste," he whispered as he dipped his tongue into her core.

Her thighs clenched and then relaxed as he kneaded them with his warm hands. She rested her hands on his shoulders and melted into the bed, engulfed in the sensations he was giving her.

Vaughn licked his way slowly up her sweet center, clearly enjoying himself if the rumble in his chest was any indication. Pleasure flickered over his face, and he whispered he was going to take her higher. He took a finger and gently stroked her, then eased it just inside her body as he continued to worship her with his tongue. He noticed her legs shaking and grinned to himself, the rumbling getting louder.

She gasped and moaned as the rumble worked its way through her, and she gripped his shoulders tighter. No, that wasn't enough. She lifted one hand to the back of his head and anchored her hand in his silky hair. She thrilled in the way it brushed her thighs as he moved his head around, then he gave one long lick and eased back to look at her. Her eyes fluttered, and she saw him grin.

He eased a second finger in, stretching her painfully but deliciously. She gripped his hair and his shoulder harder, not realizing she was digging her nails into his skin hard enough to leave marks. He didn't seem to notice as he curled his fingers inside her and began to massage that sweet spot deep at her core.

She cried out as he began to flick his tongue even faster, her legs trembling with pleasure. She couldn't help but whip her head side to side, unable to believe how amazing this was. Nothing on this earth should feel this good. She couldn't take much more; she was going to explode.

"Vaughn, Vaughn," she cried, "I can't, I can't!" She gasped as he growled and heated his tongue to an almost intolerable level. She saw her world draw to a pinpoint before it exploded, and her body arched off the bed as the orgasm racked her.

He growled again in triumph and continued to draw his tongue against her, lapping up his victory.

She let go of his hair and shoulder, dropping her arms at her side as the tremors rocked her body, and she continued to shake and quiver. The room slowly came back into focus as he lifted himself and sat up on his knees above her. She blinked and took in the sight of his body. Long, hard, and absolutely ready for her. She was more relaxed than ever in her life but still wasn't sure how this was going to work. But oh baby, was she ready to try.

She reached for him, and he gladly leaned down to her as he kissed his way up her neck and to her jaw, nibbling at the corner of her mouth while he slowly slid inside her. He was stretching her in a way she didn't think was possible. The burn was delicious, and she widened her legs, ready to give him more room.

He somehow managed to slide all the way home and moaned something unintelligible, but it sounded like a commentary on how wet and tight she was. It may have been magic, but it had worked! She gasped as the breath left her when he slowly pulled back and began to move inside her. He covered her mouth with his as she gasped, and their tongues mingled.

He started to thrust harder, and her hands found his broad back and gripped tight. She lifted her legs and wrapped them around his waist, allowing him to go further. She heard him moan and smiled as she remembered he wasn't the only one who could give pleasure here. She arched her back to take him in even deeper than she thought possible, and he trembled.

Suddenly, she heard a rustle, and there was a sharp gust of wind as his wings unfurled behind him. She stilled beneath him and stared in awe at how beautiful they were. The light from the lamp was low but enough to cause the gold to spark and wink at her over his back. She reached up tentatively to stroke the top of one, which caused him to purr, and then there was air on her back. Her eyes grew wide as she realized he had lifted them up and was holding them in the air above the bed.

"Holy crap! Vaughn, what the..?"

He slammed her against the wall, halfway to the ceiling and grabbed her legs to steady them around his waist. "Now you've done it," he growled at her. He started pumping his wings in time to each thrust, which forced him into her so hard she thought it would split her in two. It was amazing!

She could feel the pressure building and knew she was going to fall off the edge of the world again. She gasped his name, "Vaughn!"

He rumbled in response. "Let go, my sweet Bridget. Fly with me," he commanded her as his breathing grew ragged and his thrusts became erratic. He was close, too.

Without warning she did fly apart and screamed as the orgasm blew through her like a late-spring tornado. It was glorious and wicked and everything she never knew she could feel. She had dug her nails into his back so hard she'd drawn blood. She noticed the warm trickle down his back as she pulled her hands up and stroked his wings where they sprouted from his back.

That was the final straw for Vaughn, as he roared his release and the sultry smell of smoke erupted from him. He fiercely claimed her mouth again as he shuddered then slowly lowered them back to the bed. He lay there over her, ending the kiss and then levering himself up to look at her while his wings folded against his back, but they didn't disappear as they had before. "Bridget," he moaned into her shoulder. "You were perfect."

Chapter 12

"Holy shit," Bridget said breathlessly. "That was, that was. I don't know what that was but holy shit."

Vaughn chuckled and brushed her hair off her face. "Well, I guess that was a compliment?" he asked, then rolled his shoulders.

Bridget's face fell, "Oh crap, Vaughn, I'm so sorry! I hurt you, didn't I?"

He smiled and kissed her hand. "No, my sweet, you didn't hurt me. I'm made of tougher stuff." He winked at her and continued, "I actually like it a little rough." His face slowly turned serious, "But did I hurt you when I…?" He paused and looked up at the wall where he'd pinned her.

Now it was Bridget's turn to laugh. "No! Absolutely not!" she said with more force than she expected. "I loved that, it was so primal, so just, wow!" She stretched like a cat after a long nap in the sun, enjoying the feeling of her relaxed muscles. She hadn't realized how tense she was until he had worked it out of her.

He grinned and told her, "Well you certainly look like you've been well used." He kissed the tip of her nose.

She froze suddenly, "Oh god, I'm not. I mean, we didn't use any protection." she stopped, berating herself internally for forgetting such a basic thing. The strong pull of his desire for her had swamped her senses. She'd been overwhelmed by her want for him in return.

He smiled gently at her, "It's okay, Bridget, dragons don't get human diseases that way. And you don't have to worry about other, um, complications; it can only happen with a bonded mate. It's a magic thing."

She studied his face, trying to determine whether to believe him or not. She decided once again to trust him. She couldn't explain it, but everything about him felt safe. *Which is ridiculous because he's a dragon.*

"Bridget, I promise, if there were any concerns in that regard, I swear I would have used protection. I would never do anything that would harm you."

She laughed in relief and then put her hands to her hair. "Ugh, I'm sure my hair looks a fright now, and I'm covered in sweat. Do you mind if I take a shower?"

He said, "Oh, I've got a better idea." He picked her up to his chest and walked out of the bedroom.

At first, she was surprised and embarrassed by this display of masculinity, but then decided to revel in it instead. "Where are we going?" she asked, lazily stroking her hands over his broad chest and toying with the ends of his hair. Jorrie was *not* going to believe her. In fact, she wasn't sure she wasn't dreaming. She picked up the faint sound of lapping water as they walked into another room before Vaughn suddenly leapt, and they were falling. She had a second to think about screaming, and then she was underwater.

Bridget came spluttering to the surface and shoved her hair out of her eyes. "What the hell, Vaughn!" she shouted when she caught her breath. She looked around and didn't see him anywhere. She was in a giant pool, but like none she'd ever seen. The water seemed to be the perfect temperature and was surrounded by rocks. No real shape, the edges meandered in a free form. Natural looking ledges were set into the sides, where a person or several could lay. She made her way to the nearest one and looked up.

She was so startled that she almost forgot to keep swimming until water flooded her nose. She pulled herself onto the ledge and stared above her. There was no ceiling! Just the open sky! How was this possible?

"Digital again." She heard the rumble echo across the cave-like area. Of course, it was a cluster of digital screens like the windows in the living room. But where was Vaughn? She'd heard him so she knew he was still in here somewhere.

She pulled her knees to her chest and wrapped her arms around them, giving in to a little shiver. He'd better show himself soon. She had a thing or two to say. "Vaughn?" she called out, hearing her voice echo off the far rocks. "Where are you?" a little more quietly.

Suddenly, a dark shape shot through the water like a bullet near her, and he burst through the surface to land on the ledge. He stood there in all his naked glory, not the least bit shy about it, lightly shaking water from his wings.

Bridget stood and stomped in front of him then poked him in the shoulder. "Vaughn, whatever your middle name is, Drake!" she scolded, "You do *not* throw a woman into a pool without warning her. What if I couldn't swim? What if I had inhaled some of the water and drowned? You jerk!" She slapped his shoulder and crossed her arms under her generous breasts. This caused them to rise a little, which naturally got his attention.

He gave an appreciative stare, then met her eyes. "Cormac."

"Huh?" she replied intelligently.

"My middle name," he replied, "It's Cormac. So, when you want to use that sexy mom voice to scold me, dear Bridget Ridgeway, you can call me Vaughn Cormac Drake. And you wouldn't have drowned. I would have made sure of that. I told you, I would never hurt you," he spoke quietly, then caressed her face. "Please forgive me; I didn't mean to scare you; it's just you wanted to get cleaned up, and I was afraid if we showered together, I'd just ravish you against the shower wall, and we'd never finish our conversation from earlier."

Her mouth went as dry as a desert at his admission. She noticed his body was standing at attention. The thought wasn't far enough from his mind. She allowed him to wrap her in his arms and pull her close. She laid her head against his chest and heard him rumble in pleasure. "I like it when you do that," she told him. "It reminds me of a cat's purr."

He snorted, "I am not a cat." Mock fierceness colored his voice.

She looked up and grinned. "Oh, of course you are. Just a big, soft, rumbly kitty who likes to be... stroked." She put motion to her words, stroking her hand up his hard shaft and running her fingers around the tip.

His eyes flashed with flames and suddenly they were flying across the cave to a smaller pool that had steam rising lazily from the surface. He lowered them into the pool, which she now realized was a hot tub, and sighed gratefully as the warm water covered her.

Vaughn grabbed her arms and pulled them over her head with one hand. The other he reached down between her legs and began to stroke her again. "Well, you, Bridget, are just a naughty little minx who needs to be taught a lesson."

She was too wound up in what he was doing to protest. Not that she wanted to anyway. She arched into his hand and whimpered for more.

He withdrew his hand, grabbed her hips and spun them around so he was sitting on a rock bench, and she was in his lap. He slowly lowered her, and she gasped as he slid in until he was fully seated in her again.

Bridget couldn't breathe, the sensations were overwhelming with the warmth surrounding her and him stretching her like this. She put her hands on his shoulders and began to move.

Tired, she thought, *so, so, tired.* She snuggled close to Vaughn in his oh-so-soft bed and laid her head on his chest.

He pulled her in close and made his happy purr sound again. After they had finished in the hot tub, he'd given her one of his shirts to put on, and they finished their chocolate cake. He had cleaned up the wine glass she had dropped earlier while she was still unconscious and supplied her with a new one.

They had talked more about how the Shadows had come back after the two-thousand-year ban on their power was lifted. Unfortunately, it had been so long since anyone had held any powers that no one realized what was happening at first. The magic was now passed down through generations. The different tribes had long since scattered and mingled, starting new civilizations. It was only within the last three hundred years that the Shadows began finding each other and forming a new faction.

"So, all this time," Bridget yawned, "Sorry, so all this time, the dragons were what, just waiting? Watching?" she said sleepily.

"Yes. We'd been waiting for the tribes that we fought with to reform as well, but they never did, so we've allied with the Wielders we can find." He had looked over at Bridget and noticed her eyes were struggling to stay open. He kissed the top of her head, "Sleep, my dear, we can finish in the morning."

He pulled the comforter up around her shoulders and held her while she fell into a deep sleep. He lay there, soaking in every inch of her face and thought about what a hard road she'd walked so far, and was sorry about how much harder it was going to get. He fell asleep himself shortly after and held her through the night.

CHAPTER 13

BRIDGET YAWNED AND STRETCHED, feeling like she'd never slept so well in her life but also feeling like she'd run a marathon the day before. She blinked her eyes and looked around. *Right, so, Vaughn, dragon, amazing sex, shadow people, check. Wow. Jorrie is never going to believe this.* She bolted upright. *Jorrie, Gabriel! Oh no,* she panicked, thinking she needed to get Gabriel to school. What time was it?

She looked around for a clock and finally saw it was already 8:30 a.m. "Shit!" she whispered; oh, she was never going to live this down.

"Good morning, sunshine."

She turned as the delicious male voice chimed and saw Vaughn leaning against the bedroom door. He was dressed in jeans and an unbuttoned shirt, looking entirely too handsome for this early in the morning. He held two mugs in his hands. Steam from the contents wafted into the air.

"Tea?" he motioned with one cup. "I remembered how you take it." He walked over to the bed with the mug, holding it out to her.

She gladly accepted it and blew on the hot liquid while she refocused. "I'm so sorry, Vaughn, but I've got to get home. I need to get Gabriel to school!" she started to get out of bed.

"Relax, I've already got it covered," he replied, putting his hand on her shoulder to keep her there. He admired the way she looked in his bed with her hair all tousled from sleep. "I sent Liam over this morning to get him there. Jorrie already had him up and ready; she was going to take him, but he opted to ride with Liam once he saw the car. Also, um, apparently, Jorrie sends congratulations." He grinned at her shocked expression.

"Well, uh, thanks. That was very kind and thoughtful of you," she replied. "I bet he loved that, going to school in a Rolls." She rolled her eyes, imaging how her son would have reacted to such an opportunity.

He smirked, "Oh, Liam didn't take the Rolls. I thought that was too ostentatious."

Bridget eyed him carefully, "So what *did* he take that Gabe was so excited about?" she asked slowly.

Just then, Liam popped his head around the door. "Morning, Bridget!" he announced cheerfully. "Glad to see you're awake and he didn't eat you. How do you take your eggs?" he asked as if it was the most normal thing in the world to make breakfast for a woman he'd just met, sitting in his boss's bed.

"Over easy, thank you, Liam. What did you take my son to school in?" she asked suspiciously.

Liam grinned at her, "Oh, just a car miss. Drake said not to take the Rolls; it would be too ostentatious."

She glared at him; she had a feeling she wasn't getting the whole story.

"Wow, Drake, you weren't kidding. She does the Mom Look really well." Liam laughed.

Vaughn snorted. "You might as well answer her. She's not going to let it go. My Bridget is very tenacious."

Liam shook his head. "No, I don't think she will. Okay, so it's not a big deal. I just thought, if I was a teenage boy and I could pick the car, what would it be? So, I took the Lambo. No big." He shrugged.

Bridget stared at him open-mouthed; her skin prickling. "You took my son. To school. My teenage son. To *high* school. In a Lamborghini?" she demanded. "I'm never going to hear the end of it. Never, ever, ever. Do you understand this? Never!"

She started laughing, and Vaughn took her cup back before she fell back on the bed and put the pillow over her face.

Liam looked a little disconcerted. "Yeah, well, he really liked it!" he said, in his most helpful voice. "His friends were really impressed, too. They all gathered round, and I gave them a look," he added hopefully.

Bridget sat up and threw the pillow at him. "Out!" she shouted.

Liam took off like a cat with its tail under a rocking chair, cackling the whole way.

She eyed Vaughn suspiciously as he was obviously trying not to laugh. "Never," she said, as she got up and stalked to the bathroom. "Never," she said again and slammed the door.

When Bridget came out of the bathroom, Vaughn was sitting in the chair she'd spotted the night before in the corner by the bookcases. He was slouched down, looking very relaxed, with his long legs crossed casually at the ankles.

Her gaze trailed up those legs that she had reason to know were very well-muscled, continuing up to his stomach and chest where she noted he had now buttoned his shirt. *Dang,* she bemoaned the view that was no longer available. She looked at his face and saw he was watching her with a sultry look.

"Soo…" she started and pulled at the hem of his t-shirt as it skimmed her thighs.

"So," he repeated quietly.

"Well, this is nice and awkward. Um, I guess I need to get dressed. I'm not quite sure where you threw my bra and my panties," she trailed off, blushing.

Vaughn slowly lifted his frame from the chair. "Ah yes, those." He pulled the remnants of the panties out of his jeans pocket, "Those met with a rather, tragic end." He smiled sweetly at her as he put them back in his pocket.

Bridget's neck joined forces with the heat in her face. "Okay, stop that!" she chided, "You can't go around destroying my underwear. What am I supposed to wear home?"

He tossed his head lazily towards the bed, where she saw her overnight bag sitting on the end.

She turned and looked back at him, one eyebrow raised in query.

"Jorrie apparently anticipated your needs and sent that back with Liam this morning. She gave him instructions to give it to you with the following phrase: 'You go, girl, and now we are even for Cabo, 2000'. A phrase I'm sure has meaning to you, but I am certainly intrigued.

What happened in Cabo in 2000, my sweet little Bridget." He stalked over to her, grinning ear to ear.

"Not anything I'm willing to share with you just yet." She snatched the bag and walked back to the bathroom. Deciding to get a little revenge on him, she looked over her shoulder and said, "But it involved a wet t-shirt contest and a *lot* of baby oil." She smiled in victory at the look on his face before the door closed. *Yeeesss! Booty dance!* She thought before doing a silly little wiggle she and Jorrie had made up that Spring Break.

Bridget set the bag on the counter then opened it to see what Jorrie had sent. She prayed it was practical and not Jorrie's wicked sense of humor packing her things.

She was relieved to see shorts near the top, along with her favorite tennis shoes peeking out from underneath. Jorrie had come through; she really was an awesome friend! Bridget sent her a silent thanks into the universe, resolving to treat her friend to a girl's weekend soon. She saw a piece of paper folded up under the handle of her toiletries bag and shook her head. She wasn't sure what type of message awaited her but decided to just go ahead and get it over with. She pulled out the single sheet of notepaper she recognized as her own favorite stationery, with little black cats prancing across the top of the page. In Jorrie's flowery, hand she read:

'Bridge, I packed your sensible things so you wouldn't have to do the walk of shame in last night's outfit, just like when you helped me out in Cabo. You are the best friend I've ever had, and I'm going to give you some advice because I love you. Stop worrying that you aren't good enough or you don't deserve this. Get out of your head. This man obviously wants you for you. Take advantage of it, you've mourned long enough. Live a little. And tell me all about it tonight. I really hope you climbed that man like a tree, if not, I don't know if I can look you in the face ever again. Love you bunches, kiss kiss, hug hug and all that.– J'

Bridget sat on the edge of the huge spa tub and stared at the note, tears welling in her eyes. Jorrie knew her all too well. She did tend to second guess herself and put off her own well-being. She hadn't dated much and certainly had not been intimate with anyone since Brian had died. Becoming a widow so young had not factored into her life plan, and she'd had to scramble to rearrange things so Gabriel never lacked or wanted for anything. He'd become her whole world for a long time as she focused on that and that alone. She wiped away a few tears and folded the note again, holding it up to her heart. Jorrie was right, it was time for her to live.

Bridget wandered into the kitchen and found Liam and Vaughn sitting at a table, looking at some files scattered between them.

Liam saw her and jumped to his feet, pulling out a chair and ushering her to the table. Once seated, he grabbed a plate for her full of delicious smelling breakfast foods. It was all warm and fragrant, and she realized she was starving.

She waited for Liam to set down plates for Vaughn and himself before tucking into the most perfectly cooked eggs she'd ever had. She noted Vaughn watching her with amusement, a piece of bacon held lazily between his fingers and sparkle in his eye.

Liam was putting what smelled like fresh apple butter on a super fluffy, steaming biscuit with his elbows on some of the files they had been reviewing.

"Oh!" she said suddenly, "I must be keeping you from your work!" She was embarrassed at how quickly she had forgotten such responsibilities.

Vaughn smiled kindly and Liam grinned around his mouthful of biscuit. "It's quite alright, my dear. One of the perks of being the boss."

"Oh, right," she said, "Well, if Liam wouldn't mind terribly running me home after we eat, I'll get out of your hair so you can get back to it."

Vaughn stared at her for so long she thought maybe she had something on her face. She reached up to wipe her mouth with the napkin, trying to discreetly feel for any errant crumbs that may have stuck there.

He leaned towards her. "I'd hoped I could get you to join me at my office today. I mentioned to you yesterday I had a business proposition for you, but with all our," he paused and grinned wickedly, "Activities last night, we never got around to discussing it."

Liam snorted and said, "Activities," under his breath.

She shot him a look that he returned with an innocent smile. She gave up and laughed, "Okay, Liam, you win. But Vaughn, I'm not dressed to go into your office. Do we have time to drop by my house so I can change into something more professional than shorts and t-shirt?" she implored.

He waved his hand and shook his head, "Not necessary. We aren't going to Chesapeake. We're going to my other company, the gaming business that Gabriel is so excited to see. That office has a much more relaxed dress code. The programmers thrive better in a casual environment. I find their creativity improves when they roam free. So, you're dressed perfectly."

Liam didn't drive them this time, citing the need to run some errands. These errands were obviously the source of some contention as they were discussed in heated whispers down the hall.

She could make out snippets and knew it had something to do with the Shadow Claw. The conversation from last night echoed through her mind. Ancient magic, dragons, some dangerous quest to be undertaken, it all seemed like the plot of one of the video games Gabriel was so fond of. She turned thoughtfully towards Vaughn, *Cloud Warrior, hmm, I wonder if...*

"Ready to go?" Vaughn interrupted her thoughts and held up the keys. "Let's see if we can get as much awe and interest as Liam did this morning."

Driving a Lamborghini in Dallas wasn't all that rare of a sight. There were a lot of large companies in the area and quite a few high rollers. Several YouTubers, young entrepreneurs and quite a few highly paid athletes. She highly doubted, though, that there were any others that were gold with black accents.

"Less ostentatious?" she hissed at Vaughn's profile as he laughingly turned in the driveway of their destination.

As he whipped into his reserved spot, she noted that the employees she could see around the area were not paying him any attention, they must be used to the sight. The building was shaded by beautiful old oak trees. It looked like a peaceful place to have lunch, with a duck pond off to the side and lots of benches to enjoy the fresh air.

Unsure how to open the door, she waited until Vaughn came around and opened it with a flourish, holding out his hand to assist her from the car. She took a deep breath and stepped out into the warm, clear morning.

CHAPTER 14

NOISE. THAT'S WHAT BRIDGET heard when she walked through the glass front doors of the building. She was expecting the usual quiet hum of workers in an office. Instead, off to the right, she saw a gaming room where it looked like a gaggle of college kids were having a battle on a large screen in the middle of the room.

Cheers and groans erupted as she saw one young woman who looked a lot like Liam turn and high-five the crowd behind her while her opponent held his head in his hands, a sign of utter defeat. The crowd behind him gave him equal amounts of conciliatory encouragement and jeers for losing. It seemed good-natured and fun.

One of the kids saw Vaughn and Bridget and waved, "Hey, Drake!" he called out, causing the others in the room to turn and look. "You missed it! Siobhan just destroyed Sam on CW4! It was EPIC!" he shouted. This caused more cheering and laughter until some of them noticed Bridget.

"Yo, Drake, who's the babe?" one of the other kids said, causing everyone to quiet down and stare at her.

Vaughn put his hands in his pockets and strolled over, gesturing with his head for Bridget to follow him. "Bridget," he said calmly, "This young man with no manners is Collin Chester, one of our brightest developers."

Collin gave her a cheeky wave.

Vaughn continued, "For the rest of you, who are no doubt wondering, the lovely woman you see here is Ms. Bridget Ridgeway. I've invited her here today to show her what we do in hopes I can convince her to join our team in charge of VR Integration."

Bridget turned to Vaughn, trying not to show the confusion that was inside her to the group assembled before her. A job? Was he talking about a job? That's not what she was expecting when he brought her here. Honestly, she wasn't sure what to expect anymore but a job was the last thing she had thought of.

"Great," muttered the victorious young girl that Bridget remembered had been called Siobhan. "Just what we need, another corporate yuppie trying to stifle us. Does she know anything at all about gaming? She looks like someone's mom," she said with a sniff.

Everyone in the room immediately quieted down and stared at Siobhan like she had grown two heads. For all their casual approach, it was obvious she had crossed some line or unspoken boundary.

Vaughn's smile was brittle, and Bridget recognized it from the day before when he had faced Melissa Payne in the conference room.

Fearing for the young lady's safety, Bridget quickly intervened. "Well, how very perceptive of you," she drawled in a sweet voice, enhancing the southern twang in her tone. "In fact, I *am* someone's mom. A very bright young man who adores the products you make here. Not only that, but I've raised him to be a very respectful young man who knows how to address people in a position of authority and to be a decent human being. I'm giving lessons to anyone interested." She looked Siobhan up and down.

"Honey, I'll give you a few for free, since you seem to be... a difficult case. Bless your heart." She grinned at the girl, enjoying the stunned look on her face before the crowd around her burst into laughter.

Some good-natured slapping on Siobhan's back occurred before she finally grinned and said, "You're alright, Bridget," and held out her hand.

Bridget shook the girl's hand and winked.

Vaughn shook his head in defeat and pulled her away from the group, promising to bring her back after they'd had time to talk.

They walked towards a back hallway with regularly spaced glass doors that allowed her to see that many of the offices were filled with bean bag chairs, mismatched furniture and computer set-ups that would make Gabe drool. Most of the spaces were filled with action figures and posters of various gaming advertisements. Stickers covered many of the surfaces, and something that passed for music blasted from some of them. It almost looked like a college dorm.

She could see people of all ages, genders, and dress styles working away at what looked like a foreign language on many of the computers. Some of the crowd from the gaming area drifted back into their own spaces, donning headphones, and getting back into whatever world-domination plot they were cooking up.

Bridget was overwhelmed; Vaughn thought she could work here? She didn't know the first thing about programming, and certainly not in the style of working these people were apparently accustomed to. He continued down the hall and around a corner where she began to see more traditional style set-ups and 'normal' looking work occurring.

Maybe here, she thought, *working as some sort of administrative assistant.* Although if that's what he had in mind, she would politely decline. She was not interested in a pity job just because she had lost hers the day before. *Wow, it was only yesterday that I learned about shadows and dragons. Feels like a lifetime ago.* She mentally shook herself and looked around her, assessing the shadows.

Vaughn gave her a curious look, then seemed to understand what she was doing. "Don't worry, dear," he whispered in her ear. "This space is warded; these are just normal shadows in this building and my home. Your home, too, as soon as Liam finishes gathering the necessary parties." He smiled to reassure her and led her to a large corner office with floor-to-ceiling windows.

Like the other spaces, the front of the office was all glass. Unlike the other spaces, he had the ability to make them opaque, which he did as he walked in and shut the door. He leaned against the door, taking in the sight of her. She was walking around, studying the view and the large glass and chrome desk in the middle of the office. It was so unlike his staid and stuffy office at Chesapeake.

She was trying to reconcile the two sides of the man, or was that three if you counted the dragon, when he came over and pulled her to his body, putting his lips on hers in a hungry, demanding kiss. She sank into his warmth, eagerly kissing him back. When he finally let her go, she stood there with a dreamy smile on her face.

"Mmm," she hummed. "You are so good at that."

He gave her another quick kiss and said "I've been wanting to do that since we walked through the front door. I can't seem to get enough of you." He let go of her body but retained his grip on her hand as he led her over to his desk and seated her in a guest chair.

He sat next to her in the other chair and smiled. "I have to say, I'm really impressed with the way you handled Siobhan. She's a real pain in my ass sometimes, but I keep her on as a favor to Liam and his family. I'm their Godfather, their parents are close friends of mine."

I was right! Bridget thought. *She's Liam's sister.* "But he's so nice and cheerful," she said, "And she's..." she trailed off, not wanting to insult the girl.

"Surly," said Vaughn.

She nodded and shrugged. "She's young, she's got a chip on her shoulder about something, she has time to work that off."

Vaughn squinted at her. "You're very perceptive. And you're good with people. Not to mention your fine attention to business details. I really admired that about you when we were working together these last six months. I knew you were smart. Jack brags about you frequently, you know. You have a great sense of when to push and when to pull back on a project and you really seem to know what a team needs to be motivated. Like back there, I was ready to scold her for the way she spoke to you, but you knew exactly how to handle her. I saw the way your team reacted to you; they wanted to perform well for you. That's what I need here. I need someone who knows how to corral these various personalities together and help us take this to the next level." He studied her face to see what she was thinking.

"A farmer," she mused out loud.

"What?" he asked, surprised by her response.

"You have a group of free-range chickens out there," she nodded towards the hallway, "You let the chickens wander around the yard, and while they are producing enough eggs, that's fine. But when you need them to give you a specific egg, you need a farmer to encourage them and feed them the right nutrients without taking away their freedom or making them feel that they are being held back."

He stared at her and then grabbed her hands. "Exactly!" he said excitedly. "This is why I knew you were what we needed, what I wanted!" His eyes flashed briefly. "I wanted to steal you away months ago but knew I needed to wait until the deal was done. Now I don't have to wait anymore."

"Yeah," she replied drily, "Because I got fired."

He chuckled, "Side benefit. That means you are available to me, and I don't have to worry about hard feelings or accusations."

"Vaughn." She hesitated. "Look, I really appreciate what you are trying to do here, but I don't want you to feel you have to give me a job because you feel sorry for me or because we slept together. I can find another job on my own, I'm sure. I have excellent references—" she stopped as he put a finger to her lips.

"Bridget," he warned, "Stop right there. Do not insult me, because I am not insulting you. This is not a pity offer. Nor is this related to our relationship. Yes!" He growled when he felt her lips move against his skin. "This *is* a relationship. I do not take revealing my other side lightly, and you, my dear, are not going anywhere. So, I repeat. This offer is being made to you because you have the skills and drive to do what needs to be done. The fact that you are gorgeous and have the most delightful scream when I—"

This time, Bridget put her hand over his mouth. "Do not say whatever you were about to say," she warned.

He held his hands up in mock surrender, and she could feel his non-repentant smile curving against her palm.

She slowly lowered her hand and stared at him. "Okay, Drake, what are you offering?"

Vaughn gave a nod and leaned across the desk, grabbing a file folder with her name on the tab. He opened it to reveal some official-looking documents. "If you check the dates on these, you will see they were drafted well before I took you," he paused, "To dinner." He grinned a mischievous smile.

She glared at him in pretend fury before taking the papers from him. She read through what seemed to be a standard employment contract, benefits seemed affordable and more than fair. Hours were flexible, with opportunities to work remotely, which would help with Gabriel's senior year, and she checked the date, noting that it had been drafted almost three weeks ago. He was telling the truth. She glanced up at Vaughn; he was studiously staring out the window as if he wasn't on pins and needles waiting for her response. She looked back down and continued to read. *Travel expenses paid, of course, mmm, vacation time is generous too, my own office, and the salary.* Her brain seemed to stutter and restart.

"Vaughn," she whispered, "This is too much." Her eyes fixated on the very large number on the second page. She looked up at him and he simply met her gaze, no emotion on his face.

"I don't believe so," he replied evenly, "Our new VP of Integration deserves to be paid well for her work. She has a very demanding boss with extreme and unusual needs; she should be compensated for that extra work."

Bridget was suddenly uneasy. "I'm not a prostitute," she said with steel in her voice. "You aren't going to pay me to sleep with you." She was just petty enough to enjoy the shocked look on his face.

"No!" he said hurriedly, "That's not what I meant at all! I just mean that I'm splitting my time between multiple businesses, and then there's the whole dragon thing, you know. Sometimes, I have to take time to fully change, and that can lead to awkward questions about where I am and where's that smoke coming from. Plus, I can be moody," he finished lamely.

She stared at him for a moment. "Moody?"

He tapped the date on the documents, "Remember, drafted before we became better acquainted."

Bridget softened; it made sense. The money was almost three times what she made before. She'd be able to get Gabriel that car without dipping into their settlement savings after all. She quickly read through the rest of the offer and looked up at him, biting her lip to keep from laughing at the hopeful expression on his gorgeous face.

"So boss," she took a deep breath, "When do I start?"

CHAPTER 15

LIGHT FILTERED IN THROUGH the large windows that ran from floor to ceiling in her new office. Bridget hugged herself, *her* new office. After she completed the official contracts, Vaughn escorted her across the hall, showing her to a space that overlooked a green wooded area, which provided some shade but still allowed a wonderful amount of sunlight to filter through. The carpet was plush and luxurious. She wanted to throw herself down on it and roll around but remained composed as she was sure it wouldn't do for the new VP to be seen lolling on the floor like a dog.

He was showing her a catalog she could peruse to pick out a desk when a man named Killian knocked and apologetically asked Vaughn for a moment. Vaughn introduced him as the Director of Development as well as a good friend. The man nodded in greeting. He had long silvery-blonde hair that covered most of his face. He had kind eyes and a sweet smile. He spoke softly and quietly with an intriguing Irish accent, something to do with a certain Goblin not picking up a battle axe the way it was supposed to.

She shook her head. She supposed she'd have to learn a lot about fantasy with this new job. *Not just the job,* she corrected herself. She hadn't really talked with Vaughn much today about the Shadow Claw. She really needed to learn more about them and why they seemed to be after her in particular. She stared into the trees, looking at the shadows between them. She studied them anxiously, looking for anything outside of the norm. She knew Vaughn had said the building was warded against them, but how far did those boundaries go? The whole property? Or just the actual building? What good was a warding around the building if they could snatch her from the parking lot? She shivered involuntarily, thinking about it.

"Cold?" she heard as hands touched her shoulders.

"Hi-yah!" she yelled in her best martial arts impression when she whirled around and karate-chopped her attacker in the throat. "Shit!" she said, watching as Vaughn doubled over, gasping for air. "Shit, shit, shit!" she said again as she awkwardly patted him on the back, encouraging him to breathe.

"I'm so sorry!" she cried out. "You scared me, and I thought you were a shadow monster, and I..." She trailed off suspiciously. She was suddenly aware that Vaughn wasn't gasping for air. He was laughing. "Not funny," she said grumpily.

Vaughn stood and straightened his shirt, wiping his eyes and continued to laugh quietly. "I don't know, I found it pretty funny." His face was full of delight at her attack. "Ms. Ridgeway, I do believe we will need to speak to HR about your assault on another employee." He grinned at her.

She resisted the impulse to stick her tongue out at him, then thought better of it and did it anyway.

His shocked face made her laugh this time around.

"Well, seeing as how I haven't 'officially' started yet, there's not much you can do," she replied haughtily.

He smiled and pulled her in for a hug. "Well then, I guess I'll just have to let the insult stand for now while I think of a suitable punishment for you later," he promised huskily.

Her body became warm and tingly all over at what he was insinuating. "Not in the office, you, fiend!" she playfully slapped his arm, stepping away. "We need to keep it professional here," she reminded him.

He let her go and nodded. "Quite right, but I repeat my earlier question before you tried to use judo to remove my head from my body. By the way, for the record, dragons are very hard to kill. It's going to take more than your questionable fighting skills to take me down." He winked. "Are you cold? I can adjust the temperature over here." He gestured to the control pad for the room's lighting and temperature.

"No," she shook her head, "I was thinking about the shadows and the wards you mentioned. Having some not-so-pleasant thoughts. Look, I know you have work to be done, but we need to finish our conversation about these shadow creatures and my role in it. I'm scared," she finally admitted.

Vaughn studied her face for a moment. Here it was, the moment he'd been dreading. He didn't want to tell her the rest. He wanted to work by her side during the day, lie with her at night, and spend the rest of the time basking in her glow. He could listen to her talk about nothing and everything. There was so much to tell her about the hard days to come. He also couldn't tell her he was already halfway in love with her.

He couldn't tell her about all the times he'd had to stop from reaching across a table and brushing her wild red hair away from her face in the months they'd spent working together. The excuses he'd made up to bring paperwork by her office when he could have easily sent an assistant or a courier. Finding a reason to brush against her so he could feel her soft skin and breathe in her floral perfume mixed with something spicy that was just her. How he couldn't stop thinking about her night and day and how he wanted to see her again as soon as she'd left.

Pumping information from Jack about his sister-in-law, who, by the way, was the widow of his dead brother. He'd had certainly caught on to Vaughn's interest in Bridget, in fact, he had encouraged it. Her brother-in-law really cared about her, and it showed what a special person she was that he wanted her to be happy and not cling to the memory of someone long gone. She was lucky to have him as well. Jack was a good man.

He studied the way the light played across her cheeks, the way it reflected in her eyes, and something shifted in him. He wasn't just halfway in love; he was all the way. And he was going to do anything and everything in his power to protect her. Even if she never loved him in return.

Bridget studied the serious look on Vaughn's face. Trying to decipher what he was thinking. His mood had turned brooding, and she realized this was another side of him she hadn't seen before. She wanted to make whatever was bothering him better, so she placed her hand on his cheek, "Hey," she whispered, "Talk to me." She watched him come back to the room, and he stared into her eyes. She smiled at him.

He gently kissed her, then said, "Lunch, let's go eat. We can talk more once you have something in your stomach."

She laughed, "Are all dragons this concerned with food? After that huge breakfast you gave me, you're trying to feed me again. Are you trying to fatten me up to roast me for dinner?" She patted her not-so-flat but not-bad-for-her age stomach. She looked back up at him, and he was grinning in a way that she knew had nothing to do with food.

"Oh yes, my sweet Bridget," he replied, "I can't wait to eat you up." He gave a corny, evil laugh and grabbed her hand, pulling her from the office towards the hall.

After grabbing some sandwiches from a little deli nearby, they settled onto a bench at a park by the office.

She took a bite and pointed at him, circling her finger in a 'go ahead' motion. "Spill," she said after swallowing the bite.

He settled back onto the bench and picked up where they'd left off the night before. "So, the Shadows, they started finding each other and uniting as a group about three hundred years ago. In the last two hundred years they've really organized and worked towards a singular purpose. That purpose is related to a prophecy that was made before the Unbinding, as we dragon folk call the event. It was thought lost when the tribes disbanded and scattered the globe, but it was rediscovered in 1801. It has been hidden away to protect it and keep our identities secret. Can you imagine modern society finding out about this?" he asked as he paused to take a sip of iced tea.

Bridget shook her head; this was a lot to take in, and she was just one person.

"Anyway," he continued, "Not too long ago, the Shadow leader, who calls himself King Azrael, by the way, bribed someone and discovered the prophecy." He took a bite of his sandwich.

"Wait," she laughed, "You're telling me that the so-called King of these shadow monsters has the same name as Gargamel's cat?" Vaughn's face went blank, and she clarified, "You know the Smurfs, the cartoon bad guy Gargamel, he had a raggedy cat named Azrael? That little bit of trivia comes in handy from time to time," she confided.

"Ah," he replied, "Funny, but no. He named himself after Azrael, the Angel of Death. And it's fitting because that's how he sees himself. As the avenger of his people, death is his ultimate tool to instill fear in his followers and keep them under his thumb. He tortures, he teases, he torments. Quite a few of them like it that way, though." He stared off after a bird that had taken flight through the trees.

"My god," Bridget whispered. "That's horrible." She set her sandwich down, losing all interest in it.

He nodded and continued to watch the bird dodging between the trunks and seeming to enjoy the warm currents. He briefly closed his eyes and turned his face to the sun, seeming to need warmth, drawing strength from the light. After a moment, he opened his eyes and sought out the bird again. He heaved a deep sigh and shook his head. It was time to quit stalling and tell her the worst. He was not looking forward to it and wasn't quite sure how to break the news.

"Although we dragons know what the prophecy says, none have been able to truly understand what it means. As with most prophecies, it's vague and more of a riddle. What we do know, however, is that it points to two people, either of whom can supposedly bring about the end of the Shadow tribe. We don't know how or in what way, but we do know that it seems it will happen sometime in the next few months. This is known to dragon and shadow alike." He paused and looked at her. She wasn't moving, just hanging onto his every word with rapt attention. "They've already found one of those two people, and unfortunately, they killed him before we could stop them. Most regular people can't see the Shadows unless they want to be seen. He never had a chance." He stopped again and looked down at his sandwich, picking at it, having no appetite. He didn't want to say this. He experienced a sickening dread building within him and his stomach twisted in knots.

"Who's the second?" she whispered fearfully, already scared that she seemed to know the answer.

He stared up into her eyes, his pleading for forgiveness. He finally replied in a voice filled with sorrow, "You."

CHAPTER 16

"**I** KNEW IT!" SHE ranted, stomping back and forth across the trail by their bench. "I just knew it was too good to be true." She walked by, and Vaughn reached out to grab her hand. She shook him off and kept up her pacing. "Of course, it's me. Gorgeous man who looks like sex incarnate takes an interest in me. Oh, and he's not just hot, he's kind, thoughtful, funny, appreciates my stupid jokes and is crazy smart. Let's not forget he's a DRAGON!" she shouted. "He thinks I'm smart, my friends like him. Hell, my son worships the ground he walks on." She threw her hands up in the air. "I was just offered the opportunity of a lifetime with a role I can kick ass at, an amazing office at a major company, a chance to travel, and my new boss fucks like a god, and I'm a damsel in some romance novel."

She whirled around and stared him down. "And now, you tell me some fucking shadow king who thinks he's the Angel of Death wants me dead because some dude thousands of years ago picked me at random to be some sort of... what? A hero of prophecy to end a race of soul-selling shadow assholes? Is that what you are telling me,

116

Vaughn Drake? Is that what the fuck, you are telling me right now?" she seethed.

He could see her shaking in her anger, and it was glorious. He decided it was best not to tell her how much he was turned on right now. He was pretty sure she wouldn't appreciate it. "Well," he said cautiously, "I wouldn't have summarized it quite like that, but yeah, I guess that pretty much sums it up." He paused, then grinned at her, "You think I fuck like a god?"

Bridget stared at him, speechless.

He batted his eyes at her, and she couldn't hold on to her anger anymore.

She laughed until she had to sit down in the grass and cried.

He sat next to her, putting his arms around her quaking shoulders. "I'm so sorry, my love," he said, "I didn't want to tell you, but you needed to know. I promised you I wouldn't hurt you, and here you are, hurting. I'm so, so, sorry, dear Bridget. I know it's scary, but I won't let anything happen to you. You are mine!" he growled.

She lifted her face and dashed away her tears. She sighed and leaned her head on his shoulder. "I'm not hurt, Vaughn," she murmured into his neck, "I'm fucking pissed."

There didn't seem to be much to say to that.

"Why?" she sniffed.

"Why what?"

"Why me? I get that this prophecy said so, but what's so special about me? I'm nobody. I'm just a woman from Texas with a teenage son, a mortgage, and three cats. What could I possibly do?" she whispered, despair seeming to swamp her.

"Bridget, don't say that. You are so much more. I don't understand how someone as beautiful and vibrant as you doesn't know how special you truly are." He gave her a light shake.

She gave him a watery smile, "I bet you say that to all the women of prophecy."

"Wielder."

"Wield what?" She looked at him in puzzlement.

"Wielder of Prophecy. That's what you are. Bridget, you aren't just a person at random. You are descended from a long line of Wielders. You didn't know because no one ever trained you. But your power is manifesting. That's why you've been getting shocked and zapped. You can wield energy and when the Shadows get near, it starts responding. You need to learn how to control it. And that's why the Shadow is coming after you harder now. They know that you are developing what you need to take them down."

Bridget held up her hands and looked at them. "Magic wielder." she tried out the words. She turned her hands over and wiggled her fingers. A slight current ran through them. "Holy cow!" she whispered and looked up at Vaughn.

He smiled. "Gabe is going to love that."

Vaughn and Bridget sat there for a few minutes in the grass, watching pigeons inch closer to their discarded sandwiches. They ignored the stares of people who walked by with two beautiful Golden Retrievers on leashes. One of the dogs strained on his leash towards them, but a low-pitched growl from Vaughn's chest sent him running the other way, dragging his owner along behind him.

Bridget laughed, "My hero, defender of damsels from shaggy dogs."

"You forgot the part where I'm amazing in bed," he said with a straight face.

Bridget laughed again, "I never should have admitted that. You aren't going to let that go, are you?" She looked up at him.

He smiled down at her and shook his head. He placed a kiss gently on her lips, then stood. He held out a hand and helped her to her feet. "Let's go back to my place so I can change, then I'll take you home and we can grab Gabriel and some of your belongings. You'll be safer at my house tonight. We still need to ward your house."

Bridget stared at him for a minute, opened her mouth then closed it. She was about to lay into him for being a high-handed alpha male when she saw a shadow drawing up behind him. She froze in place and noticed Vaughn's body tense as well.

He whirled to face the shadow as it widened into a man-shaped form. Vaughn whispered, "Stay behind me."

Bridget nodded; she didn't want to go anywhere near it.

Out of the shadow, stepped a man. He was dressed nicely and looked like a suburban dad, nondescript and fairly forgettable. His green polo shirt was neat and wrinkle-free and tucked into a pair of pressed khakis. He wore tan loafers that reminded her of her junior high math teacher. If they hadn't seen him step out of the shadows, he could have been any random guy they passed on the street.

He was like some weird Ned Flanders demon. Half Simpson's character, half Hellspawn. She almost expected him to greet them with a "Howdy-doo!" or some other neighborly welcome. He smiled like he didn't have a care in the world except for how green his lawn was.

He finally opened his mouth. Here it was, the words of evil incarnate, something vile and foul, no doubt!

She braced herself when he said, "Well, hey y'all!" cheerfully with all the sweetness of a piece of bubble gum. She peered around Vaughn's back, checking to see if the shadow was still there. It was. Was this guy for real? How could no one else see the shadow behind him? She then remembered Vaughn said most people couldn't.

"Well, I sure do apologize for sneaking up behind y'all like that," he continued, "I normally like to give a little notice I'm popping by." He laughed as if this was a normal occurrence, and he'd stopped over for a quick beer with friends.

"What do you want?" sneered Vaughn.

"Whoa, fella, hold your horses," the man laughed, "That's no way to treat a friend!" He smiled at them and tried to peer over Vaughn's shoulder at Bridget.

She ducked her head so he couldn't make out her face. She listened as Ned continued to speak.

"I'm just looking for a friend now, y'hear? She's a sweet little gal, the widow of a dear friend of mine. I'd heard he passed on some time back, but I just hadn't been able to get out this way to pay my respects. His name was Brian Ridgeway, wife was Bridget."

Bridget fought to stay quiet as all the blood in her body turned to ice. How did he know about Brian? She squeezed her eyes closed and dug down deep, trying to remember if she'd ever seen him before. He was so generic-looking; it was hard to remember if she'd ever met him. Maybe in passing? She couldn't recall. She hoped it wasn't true, and Brian hadn't really been friends with a demon intent on killing her.

She felt the rumble rip through Vaughn as if he could sense her fear and despair.

"What do you want with Bridget?" Vaughn demanded.

She could feel him restraining himself by the tension in his back. He was barely holding on when she knew he wanted to rip this guy to shreds. *It's too public,* she realized. *It's the middle of the day in a public area. If Vaughn attacks, someone could see, and that would be a problem.* She looked around her wondering if there was any means of escape or somewhere they could hide. She realized that it was futile; he controlled shadows. He could find them anywhere out here.

She had an idea. She stepped around Vaughn, gathering her courage and put on a syrupy smile. "Well, bless your sweet heart!" she crooned to Ned in her most exaggerated Southern style. "What'd you say y'alls name was? I'm Syliva, and this here's Donald. We know that sweet little Bridget you're talking about, but I sure don't remember seein' y'all before," she continued.

Ned looked at her with confusion and then smiled back. "Much obliged, Ms. Sylvia. See, I knew Brian through our work together at the Base years back. Y'know Carswell?" He named a joint reserve base not far from here.

"Oh, sure thing, sugah," she continued, feeling Vaughn's gaze on her face, "Just a shame they shut that place down."

Ned nodded knowingly. "Well, me and Brian, we used to grab a cold one after work sometimes and he would show me pictures of his bride-to-be. He invited me to their wedding even. Such a sweet couple! Quite a stunner that Bridget gal." He winked, getting into his story.

"Well, I transferred out after that and hadn't seen him since. Heard he'd passed away and wanted to pay my respects to the missus."

Bridget knew this creep hadn't been at their wedding, and Brian hadn't worked on the base until *after* they were married. "Well, golly mister, I'm sure sorry you just missed her. She was here not even five minutes ago. She was walking her dog with her cousin. They went that way down the trail." She pointed in the direction of the dog walkers, hoping they'd had enough time to get out of the park. "I'm sure if you hurry, you can catch them!" she urged.

Ned squinted at her, trying to decide if he believed her, then nodded his thanks and turned to go.

"Wait a minute, mister," she called, "Didn't catch your name! If you don't find her, I'd sure like to let her know who called looking for her!"

The man gave an oily grin and told her, "Bob, ma'am. Bob Smith." He turned and strolled down the trail as if he had no cares at all.

Bridget waited until he'd rounded the path out of view and let out a shaky breath. She looked up at Vaughn and couldn't read the emotion on his face.

She expected a scolding, but he surprised her by wrapping her in his arms and whispering, "My little warrior." before kissing the top of her head. "That was brilliant," he said with pride. Then he shook her, "Don't ever do that again!"

She swallowed hard and nodded. "I think I'd like to go pack now," she said meekly.

CHAPTER 17

Bridget was quiet on the drive back to Vaughn's lair as she thought of it. His underground lair where he hid like a superhero. And the cave where the pool was, Gabe would probably lose his mind. She worried over and over in her mind what she was going to tell him. "Cave," she said suddenly and looked at Vaughn. "That's why you live on a sublevel?" she asked him laughingly. "Because it reminds you of a cave? Is that a dragon thing?"

He gave her a brief smile before returning his gaze to traffic. "But of course, my dear, where better to spirit away helpless women offered up to appease the almighty beast."

She smirked. "How did Ned know where we were?" she wondered. "Ned?"

She explained how the shadow reminded her of Ned Flanders from the Simpsons, and it was easiest to think of him that way, "Because his name sure as heck wasn't Bob Smith," she clarified.

He was quiet for a moment and said, "It fits. I think since they know who you are, they zero in on areas where your presence has been strong. It's a tracking technique they have and something that makes them especially dangerous. I have a feeling they are scouting and testing the waters to see if they can confirm you are the Wielder of Prophecy before alerting their king. He wouldn't like being called out for a false alarm."

Bridget sat in silence while she thought that through. It made sense in a way: don't send out the big guns until you're sure of your target. She guessed shadow travel wasn't an exact science. She smirked; it wasn't really even a science. "How do you know all of this?" she turned to him. "Is there like, a manual or something? Can I read about this to try and catch up on what's going on?"

He glanced at her as he turned into the parking garage and waved at the front doorman. He pulled into his spot and looked over. "Yes and no," he said. "It's complicated." He held up his hands as she started to protest, "It's easier to show you."

She wondered what that meant and followed him out of the car. She paused and looked back at the line of fancy, shiny cars. She glanced over at him and asked, "How many of these are yours?" gesturing at the millions of dollars' worth of classic and high-powered machines.

He stared at the ceiling as if the answer was written there. He sighed and shuffled over to her like he was expecting a scolding. "From where the Rolls usually is down there at the end, to that black SUV over there."

Bridget counted the cars, "You have nine vehicles? Who needs that many?" she mused out loud.

He grimaced.

She smirked, "You have more somewhere else, don't you."

He threw his hands in the air. "Dragon. Hoarding. It's a thing. Don't judge," he ground through his teeth. He turned around and stalked to the door; she trailed behind him, laughing.

She took his arm when she caught up to him at the elevator, oddly relieved when he twined his fingers in hers. He wasn't really mad, she realized. Just a little embarrassed to be called out. "I think it's cute," she said, kissing him on the cheek. She saw him smile and knew she was forgiven.

They entered the bedroom, where he pointed her to the little library corner and told her to have a seat while he changed. Then he would show her the material he had.

She went to the chair and snuggled into it, staring at the shelves and trying to decipher the titles. What did Mr. Hoards-A-Lot like to read? She was surprised to see such a wide variety on the shelves. He had fiction and non-fiction, studies on various religions, classics and even one romance novel paperback that was down in the lowest corner of the shelves, almost hidden.

Intrigued, she got up to examine it closer. Pulling it off the shelf, she read the spine, 'The Miller's Daughter', and turned it over to see the cover.

Her jaw dropped. "I knew it!" she giggled. She had always thought Vaughn looked like a cover model for a spicy romance novel, and here was proof. He was posed dramatically on a cliff, brooding, his long black hair blowing behind him in a windstorm. A blonde woman with enormous breasts heaving from her low-cut and totally impractical gown was draped sensually in his arms. A large mill stood alongside the river at the base of the cliff, no doubt where the girl he was about to ravish lived.

She studied his face, his strong forearms and the planes of his chest. Oh yes, that was absolutely Vaughn. She was planning to tease him about it when she noticed the book seemed to be rather old, the edges of the pages yellowed. Curious, she opened it to the copyright page and looked for the date. Her finger trailed down the page until she found it. *That can't be right,* she thought. She walked over to the lamp; surely it was the dimness of the room that was making it look like that. *1974,* she read. She slapped the book closed and looked more closely at the man on the cover. Maybe it was a relative? She studied his face again, the jawline, the set of his mouth.

"Bridget?" she heard.

She gasped and whirled around, clutching the book to her chest.

Vaughn was standing at the door to the huge walk-in closet. He had changed into jogging pants and a t-shirt that did nothing to disguise the strength of his chest and the bulge of muscles on his arms.

She glanced at the book in her hands when his eyes locked on it. She pulled the cover away from her body and looked again. It was totally him. "Well," she cleared her throat, "That certainly confirms one theory."

He walked silently to her, his face impassive, revealing nothing. He stopped inches from her and looked down at the book, gently pulling it from her hands. He arched an eyebrow at her, inviting her to continue.

"I uh, well, I, um." *Just say it, stupid! He is the one who needs to explain things,* she scolded. She squared her shoulders and met his gaze evenly. "I've always thought you belonged on one of these covers. I thought there was no way a man as handsome as you could actually be real. I was browsing your books here and noticed this tucked away like it was hiding. I was curious. Your turn. 1974? I wasn't even born yet, and you?" she finished. She snatched the book from his hands and flipped it to the copyright page, putting it in front of his face.

He slowly pushed the book down and sighed. "Yes Bridget, that's me. I hated that cover, but I guess you can call it vanity that I kept a copy. How do you think I have amassed all that I have at my apparent age?" He turned away and strode to the bed, sitting and staring at her with an indecipherable look on his face.

Apparent age? Bridget walked to him and ran her hands through his silky black hair. "Vaughn," she whispered, "I don't care about the busty blonde bimbo. I just want you to be honest with me. How old are you?"

Vaughn closed his eyes for a moment and opened them. "I was born in 1742," he replied softly. "You asked how I know so much about the Shadow resurgence?" he met her gaze.

She nodded, her face giving away nothing of the numb feeling that was spreading through her.

"I lived it."

Okay cool it, so he's a little older than you, he's really freaking hot for his age! But he's like ANCIENT, she argued in her head. *But he's kind and sweet, he likes your jokes, he gets your jokes.*

"I don't care." she heard herself say. "I don't," she continued, "I just know that I care about you. You seem to care about me, and that's all that matters." She ran her hand over his cheek, and he turned his head, pressing his lips to her palm.

He gently bit down at the base of her thumb. "Bridget." he breathed warmly. "I don't deserve you," he whispered, his voice growing husky.

"No," she said briskly. "You don't, but I guess I'm willing to make an exception for my Sex God," she said, trying not to smile.

His gaze shot up to hers, his lips curving into a decidedly feral smile. "Oh, you saucy little wench, I have a mind to bend you over and punish you for that one," he rumbled at her.

Bridget met his gaze squarely, "Bring it, Cover Boy."

Sometime after ripping each other's clothes off and biting or licking every square inch of each other's skin, they ended up gasping face down on the covers. Her head near the foot of the bed, him diagonally, his legs draped over hers.

He propped his head up and, grinning, slapped her lightly on her beautiful bare behind.

She shrieked and turned to glare at him. "You'll pay for that," she declared, "After I get the ability to use my legs again." She flopped back down on the bed.

"I do have to say, dear sweet little Bridget," he practically purred near her shoulder, "I love this little tattoo on your back. Very apropos."

She groaned. "Shit, I forgot about that. I don't see it every day. A little souvenir of that trip to Cabo." she explained.

"A dragon," he said quietly, tracing the outline of the small tattoo in the middle of her back. He gently lifted her wrist and placed a kiss on the three black pawprints on the inside of it. "And these?" he inquired.

"My cats," she explained. "I have three black cats, Dante, Poe, and Lovecraft. Next to my son, they're my heart. They've been there for me through thick and thin and although they can be assholes, they are still my other babies."

"Very literary of you," he said. "So, a horror fan?"

"Mmm, more of anything odd or a little unusual. Horror, sci-fi, thriller. I was a hard-core goth for most of high school. You would have laughed at my black jeans and combat boots." She rolled over and stared up at him.

He smiled. "Oh, I need to see pictures of that."

She shook her head. "Nope. Not gonna happen. That part of my life is long gone. Thank goodness there were no cell phones or social media sites then. I would never live that down."

He leaned in close. "Challenge accepted," and kissed her gently.

Just then, they heard the front door open and close. "Mom?" She heard Gabriel call out to her in a panicked voice.

CHAPTER 18

"G ABE!" SHE GASPED AND leaped from the bed with a strength she didn't know she possessed. She was almost to the door when strong arms wrapped around her waist, and she was yanked back against Vaughn's hard body. "Let me go!" she growled at him, slapping at his arm, which was locked like an iron band. Damn the man and his muscles, that's her baby!

"Clothes," he hissed in her ear.

She stopped struggling and remembered that, yes, she was stark naked. She nodded, and he carefully released her. She turned and ran for the pile on the floor and sifted through it, getting dressed in record time.

Somehow Vaughn beat her to it and was out the door before she could fasten her bra. *Stupid thing, absolutely invented by a man as some sort of evil torture device,* she grumbled. She quickly threw her hair in a ponytail and ran out after Vaughn to find her son. She found them in the living room, Gabe sitting on one of the sofas, Vaughn next to him, with a hand on his shoulder.

Gabe looked up and saw her before jumping to his feet. "Mom!" he said again and ran to her arms.

"Baby!" she soothed as she wrapped him in her arms and held him tight. "Shh," she cooed, "I've got you." She looked over at Liam and glared at him as he stood awkwardly behind the couch, her son's backpack in hand. "You," she ground out between clenched teeth. "Talk. Now."

Gabe leaned back, waving his hands. "No, Mom, no, it's not Liam's fault! He got there just in time."

She turned her gaze to her frightened son and smoothed his hair back. "What happened, Gabe?" she asked softly.

He trembled and hugged her again. "They almost got me."

She looked helplessly at Vaughn and then Liam, pleading for them to tell her what was happening.

Liam walked around the couch and led them both to sit down. He sat close by on the chaise, sitting on the edge like he might need to jump up at any minute.

"Well," he started haltingly, searching Vaughn's face and receiving a go-ahead nod, launched into his tale. "I got a call from Vaughn earlier about the, uh, visit you experienced at lunch today and he was concerned for your safety. So, knowing you were going to go over to get some things, I went ahead to pick Gabe up from school, you know make sure he got home quickly so we could move fast. I got there and he was hanging out back with his friends. Everything seemed normal, so I pulled the Rolls up to the curb and walked over. You guys had the Lambo so I figured he'd seen the Rolls before and would be comfortable with it. The guys all wanted to check it out, so I was showing them some of the special features of the car and maybe I was a little distracted, but I looked up and saw Gabriel walking away with a shad... uh, shady-looking person.

"I ran over and was able to wrestle him away. I didn't want to take him to your house in case they were watching, so I brought him straight here. I didn't explain too much, just that someone was looking for you and may have been trying to take him to get to you." Liam lapsed into silence, hanging his head in shame.

Bridget patted Gabe and smiled at him, kissing his forehead, before she stood and went to Liam.

He sighed, and his shoulders tensed.

She sat and wrapped her arms around him before kissing his temple. "Thank you. You saved my baby for me. I can never repay you."

Liam jerked his head up, "But Bridget, they almost got him right under my nose!"

She shook her head, "No, Liam, had you not been there at all, they absolutely would have him now, and I'd be a complete wreck. Because of you, he's here safe and whole. I kind of love you right now!" She kissed him again, hugging him tightly.

He rested his hand on her arms and leaned into the hug, making a low purring sound.

Vaughn studied Bridget, hugging Liam and heard her declare she loved him. He knew it was a motherly kind of love, but the growl seeped out of him regardless. He was jealous.

Liam, knowing what it meant, jumped up as if he'd been scalded.

Gabriel looked around in confusion and said, "Was that thunder?"

Bridget, who knew where the sound came from, stared at Vaughn with a cold expression he couldn't quite figure out. She cut her eyes over to Gabe, and he understood. She was telling him to cut the dragon crap in front of the kid. He was already freaked out.

"Hey buddy," he patted him on the knee. "I know you like games, but how do you like swimming?" he asked.

Gabriel's face lit up. "I love it! This building has a pool?"

Vaughn chuckled, "Even better, my man, I have my own pool. It has a water slide, a hot tub, and an overhead screen for watching movies or letting in some sunlight."

"Wicked!" Gabriel said, jumping up. "Um, that's, if it's okay with my mom. Is that cool, Mom?" he turned to her with his best pleading face, batting his eyelashes and pursing his lips like a fish.

Bridget smiled, glad to see the trauma being pushed behind him through the resilience of youth. "I'm cool buddy, oh, but he doesn't have a suit." She turned to Vaughn.

He smiled. "I'm sure Liam has something that would fit him."

Liam nodded enthusiastically.

"Liam, why don't you get Gabe suited up and take him in there while Bridget and I talk next steps."

Gabriel ran after Liam like a rocket, peppering him with a million questions about the pool.

Bridget was pretty sure she heard something about cannonballs and shook her head. When they were safely out of earshot, she collapsed in Vaughn's outstretched arms, grateful to have someone to hold onto for the first time in years while she fell apart. "Vaughn," she cried, burying her face in his shirt.

"Shh, Bridget, love," he comforted her. "I know. I know." He rocked her back and forth.

When the tears subsided, and the fear had worked its way from her, she sat up and wiped her face. "I'm sorry about that. I keep crying in front of you. I'm afraid I'm not a pretty crier."

Vaughn simply held her face between his hands and kissed her tenderly. "It's okay, my sweet Bridget, no one cries pretty, but you are still beautiful, and a little red nose can't change that," he said, tapping her on said nose.

She laughed and rubbed it, "Well thank you for lying to me kindly at least."

He smiled. "You okay?"

She nodded yes, and then her face went cold. "But those bastards who tried to hurt my baby won't be. It's time we turned the tables and began the hunt for them. No one touches my child and gets away with it." Her eyes lit up with their own kind of fire.

He was mesmerized by this side of her and was about to promise her the world when she started laughing. He joined her as they both heard Gabe yelling the time-old phrase of all teenage boys, *"Mom! Come watch this!"*

After watching the requisite number of tricks and splashes that Vaughn had joined in on, Bridget called a halt to the hilarity. She looked at Vaughn and caught him staring at the hot tub. The memory of their night there made her flush a little and she knew by the look on his face he was remembering it too. She nudged him with her elbow while the other boys were drying off. "Hey, I need to get my things from my house," she reminded him. "I need to feed my cats too."

He smiled, "Already taken care of."

Bridget lifted an eyebrow and shook her head. He was being high-handed again, but she knew he was worried about their safety outside of his home or office. "Okay, so what can I do?" she asked, "How about I cook dinner?"

Liam's face lit up; he liked that idea, she could tell. He was probably ready for a break from playing butler, babysitter, chauffeur, and whatever other chores Vaughn set him to.

"Mom," Gabe called, "We had lasagna on the menu at home, I was looking forward to it, any chance of that still happening?"

Liam ran over, "We have everything you need for that!" He was almost vibrating with enthusiasm, "Anything we don't have, I will go get right away. Come here; the pantry's this way." He grabbed her hand and started dragging her to the kitchen.

Bridget laughed and followed behind the eager man. She realized despite his large size and many jobs, he still seemed pretty young himself, not quite close to her age. Although, as she'd just learned with Vaughn, age was just a number. She smacked herself in the forehead, why hadn't she realized before when she heard him purring? "Liam, are you uh, well, I'm not sure if this is rude or not, so I'm just going ahead with it, but are you a dragon too?"

Liam stopped in his tracks and turned to look at her. "I guess the dragon's out of the bag," he chortled. "Yeah, I'm the youngest in North America," he said with obvious pride.

Bridget smiled at that statement, but she was confused. "Hang on though, I met your sister today, is she older than you then?"

Liam's eyes flashed with amusement, "No way, she's my baby sis, but with dragons, only the oldest can turn. It's why she's so..." he looked at the ceiling. "Well, you met her, she's pissy, right?"

She laughed, "I guess that's one word for it. She was a little surly and seemed to have a chip on her shoulder about something. Makes sense." It did make sense. Her older brother was a dragon, and she had to settle for what, watching him grow up with wings and talons while she played with Barbies? Yeah, Bridget suddenly had a lot more sympathy and understanding for Siobhan.

"Don't go feeling too sorry for her, though." Liam cautioned, "One, she hates that, and two, she didn't come away empty-handed. She's got Wielding power." He turned and trotted off towards the pantry again. Eager to get the feast underway.

CHAPTER 19

SHE FOLLOWED LIAM INTO the kitchen to ask about that when the front door flew open, and a whole herd of people walked through the door. Bridget recognized many of them as some of the game developers from earlier today, her new staff. She had a moment to wonder why they were there when she realized they had brought some of her belongings from her house. She was confused about how they could have gotten in and knew what to grab when she saw a familiar blonde head bobbing in the crowd.

"Jorrie!" she shouted as the woman rocketed through the group and launched herself at Bridget. They hugged each other tightly as the others milled around the kitchen, digging in the cabinets looking for snacks.

"Hey guys!" she heard Liam call out over everyone, "Bridget's making lasagna. Who's staying?" A sea of hands shot up in the air around her. Liam grinned at her then winked at Jorrie who ignored him.

She looked at Jorrie and said, "We need to catch up but looks like I need to make a grocery list, and you have to help me. And tell me why you're ignoring Liam."

Bridget was in the kitchen with Jorrie having just compiled a list of things they would need to feed the army that had arrived, when Vaughn walked in, toweling his hair dry and looking delicious in a pair of sweatpants and no shirt. Bridget leaned over and closed Jorrie's mouth, whispering, "You're drooling."

Jorrie looked at her friend, looked at Vaughn, then back at Bridget. "And you're not!" she suddenly hissed. "You did it! You little tramp! You climbed that man like a tree, just like I told you. Hell yeah, girl! I thought you looked awfully relaxed!" She high-fived Bridget, who had to count to ten to distract her from murdering her best friend for saying that out loud.

Vaughn moved towards them, a glass of wine in each hand. He set the wine down in front of them, wrapped his arms around Bridget's waist, kissed her on the temple and grinned at Jorrie. "Oh yeah," he smoldered, "She climbed me up, down, sideways and every way in between. She called me a Sex God." He danced back in laughter as Bridget whirled around to slap his chest.

"I knew I shouldn't have said that to you," she hissed while Jorrie stood stock still at the counter staring.

"Sex God," she whispered.

Bridget laughed at the expression on her friend's face. For all her bravado and straight talk, it looked like Vaughn found the perfect way to quiet her down. She turned to him again, "Go put on a shirt, Sex God, I think you're distracting her."

He mock-saluted her and turned on his heel to head back to the bedroom.

Now that he was out of sight, Jorrie seemed to break out of her trance. She picked up the wine and gulped some down. "Bridge," she started, seeming at a loss for words, "That man. So hot, muscles, mmm. Please tell me it was as good as he looks."

Bridget leaned over to her friend and whispered, "Better."

Bridget and Jorrie were sitting in the living room, surrounded by Gabe and the crowd that had kindly delivered essential items from her house with Jorrie's help. The silver-haired man, Killian, among them, speaking quietly with some of the team.

Gabe, having learned that many of the group were developers for Vaughn's gaming company, was in heaven. He was pestering them with a ton of questions, which they seemed to enjoy, when a voice rang out.

"Hey kid, Gabe, right?" It was Siobhan. Bridget hadn't seen her come in. "So, Bridget's your mom?" she asked him.

Gabe nodded his head. Bridget saw the instant puppy love sweep across his face. *Oh boy.*

"Nice. She's a cool chick. For an older person." Siobhan winked at Bridget. "Word is, you're pretty good at Cloud Warrior," she stated in a challenging voice.

Gabe tried to play it cool, "I can hold my own."

"Ever beaten GreenPrincess1?" she asked with a small smile.

Gabe's eyes lit up, "No, I've always wanted to play her, but she's never on when I'm on. Have you ever played her?"

Siobhan spread her arms, and the others let out a collective "Ooh."

"Dude, I *am* GreenPrincess1," she said. "You ready to go?"

Gabe's eyes went round, and he looked like he had just been confronted with the face of God herself. He nodded mechanically, then followed Siobhan and the others to a large gaming room down the hall.

Bridget heard the sounds of Gabe's favorite game booting up and the excited cheers as they settled in to join or spectate the match. She smiled, grateful to the team for distracting Gabe from earlier events. She wasn't sure how much she could tell Jorrie and wondered where Vaughn had slipped off to.

The door opened, and Vaughn walked in, trailed by Jack. Vaughn didn't look very happy. In fact, he looked downright thunderous.

Bridget was about to inquire when she heard a chorus of me-ows and growls. "My cats!" she squealed, running over to relieve Vaughn of the two carriers he had. Jack had the other, and a bag of what she assumed were essentials for her babies. "Oh, thank you, thank you." She kissed Vaughn repeatedly.

"Hey, don't I get some of that? I carried Lovecraft!" Called Jack.

"Of course you do!" Bridget laughed, running over to hug her other favorite man.

"Yeah, you carried him because he bit me," snarked Vaughn.

She whirled back to Vaughn and snatched his hands, looking for the bite. "You need to wash that right away," she worried, "Cat bites can get infected if not properly treated. He was probably just scared, poor baby didn't know what was going on." She continued to look at his hands but didn't see any marks.

She looked up at him questioningly, and he whispered in her ear, "I heal quickly. Dragon perks, remember?"

She nodded and glanced at the others; they were focused on calming down the angry felines. "Where can we put them?" she asked Vaughn, "I don't want them to run around and destroy things. They're like ninja scientists. Under foot, trying to kill you, constantly checking on gravity. Why did you bring them here? Someone could have just fed them."

He smiled and pointed down another hallway. "I had Liam set up a little room just for them so they would have some space to chill out and get used to being here. We don't know how long you're going to be here." He opened a door to something that looked like an ad for cat Nirvana. Scratching posts, cat trees, a fancy litter box that seemed to clean itself, and lots of comfy beds. Toys everywhere.

She could see three noses poking out of their carriers, eager to explore the space. "Vaughn, this is just too much for a night or two." She turned to him. "Thank you, though." She took the carriers into the room and opened the doors. Poe shot straight out of his and up the ramp to the highest perch. Dante and Lovecraft held back for a minute, preferring to get the lay of the land before venturing forth. "We'll let them settle in first, and I'll check on them later. I need to see if Liam is back with the supplies to feed this army you've brought over."

Jorrie and Jack cornered Bridget in the kitchen, they'd volunteered to help her feed the large group so they could get her alone to question her.

"Alright, Bridget," Jack started, "You've dodged us enough. Exactly, what the hell is going on here?" He stared at her, concern in his eyes.

Jorrie set down the cheese she was grating and leaned a hip on the counter. "C'mon, Bridge, you're being very cagey about all of this.

When you went on the date last night, I told you to have sex with the man, which I'm very proud of you for, by the way, but I didn't mean you should move in with the guy the next day! I mean, what the hell girl? That's way too fast." Jorrie looked at Jack for confirmation.

He nodded and added, "Babe, Bridget, you know I love you, and I want what's best for you right?"

Bridget nodded, staring at the floor, wondering where to start and how much she could tell them.

Jack continued, "Look, I only want you to be happy. Vaughn is a great guy. He really cares about you, and I'm glad he finally got around to asking you out. He's been mooning over you since the day he met you!" Jack rolled his eyes.

Bridget looked at Jack in surprise. "You knew the whole time? I thought you just found out!" she said incredulously. Jack had a reputation as the *worst* secret keeper in the world. Especially if he'd had tequila. Bridget looked at Jorrie to get her take on it and saw Jorrie was suspiciously busy grating cheese again.

"You both knew," she laughed. She set down the spatula she'd been using. "You come in here questioning me when you both knew what was going on? What else do you know?" she demanded.

"Nothing!" Jorrie said, holding up her hands. "Look, I could tell Jack knew something. You know how he is with a secret."

Jack nodded and mouthed, *the worst,* at Bridget, which made her smile.

"I made him go out to Margarita Madness with me and plied him with enough tequila to get him talking. He told me Vaughn was interested in you, and how he kept talking about you and asking questions.

How he would invent some reason to be around you. And you were so blind to it all! It was honestly just so sweet and romantic," Jorrie sighed. "I knew, if you knew, you'd just close him out and be awkward around him until he finally got around to asking you out. He's the only man since Brian that I've seen you even remotely interested in, and it needed to happen."

Bridget stood there for a minute then smiled at her friends. "I love you guys. Seriously. But don't *ever* keep secrets from me again!" She threatened them with the spatula.

Jack pretended to cower in fear while Jorrie just rolled her eyes. "Okay, your turn, spill!"

Bridget thought for a minute and shook her head. "Look, guys, I haven't moved in. We're just staying a night or two for safety reasons. I need to talk to Vaughn first. Some of these secrets are not mine to spill. Let's get through dinner, and then we can all sit down and talk together, and then figure this out. Can you trust me for that?" She got two hugs as an answer.

CHAPTER 20

DINNER WAS A NOISY, boisterous affair, as expected. She was glad she'd made as much as she had. She thought she'd made too much, but after seeing how all the 'kids' ate, she understood how a frat house mom must feel. She smiled at them, so easy with each other, including Gabe in conversations like he was part of the team. She could tell they'd had large group dinners here before as they all settled in like they were home. It made her unexplainably happy to realize she was now part of it and they'd accepted her easily.

Of course, Gabe managed to seat himself next to Siobhan and was recounting his epic tournament prowess to her.

"Gabe," she called to him, "Eat your dinner and quit pestering Siobhan."

"Bruh!" he turned to her. His eyes widened at the calm expression on her face, "I mean, um, yes, Mom. Ma'am."

She winked at him, and the rest of the table erupted in laughter.

One of the guys, Marco was his name, slapped Gabe on the back and told him, "Rookie mistake, man."

Jorrie, eyeing Siobhan, leaned over and whispered, "If that girl hurts my little Rutabaga."

Bridget whispered back, "You hold her down. I'll rip her heart out." Vaughn choked on the bite he'd just taken, and Bridget realized he must have heard them. She winked, and he smiled.

He leaned over to them, "You two she-lions better not pounce too quickly. Siobhan's a good girl. She won't hurt him."

Jorrie looked Vaughn in the eye. "Hey, I watch a lot of DateLine. She'll never see it coming." She sat back in her chair.

Bridget blinked prettily at Vaughn as he shook his head. "Speaking of things we don't want others to hear, we need to sit down with Jack and Jorrie. I haven't told them much, and they really need to know. Not my secrets to tell, though, so I asked them to wait for you."

He nodded and kissed her cheek, "Thank you," he breathed in her ear. Vaughn stood, "Alright, you hooligans." He was met with jeers. "The grownups are going to have adult conversations; you guys clean up. I mean all of it!" He looked around the table. There was some grumbling, but it was good-natured. "Those who cooked don't have to clean."

He took Bridget's hand and pulled her from the chair, nodding at Jorrie and Jack. "Liam, Killian," he called, "With me."

"Hey, Liam didn't cook!" called out Marco.

"I bought the groceries!" Liam shot back.

The others laughed and began to stack dishes. Bridget, Jack, and Jorrie grabbed their wine glasses and followed Vaughn down the hallway to a large library, Liam and Killian trailing behind. Once they were all settled down, they began.

Well, Vaughn started off by staring at the ceiling and humming.

Bridget elbowed him in the ribs and motioned with her head that everyone was waiting for him to open the discussion.

"Sorry," he said, "Was trying to decide how much to tell."

Jorrie leaned forward, "All of it, Mr. Sex God."

Jack choked on his wine, and Jorrie had to slap him on the back.

Vaughn stared at Jorrie and then at Liam, who was seemingly fixated on the table near him, obviously trying not to laugh. "Mouth. Shut," he growled to Liam, who nodded quickly. Vaughn looked at Bridget; she was biting her lip. "How much do you trust them?" he asked.

"With my life," she replied without hesitation.

Vaughn sighed and settled back into the cushions, pulling Bridget closer and kissing the top of her head. "Okay, all of it then," Vaughn told them about the Shadow Claw, their leader, the great battle for domination and subsequent removal of powers. He shared how they were making a resurgence and about the prophecy that had endangered Bridget's life.

Bridget could see they were growing more and more skeptical, so she added in her part. About the shadows coming for her, about them trying to grab her in the parking garage, at the restaurant, in the park, and how they'd made a play for Gabe today at the school.

At that part, Jorrie jumped up and threw her arms around Liam's neck. "Thank you so much, thank you for taking care of my Rutabaga."

Liam glanced at Bridget as he hugged her back and mouthed, *Rutabaga?*

She shook her head in a don't ask motion and looked at Jack. He was quiet and thoughtful.

"Bridge," he began slowly. "This explains so much." He looked up at her, tears in his eyes. "I've seen the shadows too."

Bridget ran over to Jack and dropped to her knees in front of him. "Tell me," she commanded.

"I first saw them the day Brian died," he began. "You remember I came to tell you; I didn't want it to be the police."

She nodded, remembering how awful Jack looked, forlorn and drenched, standing on her doorstep in the pouring rain, not caring he was soaked to the bone.

"I was standing there, and I thought I saw a shadow moving across the wall behind you. It didn't make sense to me then. The world didn't make sense. You dragged me inside and sat me down. Gave me a towel and a cup of hot tea. You were so worried about me, but then I had to tell you. You broke down and were crying in my arms. I didn't tell you, but I saw the shadows again. They were hovering in the hallway like they were just watching you. They slowly drifted away. I've seen them several more times since then, hovering, watching." He hugged Bridget. "I'm so sorry I never told you, I thought I was crazy, like I was imagining things. I should have spoken up sooner."

Jorrie came over, refilled Jack's wine glass and wrapped her arms around them both. The three friends sat there, silent, sharing their love for each other.

Vaughn watched them and debated how he would share the rest. He remembered how Bridget had reacted when he'd proven the existence of dragons. He didn't know if he could handle two more hysterical people tonight.

Killian, hovering behind him, chimed in. "If they have been aware of her all along, why wait so long to make a move? Why now?" he asked.

"They weren't sure?" Vaughn replied, not convinced of that answer. "Like the rest of us, they had multiple people they suspected, but they had to be certain. Moving too soon could alert the dra..., umm, others, what they were planning. Or they were waiting for her to manifest. Show off her Wielding."

"Wielding?" asked Jack.

Killian stepped forward and shot silver flames across the room that looped back around into sparkles and flitted about like fireworks. The others stared at him in awe. "Wielding magic," he murmured.

Liam grinned and rumbled, drawing a glance from Jorrie, who took her seat and gazed at them shrewdly. "There's something else you aren't telling us. Something even bigger you are keeping back."

Bridget nodded, "Jorr, Jack, you know I love you both, so please believe me. This next part? It's going to blow your minds, but you have to believe it's real and stay calm, okay." She turned back to Vaughn, "If you're ready."

Vaughn sat forward and dropped his head, then looked up with flames in his eyes. Jack flinched, and Jorrie sat frozen. He tilted his head back and blew three perfect smoke rings towards the ceiling. The others watched them rise in fascination and looked back to Vaughn. He smiled to reassure them, then stood. "My kind have been around for as long as the Shadow Claw," he intoned, "Even longer. We are the guardians of the old magics and the protectors of the Wielders. We are…”

“Oh, jeez, Vaughn,” interrupted Liam. “Quit being so dramatic about it, you’ll scare them!” He whipped off his shirt and rolled his shoulders. He gave a little shimmer and green wings unfurled behind him. He flapped them lightly and looked around.

“We’re dragons, okay? Just dragons. Nothing woowoo scary, we don’t eat virgins, we don’t ask for sacrifices, we rarely plunder and pillage kingdoms anymore. And no, there is no secret weakness in our scales when we are fully changed. Killian’s a Wielder, I’m a dragon, Vaughn’s a dragon. Simple.”

Jack raised his hand, “Okay, um, thanks, but sorry, scales? Dragons? Yeah, that’s just a teensy bit scary.” He pinched his fingers together to emphasize how teensy. He glanced at Liam, then widened his fingers.

Jorrie stared at Liam, speechless. She looked back at Vaughn, who seeming to understand, also took off his shirt and spread his wings. His wings were much larger than Liam’s, and the gold flickered in the light of the library. Jorrie, who had jumped to her feet when Liam spread his wings, abruptly sat back down.

Jack squeaked a little, “See? Scary!” staring at Vaughn’s deadly looking talons.

Jorrie slowly stood again and started towards Vaughn, but halfway, she changed course and walked to Liam instead. She tentatively reached up towards one of his wings but pulled her hand back.

Liam gently took her hand and smiled. She took this as a sign of encouragement and slowly stroked her hand across the arch of his wing, where it came over the top of his bare shoulder. He made a low, rumbly sound, like a purr in his chest.

Jorrie's face broke into a giant smile. "Holy shit," she whispered and stroked the other one.

Liam's rumble grew louder, and his eyes closed, a smile etched onto his face. She stopped, "I'm sorry, does that hurt?" she snatched her hands away.

Liam grinned at her, "On the contrary, it feels amazing. In this form, our wings are quite sensitive, and a woman's touch is very... sensual." He adjusted his stance and cleared his throat.

Jorrie's hands flew to her mouth. "Oh my god, I didn't know. I'm so sorry! I didn't mean to," she stammered as her face grew hot, flushing as red as a tomato.

"I'm not sorry, you have very soft hands." Liam grinned, his bright green eyes twinkling with impish glee.

"Okay, lover boy," Vaughn laughed, "Knock it off. Quit mesmerizing the fair maiden, and let's get back to the business at hand." He turned to Jack. "Jack, I love you, man, but you aren't stroking my wings." He winked.

Jack blinked for a second, then laughed. It was just what he needed to bring him out of his scared stupor. He stood, wiping his hands on his slacks. "Okay, well I think I need something a little stronger than wine after that demonstration." He looked between Vaughn and Liam, both standing there shirtless, wings spread, handsome as sin. "Got any whisky?"

Vaughn nodded, tucked his wings in and headed off to grab the liquor.

Bridget wandered over to a still shirtless and winged Liam, who was watching Jorrie as she prowled the room, looking at the books and artifacts.

She glanced at Liam's wings and said, "You know, I guess I didn't realize you were different colors. Makes sense, though, just like humans have different hair and skin colors, you would have different scales."

Liam nodded, stretching his wings a bit before pulling them back in. He pulled his shirt over his head and cleared his throat. "Yeah, I guess there is a lot you haven't had a chance to ask Vaughn yet. What with you guys being so, busy." He grinned at her.

She blushed, thinking about how vocal they had been last night. "Do you live here, Liam?"

"Not technically. I have a house not far from here but I'm here most of the time, so I do have my own room. Although I'm going to be bunking with Gabe for a while until we figure this out."

She hugged him in thanks, smiling at him.

He smiled back before his eyes wandered back to Jorrie, who had joined Jack in speaking to Killian.

Bridget smirked; he was playing with fire if he was looking in that direction. Then again, he was a dragon— who knew better how to handle flames. Speaking of, "Can you breathe fire?"

Liam looked back at her, "Well, I can only do it in full form. Vaughn can do it fully human which is really rare, and only the strongest of us can do it."

"Full form?"

"Yeah," he nodded, "It's when we drop the human shape altogether and go full dragon. It's wicked cool and really fun. We don't normally show humans that form, though. Usually, only for mates, wielders we work with, and family. Like, I'd show my sister but not many others." His eyes tracked to Jorrie again.

Bridget cleared her throat.

He looked back at her, grinning. "You should ask Vaughn."

"Ask me what?" Vaughn inquired, walking into the room, whisky decanter in one hand, glasses in the other.

Bridget looked at Liam and he nodded in encouragement. "I was wondering if you would show me your full form," she said tentatively.

Vaughn's hands tremored and he tightened his grip on the glasses to keep from dropping them. He could just replace them if they broke, but he didn't want anyone to see how much her asking affected him.

He glared at Liam, who was trying to look innocent. "Oh, well, there's not enough space in here," he replied and set down the liquor. He opened the decanter and sniffed the heady aroma. "Yes, this will do nicely."

She walked over and put a hand on his arm, saying nothing.

He stared at the glasses for a second, then met her gaze. She was so beautiful it was painful. He knew why Liam had pushed her to ask. Liam thought Bridget was his true mate. But it was much too soon for that discussion. He'd have to caution Liam, the little meddler, about spreading that around. If the Council got hold of that snippet of information... He shuddered.

"That wasn't a real answer," Bridget whispered. "But I'll let it go for now."

He nodded and poured. He passed drinks around, glaring at Liam when he handed him a glass. Liam only smirked in response. Vaughn shook his head. *Kids.*

Jorrie, watching the interchange, spoke up. "Hey, is he old enough to be drinking that?" nodding at Liam.

Vaughn and Liam both burst into laughter.

Jorrie looked back and forth at them, "What's the joke?" she said.

Bridget smiled, "I know Liam looks like a college kid, but he's probably older than you. Am I right, Liam?"

He nodded at Jorrie. "Yeah, I'm young for a dragon, but I was born in 1969. Moon year, baby." He saluted her with the glass.

Jorrie stared for a second, threw back her entire glass and held it out for a refill. Liam obliged by sauntering over and pouring, giving her a sultry smile.

"If you're done?" Vaughn rolled his eyes.

Jack snickered, and Jorrie blushed.

Liam went back to leaning on his bookcase, but not before he winked at Jorrie.

Killian snorted, startling Bridget, who had almost forgotten he was there.

Vaughn rolled his eyes again and put his hands over his face. "Back to the Shadow Claw," he muttered.

CHAPTER 21

THEY TALKED LATE INTO the night, stopping to grab some snacks and for Bridget to feed the 'wee beasties' as Liam had called her cats. They seemed to be settling into their room just fine and were purring up a storm when she left. She peeked in at Gabriel; he had fallen asleep on the couch in the gaming room.

Most of the others were gone. Marco was asleep in a chair. Siobhan was sitting in the other corner, reading a book. Bridget noted someone had pulled a blanket over Gabe. She caught Siobhan's eye, nodding. She nodded back, and Bridget returned to the library. Gabe was being well looked after and protected. She appreciated that most of all.

Bridget walked in, seating herself in Vaughn's lap, giving him a deep, sensual kiss. "Thanks," she whispered.

He smiled, "I don't know what I did, but tell me so I can do it again."

She laughed and slid onto the cushion next to him, snuggling into his side. "Mm, nope, moments passed. You just get the one."

Vaughn squeezed her and tickled her, whispering, "You're going to pay for that." A smile full of dark promises graced his lips.

Bridget's heart rate skyrocketed, remembering her last 'punishment'.

"If you're done," Liam mimicked Vaughn's tone from earlier.

Bridget launched a throw pillow at him with scary accuracy, pegging him right in the face. "Little League Mom," she smirked at his stunned expression.

"Okay, children," trilled Jack. "So, we've established a lot of knowledge and understanding about the Shadows, their King, Wielders, dragons are real, we know Vaughn hired Bridge so he can shag her when he wants, and Bridget and Gabe are in danger. What we haven't done is discuss what the next steps are." He leaned back and arched one of his perfectly manicured eyebrows. "Did I miss anything?"

They all stared at him before Vaughn cleared his throat, "Hmm. Very succinct, and yes, we need to decide our next steps. I've already brought Bridget and Gabriel here for their safety until we can make their home safer. This house is warded, my office building and cars are warded. I have sentries keeping watch; should the Shadow King set foot in this state, we will know. Short of taking the fight directly to them, we are doing all we can until we fully decipher the exact nature of the prophecy and what Bridget is supposed to do."

Bridget yawned.

Vaughn smiled at her indulgently, "I think we've done enough talking for one night. I'm going to take sleepy head here to bed. You guys are welcome to stay if you want, there's plenty of rooms in the guest wing," he said to Jorrie and Jack.

They both nodded. The combination of alcohol and shocks they'd had today wiped everyone out.

"Liam," murmured Vaughn. He scooped Bridget up in his arms, her head lolling against his shoulder.

Liam gestured to Jorrie and Jack to follow him to the guest rooms.

Vaughn gently laid Bridget on his bed and stepped back, just needing to look at her and know she was safe. He liked the way she looked in his home, in his bed. Her hair tousled and her face relaxed, a small smile resting on her soft lips. His heart clenched at his need for her. She wanted to see his full form. He shook his head, he'd never, in his long time on this planet, shown his full form to anyone other than other dragons, and some of the Wielders he'd worked with. He was old-fashioned, he guessed. Vaughn had never taken a mate. He had no family— his best friend Killian and his godson Liam were the closest he had.

He looked closely at Bridget. Was she the one? Why her? Why now, when everything they held dear hinged on keeping her safe and teaching her to use her unknown skills to stop the Shadow Claw? He leaned over, gently removing her shoes, knowing she would be more comfortable that way. As he unbuttoned her shirt, he skimmed his fingertips over the tops of her breasts where they were spilling out of her bra.

She sighed deeply, and he stilled, not wanting to wake her. He continued to unbutton her shirt and slid it out from under her. He slid her shorts off, smiling at the matching panties and bra. Who knew his Bridget was such a stickler for that? He put his arms under her, working to unclasp her bra, wondering why they needed to have so many hooks.

He finally got the clasp to release and eased the lacey material away from her body. She shivered slightly as she was exposed to the cool air in the room. He snatched one of her nightgowns from the chair where she had laid it earlier. He shook it out to slip over her head when his gaze caught on her breasts again. The chill in the room had caused her nipples to peak and looked entirely too tempting to him. "I'm going to hell," he whispered, pulling off his own clothes and lowering himself to her side.

Bridget wasn't sure if she was awake or not. Her eyes were closed, but she was feeling the most wonderful sensations. She sensed a warm, masculine presence wrapped around her body, and it was so right. She sighed and breathed the name that went with the spicy, smoky aroma she loved. "Vaughn."

He heard her whisper his name, and his heart leapt at the sound. He continued to press small kisses over her body, and she began to stir. He lifted one lovely leg and placed it gently around his waist. He ran a finger down her center and found her warm, wet, and receptive.

She shivered again and moaned.

He positioned himself at her entrance and slowly slipped just inside. Her eyes flew open, and he swallowed her gasp with a kiss as he thrust forward, sheathing himself in her. He lay there for a moment, fully savoring the feeling of her body warm and silky around his. She was so completely perfect for him.

She whispered his name again, pleadingly.

He looked into her eyes and saw a fire there that matched his own. He whispered, "Bridget." as she wrapped her arms around him, pulling him down to her. She had slipped her other leg around his waist and raised her hips to meet him. He understood and began to move inside her again, but slowly. He wanted to savor this sweet moment, feeling everything.

They made love gently, savoring each other, taking in every second as if it was the first time. This was so different from their frenzied, powerful coupling before. Vaughn wasn't sure what made this so much more special, but his heart was warming in ways it never had. He was old, he'd been with other women, but never like this. Never this soft exploration, this melding of hearts. *It's because she matters*, he realized. He wrapped her in his arms tightly as his heart filled with heat and he shattered at the same time.

Bridget cried out, too, as his heat swamped her and brought her own release. They both lay there, quietly breathing each other in. She snuggled up to him, and he curled his arms around her. She fell asleep quickly and peacefully, but as she drifted off, she thought she heard him say, "I love you, Bridget."

Bridget woke with a smile on her face. She was warm and sated. A wonderful feeling. She remembered Vaughn being so sweet, carrying her to bed and being oh so careful trying to undress her and put her in a nightgown. Like something treasured. She grinned at the sight of that gown still lying on the chair where he'd dropped it after he'd been too tempted by her naked body. If this was how she'd feel waking up naked, she'd never wear a nightgown again. Vaughn was warm and soft against her back.

They'd fallen asleep in each other's arms, and at some point, she'd ended up facing away from him, so he'd wrapped a strong arm around her. She eased herself back over, so they were face to face. She studied the soft curve of his lips, the angles of his jaw. The dark lashes that framed his beautiful eyes. He really was just too incredibly handsome, and she couldn't believe this gorgeous thoughtful kind man really wanted her.

Loves you, her mind supplied helpfully. She thought about it for a minute. Had he really said that? He sometimes called her Bridget love, but that was a term of endearment. Kind of like calling someone baby, honey, or darling. *No, he said I LOVE YOU! Three whole words, three syllables, three distinct sounds.* She wished her head would shut up and just let her enjoy this moment.

"You know it's rude to stare." Vaughn whispered without opening his eyes.

Bridget jolted at being caught, whispered back, "How did you know, your eyes were closed. Is that some sort of dragon voodoo?"

He opened his beautiful blue eyes, pinning her to the spot. "You were thinking too hard again." He smiled and brushed her hair from her face. "Good morning my sweet, did you sleep well?"

She kissed him lightly. "Why, yes, Mr. Drake, I had a warm handsome man here to keep me company all night long."

He growled at her and flung the blanket over them while she squealed in mock terror.

Sometime later, they lay panting, her head on his chest, him running his hands lazily over her back. "I suppose we should check on the others," he finally sighed.

Bridget stretched like a cat and yawned. "Mmm. A responsible Sex God." She giggled.

He pinched her arm and laughed. "You aren't letting that go, are you?" he teased.

She shook her head no and sighed. "I'm glad the other rooms are on the other side of the house; I'd hate to think we had an audience. But I'm sure we need to get up and feed whoever is still here." She smelled coffee brewing and added "Although it seems someone has made a start." They took turns taking a shower and getting dressed.

When they stepped into the breakfast nook, they found Siobhan, Marco, and Gabe sitting at the table, plowing through a stack of pancakes.

Liam was in the kitchen with Jorrie, showing her how to flip a pancake high. They were laughing and standing very close together.

Bridget looked up at Vaughn and smiled.

He shook his head, asking, "Where's Jack?"

Jorrie answered, "Probably nursing a hangover. You know he's not his best the morning after."

"I resemble that remark," Jack said, coming around the corner, looking a little worse for the wear. He sat down and put his head on the table. "My kingdom for some coffee," he moaned.

Bridget took pity on him and fixed him a cup, setting it down by his nose.

He inhaled the aroma and sat up, taking her hand. "My darling angel, why don't you run away with me." He kissed her hand.

She kissed the top of his head, "You're engaged, remember?" and walked away to fix herself some tea.

Once everyone was settled at the table, Gabe turned to Vaughn. "Mr. Drake, it's really nice of you to let us stay here last night. So, thanks for that. I know there's something going on, and I'm being kept in the dark here, but I'm sure it's some adult crap that you guys think I'm too young to handle yet, so I'm going to respect that for now. But I need to know, what are your intentions with my mother?"

Jack choked on his coffee, Jorrie grinned at Liam, and Bridget put her head down on the table.

Vaughn, however, took the question seriously. He stood and walked around to Gabe, indicating he should stand as well. "Gabriel, I appreciate your respecting our boundaries on the other matter. Your mother's main goal is to keep you safe, so that is mine as well. When she deems it necessary for you to know all, you will. Until then, she's running that show. As to your question about my intentions, well that's an easier answer. Your mother is a smart, talented, beautiful, amazing woman. So, I've taken advantage of that by making her the new VP of VR Integration at Cloud Warrior Gaming.

"I hope you agree that your mother is deserving of happiness in her life as well, so as the man in your household, I'd like to ask your permission to court your mother to see if I can give her that. I'm not going to try to take your father's place. No man could ever do that. But I hope you will see how much I want to be in your lives in my own special place. So, Mr. Ridgeway. Do my intentions seem clear enough for you? And do I have your permission to date your mother?"

Gabriel stood there for a moment, obviously giving serious consideration to what he'd just heard. Finally, he nodded, but he leaned in close to Vaughn. "Yes sir, I'm okay with you dating my mother, but know this if you hurt her," he paused, "I'll sic my Aunt Jorrie on you. And she watches a lot of DateLine."

Bridget wasn't sure whether to laugh or cry at the scene before her. The respect Vaughn had shown Gabe, treating him like a man. It was so sweet and thoughtful. Gabe had obviously picked up on Vaughn's sincerity. The kid had a good BS meter. It was the last line, though; they all burst into laughter.

Jorrie laughed so hard that tears poured down her face. "That's my Rutabaga!" she shouted.

Gabe mortified, turned and hissed at her, "*Aunt Jorrie!*"

This caused her to laugh harder. "I'm sorry, baby." she gasped. "I've raised you well!"

Gabe turned back to Vaughn, shrugging off the embarrassment of the childhood nickname in front of his idols. "Mr. Drake, sir."

Vaughn held up a hand, "Just call me Drake, Gabe."

Her son smiled, "Okay, Drake, I was also wondering if we were still on for today? You mentioned letting me and some friends beta test Cloud Warrior-4?" He smiled hopefully.

"Indeed, I did!" Vaughn smiled back. "A promise I intend to keep. I think we said 1:30, right?"

Gabe nodded vigorously.

"Fantastic, that will give us all time to get there and get everything set up. I'll have some pizza delivered, there's plenty of drinks in the café, so you guys will be all set. Marco, Siobhan," he called to his staff, "Can you two run ahead and get things set up for our newest beta testing interns?" he smiled.

Marco grinned, "Fresh meat! Awesome!" and grabbed his jacket and helmet from the bench by the front door. "C'mon Von-Von, I'll give you a lift."

Siobhan punched him in the arm. "I told you never to call me that," she growled, "But I do like your bike." She threw a wave over her shoulder, "See you there in a bit, Gabe!"

Bridget frowned as she watched Gabe track the slinky girl's form out the door. "Gabe," she called to him about to warn him off from the puppy crush he obviously had on her.

Liam walked in front of her and put his arm around Gabe's shoulders. He winked at Bridget and said, "C'mon man, come help me with the dishes, and I'll tell you why you'll never get anywhere mooning after my sister," as he steered the teen back into the kitchen.

Bridget watched Liam bend his head closer to Gabe and give him some man-to-man talk. She sighed with a little sadness in her eyes.

Vaughn put an arm around her shoulders and his chin on her head. "I'm sorry you're sad," he said quietly.

Jorrie rubbed her back.

"I'm not sad." she sniffed. "Okay, maybe a little, but I'm more grateful. Gabe hasn't had a solid male role model in his life since his father passed, and I've tried filling that void, but I can't talk to him about girls and flirting. It's so sweet of you and Liam to help with that. He absolutely adores Liam, you know. He adores you, too." She looked up at Vaughn.

He smiled, "What about Jack? I know he's been there for him."

Jack sighed and gave an exaggerated sashay over. "Well, I gave him great advice about not mixing stripes and patterns, but when it comes to advice about the fairer sex, I'm afraid I much prefer a five o'clock shadow. Although I did teach him how to tackle and throw an uppercut." Jack laughed. "I know what you mean, though. Gabe needs someone to confide in about that stuff, and gay Uncle Jack wouldn't be the first choice. I'm not hurt. I know my place."

He joined the group in a hug, then backed up and clapped. "Now unless you have any hot gay dragons lurking around, I haven't met yet, I'm going to run home and make sure my fiancé hasn't abandoned me." He winked, shook Vaughn's hand and mimed a phone. "Call me once we are ready to plan Shadow Extinction. They messed with the wrong family."

CHAPTER 22

BRIDGET SAT ON A stool at the back of the large rec room at Cloud Warrior Gaming, listening to the noise of seven teenage boys plus a few men, who might as well have been teenagers. Gabe and his friends were battling Vaughn's developers in the newest unreleased edition of Cloud Warrior. Gabe would be the king of his friends for a while with this coup. She hoped it didn't go to his head.

"Pepperoni, madame?" a slice appeared in front of her, Vaughn smiling as he offered it.

She took the slice and gave a stiff head nod. "Thank you, kind sir." she sniffed. They both grinned at their silliness and turned to watch the kids. "They are having an absolute blast," she said, "You may not get them out of here."

Vaughn nodded and replied thoughtfully, "That's a good thing though. That means the game is doing what we intended and bringing people together, bringing them into the realm we've created. They are living inside of that world, working to defend it."

Bridget tilted her head. "Hmm, hadn't thought of it like that before. Still, I have to ask," she looked at him, "Cloud Warriors, they're dragons and dragon riders. A little on the nose don't you think?"

He smirked, "Hiding in plain sight."

She laughed, "So are *all* of your employees dragons, or wielders?

He shook his head, "No, not all, although a good number of my employees worldwide are, most of the staff are just really talented people with great imagination." He nodded at Liam and Siobhan, "Obviously you know about them. You met Killian, Marco too. Jackson and Della over there are dragons. You haven't met her yet, but Betsy in HR is a dragon, and Henry in accounting is a wielder. There's a few more in the design department."

Bridget thought about it a moment, then looked at Vaughn. "A dragon named Betsy?"

Vaughn invited Bridget back to his office to grab some papers he claimed he needed. She figured it was really to get a break from the noise. They quietly sat in some small chairs by the window, enjoying the sun shining and the warmth it gave in the cool air-conditioned space. You just had to have AC in Texas in the summer, non-negotiable. Even though it was still a few weeks away, the temperature outside was nearing cremation levels.

He watched her sitting quietly. He knew she must have more questions but hadn't asked.

She must have sensed he was willing to talk though, because she sat up straighter and her expression turned serious. "I was wondering, can I ask you more about dragons?"

He waved a hand in a go-ahead signal, stretching his legs and basking more in the sun.

"The colors," she started, "Do they signify anything? I know your scales seem to be black and gold. Liam's were green. What other colors are there? Do they mean anything? Do you have any additional powers, senses, abilities? Can you fly in any form? Do you have live births or lay eggs?" she said the last with a blush on her face.

Vaughn roared in laughter. "Well, my dear blushing maiden, I will answer all of your questions, but let me start with the last. Neither. In case you hadn't noticed, I'm all male." He leaned over the table and growled like he was stalking her. He blew a cloud of smoke and warmth across her neck and placed his mouth right next to her throat.

She swallowed carefully, suddenly reminded that he could quickly turn into a vicious beast if needed.

He sniffed her neck and licked up the smooth column of her throat to her ear.

Bridget let her breath out in a whoosh and Vaughn sat back down. Smiling and looking pleased with himself. She let out a shaky laugh and crossed her legs at the sudden dampness she had there. Okay, kinda scary, but dear lord that was sexy. He knew it too. She looked him in the eye and only raised an eyebrow. "Are you, must have slipped my mind."

He rumbled low in his chest, and she worried she was going to leave a damp spot on the chair. "Well, my darling, I will be sure to remind you at the first opportunity. Unfortunately for me, all of this glass and a horde of teenagers down the hall does not lend itself to the things I want to do to you."

She swallowed hard.

He pointed to himself and whispered, *"Sex God."* He winked and continued, "As to your questions, let's see. Colors, yes, there are multiple colors and as you guessed, they do mean different things. They're generally associated with the powers of the Wielders they most closely affiliate with. Liam, for example, is a green and Siobhan's power follows the family line which is warding and protection, and of course plants. They take after their mother. Marco is red, they are the warrior daredevils of the species. Reds and their wielders have a thing for speed and danger. As you'd expect, fire is their element.

"What else, silver dragons and their wielders are mostly skilled in spell work. They can weave amazing illusions and redirect light, almost like a mirror. They are tricky. Killian is silver. Oh, and the browns, as you might have guessed, are affiliated with earth and stone, they tend to be shy and quiet. And finally, the blues with water, storms, rivers, oceans and such. The myths did get a few things right." He shrugged.

"Black?" Bridget said.

He looked around like he wasn't going to answer at first. He sighed. "Black dragons are affiliated with raw magic. Not much is known about their abilities."

Bridget looked at him in confusion. "But you're a black dragon. Aren't you?"

He nodded.

"Then how is there not much known?"

He stared at her then said, "I'm the only one. I keep that information close to my chest."

Bridget pondered that. Obviously, there was more to this story, but she didn't want to push him yet. "What about the rest of my questions, sir?" she asked with mock primness.

He smiled, knowing she was purposely changing the subject, and he was grateful. "Other abilities, yes, many dragons can do similar magic to the Wielders, but they are usually stronger at it unless the dragon is very old. We can all do partial transformation. We can all breathe fire, except for the blues. They do steam and are very sensitive about it, don't ask," he added.

"We can carry one or more people when we're in our dragon forms. When a wielder and a dragon are touching, it amplifies both of their powers. They can develop a psychic bond, too, which comes in handy. Another thing the myths got right. The bond exists with mates... life partners. Which brings me to that other question. We reproduce with humans usually so we can keep the human form in our bloodline. Women carry the baby the normal nine months, there is nothing at birth that would give us away. Dragons don't usually mate with each other. They're too territorial and grumpy." He smiled. He was only kidding a little.

"Yoohoo! Bridge!" she heard coming down the hall. It was Jorrie. "Are you decent? Do I need to cover my eyes?"

Vaughn rolled his eyes. "We're in my office," he called out, "We're naked and in the throes of wild passion on my desk. Enter at your own risk."

"Hot damn!" Jorrie laughed. She entered the office with her hand over her eyes, the other outstretched to keep her from running into anything.

Bridget shook her head, laughing. "It's okay, Jorrie, you can look."

Jorrie dropped her hand and looked around. She whistled and said, "Swanky! Nice digs, Drake." She walked around looking at the view and pictures.

Bridget could tell something was bothering her. "What's up, Jorrie? What's on your mind."

Jorrie sighed.

She was obviously reluctant to bring it up but it would come out soon.

"It's Payne," she finally said.

"Where? What hurts?" Bridget asked, confused.

"No," Jorrie laughed without humor, "Not pain like I'm *in* pain, Payne, as in Melissa. You remember Major Payne?" Jorrie hesitated. "I can't work there anymore. There's no way I can keep working for that bitch and not say something or maybe make her disappear." She looked up at Bridget. "Every time I think about that swamp hag, I start plotting her murder." She stared at the floor, twisting her hands. "So, I was wondering if you would write me a reference so I can start looking for another job?"

Vaughn sat back and steepled his fingers. Bridget had reassured her friend she would help, but he wanted to help her as well. He liked the spunky lady, and she was Bridget's best friend. He suddenly had an idea. "Jorrie!" He jumped up. "What do you do there?"

She looked at him curiously, "I'm the foreign accounts liaison. I speak five languages, in addition to English, so I usually coordinate activities with our partners overseas."

Vaughn snapped his fingers and ran around his desk. He turned on his laptop and began furiously typing. Jorrie and Bridget exchanged a look.

"Vaughn?" Bridget inquired.

He held up a finger indicating they should hold on. After a few minutes he printed out some pages and waved them over. "Jorrie, as the owner and CEO of Drake Enterprises, I would like to congratulate you on your offer of employment as Director of Foreign Relations. I will need you to work closely with our new division's VP, one Ms. Bridget Ridgeway, as we are launching a new global VR operation. I trust the benefits and pay would be to your satisfaction?" He sat on the edge of his desk, grinning at them.

Jorrie looked at Vaughn and stared down at the pages in her hand. She read through them, and he saw several emotions cross her face. She finally settled on anger.

What? He was confused. Why was she mad? He thought she would be perfect for the role, it would give her the chance to be with Bridget, and she knew about the shadow situation for which she'd already proven she had valuable insight. She was a sharp lady, and he valued people like her, independent thinkers who didn't back down from roadblocks. He looked at Bridget and saw she was watching Jorrie, too. She also saw the anger on her face.

"Jorrie!" Bridget stepped in front of her, "Slow your roll firecracker. It's not what you think. Vaughn doesn't do pity. He offered you this because he knows you are sharp. He values independent thinkers who don't back down. Plus, he thought you would be perfect for the role. We can be together, and you can really help us with our fight against the shadows. I promise Jorrie, he's not trying to demean you. This is a good thing."

A strange look crossed Bridget's face. She turned and stared at Vaughn. *Where the hell did that come from,* she thought. *How did I know all that?* She saw that Vaughn's face had gone pale, and he was staring at her like she had turned purple. She was suddenly a little nauseous and sat down quickly.

He jumped up, "Bridget, are you okay?" Concern was etched into every feature.

She waved him back, "Yeah, yeah, fine, just a little dizzy all of a sudden. My head feels weird."

Vaughn dropped his hands like he'd been shocked. "I'll, uh, go get you some water," he stammered and rushed out of the room.

Jorrie watched him go, "I don't know what just happened there, but something sure as hell spooked that man."

Bridget couldn't help but agree.

CHAPTER 23

VAUGHN PULLED HIMSELF TOGETHER and brought Bridget a bottle of cold water.

She gratefully sipped it, claiming she was much better.

Jorrie had apologized for misjudging his kind offer and accepted the position, signing the offer with a flourish. She was so excited that she emailed her resignation letter from Vaughn's desk and stabbed the send button with a vicious glee.

He showed her the empty office next to Bridget's and told her she had free reign to set it up and get him a list of supplies she needed, mentioning the catalog he'd already given to Bridget. She seemed mollified so he left the two of them talking about color schemes and standing desks. He sought out Liam and Killian in the rec room where the little party had started to wind down.

Liam grinned at his boss as they walked to the café area, giving him an update. "It's a hit, boss. They loved it as predicted. The ogre dimension was epic; they ate it up. Real stroke of genius that."

Killian nodded in agreement; his team had done well.

Liam's smile slowly turned into a frown as he watched his boss and mentor pacing across the café floor. He looked like a man haunted rather than someone celebrating success. "Boss." No response. "Drake," he tried again. "Vaughn!" he said louder and grabbed his shoulders.

Vaughn responded by grabbing Liam, bunching his shirt in his fists and snarling. He was breathing heavily and looked wild.

Killian pulled Vaughn back while Liam patted him on the chest, "Vaughn, Vaughn, it's me. What the hell, man, you're kinda freaking me out." He spoke soothingly.

Vaughn finally relaxed his grip and thrust both hands into his hair. "She heard me," he whispered. "Bridget, she heard me."

Liam looked at Killian in confusion, and the wielder just shrugged. "Yeah, man," Liam spoke slowly and clearly, not wanting to spook this dangerous man in front of him. "She hears you all the time. Every time you talk to her, she listens."

Vaughn waved his hands impatiently in Liam's face. "No, no, not listens to me. She *heard* me," he pointed at his head. "I offered Jorrie a job here and —"

Liam broke in, "Jorrie? Here? Did she accept? What's the —"

"Not important!" shouted Vaughn, startling some of the kids walking to the bathrooms down the hall. He waved them on with a smile. He turned back and took a deep breath. "Sorry, this just has me off balance."

Killian nodded and wisely kept quiet. He'd never seen Vaughn this worked up in the decades he'd known him.

"I had offered the job to Jorrie, but she got angry. I wasn't sure why, but Bridget knew. Of course, she did. That woman is simply amazing! But she stopped Jorrie and started telling her about how it wasn't pity and the reasons why Jorrie would be great for the job. But," he grabbed Killian's shirt this time, "I didn't say any of it out loud. She got it from my head."

Vaughn watched as Killian looked at him in confusion and saw the moment it clicked.

"Oh shit," Liam said under his breath as he also understood.

Vaughn nodded. He agreed.

"There you guys are!" came Bridget's cheerful voice. She found her boys in the front lobby by the massive glass doors. Vaughn was listening to Gabriel as he chattered ninety miles an hour. She noticed Liam and Killian retreating. The lobby was full of the parents of Gabe's friends as they came to pick them up.

Vaughn smiling, walked around, handing each kid an envelope, thanking them and their parents for coming today to participate in the beta testing program. He promised them all an advance copy of the game and indicated the envelope was a little thank you for their time and efforts. He also mentioned the summer internship programs they had for high school seniors thinking about careers in coding, programming, and developing.

Jorrie leaned over to Bridget. "That man is smooth like silk."

Bridget nodded. He was very smooth. He had a way with people—of making them feel important. She sighed a little.

Jorrie laughed. "You've got it so bad for that man," she said in a singsong voice.

Bridget smiled and turned back to the scene before her. "Yeah, Jorr, I do."

"$500 mom!" Gabe said excitedly from the back seat of the SUV as they drove back to Vaughn's place. "He gave us all $500 and promised us a copy of the game before it's in stores, *and* he told us he would have us back for future beta programs!"

Bridget smiled; it was only the fifth time she'd heard it since the others had left. "That's great, baby. That was very generous of him, wasn't it?"

"Hell yeah!" Gabe said, then as his mother caught his eyes in the mirror, "Uh, I mean, thank you Mr. Uh, I mean, thanks, Drake, I really appreciate your generosity today and for including me in the program. I look forward to future opportunities with you."

Vaughn laughed; Gabe was quite a character. He could definitely see his mother's fire in him. "You are quite welcome Mr. Ridgeway, now I expect that at least some of that money goes to your college fund. After all, we must be responsible. You can't buy a Lamborghini if you blow all your money on pizza and arcade games." He winked at Bridget before turning his eyes back to the road.

She studied his profile thoughtfully. Whatever had spooked him at the office seemed to be resolved now. There wasn't a hint of what was going on remaining. Maybe she had imagined it because of that dizzy spell. She had tried to ask Liam about it in the lobby, but somehow, he'd melted into the crowd, and she lost sight of him. Almost like he was avoiding her. Maybe he was avoiding Jorrie. It might get a little awkward the way they had been flirting and would now be working together. She heard Gabe in the backseat still chattering on, this time about how impressed 'the guys' were with meeting the actual GreenPrincess1. She rolled her eyes. Siobhan. Well at least she had kept a professional distance during the party. She realized Vaughn was looking at her. "What?" she said, focusing on him.

He chuckled, "I asked if you wanted to go out tonight for dinner or order in. You've been through a lot, and you weren't expecting to cook for a horde last night. I thought you might be tired and not want to mess with figuring out what to eat. Or if you like, I can do some steaks." He glanced over at her and saw her gaze riveted to the side mirror. "Bridget? If you don't want steak, it's fine, I just..." He trailed off as he glanced in the mirror and saw why Bridget was staring.

Behind them, in an SUV similar to theirs, was a group of men. Nothing unusual about that except they all had swirling black shadows where their faces should be. "Damn," he said under his breath. He stomped the accelerator and cut through traffic to get away from their tail. The car was warded, so they couldn't hurt them inside of the vehicle, but that didn't mean they couldn't follow them or run them off the road.

"Hey, where's the fire, Verstappen?" Gabe laughed from the back.

"Gabe, get down now!" shouted Bridget, seeing a gun pointed at them from the car next to them. The person in the back seat also had a shadow face and was aiming at them from the open window. She ducked and screamed, "Vaughn!" as the person fired. She waited for the glass to shatter, but it never came. She peeked and saw the bullet stuck in some sort of green webbing that faintly glowed around the window. She tapped it gently, and the bullet fell to the road below. She turned back, checking on Gabe. He was hunched down on the seat, out of view of their attackers, terrified.

Her anger boiled at seeing her child having to duck from bullets. She noticed a strange static come over her again, like after she'd been zapped before. She looked at her hands and saw little arcs flowing from finger to finger, dancing happily between them. Only a faint tickle, nothing like the pain she'd experienced before. The energy swelled in her, and she smiled. She knew what to do with this.

Vaughn was well and truly scared. Not for himself, he could handle them fine. But Bridget and Gabe were in danger. He was also pissed; they had shot at them. He could feel his dragon heating up, demanding retribution. He was about to exit the highway when he experienced a pull on his power. The hairs on his body stood on end. He glanced over at Bridget and saw her eyes had turned black and electricity was arcing between her fingertips. He opened his mouth to warn her when she threw her hands out, and a clap, almost like thunder, sounded. All the cars in a two-hundred-yard radius suddenly died and came to a rolling stop. It was like someone had drained all the power from them.

Bridget looked at Vaughn in alarm. Then her eyes rolled back, and she passed out.

"Bridget!" he yelled.

He kept driving and swung the SUV off the highway toward downtown. Fortunately, it was Saturday, so they were able to get to his street quickly without too much traffic. He flew into the garage, heading for his spot by the door. He rushed around to Bridget's side, flinging her door open.

"Gabe!" he said quickly to the terrified kid, leaning over his mother, begging her to wake up. "I know you're scared, buddy, but your mom is okay, I promise. She just tapped into a huge amount of magic before she was ready, and it wore her out. Help me get her inside. Come on Gabe. You can do this. You are strong."

Gabe shook his head, and tears began to fall down his face as he continued staring at his mother.

Vaughn understood. He already lost his father tragically; now he'd been shot at, and his mother was unconscious. He was freaking out, poor kid. "Gabe, look at me," Vaughn commanded in a stern voice.

Gabe looked at him sharply.

"What did I promise you? That I wouldn't let anything hurt your mother, right? Yeah?"

He nodded.

"Okay, good, that's right. I love her, and I promise you this on my life. She's fine. She just needs rest right now, okay? Do you trust me?"

Gabe nodded again, wiping his tears. He jumped out and grabbed his mom's legs, helping maneuver her out of the car.

Vaughn picked her up, cradling her against his chest. Gabe shut the doors and danced around them, trying to see her face. Vaughn tossed his key card to him, so he ran ahead to call the elevator, and once on Vaughn's floor got them in the front door. Vaughn rushed Bridget into the bedroom.

He laid her gently down on the bed and whipped out his phone. Liam answered promptly. "It's Bridget," he said breathlessly. "She tapped into my magic and used it without really understanding it. She's unconscious. Bring Siobhan."

It only took twenty minutes for help to arrive but to Vaughn, it was years. He quickly gave Siobhan a rundown of what happened. She nodded once and walked into the bedroom without another word. He didn't tell her how he thought Bridget was able to tap into his magic, that was more than he could handle.

Liam sat down next to Gabe, not saying anything, just giving him a hug.

Vaughn hadn't talked at all while they had waited. He walked over and sat on the other side, looking at the boy and seeing questions in his eyes. "Gabe," he sighed. Bridget was going to kill him for this, "We need to talk."

CHAPTER 24

B RIDGET CAME TO SLOWLY, her head pounding, her vision fuzzy. She groaned and stirred, feeling like she'd been hit by a truck. She heard someone shift on the chair next to the bed and turned to look. "Ugh," she groaned again. Why did that hurt so much?

"Welcome back," came a female voice.

She tried to focus and found that if she squinted, she could make out Siobhan leaning over her. "What hit me?" Bridget croaked.

Siobhan snorted, "From what I hear, a couple of thousand kilo-watts of electricity."

Bridget was pretty sure that wasn't a thing, and it hurt to think about it, so she ignored it. "My head," she managed.

"Yeah, that happens when you overload on magic like that. You should take it slowly when you first start out. Sending a shockwave like that is totally badass, don't get me wrong, but not good for a first-timer." She used a cool rag that was heaven on Bridget's forehead, wiping away the sweat collecting there.

Bridget vaguely recalled some of what Siobhan was talking about. "Gabe? Vaughn?" she whispered. Whispering was good. It didn't hurt as much.

Siobhan smiled, "They're fine, thanks to you. To hear Gabe tell it, you looked like Storm from the X-Men. His mom is a bona-fide superhero."

Bridget smiled weakly at that. "So hot," she whispered. Her surprise at finding Siobhan there had worn off; now, she was more aware of her misery.

Siobhan nodded, "Well, that's to be expected. I can help, though." She closed her eyes, holding her hands out, palms down, and suddenly Bridget's body was wrapped in ice. It was heaven.

"Ooh," Bridget sighed. She blinked; her vision had finally cleared. She tried to sit up, but her head throbbed. "Got anything for the nails being driven into my skull?" She didn't have to try hard to sound pathetic. Siobhan put her fingers on Bridget's temples, and suddenly her head was whole again. She was human once more.

Bridget sat up slowly and looked at Siobhan with wonder. "Wow," she said in a normal voice. "You're pretty handy to have around during a migraine."

Siobhan rolled her eyes and stood. "Yeah."

Bridget grabbed her arm. "I don't mean to belittle you. I just make stupid jokes when I'm on edge," she admitted. "Thank you. Truly, thank you for helping me. I'm impressed with your abilities. Maybe you can teach me how to not fry my brain in the future? I don't know what I did or how I did it. I remember I was staring at a bullet hanging outside the car window, and then I was angry at those shadow bastards for trying to kill my son. After that, I remember crackling and boom, I woke up here in Vaughn's bed. Again. I'm making a habit of this," she muttered the last part.

Siobhan smiled, patting Bridget on the shoulder. "You're welcome." She walked out of the room.

A giant dog barreled in and jumped on the bed. No, not a dog, she realized. It was Gabe. He was bouncing around, ecstatic to see she was okay. He was talking so fast she could barely make out what he was saying, but she caught enough to know he was glad she was alright. She was now a badass superhero, he was fine, and Vaughn was going to show him how to grill a steak.

She laughed and put her hands on his face. "Love you, bug."

He stopped bouncing. "Love you, too, Mom."

They smiled at each other for a minute, then she said, "Well I guess we need to talk about what happened. But we can't wait until after dinner. So Vaughn's going to grill steaks, huh? I didn't see a grill anywhere. Do you mean he's doing them on the stove?" She was trying to buy time to figure out how to explain this to him. He oddly didn't seem fazed by what had happened.

Gabe grinned at her, "Of course not, Mom, he's going to use his fire breath."

Vaughn was in the kitchen, putting salt and pepper on the steaks and wrapping some potatoes in foil. He had wanted to run to Bridget's side when she came to, but knew she'd need some time to reassure herself that Gabe was okay. He needed some time himself to really come to terms with what had happened today. For her to tap into his thoughts and then channel his magic meant one thing. He had avoided this complication for the majority of his life for a reason. If he didn't admit it, maybe he could ignore it a little while longer? No, that was foolish thinking. He just needed more time to figure it out before the Council became aware. Once they were, he would no doubt be summoned before them to discuss it. That was something he was most decidedly not looking forward to. He sighed. Who was he kidding?

He knew it deep in his heart. Bridget was—

"Vaughn. Cormac. Drake."

He whirled around and saw Bridget standing in the doorway. Arms crossed, foot tapping, fire in her eyes. He saw Gabriel peeking around her, frantically waving and wide-eyed.

Pissed. Bridget was pissed.

Bridget stormed across the bedroom throwing him furious glances while he sat on the bed, ankles crossed, hands folded demurely. She wasn't falling for the innocent schoolboy look, and he knew it, but he dared not do anything else until the dam was ready to break.

She whipped around and hissed at him. It was impressive. "You told him. You knew that I, no, just." She stared. "How dare you!" she said in a deadly quiet tone. She stood in front of him. Hands on her hips this time, daring him to speak.

"Bridget, my love, I had to."

She snorted.

"It's true," he implored her. "Look, you were out cold, Gabe was freaking out, I called Siobhan over here while Gabe was begging me to call 911. What was I supposed to do? Explain to the cops, hey, my girlfriend fried her brain with magic and won't wake up?"

She shrugged. "Not your place."

"The fuck Bridget? He saw you wield a big ass EMP to take an entire section of roadway out." He was getting angry now. He stood up and leveled his gaze with hers. "Your son was terrified. I was terrified. I thought I lost you. I had to reassure him somehow that it was all going to be okay. He's a smart kid, Bridget. Give him some credit. He'd already figured out quite a bit of it on his own. Liam and I just filled in the gaps. He was totally cool with the whole dragon thing. Handled it better than you did. The kid thinks he's living with legends. Seriously, he's fine, chill."

As soon as the last words left his mouth, he knew it was the wrong thing to say. At no point ever in the history of someone telling a woman to calm down, did she calm down. The dam broke.

"AAAAHHHH!" Bridget screamed wordlessly at him. She jabbed her finger in his chest. "You are *not* his father; you do *not* get to make decisions for him. That is my job. *Mine!*" she slammed her fist against her chest. "I was the one who had to be there to pick up the pieces when his father died. I'm the one who had to put aside my own pain, my own misery and keep him together. You had *no right* to tell him about any of this." She was sobbing. Angry, miserable and scared.

He understood now. She wasn't angry with him for telling Gabe; she was angry that he had to be told. That he had been exposed to any of this. Vaughn was just the target of her anger. "Bridget, my love," he began quietly.

"Stop it!" she yelled. "Stop calling me that!"

He looked at her, confused. "Bridget? But that's your name."

She turned away, wrapping her arms around herself. "The other part." She spat the words over her shoulder. "I'm not your love."

Vaughn's eyes flamed up, and smoke poured from his nostrils. He marched over and spun her around, growling at her.

"Oh, quit with the scary dragon stuff, will you? You don't get to say that to me." She tried to pull away from him, but he held on.

"Yes, I do," he growled.

She tried harder, broke away, and then walked to the door.

"Where do you think you're going?" he growled again.

Her shoulders dropped, and she looked back at him. "Home," she whispered, reaching for the doorknob.

Bridget heard the flap of wings about a second before she was yanked off her feet and shoved against the wall, almost to the ceiling. Vaughn had pinned her there, his hands on her waist. His massive wings stretched out, fluttering gently to keep them off the ground. He held his hurt gaze level with hers. She could feel his breath, super-hot on her neck.

"You. Are. Not. Leaving," he snarled at her.

She jerked her head back in fear, banging it on the wall. This overcame her shock at her situation and brought back her anger. "Ow! Damn it, Vaughn, this is childish. Put me down and talk to me like a human."

Now his head snapped back, and the flames in his eyes flickered for a moment.

She saw they were replaced by fear. He was terrified of her leaving. She didn't understand it. They'd only been together for a few days, and yes, they'd been magical, but what was this? Why was he in such a panic over the thought of her going to her own house to unwind and have some space? "What the hell, Vaughn, is this some sort of dragon territorial thing?" she demanded, doing her best to look angry while her feet dangled at least four feet off the floor.

His eyes flickered again with uncertainty and fear. "Yes, no, kind of, you can't leave me!" he said.

"And why the hell not?" she shouted again, "Am I some sort of prisoner here? Why do you care?"

Vaughn let out a frustrated growl, "Because."

She rolled her eyes, "Not good enough."

He gritted his teeth, then shouted, "Because I fucking love you, Bridget!" Then whispered, "I love you." He slowly lowered them both to the ground. He set her gently on her feet and backed away, his wings dragging on the floor. He held his arms listlessly at his sides, looking like his world was ending. "Please," he begged her, "Don't go. I love you. Don't leave me." He dropped to his knees then, and his wings crumpled around him.

Bridget stood there in shock, staring at him. It swirled through her head. Love? He loved her. This strong, virile man, who ran international mega companies, who was a fierce beast and fighter, made love like a man possessed, treated his staff like they were his family, and could speak to a crowd while having them eat out of his hand. This man was absolutely undone with the love of her. Everything he'd done had been to protect her and Gabriel.

Jesus, Bridget, she thought, *you're such a fucking idiot.* She walked over and dropped to the floor in front of him. She lifted his head with her hands and saw the tears in his eyes. She could see it had cost him a lot to admit this to her. He was caring for her the best he could in extraordinary circumstances, and she had thrown it in his face. He seemed so vulnerable. Her heart ached, and she ran her fingers through his hair.

He rumbled in his chest quietly and turned his face to her palm. Breathing warmth into it.

"Vaughn," she whispered, and he looked up at her, like he was frightened of what he might see. Overwhelmed with emotion and realization, the tears came to her eyes. "Vaughn," she whispered again and leaned her forehead against his. "I'm so sorry. I'm not going anywhere. I wouldn't admit it to myself, but I will to you. I love you. I absolutely love you, too." She pressed her lips to his.

CHAPTER 25

AT HER ADMISSION VAUGHN shuddered and wrapped his wings around them both, pulling her into his lap. It was like a warm cocoon, and she snuggled into his chest while he rested his chin on her head, holding her tightly. They were quiet for a while. Then he softly told her about when a dragon and their human side both fell in love with someone, and that person loved them in return; it became a magical bond, and they became mates. He told her that she was his mate. His destiny and the only one he could ever love. He shared how he'd realized it was happening when she'd picked up on his thoughts at the office and she'd channeled his magic in the car. He told her about how his heart was so connected with hers now that without her, his magic would wither away, and he'd lose the ability to change into a dragon. He talked about how fiercely protective dragons were and how an insult to a mate was an affront to the dragon.

Bridget sat quietly, taking it all in, listening to the rumble in his chest, the beat of his heart that was so strong and full of life. She'd never thought of loving anyone again after Brian, and she'd certainly never thought to be loved like this in return. This was on a different level.

She learned that now that Vaughn had recognized her as his mate, there was no way for him to ever be mated with anyone else. He'd told her there was a process to mark her; it involved sex and blood of course. She wasn't surprised.

She was ready to go for it right now, but he declined. They had time. He wanted to make it special for her. They only got one shot at it, and he wanted her to know the full extent of what she was getting into before she committed. Bridget knew it didn't matter what else there was. She knew it deep in her soul. This was right. This was meant to be, and she was going through with it.

Bridget was in the kitchen chopping vegetables for a salad because even though dragons were meat and potato creatures, she had a growing son to try to shovel healthy food in. That was her job, wielder of vegetables. She heard a cry of amazement and saw Gabe cheering as Vaughn used his fire breath to light the oversized fireplace in the dining room. He kept it going until the grate he'd placed there was hot enough and put the steaks on. She had wondered why there was such a large fireplace in the dining room of all places, but now she understood. She remembered her first night here when Vaughn had made a joke about cooking on an open flame. She rolled her eyes. Dragons. She glanced over again.

Now, Vaughn was showing him how to check for doneness. Her heart filled with joy to see them bonding over guy things. Gabe needed this. She needed to ease up and let people help her. Vaughn obviously enjoyed being around Gabe; he must have needed it too. Surrounded by friends, he'd been alone for hundreds of years.

Earlier, when they'd come back into the kitchen, Gabe had hugged her, whispering that it was all going to be okay. He'd begged her not to be too mad at Vaughn.

She whispered back that she'd only yelled at him a little, and everything was going to be okay now.

He looked at her, "Does he make you happy, Mom?"

She'd nodded. Yes.

"He loves you."

"What do you think about that?"

He tilted his head, looking just like his father in the moment. "I like it, Mom, I like it a lot. And if you want to love him back, I'm good with that too."

She hugged her baby and told him, "I do love him."

He shrugged and warned her not to do any mushy crap in front of him.

Vaughn had heard the last part, so of course he dipped Bridget over his arm and kissed her right in the middle of the kitchen.

Gabe had pretended he was gagging and throwing up, but she had seen the smile on his face. He really was happy, and that was all she needed.

They sat down at the table, just her, Vaughn, Liam, and Gabe.

"Where did Siobhan go?" she asked as she added more salad to Gabe's plate than he had originally taken. She heard him complaining under his breath about the vegetable enforcement officer and added salad to both Liam and Vaughn's plates as well in solidarity. They wisely didn't comment and tucked into the food.

"Oh, she left when the fireworks started," Liam said then jumped. Vaughn had obviously kicked him under the table. Liam grinned while he rubbed his shin.

Bridget laughed, "Well, I just wanted to thank her again for helping me earlier. It was amazing, really."

Liam smiled with pride. "Yes, my baby sister can do amazing things. She's not really supposed to be able to heal, but she's worked out some things that turn warding into healing spells. Vaughn thinks she's really gifted; I just think she's too stubborn to accept she can't do something." Liam put a bite of steak in his mouth and smiled his boyish smile.

Bridget couldn't resist teasing him a little. "You know she reminds me a lot of Jorrie in that way, stubborn, beautiful, won't take no for an answer. I can see why you like her." She derived a small about of pleasure from seeing Liam flush and take a big gulp of his wine.

"Hey," said Vaughn, "You peasant. That is a very nice Bordeaux. It's meant for savoring, not chugging." He winked at Bridget.

Gabe looked up from his potato, a piece of cheese hanging from his mouth that he was trying to catch with his tongue. "Wait, Liam, dude. You like Aunt Jorrie?" he said incredulously. "Weird. You know she can curse you out in five other languages and probably knows, like, a gajillion ways to kill you and hide the body."

"So I've heard," Liam said dryly. They all laughed then, and Bridget couldn't help smiling when the warm feeling of family settled over her.

They adjourned to the living room to watch a movie. Once they had picked something to watch, Liam and Gabe made noises about popcorn despite the large meal they had just inhaled.

Bridget was quite sure Gabe had a hollow leg and it was obvious Liam hadn't grown out of his yet, either. Since it wasn't a school night, and quite frankly, what boy didn't deserve to stay up late and gorge on snacks after being shot at, she didn't protest when they came back with popcorn, soda, and a bag of M&Ms. She just smiled and settled in the comfort of Vaughn's arms while the sound of a high-speed chase filled the room as the movie started.

The credits were rolling, and Bridget stretched, glancing over at the boys. Liam and Gabriel were passed out on the other couch. Both heads back, mouths open, snoring slightly. A bowl of popcorn, half-eaten, sat between them. It was so adorable she did the only thing a mom in her position could do. She grabbed her phone and took a couple of photos of them. She sent the best one to Jorrie with a little heart-eyes emoji. She knew Jorrie would get a kick out of it, and she did, responding with a crying, laughing face. She heard Vaughn laugh quietly behind her as he leaned over her shoulder.

"You bad girl," he whispered, kissing her neck.

She turned to him, "Hey, I gotta get my blackmail material anywhere, and any way I can. He's at the age now where me taking his picture is so embarrassing, he's going to die," she whispered back. She sighed, "I hate to wake him, but he really needs to sleep in a bed tonight."

Vaughn waved a hand and shooed her away. "I got this." He leaned over and tapped Liam lightly on the shoulder. He was instantly awake without a sound. Vaughn pointed at Gabe, then pointed at the back bedrooms in the guest wing. Liam nodded and stood. He stretched, then scooped Gabe up effortlessly and put him over his shoulder like a sack of potatoes.

Her jaw dropped. Her hands came up on their own, and she snapped another picture. This one showed Liam's bulging muscles and tight butt as he walked down the hall. She sent that picture, too and this time, Jorrie was the one who supplied the heart eyes.

She started to clean up the mess when Vaughn scooped her up and threw her over his shoulder the same way Liam had with Gabe. She began to protest when he ran his hand up her calf to her thigh, then smacked her firmly on her butt. She was so caught off guard she forgot what she was about to say.

"So, Bridget, my love," Vaughn said. "If I remember correctly, I believe some punishment is in order from earlier in my office. Let's go work this out in the boardroom. I mean bedroom."

She laughed all the way to the door.

When he got to the bed, he heaved her back over his shoulder and threw her down on the bed so hard she bounced.

She yelped, then fell back laughing again. She looked at Vaughn and saw him watching her with a tender expression on his face.

"I love the sound of your laugh," he said. "I love watching your hair fall in your face, the way you bite your lip when you're thinking hard. I love the quick little breaths you take when I kiss your neck. I just love you, Bridget. I love you so much," he finished in a whisper.

She got up on her knees and began to remove his belt. "Show me," she said with a sultry smile that instantly got him hard.

Vaughn took his time undressing her so he could watch the slow reveal of her soft skin. He reveled in the way it seemed to glow in the dim light. He found himself wanting to rip her clothes off and take her now, but he quieted those thoughts and kept his hands gentle. She was a thing of beauty, and though she seemed tough and fiery, he knew she was also fragile, and needed to be cherished. He leaned back, pulling his shirt over his head and hissed as her hands fumbled at the button on his pants.

She kept her gaze locked on his as she slowly and tortuously lowered the zipper.

He was dying. It was like all the air had been sucked out of the room. He could feel himself straining under the pressure of her hands on him.

She slid his pants down his legs, and he gasped as she quickly darted forward, biting him lightly on his hip. "Mm," she said, "I was right; that hip was delicious."

His eyes almost rolled back as she pressed light, fluttering kisses along the top of his boxers to his other hip, where she lightly sank her teeth into that one as well. "Bridget," he whispered in a strained voice. "I had no idea you were so... bitey."

She smiled up at him and slowly inched the last of his clothing down his body. She watched as he sprang free and braced himself.

He shuddered when she wrapped her warm hand around the length of him. Dying. Yes, he was dying, and there was no way he'd rather go.

She stroked him and watched as he quivered, spreading the small drops that were seeping out with the pad of her thumb. "You're always so in control, Vaughn," she said quietly, "Let me have a turn." She leaned forward, and he moaned as her soft velvet lips close around him.

He bucked his hips and almost lost it there. The woman was trying to kill him, he decided.

She put one arm around him and squeezed his butt, humming in pleasure around him. She slid further down his length, and he let loose a strangled cry. She reached underneath and lightly scraped her fingernails over his balls.

He was pretty sure he heard angels singing. This beautiful creature before him was pure sin wrapped in velvet.

She began to glide back and forth on his shaft, sucking and flicking her tongue over the head.

Her fingers dug into his backside as she continued her happy little humming noise, and she moved faster and harder. "Bridget," he gasped, "If you keep doing that, I'm not going to last!" Her shrug and a small laugh in her throat had him growing impossibly hard. He wasn't going to make it. "Bri- Bridget!" he cried out, feeling that last tense moment before he knew he couldn't stop. She flicked her tongue over the slit, and he lost it, jetting his pleasure down her throat. As he spasmed in her mouth, he found his hands in her hair, reveling in the silky texture as it brushed his thighs. His legs were shaking as she gave him one last long lick and settled back on her knees like a satisfied cat. He sank on the bed next to her, trying to remember how to breathe. He turned to her and said, "I like it when you take control. But now it's my turn."

Bridget gasped when he pushed her onto her back, yanking her arms up over her head. She hadn't wanted anything from him in return; she'd only wanted to repay some of the pleasure he'd given her. To take some control from his massive shoulders for a little while and let him just enjoy. The look in his eyes said there would be none of that.

"Vaughn," she begged, "You don't have to. I just wanted to give to you."

Smoke filtered slowly from his nostrils, and he let the flames in his eyes roam her body. He looked in her eyes again, and she knew she was lost.

"Oh, but my love, this is you giving to me. Because there's nothing I want more right now than to have a little bite of you." He leaned in and kissed her fiercely, then smiled a wicked grin showing his fangs.

"That's new," she said, trembling bravely. When he lightly scraped his now razor-sharp teeth over her neck, she began to get a feel for what the mating ritual would be like. She trembled thinking about where else he might place those teeth.

As if he was reading her mind, he lowered his face to her breasts and scraped his fangs across them as well. He pricked one hard nipple with the tip of a fang and held her down as she almost came off the bed. "No, little one," he growled, "You're not the only one who gets to be bitey." He began to roll her nipple in his mouth, nibbling and sucking until she realized her body was going to overheat again. He generously paid tribute to the other side while her hands flexed in the shackles of his, still locked over her head. He finally let go as he slid down her body, and she gripped the sheets instead. "Watch me," he commanded as he pushed her legs apart.

She tried to resist, not wanting those fangs anywhere near her tender parts, but he overpowered her and held her thighs wide.

He ran a finger down her center, parting her lips and saw the moisture already there for him. He leaned down and gave a small lick, then a feral smile as her hips bucked. He locked eyes with her, then turned his face to her thigh and scraped his fangs down the tender flesh there.

She squirmed again, and he laughed his rumbly dragon laugh. More moisture flooded her in response, and he stabbed at it with his tongue. He lapped at her and circled her clit, his tongue warm and impossibly soft. She clenched and unclenched her hands in the silky sheets, unsure if she could take much more. She looked down and saw him watching her with those flaming eyes. She froze as prey does when a large predator gets them in sight. She shivered, and that earned her another rumble, and he blew warm air onto her. Her back arched, and her legs began to shake. She was so close, and he was doing amazing things that she almost couldn't stand. Suddenly, the tip of his fang scraped across her sensitive bud, and she exploded.

He greedily latched his mouth to her, sucking it all in as she had taken him.

She screamed, experiencing wave after wave of pleasure. She finally stilled, gasping for air. He lay there, draped over her legs, his head on her thigh, nuzzling her skin and making purring sounds. This was a satisfied dragon, and he was all hers.

CHAPTER 26

AFTER A WHILE, VAUGHN sprang from the bed and picked her up over his shoulder again, walking into the bathroom. She gave a feeble protest, but her legs were still too weak to get there under her own power. She heard him turn on the shower, and he walked into the steamy stall and plopped her down under the spray.

"Hey!" she shouted as the water hit her full in the face, waking her from her stupor.

"Sorry," he grinned, not looking the least bit apologetic. "But you were such a dirty girl, I knew I needed to get you clean."

She looked up at him, black hair slick and wet, water coursing down his chest. How many fantasies had she had about him looking like this in the office? She'd lost count, but the reality was so much better than her imagination.

"Glasses!" she suddenly said.

He looked at her in confusion.

"Where are your glasses? You were wearing glasses at Chesapeake and when you came to my office, but I haven't seen you wear them since."

Vaughn looked down at his toes, he seemed a little embarrassed.

Her big, strong dragon, bashful about glasses? She smiled.

"They weren't real," he admitted, "I only wore them to try to look more professional. I've learned that people don't take you as seriously as they should when they think you're just a male cover model. Having a little issue like needing glasses made me seem more approachable."

She'd had fantasies about those glasses on him. Those and nothing else.

He grinned, picking up on what she was thinking. "Bridget," he chided as he picked up a shower poof and squirted her creamy summer-scented body wash on it. "Having some naughty librarian fantasies, were we? I think one night we are just going to have to list all of your dirty thoughts about me so we can act them out."

Bridget's mouth went dry despite being surrounded by water.

Vaughn stepped closer and began to run the soap over her body in light circles.

She relaxed into the warm steam and almost hypnotic motion of the puff as he turned her around and began scrubbing her back. She was ready to purr herself.

He wrapped his arms around her, placing her slippery skin against his own slick chest.

She leaned into him and enjoyed the warmth of his body, his lips trailing kisses down her neck. She was going to offer to wash him when she felt him hard and ready against her backside. She looked up at him, over her shoulder. "Already?" she asked.

"Quick healing," he reminded her.

Oh crap, she thought, *makes so much more sense*. She arched her back into him as he slid a finger between her legs and stroked her.

"Still wet for me, my love?" he purred in her ear.

She nodded breathlessly and wiggled against him, begging for more.

He obliged by bending her over the bench at the back of the shower and worked the tip of his shaft into her warmth. With one hand on her back and the other on her bottom, he pulled back slightly and, just when she started to squirm for him, slammed himself to the hilt.

She screamed in pleasure, and he pulled back again. "Please, please," she cried out, wanting him to fill her again.

He wanted to give her whatever she wanted, so he began to slide in and out, angling up a little to hit that sensitive spot inside.

She could feel everything begin to spiral, the warm steam lying heavy on her skin, the pressure, it was too much, and she finally fell apart around him.

He continued to pump into her, and she continued to shatter. When her arms wobbled, and she couldn't hold herself up any longer, he pulled back and spun her to face him. He picked her up and put her against the wall, "Hold on to me," he told her.

She gratefully draped her arms around his neck and her legs around his waist, sinking down onto him with a delicious slide.

"My love," he whispered over the pounding water, his head next to hers.

She lifted her lips and sought his out. They devoured each other while he began to move again. Bridget thought she couldn't possibly imagine feeling anything wilder and more wonderful than this right here. The pleasure spiked again, and when he began to lose his rhythm, she knew he was close. She leaned forward and bit down as hard she could on his shoulder, causing him to roar so loudly she swore the walls shook.

He emptied himself into her, moaning with pleasure until finally he stilled. Vaughn put his forehead against the shower wall. Bridget hung limply in his arms. His breathing finally steadied, and he looked at her. "What you do to me, my love, my little dirty girl."

She looked at him and, with a straight face, said "Sex God."

After they dried off, Bridget went to grab a nightgown. She didn't mind sleeping nude with Vaughn, but she needed something between their skin, or she was afraid she wasn't going to get any sleep tonight.

"Hang on." He grabbed her hand. "Get dressed, and dress warm," he told her. She gave him a puzzled look and he brushed her hair from her face, tucking it behind her ears. "Just, please, Bridget, trust me. This is important."

His face was serious, so she nodded and did as he asked. When she was ready, she wandered out to the living room, finding him staring at his digital windows. He was studying the night sky and the few stars visible above the light pollution of the city. She quietly took his hand, standing there until he was ready.

He squeezed her hand in appreciation and told her, "I want to show you more of my world."

She smiled, "Whoa there Alladin, I've already seen all of your world." She looked him up and down.

He chuckled, "Smartass." He kissed her on the nose and grabbed a blanket from the back of the couch. He pulled her to the front door and the elevator.

"Where are we going?"

"Out."

She watched in curiosity as he pushed the button for the top floor instead of the parking garage. He smiled and winked, so she decided to play along. As they reached the top and exited, he took her to a door that was only accessible by a card reader. Somehow, she knew his card would work before he even proved her right. "You own this building, don't you?" she asked quietly.

He nodded. They went through the door and up two flights of stairs to another door. He slid his card again and paused with his hand on the door. "I forgot to ask," he turned to look at her, "Are you afraid of heights?"

She slowly shook her head— no.

He nodded and opened the door out onto a rooftop terrace.

Holy shit! This man has a freaking patio, on top of a skyscraper, in downtown Dallas. She walked around amazed, taking in the sights. The air seemed so much cleaner here. The views stunning. She kept cautiously back from the edge but then noticed, "There's not a lot of wind up here like I expected." She turned to face Vaughn and found he had removed his shirt and had his wings outstretched.

He rolled his shoulders, eyes closed, and turned his face to the sky.

"And what about other buildings. Can't people see you?"

He shook his head, "Wards." He was enjoying the night air on his wings.

She walked over to him and stroked one wing. He smiled and opened his eyes. "Is this what you wanted to show me?" she asked softly. "It's amazing. I'm sure there's not a lot of places in a major city where you can just be yourself."

He pulled her close to him, appreciating that she understood exactly. After a few minutes of just enjoying each other's closeness, he stepped back and motioned to a large, empty space behind him. "Stay here, Bridget. I need to show you something else, and I don't want you to be frightened. Okay?" He turned back, searching her eyes.

He looked vulnerable again, and Bridget understood. He was going to fully transform for her. Show his dragon to her as he had never done for anyone else. This was a moment of full and complete trust; it meant everything to him. She nodded and put her hands in her pockets. "I'm here, Vaughn, I'm not going anywhere." They both knew she meant more than just this spot and moment.

His shoulders relaxed, and he turned, walking to the empty area. He took off the rest of his clothes, setting them aside. He stood for a moment, face tilted up, eyes closed again and fluttered his wings. Then he looked at her, and his eyes were pitch black. There was a dark, wavy shimmer around him, like a heat mirage on a long highway in the middle of summer. He went out of focus, and the shimmer expanded.

Before her was a massive, black dragon with golden claws and giant metallic wings. He was so tall she had to tilt her head up to see his enormous head. Deadly looking spikes lined his long neck and wide back, his huge feet sporting wicked talons. A lengthy whip-like tail shifted restlessly behind him, making a slithering sound on the concrete, the deadly barb on the end sounding like a rattlesnake. In this form, his wings were so large they rivaled the billboards on the sides of the highway.

Bridget stood there staring, a scant moment of terror, before gathering herself. She'd been attacked by a shadow monster. She'd experienced death, pain, and heartache. She'd used magic to fight for her life. She was not going to let this beast before her separate her from the man she loved because this *was* the man she loved. She took a step forward, unsure if he could hear her or communicate this way. Probably something she should have asked before he changed. She remembered their budding psychic connection. It was supposed to be stronger in his dragon form.

Can you hear me? She thought at him, hoping this was how it worked. He rumbled in his chest, and she took that as a good sign. *You're beautiful!* She thought in awe, hoping to convey to him how moved she was.

He lowered his massive head and looked at her with eyes the size of car tires. He snorted a smoke ring at her, making her laugh.

"Cut that out." She gently smacked his neck, and he snorted again.

He purred softly, which shook the rooftop.

"How do you not collapse the building under your weight?" she asked him.

He rolled his eyes.

"Oh yeah, magic."

Are you trying to say I'm fat, little one? She heard in her head. It was his dragon voice, deep and raspy.

No way, not me! Not me saying a thing about your size, she smiled at him.

Good, he rumbled, *Dragons are very proud, and we do not take kindly to insults about our best form.*

She looked him over and stepped closer, running her hands over his scales. They were smooth and shiny, not soft but not sharp either. She looked at his nearest eye, watching her movements and walked to his snout. She leaned over and saw his sharp fangs poking out from his lips.

I am not a horse to be evaluated, he grumped at her.

She stifled a laugh so as not to offend him. "Why, Mr. Dragon, what large teeth you have."

He rolled his flame-colored eyes, *All the better to eat you up if you keep sassing me.*

They both laughed.

What do I call you? she asked curiously.

Stormageddon, Dark Lord of All, he replied haughtily.

She blinked, then laughed. *Nice try, smartass. I know that reference.*

He shrugged, which in his dragon form was more of a ripple of muscle. *I'm still Vaughn, but if it helps you to separate us in your mind, you can call me Drake in this form. We all have a human name and a dragon name. There's no separation otherwise,* he explained.

She nodded. "So now what, Mr. Dragon? Drake," she said, looking down the length of him, marveling at his sheer size and power.

Now, my love, we fly.

CHAPTER 27

BRIDGET HELD ON TIGHTLY as they soared through the night sky. *THIS. IS. AMAZING.* Underneath her legs, Drake rippled a shoulder.

You don't have to shout, he grumped at her.

Sorry, she thought back quieter. *This is ahhh-maaazzziiinnng* she drew out the word.

He bobbed a bit in flight as if to warn her he would drop her if she kept being a smartass. She leaned forward and wrapped her arms around his neck. She knew he never would and was just being playful. He rumbled in response to her hug.

She sat back up and continued looking around. She could make out the highway below them. It seemed they were following it north. The night air blew through her hair, tangling it hopelessly, but she didn't mind. She was flying on the back of a huge black dragon. How many people could say that?

You're the only one, he thought quietly.

Her heart swelled for a moment, thinking about the meaning behind that simple phrase. It was an honor, she understood, one reserved only for mates or battle partners. Drake angled slightly west as they flew over the city of McKinney. Already? She was amazed at how far they'd come. How fast was he going? She decided she didn't want to know, really.

Good choice, he chuckled.

"Alright, Jumbo Jet, where are we going?" she asked aloud, and his left ear wiggled.

She had to admit his ears were adorable in this form. Peaked like a cat but longer, they could rotate and swivel to focus on whatever he was listening to.

Ugh, she heard him groan at any part of him being called adorable.

"Sorry, my fierce, vicious looking beast," she consoled him.

Much better, he agreed, *and the answer to your question is Lake Texoma.* Drake started to lose elevation, and she saw they were now circling over the lake.

Where on earth are we going to land?, she worried.

Hold on, he thought to her, dropping low above an island covered in trees except for a large bare patch in the middle. He gently lowered himself to the ground like a giant butterfly and settled in. He laid his neck on the ground so Bridget could slide off and then sat back up. He had his massive paws primly placed in front of him, his tail wrapped around them neatly.

Bridget tried very hard to keep the comparison to a proud cat from her mind, as she knew Drake would not appreciate it. She looked around. Although it was late at night, the moonlight allowed her to see the surrounding area. "So, what is this, like your own island? How do you keep people away from here? How do you keep them from seeing you?" She whirled and looked at Drake, watching the way he tilted his head with the wind, letting it rush over his scales. She understood why he came here. The island's cliffs were sheer. There was no way to anchor a boat and come ashore without some massive undertaking, which she was sure was something he discouraged.

Clever, he thought, *that's precisely why I chose it. It's warded, so people can't see me when I'm here. When I'm not here, it gives off a strong stay-away vibe to any would-be trespassers. On paper, this place is documented as a protected nature preserve for endangered species under the care and protection of Drake Enterprises. One of our many charitable works. I come here when I need to spread my wings and get away from it all. I love basking in the sun here in the summer. Something about this place calls to me.* He fluttered his wings a little, then stretched out on the soft sand. *Come here,* he called.

She obliged and spread the blanket between one of his paws and his head. She sat down, snuggled into him, and enjoyed the closeness of the night air. She shivered a little and wished she'd dressed a little warmer. The wind off the lake carried a slight chill.

I can fix that, he said. He propped a wing around her, blocking the wind. It reminded her of the night prior when they were wrapped in his wings while he'd told her about dragon mates. His scales behind her began to warm, and she realized he was heating it for her, like a giant electric blanket.

She snuggled closer to him, grateful for his thoughtfulness. *Do you like to swim?* She thought suddenly, *I mean, I know you do in your human form, but what about as a dragon?*

He chuckled, *of course, I'm a fantastic swimmer. Another reason I like to come here. This form doesn't fit in my pool at home, much to my dismay.*

She had another thought. *How do you keep people from seeing you when you swim though? Surely, something as big as you moves a lot of water. I'm assuming you can't breathe water, so you'd have to come up for air, too.* She felt, rather than saw him roll his eyes.

Yes, he said patiently, *we have to breathe air, although we can hold our breath for a long time. But we use a simple glamour to hide ourselves, like a perception filter. It's dragon code, per our ruling Council. No unnecessary exposure. You do have some that slip up now and then. Like my cousin, Corran. That idiot. He loves playing tricks on humans over in Ireland. You probably know of him.*

She shook her head. She didn't know anyone in Ireland, much less a dragon named Corran.

Drake chuffed, *yeah, you do. You just probably know him as the Loch Ness Monster.*

"Shut up!" she yelled, slapping his scales.

He chuckled, the rumble echoing over the water.

No freaking way! So, the Loch Ness Monster is real? Just a dragon with a penchant for pranks instead of some ancient sea serpent? Get out of town. She sat back, thinking about it and laughing. Oh, man those monster-chasing shows would never live it down if they knew it was a dragon intentionally messing with them. *Anyone else I should know about?* She inquired of him sweetly.

He chuffed again. *Well, there's Pedro, down in Mexico who has a penchant for goats and can shrink down really small.*

"Chupacabra!" she crowed, laughing.

He nodded, *go up North East, Vincent likes to leap from buildings in partial form, flying around being mysterious.*

"Mothman?" she cackled, "Oh, this is just too good. So, what, all monster sightings around the world are just dragons who've got jokes?"

No, not all of them. Bigfoot isn't a dragon. At least, not that I know. And Yetis aren't dragons. Pissy creatures, moodier than dragons, honestly, he sniffed in disdain.

I can't imagine, she thought dryly. He growled at her, and she kissed his scales again to mollify him.

"Vaughn Drake," she whispered, "Tell me about your family."

He sat quietly for a moment, then described his mother, Mirra. A silver dragon, a quiet beauty, whom everyone agreed was the kindest of all, but stern when she needed to be. She was graceful and fair. His father, Ivan the Red, was rough and ready. A black-haired warrior like him. They loved each other with a passion for the ages. He'd had a wonderful childhood. Lots of cousins and other dragon children to romp around with. Getting into the usual general mischief that most kids do. He told her of the day the Shadow Claw had invaded his village, and although he was almost a man by then, his father wouldn't let him fight. He hadn't yet made his final transformation; only then could he be trained in the specifics of his color specialty. They didn't know yet what color he would be.

"Wait," Bridget interrupted. "Dragon children are the same color as their parents, yeah?"

He nodded.

"So why aren't you silver like your mother?"

He sighed. It was because his father was a red dragon, not a wielder; they weren't sure which parent he would take after.

"Hold up again, I thought you said dragons didn't mate with other dragons."

Usually, they don't, but my mother and father were the exception. My father was so fierce that only another dragon could tame him.

She nodded; he seemed like a mixture of both of his parents. Fierce and kind.

He continued to tell her about the day the Shadows came. His father and mother had both fought hard, but suddenly, the Shadow King himself had appeared behind his mother before she could turn. He'd slit her throat. Bridget winced and mourned at Vaughn's pain at the memory coming through their connection. His father, enraged, tried to kill the Shadow King, but he had dissolved into shadow again. How do you kill something that has no form or mass?

The shadows withdrew, and his father had fallen to his knees, holding her body. *You remember what I told you happens when dragons lose their mates;* he reminded her quietly.

She nodded sadly.

It had killed his father. Vaughn, standing there watching this scene unfold and being helpless to do anything about it, had cried. Seeing his mother's blood in a pool by his feet and his father's lifeless body at her side, he vowed vengeance on the Shadow King. That he would avenge their deaths. In his rage, he changed into full form for the first time. Everyone was shocked. His scales were like polished obsidian; his eyes were like flames and even stranger; he shimmered with golden wings.

There had never been another black and gold dragon before that, he confided. Black dragons had been thought extinct when the last one had died over a thousand years before. His two-tone scales had shocked the dragon world, and he'd been sent before the ruling body, the Dragon Council. They'd examined him, not sure what to make of it. He was kept under strict observation and trained in the multiple guilds of dragon skills to find where his talents lay. It turned out to be brute strength and raw magic compared to more refined skill sets. He was a fierce and deadly warrior, his rage fueling many fights. The Council had wanted to keep him there, a tight leash on him, but he railed and fought, demanding his freedom.

He was finally granted it after many years, under certain terms. He'd agreed and set out to see the world. He'd wandered a bit until the 1940s when he settled in Dallas. The bustling city had appealed to him, but by then, the fire of his rage had been tempered. He'd already proven business savvy and had built up a large amount of savings. He'd stayed because Dallas just seemed right. It was meant to be.

What is the Dragon Council, and what were the terms? she asked.

He chuckled, *so many questions, my shining star. Tomorrow is soon enough for answers. Let's get some sleep, and we'll start again in the morning.*

Bridget nodded, feeling the pull of sleep but wanting to keep listening to his fascinating history. He pulled her closer under his paw and turned his long neck around so she was completely surrounded by him. He pulled his wing over the top like a canopy, and she relaxed. She was safe here; nothing would harm her while she was with her dragon.

His rumbling purr and radiating warmth soon lulled her into a deep sleep.

CHAPTER 28

THE SUN ROSE AND warmed the day like a smile upon the land. The rays spread out across the horizon and stole away the shadows. *Okay, now I'm being fanciful,* Bridget thought, *spend one night on an island with a dragon, and suddenly you're writing poetry.* She heard a laugh behind her.

"You know, I prefer sonnets myself," Vaughn said. He was hopping around on one foot, trying to get his shoes back on while standing on the roof of a skyscraper.

She laughed at how ridiculous it all seemed. They had slept until the sun had warmed them both and, after Drake took a quick dip in the water, flew back.

He had flown high enough that she was able to trail her fingers through the few wisps of cloud remaining before the sun burned them off. It was a thrill she'd never forget.

"I'm still not sure I forgive Drake for shaking lake water on me like a dog."

He was finger-combing his hair in the reflection from a nearby window. He laughed, "Well, I needed to dry off so you weren't slipping around."

Mmm-hmm. She heard Drake's raspy laugh fill her head as Vaughn grinned at her.

She walked over and placed her hand on his arm. "Thank you, Vaughn. Thank you for sharing that side of yourself with me. Thank you for trusting me and loving me enough, to be yourself fully with me. I know now what it means to you."

He pulled her in and kissed her softly. "Thank you," he whispered back to her, "Now let's get these kolaches inside before the kids eat us out of house and home."

She nodded, following him downstairs. "Honey, we're home." Bridget called out, walking in the front door.

Gabe and Liam were standing in the kitchen, digging through the pantry. They both poked their heads around the corner and spied the large bakery box Bridget carried. They smiled at each other and made a beeline for it.

"Whoa!" Vaughn stepped in front of them, holding up his hands. "Plates, and save some for your mom!" he called as they rushed off with the box, like goblins eager to hide their treasure.

"Yes, Dad!" Liam called back with a hint of sarcasm, Gabe cackling like a co-conspirator.

Vaughn rolled his eyes and turned to Bridget. She was beaming at him. He liked that look on her face. He decided he never wanted to see it go away. He took her hand and led her to the dining room. "Let's see if we can get some of that before they finish it all."

"Mmm," Gabe mumbled around a mouthful. "I love the ones with cheese and jalapeño."

"Gabe," warned Bridget.

He swallowed, clearing his throat. "Sorry, Mom." he grinned at her and mimicked a sing-song voice, "No talking with your mouth full." He looked over at Liam, "Moms, am I right?"

Liam laughed, "You think she's bad? My mom would have smacked me in the back of the head. And Drake, well, he's just as stuffy about manners." He dropped his voice to copy Vaughn's, "Pick up the trash from your room. Don't forget to pick up the dry cleaning, quit staring at that young lady's—"

"And that's enough of that," Vaughn interrupted.

Gabe was still snickering when a frantic knock beat at the door.

Vaughn leapt to answer it, moving with a speed Bridget wouldn't have believed possible if she hadn't known about dragons. When the door opened, Marco rushed in, closely followed by Siobhan and Killian.

"Drake, man, you're okay!" Marco breathed, patting him on the shoulder like he wasn't sure he could believe his eyes. "What is wrong with you guys!" he yelled. "We've been trying to call you all morning!"

Liam grimaced, "I forgot to charge my phone last night, battery is dead."

Bridget and Vaughn looked at each other. They had both left their phones in the bedroom last night when they went on their adventure. They hadn't checked them since they'd returned. Vaughn turned to Marco, demanding an update, while Bridget ran to the bedroom to get hers.

She pulled it off the charger where she'd left it and saw dozens of missed calls and text messages. Most of them were from Jorrie and Jack. Quite a few texts from her friend group as well. Glancing through them, she came to understand something drastic had happened early that morning, and no one knew where they were. She debated briefly about who to call first, but by this time, they were probably together. She dialed Jorrie, who answered on the first ring.

"Bridget? Bridget! Please, God, let that be you!" she shouted.

"Jorrie!" Bridget shouted over her friend, "It's me. I'm here. I'm fine." She heard Jorrie let out a breath.

"Thank God, oh thank God. Jack! She's fine. I have Bridget on the phone. She's fine."

Bridget heard an engine revving and pictured them speeding down the road in Jack's classic Mustang.

Jack was shouting, "Where is she, are they at Vaughn's? Let her know we're almost there."

She heard tires squealing as they went around a corner fast. "Yes, I'm at Vaughn's, I'm here, he's here. Gabe and Liam are here. We just didn't have our phones with us."

Jorrie was quiet for a minute. "Bridget, I'm so sorry. I know how much that place meant to you."

Bridget's mind reeled. What place? What was Jorrie talking about? She heard a car door slam.

"We're here," Jorrie said breathlessly, "We'll be right down." The call disconnected.

Just then she heard Gabe wail loudly as if in pain. Bridget dropped the phone and ran back to the living room. What the hell had happened? She said "Jorrie and Jack are in the garage, they…" she trailed off.

Gabe was sitting on the sofa, looked shell shocked, and Vaughn was pacing the floor, fury waving palpably off of him. His talons were snicking in and out, and smoke was pouring from him like a chimney. Marco and Killian were standing between them all, clenching their own fists.

Gabe looked up at her and sobbed "Mama!" She ran to him, wrapping her arms around him. He held onto her, shaking, and crying. "The house Mom, the house." It was all he could say.

She looked to Vaughn for answers. All she could get from him was black waves of anger and something about Shadows and her house.

Another burst of frantic knocking on the door sent Killian rushing to open it. Jack and Jorrie burst in like a whirlwind and ran straight to them.

"Aunt Jorrie!" Gabriel wailed, throwing himself into her arms.

Jack picked Bridget up and squeezed her so hard she couldn't breathe. He put her out at arm's length and looked her up and down—for what she wasn't sure, but he seemed satisfied and pulled her back in.

She could hear Jorrie crooning to Gabe the way she had when his father had died. She rocked him like a baby, and it was telling of his state of mind that he didn't protest. Bridget couldn't take it anymore. She backed away from Jack and started speaking, softly at first, "Look, I appreciate you all being here, and I'm so glad we are all here and okay, but I have yet to know what actually happened because no one seems to be able to give me a straight answer." Fear got the best of her, and she shouted, "So will all of you, just stop and *tell me, what the fuck is going on!*"

Everyone froze and stared at her in shock. It was quiet except for the sniffling coming from Gabe.

Vaughn rushed to her side. "Bridget, my love, I'm so sorry." He pulled her gently to his chest. "The Shadow Claw, they retaliated for our escape yesterday, and now they're playing hardball. My darling, they set fire to your house before we could finish warding it. I'm afraid there's nothing left."

Her stomach plummeted to her toes, and her knees gave out. Only Vaughn's quick reflexes allowed him to catch her and stop her from hitting the carpet.

"I've got you." he whispered soothingly, holding her upright.

"My," she cleared her throat, finding it suddenly clogged with tears, "My house?" she asked pitifully. He nodded and hugged her tighter. "Everything?" she whispered, and he nodded again.

It's all gone, she thought. *All of my things, Gabe's things. His baby pictures, my wedding photos, all I have left of Brian and our life together.* "Oh my God." She sobbed into Vaughn's chest, feeling his rumble, trying to soothe her. It was sweet, but it didn't help.

Gabe walked over and hugged her from behind. Vaughn adjusted his grip and wrapped his arms around them both. Laying his cheek on Gabe's head. She sighed. Now it helped.

She had to be strong again. She couldn't fall apart. She still had Gabe. She still had Vaughn. Her cats were already here. She could get new clothes, a new car. She could take more pictures of Gabe. She would always have Brian in her heart. She leaned back and gave Vaughn a watery smile. *I'm okay,* she sent him.

My love, he replied, his anguish evident. His sorrow and remorse at not prioritizing the warding, swept through their connection.

"No, Vaughn, it's not your fault," she whispered, trying to reassure him. "You kept us all safe. We might have been there if you hadn't insisted on us staying here in the interim. Now I guess I'll have to figure out where we will go." She blew out a heavy breath, calculating in her head what she would have to replace.

"You'll stay here. With me," he told her firmly. "Gabe can pick any of those back bedrooms he likes, and you would of course stay in my room, our room. You can change anything you want. Please Bridget, I want you both here more than anything, where I can keep you safe."

"Oh, no, Vaughn. We couldn't possibly impose on you like this!"

He tilted her chin up and brushed a kiss across her lips. "Bridget, I love you. You love me." *You're my mate. Be honest, there's no point in you finding another home when you're going to be moving in with me eventually anyway. We would just make our current situation permanent. Don't you want to wake up next to me every day?*

His words and thoughts made sense to her, but the thought of surrendering to him fully and letting him make this decision on her and Gabe's behalf was hard to swallow. Her need to protect her son at all costs was at war with the sense of independence she'd been so proud of for the last few years. Being a young widow had its challenges. Additionally, being a single mother had raised those stakes even higher. Logically, it made sense to take Vaughn up on his offer, but emotionally, was she ready to shift her entire world to intertwine it with his?

She looked into his deep blue eyes. They were anxiously searching hers for an answer.

She smiled softly. Every answer she wanted was there in his face. She'd let him mark her as his mate that morning when they woke. As a result, she felt more connected to him than she'd ever felt with another person. It was as if their very souls were woven together. She could feel what he was feeling and right now that was love and devotion. She needed to let go of being stubborn and strong because she had to, and let someone love and care for her because she could.

"Vaughn!" came the sharp snap of Killian's voice.

A black eyebrow raised in question at the silver wielder who was rarely heard speaking, much less snapping at his friend.

"Are you linking with her psychically?" Killian demanded.

Vaughn's massive shoulders heaved with a deep sigh. He'd hoped to keep this secret a little longer to avoid the Council catching wind. It seemed the dragon was out of the bag. The others were looking at the two of them, waiting to see what the fall out would be from the question.

He nodded. "Yes. We are."

Killian stared at him consideringly, his one visible eye intensely focused on his friend. He tossed his hair back and grinned. The sudden view of his entire beautiful smiling face shocked the others. "You marked her, didn't you? She's your mate."

All the dragons in the room gasped, and Siobhan's jaw dropped.

CHAPTER 29

Bridget looked around the room at the shocked faces. She wasn't sure where to start.

Liam did. "Your *mate*?" he hissed. "When did that happen? What about the Council?"

Vaughn shook his head, "This morning, and screw the Council, they don't own me."

Marco shook himself. "Well, uh, congratulations Drake, none of us ever thought that would happen, sir and uh, well, congrats man." He shook his head and mouthed the word 'mate' to himself.

Siobhan slowly shook her head side to side. "Wow!" she whispered, then grinned at Bridget.

After a moment of hesitation, Gabe walked over. He'd been sitting with Jorrie again, watching everything. He walked straight to Vaughn and looked him in the eye. "Mate?" he asked.

Vaughn nodded and bowed to him. Bridget eyed him warily, but Gabe surprised them by breaking into a grin and holding up his fist for a bump.

"Nice," he said. "Can I pick the far back bedroom? The one at the end of the hall with its own bathroom?"

Bridget laughed and Vaughn winked, giving Gabe a thumbs up.

Vaughn then steered her away from the kids and sat her on the couch.

Jorrie and Jack were both sitting there, eyeing her strangely. Jack had a smug smile on his face, Jorrie looked pissed.

Bridget sighed, "Okay, look, guys, I'm really sorry I didn't have my phone. I didn't know you were trying to reach me. Vaughn and I were—"

"Getting mated?" Jorrie interrupted with false sweetness.

I'm really in for it now, Bridget sent Vaughn, *when she gets that sugar isn't as sweet as me tone in her voice, you might as well make funeral arrangements.*

Vaughn's nostrils flared in amusement as he tried not to laugh. He was sure it wouldn't help the situation. "Look, Jorrie," he began in his most reasonable voice.

She held up a finger, "Do *not* look Jorrie me. Now. One of you. Start talking. What the hell is mated? Is that like dragon for married? Bridget? Tell me you did not go marry this guy. Tell me you did not get married without me there." Tears welled up in Jorrie's eyes.

Bridget grabbed her hand. "No, no, Jorrie, you know I would never do that without you! Mating is like, a magical bond between a dragon and their partner." She looked to Vaughn for help.

For a second, he considered sitting back and let her continue to stumble through the explanation because it was kind of cute. But he also valued breathing. He didn't want to jeopardize that. It wasn't overrated. He took her hands and looked into her eyes while he explained.

"A dragon bond is when a dragon and his human form, recognize their soulmate. They both love the person beyond all reason and more than anything else in the world. They put them above all others and would move heaven and earth to be with them. There's a ritual they perform to mark them as mates, and it connects their souls in a spiritual, magical sense. Their lives are now intertwined, and if part of that connection is broken, the magical side of the other ceases to exist. Most do not survive the loss of a partner they are so closely joined." Vaughn finished speaking and looked from Bridget to her friends. He realized the room was quiet, and everyone was staring at him.

That was beautiful, she told him.

Vaughn continued out loud for the benefit of her family. "What it means for us is that my heart recognized Bridget as the one my soul has been waiting for. I love her; I would die for her. I have waited a long time alone for her, and I will never leave her side. No one can keep us apart. She is my everything. And she loves me too. Somehow, this amazing creature loves me in return. I don't deserve her." He smiled at her, and she smiled back at him.

They leaned towards each other, about to kiss, when Gabe shouted, "Mushy shit! Ugh!"

Laughter bubbled up from everyone, and normal conversation started again.

Jorrie took Bridget's hand, "I'm so sorry, sweetie. I love you so much, and I was afraid you were maybe being taken advantage of. I know Vaughn's a good guy, but I didn't want you to end up on an episode of DateLine. That's how it always starts! I'm so happy for you guys. Oh my God. I'm gonna cry!"

Bridget hugged her friend and turned to Jack, who had been quiet the whole time. He had a hand over his face, and she couldn't tell what he was thinking. "Jack?" she shook him gently.

He dropped his hand, and his eyes were full of tears. "What? Can't a man cry in peace at the like most romantic damn thing he's ever heard? Dammit, Bridge, that was seriously just like the most. I can't even!" He waved his hands and pulled out a handkerchief to wipe his face.

She grinned; his response was so Jack. More importantly, she could tell he was genuinely happy for her. She had been concerned about how he would feel about her moving on from Brian, but she knew Jack wanted her to be happy. They had been good friends before her marriage to his brother, and she was grateful for his continued support.

Vaughn looked a little lost and patted Jack on the shoulder in awkward support.

Bridget bit her lip; this would be good.

Jack sobbed, throwing himself in Vaughn's arms. "Take good care of my Bridget!" he wailed, dialing up the theatrics. "She's my best girl ever and I'm just so happy for you both. It's amazing how two hearts can find each other this way." He dashed some tears on Vaughn's shirt.

Vaughn looked helplessly at Bridget and Jorrie; they stared back with sympathetic expressions.

"I just, I just," he continued, "Want to wish you the best and all the happiness and know if you ever break her heart," Jack's tone suddenly turned deadly, "I'll kill you in your sleep." He removed the knife from

Vaughn's throat and kissed him on the cheek. He sat back, crossed his ankles and smiled sweetly, tears gone.

Vaughn sat still, trying to figure out what just happened. How the hell had Jack just pulled a knife on him without anyone in the room sensing it or intercepting. He eyed him shrewdly, deciding to roll with it. "Message received."

Jack nodded gracefully and flicked the knife through his fingers with ease.

Marco and the others exchanged glances and wisely stayed silent.

Did you know about that? Vaughn sent Bridget.

She smirked at him. *Yup. He uses that flamboyant routine to catch people off guard. Works every time. He's not going to admit it, but Jack is quite the badass.*

Vaughn eyed the man he considered his future brother-in-law with a new appreciation. He leaned over and kissed Jack firmly on the mouth. "Welcome to the family."

Another round of laughter filled the room and once everyone was reassured, Vaughn took Bridget and Gabe to a few nearby stores to get some essentials. He insisted on replacing Gabe's computer and school supplies immediately even though there were only two weeks of school left. Bridget tried to protest, but he was resolute on this, and she gave in quietly to make sure Gabe was taken care of.

The rest of the afternoon passed in a quiet blur of phone calls with the police, her homeowner's insurance, and various friends reassuring them that she was okay. Brian's parents were glad to hear they were unharmed, but not necessarily thrilled that she was going to be living with her new boyfriend. She wasn't terribly worried about them, they'd not been very accepting of Jack when he'd come out in their college years, and she hadn't forgiven them the hurt they'd caused him.

That evening, as they lay in each other's arms, Bridget asked Vaughn to start training her on how to use her magic appropriately. "Yesterday the Shadow's attacked and I almost fried my brain. Today they tried to kill me once more. I need to be able to defend myself, without doing their job for them."

Vaughn hated that she needed to learn defense, but promised he'd have Siobhan over the next day to start teaching her as well.

Bridget found out the hard way that Siobhan was quite an unsympathetic task master. She drilled Bridget over and over again in simple spells, controlling her draw on magic, and holding a flame steady. Although Bridget could perform basic glamour type magic that all Wielders could do, she was unable to control any of the usual elements that other Wielders managed.

"I don't get it. What kind of Wielder are you? You're not any usual color and you aren't black like Vaughn. If you were, your powers would just be controlling raw power. You have something specific, but I can't figure it out. Hang on." The prickly woman pulled out her phone and her fingers flew across the screen as she tapped out a message. "Okay, Killian is going to join us. He might be able to figure this out. Now, back to training!"

"Yes ma'am!" Bridget replied wearily. The magic itself wasn't difficult to perform, but channeling power from the Earth and from Vaughn were two completely different skill sets and much harder than she could have imagined.

After another half hour, the quiet silver-haired man slipped into the gym where they were practicing and leaned against the wall. He'd been there for at least ten minutes before either of the women noticed him.

"Dammit Killian, I hate it when you do that!" Siobhan complained. "Why can't you just walk into a room and announce yourself like a normal person?" Her tone indicated she didn't expect an answer, and he didn't give one.

Bridget studied him as he studied her, circling her like an appraiser evaluating a fine piece of art. "Well?" she arched her eyebrow at him.

He nodded, and pushed his hair back behind his ear so she could see his whole face. "Light," he said simply, as if that explained the entire mystery.

She noticed he had very full soft lips with a cute little ring piercing the lower one. "Light what?" She was distracted by the way the light winked from the small ring and twinkled in his warm hazel eyes. He had an Irish lilt to his voice. Vaughn had told her that Killian had been born and raised in Ireland but had moved to the United States decades before to work with him. He was Vaughn's oldest friend. He'd always been quiet, but when he did speak, he was blunt and to the point.

He sighed now. "Light magic. It's what you have. You're a Light Wielder. You have energy and light powers. You keep getting shocked because your power is responding to the Shadows around you. You can push or draw energy. From what Vaughn said about your outburst the other day, you pushed out a massive wave of energy after you pulled it from him. Like an EMP wave. Pretty impressive actually." He was grinning.

Bridget rolled her eyes. "So, I can shock myself and knock out car batteries. How is that going to help?"

"That's what we have to figure out isn't it. Shock me," he said matter-of-fact in his quiet voice.

"How?"

He shrugged. "Think of the Shadows and what they did to your house. Then when you feel it building, let it loose instead of holding it in."

Bridget concentrated on how it had felt when the shadows surrounded the car and when she learned about her house. She felt anger building, and her skin started to tingle. The hairs on her arms and back of her neck rose, and the air around her became charged. She lifted her hands and watched the small blue arcs dancing from finger to finger, fascinated that it simply tickled.

She was about to touch Killian's arm when Liam walked into the gym, making her jump. The arcs flew from her fingers and lanced through the air towards the green dragon.

He didn't react in time and the jolt smacked him square in the chest. He fell backwards, landing on his bottom, a stunned expression on his face. "Um, ow," he managed to squeak out.

Siobhan was laughing so hard she almost fell onto the floor with her brother. Tears were falling from her eyes as Liam glowered at her while he rubbed his chest.

"Oh my god Liam, I'm so sorry!" Bridget ran to him and held out her hands as if to assist him.

He scooted rapidly backwards to the wall, holding out his own hands to ward her off. "I'm good! I'm fine. Please don't help me."

A warm, rich chuckle that turned into a full laugh filled the room as they all turned to Killian in surprise.

Bridget started to laugh with him and soon they were all on the floor wiping tears away.

Vaughn walked into the room a few minutes later and shook his head slowly at the group there. As he turned to walk out, Bridget sent another spark across the room, striking him right on the butt. His shocked facial expression when he whirled around had them all dissolving into giggles again.

CHAPTER 30

I T HAD BEEN SEVERAL days since the attacks on Bridget and the Shadow Claw showed no signs of slowing down. Attacks on other dragons and wielding families were escalating. Vaughn had called a meeting at the Cloud Warrior offices so they could use the education center, they needed space, and there wasn't enough room at Vaughn's home. Bridget, Jorrie, and Jack sat along the back wall, talking softly while the room filled with dragons and wielders. Many of them Bridget had never met. She saw a few familiar faces and they greeted her with a friendly nod.

Vaughn finally strode in, followed by Marco, Killian, and Liam. Vaughn took his place at the front of the room with Liam and Killian. Marco sat in the front row next to Siobhan. He took her hand in his and she gave him a smile.

Bridget wondered if the two were serious. She laughed to herself, being in love apparently made her want to fix everyone up. She was glad the girl had someone that tolerated her prickly nature.

Vaughn tapped the lectern at the front of the room to get everyone's attention. There was an excited buzz in the room, and she noticed many heads turning to stare at her. Vaughn tapped again, and the conversations continued to build in volume.

Liam put his fingers to his lips and blew a shrill whistle that caused everyone to put their hands over their ears and look at him. "Oi!" he shouted. "Drake's talking."

He looked at Liam in amusement and nodded his head in thanks. He turned to the crowd. "Brothers and sisters. I bring you here today with urgent news. As many of you know, the time of the Prophecy of Shadow is nearly upon us."

Bridget saw many heads nodding in agreement.

"Many of you are also aware that the Shadow Claw grows bolder by the day. They are now attacking in broad daylight, no longer discreet. The time has come for us to take action. We must go on the offensive if we are to defeat them."

A chorus of frustrated voices filled the room as dragon and wielder alike expressed their anger at the recent attacks.

Vaughn raised his hand to hush the crowd. "Now, we need to start by, uh, yes?" he nodded at a young lady in the second row who had politely raised her hand.

She stood and looked around at her fellow dragons. "Sorry to interrupt, Drake, but I think before we get into that, shouldn't we address the dragon in the room?"

Vaughn looked at her, confused, "What do you mean?"

She laughed, "Sir, is it true? Did you take a mate?"

The room erupted into noise again, and Vaughn looked at them as if they were crazy. He couldn't fathom why this many of them were so interested in his love life.

Liam whistled again to get the room under control.

"Okay everyone, I can't imagine for the life of me why this is so interesting to you all. Really, I can't, but yes, it's true. I have taken a mate."

Bridget noticed a few sad faces on some of the ladies in the group and smirked.

Vaughn continued, "Since this seems to be a manner of great importance, I guess introductions are in order. Bridget, my love, would you join us up here?"

She froze, oh crap. This was happening. She stood, made her way to the front, and stood next to Vaughn.

He placed his arm around her waist, *breathe, you got this.*

She squared her shoulders and held her head up high. She did have this. "Hello, everyone. It's lovely to meet you all. Some of you I already have the pleasure of knowing, and I look forward to getting to know the rest of you as we work to kick some Shadow ass!" The room erupted in cheers and roars as they enthusiastically agreed.

That's my girl, Vaughn thought with pride.

Bridget turned and noted one person who was not cheering. An older man stood at the back of the room. She could have sworn he wasn't there earlier. She nudged Vaughn and nodded her head at him. She saw his gaze narrow and lock in on the man, and then all color drained from his face. The rest of the team seemed to sense something was amiss and turned to see what he was staring at.

The man walked down the middle of the aisle and came to a stop in front of them. The room was dead silent. He looked up at Bridget and said, "Prove it."

She looked at him closely, trying to see what the goal was here. Was he off his rocker? What was he asking her? She looked at Vaughn, but he was still staring at the man as if he'd seen a ghost.

The man spoke again, "I challenge the legitimacy of this mating. Prove the bond or let the lie be clear for all to see."

Suddenly she understood. He didn't believe she was really mated to Vaughn. She rolled her eyes and pulled down the collar of her shirt. Showing a small black dragon branded onto her collarbone. It had hurt like hell, but really was no worse than a tattoo. Murmurs went through the group.

Everyone was staring at her with a look of reverence. Even Jorrie and Jack were wearing matching expressions of tenderness.

The man who had issued the challenge strangely had tears in his eyes. He walked up to Bridget and took her shoulders in his hands. He was smiling. "Brilliant," he said. "I'm so happy to meet you, Bridget. Welcome to the family, Daughter," he said embracing her.

Bridget stood there, shocked, then turned to Vaughn.

His eyes were bright with unshed tears. He nodded and shook the man's hand, uttering one word. "Father."

CHAPTER 31

*F*ATHER?

Yes, Bridget, that is my father, Ivan the Red.

What. The. Fuck. You said your father died after your mother was killed.

Yeah, well, obviously, I was wrong. I don't know how this is possible.

Ya think? I'll tell you what I think. I think we better start talking and figure this out.

I agree. I've only been thinking my father was dead for over two hundred years but somehow, he just waltzed in here, challenged you, and then welcomed you as his daughter? I'm seriously thinking I'm in some episode of the Twilight Zone here.

Because that's comforting.

I love you, smartass.

Love you too, Sex God.

"Are you two done?" asked Ivan the Red, Vaughn's magically undead father.

Bridget gave Vaughn side-eye; *can he hear us?*

Ivan laughed. "No, you lovely creature, I'm not reading your mind, but it was obvious you two were speaking to each other. I'm going to have to teach my daughter a better poker face!" The smile left his own face. "I'm sure you're wondering how I'm here."

Vaughn nodded in silence.

Bridget took charge, grabbing them both by the arm and called out to the group, "If you'll excuse us, a quick sidebar is needed here. We'll be right back." She walked them out of the education room and down the hall to Vaughn's office. Once there, she steered father and son to the guest chairs and sat across the desk from them. She decided a little distance couldn't hurt. She grabbed the remote and opaqued the windows. She pointed at them both and said, "Speak."

Ivan laughed and slapped his leg. "Oh, son, I can see why you snapped this one up. She's a firecracker!"

Vaughn smiled and replied dryly, "You have no idea."

The two men looked each other over for a bit. Bridget took the opportunity to compare them. She could certainly see where Vaughn got his good looks, but Vaughn was softer somehow. Must have been from his mother. He had thick black hair like his father, but his was wavier and fuller compared to his father's straight locks. Definitely the same arrogant nose. Vaughn's lips were fuller.

Vaughn finally spoke, "Father, please understand, I'm grateful to see the rumors of your demise were false, but," he faltered.

"What the hell am I doing here alive?" Ivan supplied for him.

Vaughn just nodded; the normally eloquent speaker was unable to formulate the right words.

Bridget raised her hand, nodded, and pointed at herself, indicating she would also like to know.

Ivan leaned back in his chair. "Well, son, it's a long story and we are short on time so let me give you the short version. After your mother died, the bond between us should have snapped. I'm not sure what happened, but I fell into a state so close to death everyone thought I was. I know you had a memorial for us, I am told it was lovely, very traditional. Thank you, son. For the first one hundred fifty years or so, I was held in a chamber below the Council in a magical stasis, they called it.

"The healers worked for years, trying to mend my spirit. When I finally woke, they spent another decade doing what you would call rehabilitation. I had to learn to walk, shift, fly, all over again. Since then, I've been learning my way around this new world you live in. I wasn't allowed to contact you. The Council was afraid if you knew I was alive you would do something rash. You know they have been keeping an eye on you since you came to the United States."

Vaughn rolled his eyes. He hated being reminded.

Ivan continued, "I was just as surprised as you were when they elected me to serve you your summons."

Vaughn leaned back and put his hand on his chin, rubbing thoughtfully. He'd been expecting a summons since he marked Bridget as his mate. He just hadn't been expecting it that fast. God, had it only been a few days? He looked at her, smiling.

She smiled back and mimicked drinking, asking if they wanted water. He nodded, and she ran to grab some cold bottles from the fridge.

Ivan gratefully accepted the bottle and drank half the contents before clearing his throat and continuing. "So, I've got a summons here for you," he mumbled, pulling an official-looking black envelope from his coat. "To appear before the Council to discuss your violation of their terms."

"Um, excuse me, violation? What violation?" Bridget demanded.

Vaughn looked at her with guilt all over his face. He'd told her his release from the Council had come with certain terms. He just hadn't told her all of them. "Well, one of the terms was that I wasn't allowed to ever take a mate," he supplied quietly.

She stared at her mate. She was pretty sure he said he wasn't allowed to have a mate. As in, he wasn't supposed to do what he had done. And he knew it but did it anyway. A thousand different emotions raced through her head as she processed this. She looked at Ivan and saw a soft smile on his face.

He reached across the desk, took her hand, and spoke softly. "Lovely Bridget. The heart wants what the heart wants. You can't tell a dragon no. The Council was foolish to instill such a term in the first place." He turned to Vaughn and slapped him on the knee with the stiff envelope, "And you were an idiot for agreeing to it!"

Bridget clapped her free hand over her mouth to stifle the giggle that wanted to burst out.

Vaughn had the decency to look sheepish.

Ivan squeezed her hand and let it go. "Now, there's some other things you need to know son, and they aren't going to be easy to hear. So, listen well."

"Father, please." Vaughn held up a hand. "I know you've more to tell us, but I need to clarify a few things."

Ivan regarded his son thoughtfully. "Always the inquisitive thinker you were. Never one to rush into a fight without analyzing all the factors first. That's why I wouldn't send you straight to warrior training despite my red powers. I thought you'd more of your mother in you, I expected you'd be silver like her. But my son, I heard things in the mountain. Strange things. I heard that you are neither red nor silver? I also imagine you want to know why the Council hid me away all those years, why they were keeping me secret."

"Exactly!" Vaughn slammed his water down. "Why was I led to believe all those years you had died? I was being kept a prisoner by the Council, too, probably near where you were held, and I never knew." He hung his head, whispering, "I never knew."

It broke Bridget's heart to see the anguish on his face. She knew firsthand how hard the death of a parent and partner were. Vaughn had thought he lost his mother and father through violence at a young age, only to find his father had been kept away by some unknown motive of this mystical Council. She walked around the desk and leaned over him. Wrapping her arms over his chest, she held him.

He lifted his head, burying his face in her neck, just breathing her in.

She heard a soft rumble and knew he was going to be okay.

Ivan gazed at the pair softly. They reminded him so much of his own mate it made his heart clench. He sniffed lightly, discreetly wiping his eyes.

"Vaughn, son, it must have been hard for you. Seeing your mother fall, then thinking I was gone too. I can't imagine how it wounded you.

That, I believe, is the underlying reason for all the cloak-and-dagger nonsense. My boy, I'm told you manifested your dragon at that moment, and it was unlike anything anyone had ever seen. I'm told it was glorious and terrifying all the same."

Vaughn turned his head away from Bridget's warmth and looked at his father. His eyes held flame in them, and smoke trickled from his nostrils. "It was. I was pure fury and revenge," he said in a low steady voice that sent chills over them. "I wanted to be the night, bringer of death to the shadows. I was death, I was pain, I was raw force and rage. All I could think about was reaching into the shadows and ripping them to shreds."

Ivan regarded his son with appraising eyes, giving a sharp nod.

Bridget shivered, and Vaughn put a reassuring hand on her arm.

"Don't you see Vaughn, that's it. *That's* why you became the first black dragon in millennia. Most first transformations are a time of happiness and growth. A time of renewal when our line continues. Yours was born of anger and hate, bloodlust and fire. That's why the Council fears you and kept you under lock and key. That's why they kept me alive and hidden away all those years; they wanted to know how it happened. How did red and silver create black. They thought it was because we were two dragons, but with me only inches from Death's door, they couldn't confirm it. When they finally revived me, they 'rehabbed' me under the guise of needing a warrior, but they were really studying me. My reputation as a fighter had gone to my head, I guess. I really believed they needed me. To resume my place on the front lines. So much had changed though. It's just been the last nine to ten years that I really understood the reason behind it."

Vaughn shook his head. "The Council wants me back. By mating with Bridget, I've fallen right into their hands."

CHAPTER 32

VAUGHN HAD RETURNED TO the gathered assembly and quietly pulled Liam and Killian aside, whispering the new plan to them. Liam's eyes widened slightly, but otherwise gave nothing away. A slight nod was Killian's only acknowledgement.

He stood once more in front of the group, and they immediately quieted down this time, leaning forward to hear the news.

Bridget and Ivan sat in the back of the room with Jorrie and Jack. "Jorrie, Jack, this is Ivan, Vaughn's father, and my, I guess, I don't know." She looked at him. "What do I call you?"

He laughed, a rumbly chuckle much like Vaughn's but deeper. "You can call me Ivan for now. We can figure out the rest later. A pleasure to meet you, Jorrie, my dear you are as lovely as a spring day, and Jack, I can see you are quite the charmer. I look forward to getting to know the rest of my family soon."

Jorrie and Jack mumbled shocked replies, then sat back as Vaughn began to speak.

"Everyone, the events of this day have indeed been shocking. First, the revelation of my mating to my lovely Bridget." A round of applause broke out, and he waved it down. "The brazen attacks on our families by the Shadow Claw." He took a deep breath, "And my own father, Ivan the Red, seemingly returned from the grave."

At this point, every head in the audience turned and stared at Ivan. Not a sound was heard.

"Thank you all for your patience while we sorted this out." Heads turned back to Vaughn, captivated by the events, wanting to know what could possibly be next. "As we discussed earlier, the Shadows have become brazen and are posing a viable threat to all our kind." Hisses at this. "Now, now, you'll all get your chance," Vaughn cautioned, "But be warned, the Shadows are operating in desperation, they no longer have anything to fear except extinction, they will ambush us, they will fight. We must be ready for anything and everything. Our forces captured a Shadow only this morning and have been interrogating him as to the Shadow's movements and goals. We hope to have more information on that front. In the meantime, I will travel to the Council to request assistance. I will leave you in Marco and Killian's capable hands to plan our defense and offense here while I am gone."

Vaughn spoke for a few more minutes, assigning duties, teams, leaders, and setting expectations. He turned the floor over to Marco, then came to the back with Liam, Siobhan, and another man Bridget had not met yet. He was devilishly handsome, and she saw a twinkle in his eyes that made Bridget suspect he was going to be a handful.

Vaughn picked Bridget up, seeming to need to touch her. She happily wrapped her arms and legs around him. He held her close for a few minutes while the others made small talk, studiously ignoring the couple.

You were brilliant up there, she told him. She could feel him smile against her neck.

Just doing what any good general would do, he chuckled, and she shivered at the feeling. *Careful little one,* he rumbled, *don't get me too worked up or I might have to take you back to my office, windows be damned.*

She smiled, *Sex God? I should have named you Sex Fiend. Don't you get enough?*

Vaughn pulled back and looked into her eyes, his bright blue ones conveying to her how much he loved her. He brushed a small strand of hair from her face. "Never," he whispered, kissing her gently.

They heard a polite cough from the newest member of the group, and Jack whispered, "Get a room, you two."

Vaughn laughed and set Bridget down. He turned to the newest member of the group and clapped him on the back. "Ah yes, Davis, this is my mate Bridget, my father Ivan, Jorrie, and Jack, you know the rest, everyone, this is Davis. He will be joining us on our trip to the Council as extra security and eyes."

Davis gave a slight bow, then winked at Jack, blatantly appreciating him. Yep, a handful.

Vaughn asked them to come back to his place to discuss their plans and arrangements further. He turned to his father, "I'm not sure how you made it here, but you're welcome to ride with us if you like."

Ivan smiled and accepted. "Of all of the new things I've had to learn, driving cars is not something I am particularly fond of yet. Give me a strong horse any day!"

Bridget laughed, then realized he was quite serious. She took his arm and steered him towards the rec room where they'd left Gabe and other kids whose parents were in the meeting.

Gabe was currently teaching some of the younger children how to play billiards. He was great with kids, she smiled. She and Brian had always talked about having more, but time went by, then he was gone. Gabe had always wanted a sibling.

She caught his eye, motioning him over. The younger kids were bummed about losing their playmate but quickly became engrossed in the game again. One of them was trying to move a ball with a steady stream of smoke. That one seemed precocious. It made her think of what Vaughn was like as a little boy. She had so many questions for Ivan.

"Gabriel, I'd like you to meet someone," she said as he sauntered over. "This is Ivan the Red, or just Ivan. He's Vaughn's father. Ivan, this is my son, Gabriel, or Gabe as we call him."

Gabe smiled and held out his hand to shake. "A pleasure to meet you sir," he said politely, using his best manners.

Ivan smiled and pulled the stunned Gabe into a strong hug. "My boy!" he said in a gruff voice. "I went from not knowing where my son was to gaining a daughter and a grandson in one day!"

Gabe looked at her in confusion.

She mouthed at him, *just go with it.*

Gabe winked; he understood the mission. "Wow, that's really cool, sir, uh, Ivan. Hey Gramps, you ever played Cloud Warrior?"

Bridget stared at the ceiling, *where did I go wrong?*

She heard Ivan laugh as he let Gabe go. "A warrior indeed." He patted Gabe's shoulder as they exited to the parking lot.

Back at Vaughn's place, the serious discussions began. Apparently, the Council was on an island off the coast of Italy, called Sardinia. It boasted a wonderful climate most of the year and had mountains as well, ideal for dragons. They would need to travel by plane to Rome and then by car to the coast, an area known as Ostia. From there they planned to fly at night to the island. The dragons would carry the humans to save time. It was normally unheard of for an unpaired human to see, let alone fly with a dragon, but these were desperate times, and the others were amenable. They booked accommodation in the town of Sassari and with that set, went to pack. They were leaving for Rome first thing in the morning on a Drake Enterprises private jet.

Bridget sat on the bed, unsure of what to do. She didn't have much to pack as most of her belongings had been torched by the Shadows. She only had some basic essentials, but it didn't bother her. What concerned her most was Gabriel. She was conflicted about what to do with him. She didn't want him to come because it could be dangerous, but she didn't want to leave him here alone. Plus, there were still two weeks of school left.

Vaughn walked in and saw her sitting on the bed, obviously working out an internal struggle. He could feel her thoughts and understood where her mind was. He sat next to her hoping like hell she would forgive him for what she would consider him being 'high-handed' again. "Bridget," he started softly, "I know you're worried about Gabe. He and I talked."

She looked sharply at him.

"Hold on!" he held up his hands placatingly. "I know you've got a lot running through your mind, and I'm trying to help. If it makes you feel any better, Gabe approached me." He noted her shoulders relax; so far, so good. Now for the hard part. "You know as well as I do he would be furious if we left him behind, but you're worried about his safety. My love, think. Where else could he be safer than with us? Not to mention four strong dragons and a wielder? You have my word; I will look after him as if he were my own." He took her hand in his and brushed his lips across her knuckles. He saw the relief in her eyes and knew he'd made it over the first hurdle. Now, the second. "As for school, that's handled as well."

She eyed him suspiciously. "Vaughn." Her tone was deceptively calm. "What did you do?"

He smiled sheepishly. "Well, I may have put in a call to Ms. Jenkins and explained that Gabriel was selected for a summer internship at Cloud Warrior, and part of that was studying foreign relations abroad. She was very excited at the opportunity after I mentioned that I would like to partner with the school for future internships. I may also have offered a scholarship stipend for their STEM program. With that, she was very understanding about letting Gabe be excused for the last two weeks to start right away. They weren't doing anything anyway; year-end testing was already done." He braced for her ire. To his surprise, she burst out laughing so hard she fell back on the bed and wiped tears from her eyes.

Finally, she sat up and looked at him. "Oh, my dear sweet dragon, you bribed the school for me."

Bridget walked down the back hall where Gabe was still bunking with Liam. She leaned on the frame and studied them as they good-naturedly threw things at each other. The room was in complete disarray, as expected. A pair of boxers landed at her feet after being launched like a rubber band by Liam. He saw her first, stood straighter, and stopped laughing.

Gabe, warned by Liam, slowly rose from where he'd been ducking behind a chair and turned to face her. "Hello, Mother," he said solemnly. "We were packing."

She picked up the boxers between her thumb and pointer finger. She looked over, waving them at Liam, "Your underwear, I presume?"

Liam's face reddened as he quickly came over to take them from her. "Sorry about that, Ms. Ridgeway," he mumbled.

She rolled her eyes. "Liam, I think we've been through enough that you can call me Bridget like you usually do." He grinned and tugged a lock of hair on his forehead.

Gabe opened his mouth, and she whirled on him, "Not on your life, bud. I will *always* be Mom to you!" She poked him in the chest with a smile. She turned to the dragon, "Liam, I'm sorry to ask, but I need a minute with my son if you don't mind."

He nodded in agreement and scurried out of the room, murmuring about checking if Jorrie had returned yet. She was going along as their foreign relations expert. It helped that she was fluent in Italian as well. Of course, so were Vaughn and Ivan, but that wasn't surprising considering the amount of time they'd both spent there. Once they were alone, she sat in one of the chairs and motioned her son to sit as well.

"Hi, baby." She smiled at him.

He smiled back. "Hi, Momma."

"I just wanted to see how you were doing with all of this. A lot has changed in the last few days, and it can be overwhelming. I guess I just need to know you're okay with it. With this," she gestured around them, "with Vaughn, the dragon aspect, this trip we are about to undertake, being away from your friends. You know this is going to be dangerous. I would understand if you wanted to stay here."

Gabriel sat for a moment, giving her words some serious thought. He looked so much like his father just now. "Mom, I love you, and you deserve to be happy. You've worked so hard for my happiness since Dad died that you didn't take time for yourself. I really like Vaughn; he's a cool guy, and I can tell he loves you a lot. I mean, being a dragon is super badass, but he makes you happy. Yeah, I know there's danger, but staying here would be dangerous too, with these shadow jerks looking for us. I'd rather be with you, helping keep you and Aunt Jorrie safe. Besides, what kid wouldn't want to get out of school early and go to freaking Italy instead!"

She studied the little man sitting in front of her. She didn't know what she'd done to deserve this wonderful human, but he was hers, and she was grateful. "Thank you, baby. He means the world to me, and so do you. I just want you to know he will never replace you in my heart. You have your own special place there." She sighed happily as she sensed Vaughn behind her.

"Nor would I ever want to replace you there," he said to Gabe.

Gabe got up and wrapped his mother and Vaughn both in a hug. They all stood there, soaking in the moment, and Gabe whispered, "I love our family."

Bridget kissed him on the cheek. "You better, he bribed the principal for you."

CHAPTER 33

THAT EVENING, WHEN EVERYONE was in bed, Vaughn lay on his back staring at the ceiling. So many emotions were warring within him.

Bridget snuggled up to his side. "Now who's thinking too hard?"

He rumbled at her, and she took the hint, laying her head on his chest, his strong arms wrapped around her.

"What's got you thinking so hard, my love?" she whispered.

"Just," he paused, "Something Gabe said earlier."

She lifted her head. "What was it?"

He made a non-committal shrug.

"Vaughn, tell me." She commanded softly.

He looked at her, knowing he couldn't keep anything from her, and said quietly. "Earlier, when Gabe said, 'I love our family' it really struck a chord with me. I haven't had a family for so long. I have my employees and friends, but not a true family like you, Gabe, Jack and Jorrie have. You're a family unit. I never knew that was something I wanted. But now, having a small taste of that, I've realized that I do. I want a family, and I want it with you. With you and Gabe and Jack and Jorrie. With Liam and even Siobhan. I want," he paused.

She nudged him gently to continue.

"I want children of my own. With you."

"Oh, Vaughn," she whispered. "You dear, sweet man. You're already part of our family. That's what Gabe meant when he said he loved our family. He's including you in that. You are part of our lives; we aren't letting you go. And silly goose, Liam and Siobhan are definitely family as well."

He closed his eyes and wrapped her tightly against him. "God, I love you, woman."

"You better! I love you, too."

He relaxed his grip and looked at her. "Bridget, about the other," he began.

She laid a finger over his mouth and crawled on his lap, leaning down to him. She replaced her finger with her lips, kissing him softly. "Vaughn," she sighed. "I don't know if it's still possible for me anymore, but I'm willing to try." She kissed him again before they fell into a familiar rhythm, making love gently before they fell asleep, knowing they faced a long day ahead.

The next morning reminded Bridget of that scene in *Home Alone* when the family wakes up and realizes the power is out and they've missed their alarm. There were people everywhere, underfoot, running this way and that. She thought she was very in the way. Looking for somewhere to be, she wandered into the kitchen. She found Jack there, leaning against the counter, staring sadly into his coffee.

She leaned on him and put her head on his shoulder. "Hey, brother."

Jack leaned his head on hers and sighed. "Hey, little sister." They stood there like that for a few minutes, just breathing.

Finally, Bridget wrapped her arm around Jack's waist. "It's Darren, isn't it."

He nodded, standing there a little longer before he kissed the top of her head and turned to face her. She was silent, letting him decide how much to say.

"You always seem so perceptive about other people's relationships," he mused, "I can't believe you couldn't see Vaughn was mooning after you that whole time." He sighed again. "It's been falling apart for a while. He doesn't understand my work, why I'm gone so much. Things I can't tell him. You know I hate secrets, but I have to keep them. He doesn't understand why I've been spending so much time with you lately; I can't tell him that either. But you and Gabe are my family first, babe. He gave me an ultimatum last night. If I left on this trip, he wasn't coming back. He moved out three weeks ago." He stared at the ceiling. "That's when I admitted what I already knew. He doesn't love me. I don't love him. I loved the idea of him for a while, wanting what my brother had, but after really seeing you and Vaughn, I knew it wasn't true love. It's better we end it now rather than move forward with a sticky legal entanglement." He groaned, "Dragon bonding sounds like a much better way to go, no alimony!"

Bridget laughed and then hugged him. "I'm so sorry, Jack. I think there was a part of you that did really love him, but I know the right person is still out there, waiting to meet you."

He nodded and saluted her with his coffee cup.

Vaughn walked into the kitchen and paused, seeing Bridget and Jack embracing. "Am I interrupting something?" he asked, backing out of the room.

"No," Bridget said, pulling him in. "Jack had a hard choice to make last night. I'm just reminding him that he's got a lot of people here who love him."

Vaughn nodded and put his hand on Jack's shoulder. "Absolutely, Jack. I know this whole thing has been rough, and I'm sorry our baggage is spilling over to you."

Jack waved it off, "No, if anything, I should be thanking you. It's really opened my eyes to possibilities, and I'm going to be better off this way. I'll be alright. Just stings, you know?" he shook his head, rubbing his chest.

Vaughn pulled him in for a hug and whispered, "I got you, brother. You're my family now, too."

Jack gave Vaughn a watery smile as he hugged him back tightly and turned to Bridget. "You're lucky you snapped him up when you did; otherwise, I'd have to fight you for him."

They all laughed, the mood seeming much lighter, although Bridget knew Jack was still hurting. She hoped this trip would take his mind off it for a little while.

Liam popped his head in, "Sorry to interrupt, Drake, shuttle's here."

Just like the movie, Bridget mused as she watched nine people trying to corral luggage and themselves into the two airport shuttle vans. The guys were loading their gear, Gabe was bouncing around like a spring, Siobhan was trying to discreetly place wards on the vans, Jack and

Jorrie were engaged in a friendly argument about who was going to ride up front with the hot driver of van two, and Vaughn was trying to direct it all. A last-minute addition to their party made it ten in total.

Davis' identical twin brother Shepard was coming along too. It was decided the rare powers the two had were needed for the fight ahead. If it wasn't for Shepard's longer hair, it would have been impossible to tell them apart as they both had impish grins and mischief in their eyes. Davis and Shepard were both born dragons, which was highly unusual as only the firstborn inherited the gene. Their parents had worked hard to keep it a secret, knowing the Council would have taken great interest in the twins. Going to Italy, right under the Council's nose, seemed like a bad idea but they had waved it off, confident they could stay under the radar. They were already getting into some shenanigans, and she knew she'd have to watch Gabe around them. They could lead him into trouble.

Feeling him before she heard him, she reached back for Vaughn's hands as he walked behind her. Every day, she was more aware of him, where he was, even when he wasn't next to her. It was safe, and she liked this connection they had.

What movie is that, my love, he asked her, linking hands and standing with his warm, hard body against hers.

She laughed, *Home Alone. You remember that movie? When they're trying to go to Paris, and they're rushing to the vans to make their flight on time?*

Vaughn laughed and whispered in her ear, "But this time, Kevin's coming with us."

She snorted, "He better!"

"Gabe!" hollered Vaughn, "Get your butt in the first van so your mom can breathe easier, okay? No Kevins today!"

Gabe looked a little confused, not understanding the joke, but complied with the order.

Bridget laughed. "I'm going to join him, so he doesn't talk the driver's ear off." She kissed his jaw and climbed into the van as well.

Vaughn stood there watching her, enjoying the way the sun lit her coppery tresses up like flames. His father came to stand next to him.

"She reminds me of your mother."

Vaughn looked at him questioningly.

Ivan continued, "She's fierce and fiery, but she's gentle and kind, and she has a big heart. Look at the family she's gathered around her. She would fight to the end for them."

His heart skipped a beat. Ivan was correct and that worried him.

CHAPTER 34

THE PRIVATE PLANE WAS about as luxurious as expected. She smothered a laugh, thinking how dragons liked fancy things. She couldn't imagine Vaughn shopping at Walmart. She glanced at Ivan, she doubted he knew what a Walmart was, but figured one glance inside and he would run the other way. She settled into her soft leather seat, stretching her legs out, and figured she was ruined for commercial planes forever.

Gabe was hunched over a table with Siobhan and Ivan, playing poker for pennies. Ivan was incredibly good, but she figured his luck would change as she suspected Siobhan was cheating a little with her magic. She looked over at the twins and saw they had Jorrie and Jack enthralled by their stories.

Liam was watching Jorrie with longing on his face. When Jorrie would glance at Liam, he would suddenly look elsewhere. Jorrie would look at him with desire until Shepard, who also seemed interested in her, drew her back into conversation. Then it started all over again. It was sweet, really. Those two just needed to heat the sheets and get it out of their systems. Good grief, she was starting to sound like Jorrie. She was not going to admit that out loud.

Vaughn suddenly appeared, handing her a glass of wine and a menu. He sat down and simply gazed at her tenderly. She smiled and took his hand. They sipped their wine in happy silence until an attendant came and asked for their order.

Bridget settled back in her seat and picked up the book she'd brought. She tried to read for a bit but soon found she couldn't focus. She looked at Vaughn. He was frowning at some files he was reading. He looked cute with his brow furrowed and lips compressed in concentration.

"Working?" she inquired softly.

His forehead smoothed out and he smiled, nodding.

"Need any help?"

He blinked, then fully focused on her. He looked down at the file and back at her again. "I guess it wouldn't hurt to have you look at these," he said as he passed her the files. "These are some of the supplier contracts for our integration program. This would be a good chance for you to get to know what you're getting into."

She started reading the files and contracts, discussing her thoughts and pointing out things he hadn't noticed while they ate. She really had a good eye for this, and he found they still worked well together, bouncing ideas off each other. They fell back into the same working rhythm as they'd developed the previous six months.

Jorrie wandered over and started giving her input as well. Soon, the work was done. He was glad he'd hired them both. They were a force to be reckoned with and could take some of the load off his shoulders.

The attendant returned to refresh their drinks and let them know there were two hours until they landed.

After the plane touched down, they loaded into several SUVs. Vaughn surprised them by detouring to some of the hot spots of Rome. He explained to Bridget, "We arrived a little early and there's a storm coming in later, so we will be delayed setting off on our over-water flight by a few hours. I told Gabe's school this was a learning opportunity and figured we should show him the sights. Let him take some pictures, get some souvenirs, and have a little fun."

She squeezed his hand, *you big softie, thank you.*

He was laughing later when he heard Gabe, Jack, and the twins whooping from across the ruins of the Roman Forum. "Sounds like Gabe's not the only one enjoying the sights."

She laughed as well. "Let's gather our kids and check out the Colosseum, then take them for real pizza."

Vaughn smiled. *Our kids.*

Dinner was full of laughter and smiles. They'd gone to a small family-owned place that Vaughn knew from his business travels. The owners welcomed him with open arms and chattered away at him like a long-lost son. Jorrie was soon an adopted daughter when they found she could speak Italian like a native. Gabe learned that pepperoni in Italy was not what he expected, and Jack was laughing like there wasn't a care in the world.

Bridget occasionally saw a cloud cross his face, but he would shake it off and jump back into the fun. She saw Davis watching Jack with desire clear on his face. *He's going to have his hands full,* she thought. Rain poured outside, but inside, it was warm and cozy.

All too soon, it was time for the journey to continue, and they left the smiling restaurant crew with a promise to stop in again on their way home. They loaded into the vehicles and began the drive to the coast. It wasn't very long, less than an hour, and they reached their destination without incident. They found a spot to park the vehicles, not far from a lookout point on the shore.

Now a tourist spot, the lookout extended into the ocean and had a large circular plaza with plenty of room for the dragons to change forms. They walked to the plaza, and the dragons began to separate so they'd have room for their transformations. As Siobhan and Bridget were the only humans there to ever see a dragon, they would ensure everyone could handle what they were going to experience. They were about to have their minds blown.

Bridget gave her friends and son some last-minute advice. "Don't forget, in their full forms, they can still hear and understand you. You just won't be able to understand anything they are saying. Remember the signals we worked out?" she asked.

They all nodded, Gabe, looking a little green around the gills. She hugged him, saying nothing, not wanting to embarrass him in front of the others.

Jack gave a cheeky salute. "Aye, aye, Captain!"

They turned to face the dragons, and Bridget sent Vaughn an all clear. She had learned that in dragon form, all of the dragons could mind-link each other. Only her mate could hear her, though, for which she was glad. She didn't want the others to hear some of her exchanges with Vaughn.

The men stripped out of their clothes, packing them in the bags at their feet. They would need them when they arrived on the island.

Jorrie dug her fingernails into Bridget's arm and hissed in her ear, "You didn't tell me about that part."

Bridget looked at her friend in confusion. "Yes, I did. They can't transform their clothes. They take them off, so they don't rip them."

Jorrie shook her head emphatically. "Not that, you didn't tell me about, you know, *that*," as she nodded at Liam and the twins.

Liam was standing there fully nude, not in the least self-conscious about it.

Bridget glanced at the other men, none of them were. Although Vaughn was by far the sexiest one, in her opinion, they all looked like they were sculpted from marble and very generously gifted. She blushed, whispering back, "I didn't know that was a dragon thing. I thought it was just Vaughn."

Jorrie swallowed noisily. "Yeah, well, he's no slouch either."

She yanked one of her friend's blonde curls. "Hey," she said with mock furiousness, "Quit ogling my mate. Besides, they can probably hear you."

Jorrie looked at Bridget wide-eyed. Liam's sultry laugh echoed over the water, proving her right.

Jack leaned forward and said in a voice he must have known would be heard, "I do not have a problem with what I'm seeing either." He locked eyes with Davis, who was grinning from ear to ear.

Bridget decided he probably meant to be heard. She wasn't going there.

Jorrie leaned in and whispered again, "When we get to the hotel, you and I are so going to talk."

Jack pointed at himself and nodded, indicating he, too, wanted in on the girl talk.

Bridget shook her head, laughing as Gabe covered his ears and hummed to himself.

"Gross," he mumbled.

She heard murmurs of awe as wings began to pop and flare out first. It was like a rainbow of fluttering scales, first the red of Ivan, followed by Liam's green, and then the twins' bright royal blue. Davis was a slightly lighter shade than his brother, which was good as it would make them easier to tell apart.

Vaughn simply stood there, his wings still tucked behind him. In the dark, the black scales blended into the night. Only the twinkle of the gold claws sticking over his shoulder gave away their presence. He was going to change last for some reason he hadn't shared with them yet. They'd agreed to change one at a time so as not to overwhelm the humans.

Davis went first, steam billowing from his nostrils, and he shook his wings. The tell-tale shimmer made the night seem brighter despite there only being a sliver of moon. Soon, he was replaced by a brilliant blue dragon. His neck was longer and skinnier than Vaughn's, his tail like a serpent. He was much slimmer, which Vaughn had said made him a better swimmer in addition to his affiliation with water. Not to be outdone, Shepard went next, appearing a similar size and shape to Davis. Their wings swirled with the colors of the ocean. Their muscles rippling under the scales, they exuded strength and power. Their talons winked in the streetlights, beautiful and deadly.

They were so gorgeous the assembled crew drew in their collective breaths and released them with sharp gusts. Murmurs of amazement came from everyone. Jack and Bridget slipped their hands into each other's and shivered in the warm air. The feelings coursing through their bodies were indescribable and overwhelming.

"Fuck!" she heard Gabriel whisper. It was such a sight to behold. She didn't even chastise him for the language.

Jorrie, who had been flirting with Shepard a bit, put her arms around Gabe's shoulders. "You said it, kid." She was trembling slightly, overwhelmed at the sight in front of her, knowing there were still three more dragons to see.

Jack was silent, captivated by the beasts rising above him. Like the others, he knew how incredibly fortunate they were to witness this mesmerizing moment. His face held a look of awe and reverence.

Siobhan was studying the twins as well, she'd seen dragons before, but apparently not blue ones. A soft smile was on her lips, appreciating the beauty in front of her.

Now it was Liam's turn, he winked, and shimmered into a large green beast. Taller and broader than the twins, he was quite intense looking. He was thicker and had more spikes on his back and tail. His scales were a rich emerald color, and his talons were darker, almost forest green. His wings reminded Bridget of a field of clover as they waved in the wind. He made a rumbling sound similar to Vaughn's, which Bridget knew was a happy noise. He was ecstatic about the opportunity to show his full form and stretch his wings.

He pranced a little on his paws, put his head down, tail up, wiggling his behind like a cat about to pounce. He bounded over and puffed some smoke rings around Jorrie, making her look like she was surrounded by wispy grey hula hoops. Jorrie and the others started laughing at the silly display. Liam's antics certainly lightened the mood.

Siobhan, however, was not impressed. "Show off!"

He turned and bared his fangs, spitting a small flame towards her, which she quickly blocked with a shield spell.

"Still can't get me asshole," she taunted, flipping him the bird.

Liam growled at her, and it looked like a bigger flame was coming when a louder growl froze him in his tracks. If a dragon could look sheepish, Liam managed it as he swung his head towards Vaughn.

"Siblings," Vaughn sighed.

Bridget heard Davis and Shepard making a strange gurgling sound, which she realized was their way of laughing. Soon, everyone was trying to stifle their laughter.

Even Liam and Siobhan were amused. They stuck their tongues out at each other, which was such a sight in dragon form that they all burst into laughter again. After everyone finally quieted down, it was Ivan's turn.

He flapped his wings once, and the shimmer took on an orange color. Soon, there was a huge red dragon standing where he had been. Ivan was much larger than the others and covered in deadly-looking spikes. He was definitely a warrior dragon. His wings whirled with reddish-orange, which shimmered and swirled like a lava flow. His fangs protruded farther from his mouth, and his razor-sharp talons, curved like scythes, scratched the cobblestone underneath them. The sound was eerie and terrifying. The humans covered their ears and shivered.

Vaughn approached his father and stood looking at him for a long time.

Bridget noticed his shoulders were shaking and she realized he was crying. She started to go to him, but Jorrie held her back, shaking her head. Bridget knew she was right. This moment was between Vaughn and his father.

Soon, she heard his voice as it carried on the wind. "Father, it's been so long since I laid eyes on this form. Never did I think to see it again."

Ivan leaned down and bumped his large nose on Vaughn's shoulder. Vaughn wiped his face and took a pose of deference.

"I am honored standing before you now, as a man, to show you my own form." Vaughn walked to the middle of the circle of the dragons. The others all lay down on the ground while Ivan stood tall.

As they watched, Bridget remembered that Ivan had never seen his son's dragon form. That's why Vaughn wanted to go last. He had something to prove to his father. *I love you,* she sent.

He turned and placed his hand over his heart, nodding. Then he was gone as the shimmer burst out, and an enormous black and gold dragon stood in the middle of the circle.

Bridget stared at her mate; he was so beautiful it was hard to tear her gaze away. The others seemed to be just as mesmerized, murmuring in awe. She finally turned to Ivan. The red dragon was standing still. Bridget realized then that Vaughn wasn't just big. He was the largest of them all. He towered over the others. His wings were twice that of the other dragons. His black scales gleamed, the gold in his wings winking in the light. He radiated strength and power.

Bridget smiled as her family's murmurs grew louder. The other dragons were amazing, stunning even. Vaughn was magnificent and twice as fierce. That was her mate, and she was proud.

Ivan circled his son, looking him over until he made it back to his original spot. He stood there for a moment, then rumbling, gave a deep bow. It seemed Ivan approved.

Vaughn's triumphant roar split the night, making everyone jump in fright. Cars nearby began to chirp as their alarms were set off. They heard shouts and screams, then lights began to go on all around them.

CHAPTER 35

LIAM JUMPED TO HIS feet, and using his teeth, grabbed the back of Siobhan's shirt and threw her on his back. She landed as if they had practiced this maneuver before, which they likely had, and faced the town. She waved her hands in a complicated series of gestures and then threw them up like a barrier.

Alarms shut off, and fog rolled between the town and the lookout point where they were standing.

"Everyone, behind us," she called. They all hurried behind the green dragon.

Bridget realized Siobhan and Liam were using their warding magic to shield them from view. They needed to get going before anyone wandered down to investigate. With any luck, the people in the homes nearby would think it was an earthquake or something.

Vaughn rumbled at the other dragons; Liam gave him a low growl. Vaughn chuffed in reply.

Bridget laughed. Vaughn had apologized, but Liam was still pissed and chastising him.

The plan was for Gabe and Bridget to ride on Drake, Siobhan would go with Liam, Davis had volunteered to carry Jack, and Shepard would take Jorrie. Liam kept eyeing Shepard as he assisted Jorrie to mount his back. Bridget saw a puff of smoke from Liam's nostrils as Shepard licked Jorrie's leg playfully and she squealed. Siobhan kicked her brother, saying unflattering things about his tail; he growled at her and nipped at her leg.

Siblings, Bridget repeated Vaughn's earlier words back to him. They shared a quiet laugh together.

Ivan would be riderless, so he was going to carry all the gear and packs. An easy task but a way for him to help.

Drake was so large he could easily accommodate the extra weight of Gabe. Since the boy was also his mate's son, he didn't mind at all. In fact, when this was over, he was going to take the boy flying without his mother. They just maybe wouldn't tell her.

Once everyone was situated, Drake took the lead, running down the pier and launching into the air. Bridget laughed as Gabe whooped in joy.

Liam followed next and glided up behind them. He was so excited to be flying again that he barrel-rolled, almost throwing Siobhan into the ocean below. When they were upright again, Bridget could hear her cursing a blue streak and threatening parts of Liam's anatomy. That girl had a mouth on her that put Bridget's to shame.

Davis joined them, moving to the left of Drake as Liam flew to the right. Jack looked like he had a death grip on one of Davis' spikes, but the grin on his face made Bridget smile.

She heard a quick scream followed by a shout of joy and knew Shepard had taken off. Jorrie was now beside her. She turned her head and saw her friend's curls flying crazily in the wind.

Ivan soon followed, bringing up the rear to guard from any threats that might come from behind. The island wasn't visible yet, but they would be there soon enough. Now, the concern was where to land this many large creatures?

They'd been flying for a while when Bridget noticed Gabe shiver. The night air was cool, and as high as they were, there was little warmth to be had. Bridget thought, *Drake, do you mind,* and she felt him rumble in agreement. Soon, he was radiating heat up to them, and they were toasty again.

"Wicked," she heard Gabe say.

Drake must have passed the message on to the other dragons because she soon heard Jorrie thanking Shepard and Jack saying something indecent to Davis. She was glad she hadn't heard the rest over the wind.

She had a feeling Jack was going to get over Darren with help from a certain blue dragon. Those two had been circling each other from the minute they met, like cats in heat. She was happy for him. He needed someone that truly cared about him, someone that understood this world.

To her right, Siobhan was carrying on a conversation with Liam. On her left, Jorrie was talking softly to Shepard, and he was chuffing in response. Gabe had fallen silent after a while, and she realized he had dozed off. That kid could seriously sleep anywhere.

They drew close to the island, and Bridget could just make out its dark shape on the horizon in the weak moonlight. She was relieved as flying over the water in the dark made her nervous. Suddenly, she heard the dragons making noises at each other and some low growling. What was going on?

We've got company, Drake told her. *Tell the others to sit low. Ivan's going to check it out.*

Bridget used their signal system to tell the others, relieved when they all complied. Leaning down over their dragons' necks to reduce their silhouette, they all remained silent. Ivan peeled away from the squad and flew left.

Bridget watched as he picked up speed to intercept whoever or whatever was coming at them. She was grateful for their extraordinary senses then, as she couldn't hear anything other than the wind and the occasional flap of wings.

A few minutes later, Ivan took up position again and Drake signaled all clear. The others sat up in relief.

Apparently, a brown dragon was out for a night flight nearby and spotted the unknown squad. She was coming to say hello and didn't mean to startle them. She knew a great place for them to land and would show them. Drake had agreed, and soon a petite brown dragon, the color of freshly turned earth, joined the squad, flying slightly ahead of Drake. They nodded to each other, and she angled right, flying down towards the island.

Bridget could smell the ocean and lush tropical flowers as they flew lower. She was relieved to be over the land again and was looking forward to standing on her own two feet. Flying with Drake was fun, but his scales weren't exactly posh Italian leather. She wondered how he'd feel about a saddle. She grinned to herself but decided against mentioning that idea to him.

The little dragon circled a large field with a few torches on the side to mark the boundaries. She made a hooting sound, indicating they could land. The squad glided towards the grass below and landed gently, although the draft from their wings blew out the light. The ones nearest the now extinguished torches blew gentle streams of fire to relight them. The passengers slid to the ground, stretching their legs and chattering in excitement about the amazing experience.

The dragons milled about while the humans gathered the bags and moved them to the side, getting out the clothes they needed when they changed back. The small brown dragon landed with a little hop and bounded over to the group. She must be very young, Bridget decided.

She hooted at the bigger male dragons, and they chuffed back at her. She gave another of her cute hops and shimmered into a young woman. The others took their cue and changed as well.

While they were dressing, the young lady had dashed off to grab her own clothes. She ran back over once she was properly attired and introduced herself as Emberly, but they could call her Em. Introductions went around, and they thanked her for the use of the field.

She was excited to meet them as she didn't get a chance to mingle much with other dragons. Most of them stayed away due to the Council and her dad being kind of protective. She looked around as if she was half expecting him to pop out of a bush and scold her.

Jorrie nudged Bridget and motioned for her to look at Gabe. He was staring at the black-haired, brown-eyed girl as if she'd hung the moon.

Bridget shook her head; she guessed the crush on Siobhan was officially over.

Vaughn asked Em if she knew how to get to the hotel; thankfully, she did. She gave them directions which was fortunately an easy walking distance. They gathered their belongings and were about to depart, thanking Em again for her kindness when she offered to walk with them. She was smiling shyly at Gabe.

Jack gave Bridget a conciliatory hug.

CHAPTER 36

BRIDGET WAS STARTLED AWAKE by a loud bang. She looked around in confusion trying to remember where she was. It all came flooding back, and she relaxed. She sat up on her elbow, trying to figure out what the bang was and saw Vaughn standing at the door with a chagrined look.

"Sorry," he said, "Didn't mean to scare you. I was trying to bring you breakfast and the door slipped when I was tipping room service." She noticed he had a tray of food, and he brought it over.

He helped her sit up, placing it over her lap. He was wearing loose white cotton pants and no shirt. Standing in front of the window with the light filtering through, they didn't leave much room for imagination.

She glanced at the food and decided he looked much yummier. Then she remembered Gabe was sleeping in the next room and tried to keep her appetite focused appropriately.

Vaughn caught her thoughts and stretched out on the bed next to her, propping his head on one arm and striking a decidedly sexy pose.

She laughed and dabbed some whipped cream on his nose. He rolled on his back, laughing with her. She loved this playful side of him. They talked quietly for a while about their plans for the day. They were to meet the others at nine in the lobby. It was a quarter after eight now, so they decided to get dressed, but by the time they got out of the shower, they were late meeting the others. The cheers and wolf whistles they received when they appeared proved everyone knew exactly why they were late.

Gabe was too engrossed in the girl in front of him to even be a little embarrassed. Em was back again and was chattering excitedly to him about the island. They learned Em had recently turned eighteen and only gained her full form about three months earlier. She was the youngest dragon on the island and was excited to meet someone her age who knew about dragons so she didn't have to hide that part of herself. The girl hopped around so much Bridget was contemplating nicknaming her Bunny.

As it turned out, Emberly thought the nickname was hilarious and adopted it. Now Bunny was telling them about her parents while the others ate breakfast. Already having eaten, Bridget and Vaughn listened intently, interested to learn that Bunny's mother and father both worked for the Council in global communications.

She offered to show them where the council chambers were, but Ivan let her know he was already aware and would be taking just Vaughn and Bridget for this first meeting. Bunny looked disappointed at first but rebounded, offering to take the others on a tour of the island. They readily agreed, and everyone prepared for their respective plans.

"This is it?" Bridget asked Ivan as they stood in front of a nonde-script-looking storefront backed up against a mountain. After seeing how grand her dragons lived, she expected something palatial from the Dragon Council building.

Ivan turned a bemused smile on her. "Well, what did you expect them to do? Hang a banner that says, 'Here there be dragons'? This is just a cover, a shell."

Bridget shrugged, turning to look at Vaughn who had been silent since they left the hotel.

He was glaring at the doors as if he wished them irreparable harm.

She knew he'd spent many years suffering under Council rule and was not looking forward to entering these halls again. She quietly took his hand, lending him her support. Although he didn't look at her, she saw his face relax, and a small smile returned to his lips. She looked at Ivan, who simply said, "Let's go."

They stepped through the doors into a dimly lit store that seemed to sell a lot of nothing. Not much that anyone would want anyway. She guessed to keep people away, no need to come in here.

Ivan gave a nod to the proprietor, who seemed to be sleeping with his feet propped on the counter. He waved them on while looking out the window to ensure there were no spectators.

Ivan led them to the back where most places would have a store-room. He opened the door and strode into a brightly lit hall that was in stark contrast to the dingy space they'd left. A short journey led to another door, this one with a high-end keypad that looked out of place. Ivan punched in a rather lengthy code, and Bridget heard buzzing as an electronic lock released and the door swung open.

They stepped into an enormous cavern with large pillars rocketing to a ceiling high overhead. Torches spaced around the room at regular intervals did nothing to dispel the darkness in the space near the roof. Here was the real Council entrance. It was carved into the mountain. *Here there be dragons,* she thought.

"Caves," Vaughn grunted.

She was staring in wonder at the huge space in front of her. There was room for several full-grown dragons to stand next to each other. She glanced at him in confusion.

"Dragons like caves," he murmured.

Ivan led them on towards an opening that led to another room with a much lower ceiling than the previous one but no less dim. The room was long and wide, more like a hallway. The walls were lined with paintings of various people whom Bridget guessed were important figures in dragon history.

They continued forward, and soon, the hall began to curve back around, eventually leading to an enormous staircase that wound down several floors. Their footsteps echoed in the massive space, sounding like an army was marching in. When it finally leveled out, they were deposited in another rounded room with several doors lining the walls. There were opulent rugs and chairs in the middle, with vases of fresh flowers and paintings on the walls. It had every appearance of a parlor in some medieval castle.

Ivan seated himself and gestured for them to do the same. Vaughn sat and propped one ankle on his knee, bouncing it slightly. Bridget decided it was impatience, not nerves.

She walked around the room, perusing the paintings. She stopped at one, looking closer at the birds in the sky. No, not birds, she realized. Dragons. Bridget went from painting to painting and realized they all displayed dragons going about their lives. She found one that depicted a battle and studied it closely. She felt Vaughn behind her, as he leaned over her shoulder.

"The Great Battle," he told her. "This shows a rendition of the last battle with the Shadows before the tribes were scattered. See how the dragons have riders, and they look like they all hold lightning bolts?"

She nodded.

"Those were the Light Wielders. The followers of Taranis before he removed all magic from the world. Well," he smirked, "All magic except ours."

Bridget rolled her eyes and patted his cheek, her proud dragon.

A door opened, and a somber-looking older man stepped into the room with them. He nodded at Ivan and turned to Vaughn.

"Mr. Drake," he said in a low voice, better suited for a funeral home.

Bridget shivered at the way it rolled over her skin.

Vaughn put an arm around her and rubbed her shoulder, sending some warmth into her.

She smiled gratefully at him as he faced the man and gave an affirmative nod.

"Follow me if you please." the sallow complexioned man ordered.

Bridget wondered when he'd last gone outside. His skin was papery, thin and as yellowed as old parchment.

Bertrand has been serving the council for hundreds of years. He never leaves these halls, Vaughn told her, confirming her suspicion.

They entered yet another large, cavernous chamber, but this one was well-lit and decorated like a throne room. Gold was everywhere, jewels sparkling in the lights, and the opulence was off the charts. Bridget resisted the urge to roll her eyes at how ostentatious it was. She didn't want to risk offending the dragons about to lay possible judgement on her mate.

It's a bit much don't you think, she sent to him. She saw him smirk. *It's like those cougars at the bars with their overdone hair, heavy makeup and flashy jewelry trying to impress the younger guys with how rich they are. Yawn.*

Vaughn was fighting not to smile, *behave yourself my love,* he cautioned. *But thank you.*

She saw the tension leave his shoulders and watched his cool, professional businessman mask slip over his face. She knew he would hold his own.

"Vaughn Drake," a stuffy voice droned. "Step forward for judgement."

He stepped forward towards a long table mounted on the dais. Five dragons in human form sat there. Two women and three men as best Bridget could tell. They all stared at Vaughn as he stood with a blank expression on his face.

Bridget started to move up with him, but he motioned her to stay behind. She noticed Ivan stood slightly behind as well. Whatever pomp and circumstance was about to happen, apparently Vaughn was to face it without anyone at his side.

"Drake," growled one particularly grumpy-looking man. His skin was a dark ebony, like a polished piece of wood. His sculpted brow spoke of an ancient lineage. "So, the prodigal son finally returns," he continued, his voice low and smarmy. "I knew it was only a matter of time before we would have to haul you back."

Vaughn snorted and turned to face the man, "Really, Baltrus, it's been well over a hundred years. I know time passes slowly for you here in your caves with your piles of wealth, but in the real world, much has changed. And I wasn't hauled here. I came of my own free will. I came to defend my actions and ask the Council for assistance."

Baltrus' face darkened in anger. "Insolent whelp!" he snarled. "You strut in here as disrespectful as ever. Your time in the 'real world' as you call it has not changed you at all. I suggest we throw him in the dungeon and leave him there."

Bridget choked back a laugh. Dungeons? Did she miss traveling in time or something?

"Oh, Balty, always so quick to throw everyone in the dungeon, really get with the times. Today's equivalent would be to take away his cell phone," said the icy blonde beauty at the end. Her accent and high cheekbones hinted at Vikings in her family tree. She pierced Vaughn with her cold stare. "I would like to hear what our little errant child has been up to all this time."

Baltrus snorted smoke in her direction. "Of course you would, Hilde, but you know he's taken a mate. Your plans to sink your claws into him won't work this time."

Bridget narrowed her eyes at the woman who apparently wanted a piece of her man.

"Children!" croaked a wizened old man who looked like he'd been sitting in his chair since the dawn of time. He had a decidedly Asian appearance, and Bridget wondered if he was the man in charge since he appeared so much older than the others. "Mind your tongues. We have company. Let us be kind and offer them a welcome." He turned to Vaughn, "Master Drake, please, do be seated and tell us of your life. What are you doing to occupy yourself these days."

Vaughn nodded respectfully and sat. "Thank you, Master Wu. It is wonderful to see you again." Vaughn began to recount his time in America and finished by describing his many companies and holdings.

The other Council members who had yet to speak nodded along, murmuring to each other. The other woman, with pale skin and silvery blonde hair, reminding Bridget of Killian, caught her eye, winking. Bridget took that as a good sign that not all were against Vaughn.

"Enough of this nonsense!" bellowed Baltrus. "What of the reason he was summoned? He broke the terms of our agreement. He must receive judgment for what he has done."

Wu sighed. "Yes, Baltrus, that is one of the reasons he was brought back, but by all means, let us proceed before we make you late for your afternoon nap."

Baltrus growled and Hilde smirked. The silver-headed woman laughed quietly while the last man, whose face was obscured by a hood, remained impassive.

Bridget studied him. *Really,* she thought, *so clichéd. A hood? A mysterious figure?* The hood turned slightly in her direction as if in response to her thoughts. Bridget swallowed. Vaughn had told her no other dragon could read her thoughts, but she decided not to take any chances and locked her snark up tight. She pictured shoving a fuzzy beast into a large chest, locking it and sitting on it. *Hope that works,* she imagined dusting her hands.

"Council, respectfully, I beg you to listen. When first you laid terms upon me, I was young, angry and full of rage. I could not foresee a future in which there would ever be a woman that could love me, and that I could love more than life in return. It took many decades before I was able to see that I was worthy of that. That there was more to me than rage. I have become wiser in my years, and I finally found peace and the one that fate has made for me. I beg you, please reconsider your demands. Although I did knowingly break one, I did so in the name of healing my soul. She has completed me and made me an even kinder, gentler man." He bowed and went down on his knee, showing a penitent posture.

Bridget had tears in her eyes for this amazing man. She hoped with all her heart the council was moved and would forgive him.

"Well, isn't that lovely?" Baltrus slowly clapped. "Look at him there, bowing, as if our opinion matters. We know your game, Drake. You knew you violated the agreement, but you drove ahead anyway, showing you have learned nothing."

Vaughn stayed down on his knees, vibrating in anger.

Baltrus opened his mouth to continue, but Wu held up a staying hand. He looked at Bridget and motioned her forward.

She stepped alongside Vaughn and unconsciously reached out a shaking hand, resting her fingertips on his shoulder.

His mind was a swirling mass of anger close to the surface. She tried to push calm into him, and to her surprise, it worked.

He turned his head and nuzzled her wrist, placing a kiss over her pulse point.

Wu nodded, and the silver-haired woman clapped and smiled. "See how she calms him," she called out. "I think a mate is exactly what he needed, and we were foolish to impose such a restriction on him."

Bridget liked this woman and smiled at her.

They heard an angry growl, and everyone turned to Hilde. She was glaring at Bridget and, between clenched teeth, yelled, "Show. Us. Your. Mark."

CHAPTER 37

N*OT THIS SHIT AGAIN,* Bridget thought to Vaughn.

He was now standing by her side, growling quietly at Hilde. All eyes were on Bridget.

Hilde smirked and stated, "If she has truly mastered this beast that you all seem to fear, she should be able to prove it easily enough."

Bridget knew they were afraid of him, but really, they were acting as if he planned to take down the whole dragon race. Maybe that's exactly what they feared.

He squeezed her hand in encouragement as she started to step forward, but he held her back. *Channel me,* he urged her.

What? she demanded, looking at him sharply. *Last time I did that, I short circuited the elevators in your building for two hours.*

Vaughn looked at her, *I know but you didn't understand it then, you do now. You've so much more control. You need to show them what we can do, how strong we are together. I have a reason for asking, my love. You know I would never do anything to harm you. I promise, you will be okay. I'll help control it from my end.*

Bridget nodded. She did trust him. If he needed her to make a show, he had a good reason.

Ivan stepped forward, silent until now. "If it pleases the Council, I have business elsewhere to attend to. I've no interest here," he stated as if he was bored with the whole proceeding.

Bridget stared at him in confusion. Why wasn't he supporting his son? Ivan did not meet either of their gazes and waited patiently for the Council to answer.

Baltrus waved a hand negligently, "Go, go, your only role was to deliver him to us, and you performed well. Be about your day."

Ivan gave a slight bow, turned, and walked out, leaving them alone in the room.

Bridget turned a bewildered stare on Vaughn, and he looked at her with equal confusion. Had the whole 'Ivan returned home to reclaim his relationship with his son' merely been a ruse to lure Vaughn here? She let her anger boil at the Council for using him, and the way they had kept him like a prisoner, away from his own family when he'd needed them the most. Suddenly, she had the cold calculation she needed to channel Vaughn's magic as sharply as the blade of a knife. She smiled darkly and raised her hands. They wanted a show? She'd give them a spectacle.

She closed her eyes and opened herself to the magic. It began whirling through her, and she welcomed it like a long-lost friend. It was warm and buzzing, snapping and crackling. Her skin thrummed as the sensations coursed over her body like an electric current. The hairs on her arms and neck stood at attention. Her scalp tingled, and she realized her hair was floating up from her head. Her eyes flew open, and she smiled at Hilde, who flinched. She heard gasps as the room went pitch black a moment before a beam of pure light shot from Bridget's fingers. It burned brightly; several of the Council shielded their eyes from its glare.

She saw Baltrus snarling, so she twisted her fingers slightly and directed them at him. Her light swirled into a flaming dragon, which leaped from her fingertips. She watched his eyes widen in alarm and gave a satisfied smirk as it passed inches from his nose. Then, she flicked her wrist and sent the light hurtling at Hilde, who squealed, jumping back from the table and ducking out of sight.

Enough, my love, Vaughn chuckled, the pride evident in his voice. *You've made your point.*

Bridget let the magic relax, and the dragon returned to her, disappearing into her fingers. The room slowly brightened again, and Hilde regained her seat.

She pulled her shirt aside, revealing the mark, and looked up at Vaughn.

"Your eyes are as black as my scales," he said with a beaming smile that stole her breath. *I'm so proud of you, Bridget, my love.* He wrapped her in his arms and kissed her passionately. Council be damned. When they came to their senses, her eyes were once again her own.

She smiled shakily at him, and he winked. They linked hands, turning to face the Council together. United as one.

Wu clapped, and Silver Hair joined him. "Well done, my dear. Well done. Mistress Hilde," Wu turned to her, "You challenged, she answered. Do you accept?"

Bridget could see that the answer would cost her some pride, tasting like sour grapes, but she couldn't deny what she'd seen.

"I concede if I must too... this... woman," she sneered.

"Bridget," Vaughn said. "Her name is Bridget. If you address my mate as anything less again, I will take great offense." He snarled and spit flame at her feet as an indication that he was deadly serious.

She saw Hilde's eyes widen; she remembered that most dragons could not produce flames in their human form, so it was an exclamation point to his statement.

"Bridget, I concede my challenge to you. You have proven to this council that you are indeed the Drake's true mate. I commend you for your excellent, um, control," Hilde concluded with a tentative smile at Bridget.

She nodded with grace and squeezed Vaughn's hand. Things were looking up.

"So. What," Baltrus said with anger in his eyes. "That only proves my point. He took a mate against our orders and a strong one. Imagine what their children could do! He should be punished, now."

Bridget was stunned, she hadn't thought of it like that.

Wu contemplated in silence before stating, "Fortunately for Drake, it is not up to you but the Council as a whole. I call for a vote to decide."

Baltrus slammed his fist on the table. "Why a vote? It is law! He was given terms; he willingly and knowingly broke them. He admits, do you not?" he growled at Vaughn.

Vaughn dipped his head in acknowledgement.

"See? We do not need to vote on this, it's clear as day."

Wu finally snarled at Baltrus, who was jabbing his finger on the table. Baltrus sat down with alacrity. "How quick you are to judge Baltrus, have you never been wrong? Were you never young and passionate once? Have you always been so stuffy and angry? I called for a vote, so vote we shall. Those in favor of prosecuting?"

Baltrus' hand shot up. Hilde wavered as if she wanted to vote against Vaughn but was a little afraid. Baltrus glared at her, and she raised her hand.

Wu nodded, "Two to prosecute, those opposed?" He raised his own hand, and Silver Hair raised hers too. They all looked at Hood who continued to sit still, remaining silent. Bridget wondered if he was asleep.

Wu nodded again. "Two for and two against. It seems, my friend Tar'n, the vote has come down to you."

Baltrus spluttered in anger.

Bridget saw the hood move slightly as if he was focusing on her. *Good God, could this GET any more cliched!* she thought. *I mean, really. Two for and two against, down to the last vote, and it's up to some Jedi wannabe hooded dude who might not even be alive under there. Could this be any more like a fiction novel?*

Vaughn snorted, catching some of what she was thinking. *Down girl,* he sent her, *two weeks ago, you didn't even believe dragons existed. And remember those myths and legends are usually based on a kernel of truth.*

She sighed, waiting. Where did he get off being so reasonable? She was tired of standing, tired of being judged. She wanted to get back home and figure out how to kick some shadow ass.

Tar'n finally stood and folded his hands. "Drake," he said in a whispery voice.

Creepy, Bridget shivered.

Tar'n continued to speak, and his words sounded like leaves rattling in the wind through the branches of a dying tree on a cold fall night. *Wow, I'm getting morbid,* Bridget thought.

The whisper asked, "Why is it you come to us now? You spoke of needing help but have yet to ask. You demonstrate this incredible bond, this show of power, knowing it could endanger your cause. But you stand before us, putting on a spectacle. Why?" The whispering stopped, and Bridget felt the warmth return to the room. She half expected to see snow falling.

Vaughn drew himself tall, nodding; Bridget realized this was the reason he requested the show of power. "Thank you, wise one. I come before you to ask your help to battle the Shadow Claw."

The Council hissed at the name. Baltrus jumped up, shouting, "You haven't changed! Vengeance in your heart! Always looking for a fight!"

Tar'n raised a hand, and he sat back down.

"Tell us!" commanded Wu.

Vaughn launched into his tale of how the Shadows had been attacking in broad daylight in front of others, trying to snatch Bridget, burning her house down and ambushing families, killing some of them. At this news, the Council burst into shouts and unintelligible words. A cold wind whipped through the room with the force of a hurricane, whipping papers into the air and blowing out the torches. The room fell silent.

A small flame appeared next to Bridget as Vaughn walked to the torches and casually relit them. The Council sat silently, staring at the hooded Tar'n. Once Vaughn had returned to his position, the whisper came again.

"Why?" it asked simply.

Vaughn rolled his lips inward like he didn't want to answer.

A cold chill swept over him, and Bridget saw frost gathering on his skin. She wasn't sure who this Tar'n was, but she knew he was powerful. She nodded at Vaughn, encouraging him to tell them. "They are after Bridget because she is the Wielder of Prophecy."

The council was silent for a moment as they regarded him. Silver Hair finally spoke. "So, you found the Wielder of Prophecy, and mated her. Well done, Drake." She laughed and applauded.

Vaughn dipped his head.

"It's not possible," said Hilde in confusion. "The shadow killed the Wielders of Prophecy years ago."

Wu nodded slightly, narrowing his eyes on Bridget. "That is true, but here she stands, enormous light wielding at her control, I wonder." He tapped a finger to his lips. He turned to Baltrus, "You are the historian, are you not? You interpreted the Prophecy and gave us the identities of both, or so you claimed. Explain."

Baltrus eyed Bridget with barely disguised malice. "There were two Wielders of Prophecy. We know the Shadows hunted down the first one fifty years ago in the Alps, buried him in an avalanche, a Jacob Slonsky, his body never recovered. Then we received word that they killed the second wielder almost nine years ago. Another man. He was killed in an accident of some kind at a military base in America, in Texas. What was the name? A moment," he shuffled some papers.

Ice wrapped around her heart. "No," she whispered. "Please, God, no." She noticed the hood focusing on her, like a physical touch.

Vaughn turned to her and said her name, but it sounded like he was underwater, muffled, far away.

"Here it is." Baltrus waved a paper in slow motion. "Brian Ridgeway, he was the other Wielder. They killed him, too."

Bridget's world crumbled around her. Brian, her Brian, was dead because of her. Because the Shadow Claw thought he was the Wielder, but it was her. It was her fault. She saw Vaughn speaking, but she couldn't hear him. *Why does he look so scared*? She thought before she hit the floor, and the world went blessedly dark.

"Bridget, come back, Bridget!"

No, I don't want to go there, that way is pain. Let me stay here, let me stay. She slipped back into the dark, gladly letting Morpheus take her in his arms to keep the pain at bay.

CHAPTER 38

BRIDGET WOKE SUDDENLY IN her bed at her old house. Gray daylight was filtering through the windows, and rain was rattling against the glass. *What the hell?* she thought.

Someone moved next to her. She turned, "Vaughn!" she cried, but it wasn't him. It was Brian.

"Mmm, Good morning, Sunshine," he said, kissing her gently.

She felt the scratching of his beard on her chin and remembered wishing he would shave it.

He thought it made him look older. She had told him it made him look like a beaver. He'd just laughed it off.

"Brian?" she asked quietly, afraid he would disappear. "Brian, it's you!" she threw her arms around him. All of that with the dragons. It was just a dream! She looked at her collarbone, but there was nothing there. She was never drinking margaritas with Jorrie again! That was the road to danger.

"Well, of course, it's me, silly goose. Who else would it be?"

An image of a gorgeous black-haired man leaning against her office door smiling from behind glasses that did nothing to hide his beautiful blue eyes, flashed through her mind. A co-worker?

"No one," she replied and snuggled into him, letting him wrap her in his arms.

Another image, the black-haired man leaning across a table, brushing her hand as they looked at production figures.

They lay there for a moment in contented silence, her head on Brian's chest, her heart at peace.

"Can't stay much longer, darling, have to get to work," he said.

"No!" she shouted. He looked startled, so she repeated softly, "No, please, just stay here with me. Never leave me."

He laughed and held her tightly.

An image of the same man on his knees, *please don't leave me, I love you.*

She laid her head on Brian's chest. "I've missed you so much," she whispered.

He stroked her hair, confused, "It's only been since you fell asleep, my dear. Did you miss me in your dreams?"

The man again, holding her against the shower wall, sliding into her, his forehead against hers, silky black hair falling around them, his blue eyes gazing into hers, them both gasping in pleasure.

"That's it. I just missed you in my dreams." She tried to smile, but it faltered.

The man, no, Vaughn, flaring his wings. Vaughn throwing her in the pool. Vaughn on the airplane, holding her hand. Vaughn in his office, her sitting on his lap, laughing with Liam. Vaughn lying under her and groaning while her hands were on his chest as she rode him into oblivion. Vaughn fist-bumping Gabe, teaching him to grill a steak. Vaughn flying through the clouds, Vaughn sheltering her on the island with his wing while they slept. Vaughn smiling at her, kissing her softly and telling her he loved her. The pain and ecstasy as he branded her as his mate.

Gasping, she sat up, "*Vaughn!*" She put her hand to her heart and found it pounding. She looked at her collarbone again, drawn by the pain there. This time, she saw the image of a small black dragon. She touched it, and her heart settled. Vaughn.

Brian slowly sat up next to her; she faced him with shame on her face.

"Brian, I," she faltered, not knowing what to say.

He smiled sadly. "It's okay, Bridget. I was hoping we would have a little longer together, but I can see now it's time to go."

She stared at Brian, tears forming in her eyes. She shook her head, *No!*

He wrapped her in his arms, holding her. "Bridget, Bridget," he soothed her as she cried, "I know you loved me while I was here. I never doubted that. But we were never meant to be forever. You were destined for greater things. He loves you more than I ever could, even though I loved you so, so much. I know you love him now, and that's okay, Bridget. You gave me Gabriel, and that was the best thing ever. He's grown into such a fine young man."

She sniffed, "He looks so much like you. More every day."

Brian smiled and stroked her back. "He's a handsome little devil, but he's brave, like his mother." He kissed her tenderly, then pulled away and stood.

"No!" she begged.

"She's the bravest woman I know, and I know she's brave enough and smart enough to understand this can't last. She knows this was not her fault. She's brave enough to let me go and move on with her life. With her fate, with her destiny. Bridget, it's time. Tell Jack and Gabe I love them and I'm proud of them."

She cried harder, "Please, Bri, no, please, no! I can't lose you again!" Her heart ached, and she knew it was about to shatter all over the floor.

He smiled and began to fade. "Go to him, Bridget, I love you." He was gone, and she was standing in the suffocating dark, unable to see anything around her.

"BRIAN!" she screamed. She screamed his name over and over again until her throat was raw. She collapsed, sobbing until she could cry no more. She pulled her knees to her chest and lay curled up, waiting for Death to take her, too.

She lay there so long; time had no meaning. Shivering in the cold and completely dark, desolate place of her grief, the blackness so thick she could feel it like a hand on her skin. Eventually, she heard the rustle of leaves in a cold wind. A chill breeze blew over her. She looked around but still couldn't see anything. She strained to hear a whisper on that wind. Maybe it was Death... finally coming for her. She searched for the source.

Fight, the whisper said. *It is for you to finish. Fight now.*

"I can't," she whispered back. "I have nothing left."

You have everything. Now FIGHT, Bridget. I command you. FIGHT!

Bridget slowly stood and looked around shivering. "Hello?" she whispered. She thought she felt warmth behind her and turned towards it. She heard the flapping of large wings. She couldn't see them, but she knew they were black and gold.

"Vaughn," she croaked, her throat sore and clogged. The warmth became stronger, and she thought she could see some light. "Vaughn." she tried harder. She heard a faint roar. "*Vaughn!*" she screamed.

Suddenly, she was enveloped in the soft feel of her mate's wings, and the warmth seeped into her bones, into her heart. The pieces came back together, and she was whole again. She gasped; *now, how do I get out of here?*

"She wakes," said Circe, also known as Silver Hair. She wiped Bridget's forehead and smiled at her patient. She wasn't the Goddess known long ago by that name but could trace her lineage there. The magic was strong in this one; she knew Bridget would come back. She looked over at Drake, a more haggard-looking man she'd never seen. When his Bridget had dropped to the floor, his roar had nearly brought the mountain down on them. There were still shifting cracks throughout the structure as it settled.

Baltrus had been foolish to ever think they could contain or control a dragon of that power. Drake had to be the way he was so he could be the one for Bridget. It was the only way. She dipped her cloth in a nearby bowl and dripped cool water on Bridget's forehead.

Bridget sighed and shifted. Her eyes fluttered and gradually opened. Squinting at the light coming through the window, she closed them again.

After the mountain almost collapsed, they'd moved Bridget back to her hotel room and placed her in bed. Vaughn slept in the chair next to the bed, Bridget's hand in his. He had refused to move from her side. Not to eat, not to drink, and not speaking to anyone.

Circe had come along to tend to the Wielder of Prophecy. "Come on, little one," she whispered in Bridget's ear, "Your Drake needs you."

Bridget turned her head to stare at Circe, no doubt trying to figure out where she was.

Circe gently turned Bridget's head towards Vaughn. She could feel Bridget's pulse flutter.

She tried to speak, but all that came out was a croaking sound. Circe helped her sip some water and she tried again. "Vaughn." She was barely able to whisper. It was faint, but it was enough.

Vaughn instantly came awake, tightening his grasp on her hand. His eyes met hers, and his world clicked back into place. He knelt on the bed and gently kissed her forehead. Tears fell from his eyes as she reached up and cupped his face.

"Vaughn, my love," she whispered.

"Bridget, my heart," he whispered back.

She smiled, "I'll never leave you." Her eyelids fluttered closed, and she fell back asleep.

Vaughn gasped, but Circe calmed him.

"It's but a natural sleep. She needs real rest. She's been fighting against fate, that one. She's exhausted, and so are you, my handsome Drake. Although, not quite as handsome as usual. Go take a shower, you smelly man. Then get some food, for she will be hungry when she wakes. And tell her family so they stop pacing in the hall. One can hardly think with all the noise."

He grinned and proceeded to do just that.

Vaughn eased open the door and took in the scene in Jorrie's room. Gabe was sitting on the floor against the wall, Bunny holding his head on her chest. Jorrie was being held by Liam as he rocked her and wiped her tears. Jack was sitting in a chair staring into space, his face a mask of pain, Davis holding his hand. Shepard and Siobhan weren't there, but he imagined they were close by. His father, well, he hadn't seen him since the Council chamber, and as far as he was concerned, the old dragon should have stayed dead.

As he strode in, everyone looked up, their faces filled with pain. It had been two days since Bridget fell into darkness, and they were all sick at heart. Vaughn had refused to leave her side, only sending them messages with unchanging news. Circe had filled them in on the finer points, and he knew that Jack was hurting almost as much as he was. Seeing him could only mean one of two things.

"She's okay!" he held up his hands to ward off their questions and fear. The tension left the room as if someone had pulled a plug, letting it swirl down the drain. "She woke and spoke a little. She's resting now, real sleep, and you can all see her after she's had some food and a chance to clean up. She's back." Tears fell unchecked down his face.

Jorrie stood, wrapped her arms around him and squeezed tightly. "Thank you, Vaughn," she whispered.

Vaughn squeezed Jorrie back and kissed the top of her lifeless curls. He hoped she'd get her bounce back soon. Bridget would worry about her friend instead of caring for herself. He let Jorrie go and turned to Gabe, who was quietly crying. Bunny was stroking his hair. Vaughn leaned down and pulled the boy up to him. Holding him tightly, he whispered, "Your mom is fine. She's okay, buddy. I know she can't wait to see you. Gabriel, I'm so sorry about your father."

Gabe cried harder and hugged Vaughn tighter. They stood that way for a minute until Jorrie pulled him down and sat with him on the bed. Rocking him and crooning her little song until he calmed down.

Vaughn wiped his face. He nodded at Liam, who smiled in relief.

"Jack," Vaughn called. The man's head slowly turned to him. He was moving like a robot, mechanical and stiff. "Jack, come with me, please."

He rose and stumbled towards Vaughn like a sleepwalker.

The men went into the hallway, and Vaughn leaned against the wall. Jack mirrored his pose and they stared at each other.

Vaughn cleared his throat and took Jack's hand in his. "Jack, I want you to know. I had no idea about Brian being any part of this until two days ago. I swear it. Please believe me when I tell you, we never knew." He squeezed his hand. "The moment she realized, Jack, she died in front of me. That's what it was. She dropped to the floor, and all of the warmth and light went out of the world. I wanted to kill them all. I almost did," he said ruefully. "She was screaming, Jack. Screaming his name. I thought my heart would shatter and I couldn't breathe. He must have been a truly amazing man to earn that kind of love from her."

Jack slowly looked up at Vaughn as if he was seeing him for the first time. "He wasn't."

Vaughn looked at Jack, shocked.

Jack shook his head. "I don't mean to say he was a jerk or cruel, just that he was an ordinary guy. He was funny and nice, kind of a dick to me sometimes, but he was my brother, that was his job. He never meant it, just sibling stuff you know?"

Vaughn nodded. He'd seen enough of that with Liam, Siobhan, and the twins.

Jack continued, "As much as I loved Brian and I miss him dearly, it wasn't him that made that marriage special. It was her." He nodded towards the room where Bridget lay. "She loved that man and made him more because of it. That's what she does. She loves people and makes them more. I know you've seen it. Look what she did for Siobhan and Liam, for me, for Jorrie, she made us all a family. It's her."

Vaughn looked at Jack, floored. He was right. That's what attracted him to her in the first place. She made rooms brighter, tastes better; she just made everything more. He suddenly realized that's how she was going to defeat the Shadows. He finally understood the prophecy and how his mate was going to change the world.

Vaughn kissed Jack on the forehead, saying, "Jack, you're the best brother a man could ever have. I love you, I love Bridget, and we are going to finish this!"

Jack smiled and hugged Vaughn. He stood back with a serious expression. "Vaughn, I need you to do something for me."

"Anything."

"You find that Shadow King, and you fucking kill him. Kill him and make sure he knows that it's from all of us. For everyone he's harmed, maimed, killed. But most especially, make sure he knows at least one death blow is for Brian."

CHAPTER 39

AFTER A LONG HOT shower, Bridget was starting to feel like herself again. *I have really got to stop passing out and waking up in strange places,* she thought. She winced as the hot water stung her knees. They were bruised and tender, probably from when she hit the floor.

A cold wind wrapped around her in the shower suddenly, sending chills over her skin. She heard whispers, sliding over the sounds of the pounding water.

She looked around the steam-filled room but didn't see anyone. The warm water removed the chill, but she shivered anyway. A knock on the door made her jump.

"Bridget? Are you okay in there?" called Vaughn.

She smiled; he was hovering like a nervous hen near her first eggs. "I'm fine," she called as she shut off the water. *Just having phantoms whispering at me and blowing cold air up my skirt,* she thought, careful not to let that slip over to Vaughn. She didn't need him worrying any more than he already was. Who knew he could be so clingy? Of course, if it had been him who'd basically dropped dead at her feet, she wouldn't have been able to breathe, much less bring down a mountain.

She smiled at that while she dried off. Her fierce warrior, so angry he'd almost destroyed a fortress that had stood for millennia. He loved her beyond reason, and all else he'd told her. She believed it. She reached for a brush, smiling at it, and remembering how, not too long ago, a different brush had started the day that changed it all. Tapping it on her palm, she walked out into the bedroom, wrapped in a robe and found Vaughn sitting nervously on a chair, waiting for her.

He sprang to his feet and rushed to her. "Are you alright? What do you need?"

She smiled, patting him on the chest. "Could you help me brush my hair?" she asked.

He nodded swiftly and led her to the bed. He sat down and leaned against the headboard, patting the comforter, inviting her to sit between his legs.

She sat with her back to him, hugging her knees to her chest while he gently pulled the brush through her hair. "Mm." She sighed in pleasure. "That feels amazing."

He smiled as he held the damp locks in his hands. They were like strands of rubies, ropes of fire, and they drove him crazy when they brushed across his stomach.

Bridget relaxed, letting the rhythm soothe her as he patiently worked through her hair in sections. Earlier, her family had all come in to visit her and reassure themselves that she was alive. She received hugs, tears, and more hugs. She thought they were going to have to remove Jorrie with a crane if she didn't let go. Even little Bunny had come in, giving her wishes to get well. Jack was somber, but it was to be expected. Of all them, the news about Brian's murder affected her, Gabe, and Jack the most.

Vaughn had told her about his conversation with Jack in the hallway, she wasn't surprised about Jack's need for vengeance. Under his silly exterior, the man was a block of steel. He'd been so steady all these years, she knew he wouldn't waver now. She'd been glad to see her friends and family, but she was also glad when they'd left. She'd had food, she'd had her family, and a hot shower. Now there was one more thing she needed. "My love," she whispered.

The brushing paused, "Hmm?"

She turned to face him, taking the brush and laying it on the nearby table. "We need to talk."

Vaughn stared at her. Those words were seldom followed by anything good, but if she wanted to talk, he would listen. He nodded.

She stared into his eyes, seeing his fear there and hated what she was about to do. "I need," she paused. He started to speak, and she shook her head. "I need to tell you what happened."

He gave her a tight smile that didn't reach his eyes, and she guessed he was probably not looking forward to this.

She'd been told she'd been screaming Brian's name not long after she collapsed. She figured it had probably hurt him badly. She needed to make it right. She told him about how it had affected her, hearing her husband's death was the result of mistaken identity, and she was the real target. How she'd felt responsible. How the cold had washed over her, and she was falling down a deep, bottomless pit. She talked about the bone-chilling certainty that she had betrayed her husband by not making him stay that day, by letting him walk out that door to his death.

She saw on Vaughn's face he wanted badly to contradict her, but he was biting his lip so he could honor her request. The dear, sweet man. She needed to hurry, before he stopped breathing. She took his hands in hers. "Vaughn, after everything went black, I woke up in my bed in my house. It was the day Brian died. At first, I didn't believe it was real, but he was there next to me. Warm and alive. I couldn't help it; I didn't want to leave. I began to believe that everything from then on had been some sort of dream, some nightmare. I didn't want to come back. I was happy."

Vaughn's head dropped, and she heard his breath hitch. He shuddered as if she'd hit him with iron fists instead of words. This was so hard, but he needed to know it all.

She tilted his chin up and looked into his eyes. "But then I saw you. It was just a flash, but I saw you. That day you asked me to lunch. You were leaning against my office door, you'd just caught me talking to myself and you were wearing those glasses, you remember?"

A ghost of a smile appeared on his lips.

"And then Brian was going to leave. I begged him not to go."

The smile fell away.

"But then I saw you again. That night, in your room. When you begged me not to leave, when you wrapped your wings around me and held me so tight. I was in your lap, Vaughn, like this." She crawled up into his lap, letting the robe fall away, revealing nothing underneath but bare skin.

He leaned forward and let his wings spread, then wrapped them around her, like the memory.

She put her forehead to his. "Brian tried to leave, telling me it was time, and I held his hand. I didn't want to let go, but I kept getting flashes of you, Vaughn. Like waves on the shore or rain on the roof, your name, your face, just kept pounding into me, and I finally let go of his hand."

She lifted his chin and kissed him. "Brian told me to let him go so I could be with you because he knew you were my true destiny. It hurt Vaughn, and my heart broke all over again into tiny pieces I thought wouldn't heal this time. He died again, and it broke me. I screamed his name over and over until my voice was gone. That's probably what you heard."

He nodded, and a single tear rolled down his face.

"Vaughn," she sighed, cupping his face and wiping the tear with her thumb. "I need you to understand how broken inside I was. I didn't want to come back. I was content to stay there in the dark and let Death take me." She noticed his heart start pounding harder and saw fear in his eyes again. "Shhh," she told him. "I don't know how long I laid there, what it was in time out here, but it was years to me. Then I heard a whisper telling me to fight. Just get up and fight, that I had everything to fight for. When I stood up, Vaughn, I could feel you. I could feel your warmth, and I called for you."

His gaze sharpened on hers, and she smiled.

"In my darkest moments, when I thought nothing was left, I sensed you and I reached for you. I heard your wings, and I screamed your name so you could find me. Over and over, I screamed until you found me. When you did, it healed everything in me that was broken."

Vaughn let out a ragged breath and pulled her against him, tightly against his chest.

She could feel his heart still pounding as he just breathed her in. "Opening my eyes, seeing your face, knowing you were the one who pulled me back. I'm," she gave a little sob, "I'm so grateful and while I know what Brian and I had was love, it was nothing like the flame that burns in me for you. I love you, Vaughn Drake. For the way you love me so fiercely. I love you so much it hurts to breathe. I'm never leaving you again, and I'm so sorry. Oh God, I'm so sorry, Vaughn. Please," she begged. "Please forgive me."

Vaughn rocked her gently, feeling her skin on his. "Bridget, my love, there is nothing to forgive. You were dealt a terrible blow. You scared me, I admit, but I knew in my soul you would come back to me."

She shook her head, "No, Vaughn, I need you to forgive me for not wanting to leave for wanting to stay. I need to know you understand. It was easier to stay there in that moment and avoid all of the pain the heartache. The falling apart and the hard moments. I didn't think I would survive it all again. But I had to. I had to survive it to come back to you. Please tell me you understand."

Vaughn pulled her away and looked at her. "Bridget, my dear sweet Bridget. I forgive you. I forgive you for wanting to avoid the pain of not wanting to pick up the pieces again. I will always love you no matter what." He smiled, and she melted.

She leaned against his lips and kissed him gently. Then it became more passionate. Her hands were at his waist, fumbling with the string on his pants.

He broke the kiss, "Bridget, it's okay, my love. You don't have to prove anything; you need your rest."

She shook her head, "No, I'm tired of resting. The only thing I want to do in this bed is feel you in me and on me. I need to feel alive. Vaughn, I need you."

He responded by sitting up so she could slide the pants down, then sat back and opened his arms to her.

She could see he was hard and ready. She threw herself into his arms and attacked his mouth with a frenzy, digging her nails into his shoulders and rubbing her breasts on his chest.

His hands went all over her, understanding she needed it hard and rough.

She came up for air gasping and he took the opportunity to latch on to her breasts, suckling and biting, almost to the point of pain. She arched her back and moaned, letting his fire consume her.

He reached between her thighs and found her wet and ready. With a growl, he positioned her over his length and drove himself into her.

She cried out then sank down further, feeling like she couldn't get enough. "I need. I need," she panted.

"What do you need? What do want?"

"I need you to take me as hard as you can!" She watched the flames come to his eyes, and a wicked grin crossed his face right before his wings flapped hard.

Bridget lay on the floor, breathing heavily. She was sure Vaughn had taken her against every surface in the room. It looked like it had been ransacked. She huffed out a laugh. She had to hand it to him. Vaughn was very creative in ways to give her orgasms. Knowing she needed it, he'd worked to get as many out of her as he could before he finally had his own release. Brushing her hair out of her face she looked around for her dragon.

He was standing by the dresser, drinking an entire bottle of water in one long pull. Hard sex was thirsty work, apparently. He sauntered over, picked her up, and dropped her on the bed.

She laughed as he handed her a bottle, too. She propped up enough to drink some of it, then flopped back down. She stretched, feeling deliciously used. "Mm. Thank you, Vaughn. You are definitely a man who knows how to give a woman what she wants."

"Is that so?" she heard him murmur.

She sighed, a satisfied, happy noise. She heard him rummaging around and wondered idly what he was doing but decided it was too much effort to sit up and look.

"Excuse me, ma'am." she heard a sultry voice.

She lifted her head and saw Vaughn standing in front of her. He was naked except for a loose tie and his glasses. She hadn't realized he brought them! Her body went tight again at the sight. "Mr. Hotness!" she exclaimed.

He grinned. "Yes, ma'am. I understand you are my new coworker?"

She grinned back, deciding to play along. "I certainly am. How can I help you?"

He tapped the glasses down his nose a bit and looked at her over the frames.

Whoa, she thought. She almost orgasmed right then.

"Well, I'd like to have a meeting and have you take some... perhaps some dictation..." He rumbled in his chest.

Yep, she was definitely about to have one. "I'm happy to help then. When would you like me to start?"

He held out his hands for hers, and she gave them to him. Faster than she would have believed, he whipped off his tie and bound her wrists. He flipped her over and pulled her to her knees, then spanked her.

She looked at him over her shoulder, shocked.

He winked, "You're not the only one with fantasies."

CHAPTER 40

TWO WEEKS LATER, THEY were all gathered for dinner, with everyone packed into a banquet hall at a local restaurant. Vaughn believed the Council space still wasn't safe, and he refused to enter. Word was sent, summoning dragons and wielders to join the cause. In addition to the group they'd brought with them, they were joined by Bunny's parents, Circe, Wu, Hilde, and many other dragons and wielders Bridget hadn't met yet.

Others went ahead to the US to rendezvous with the team in Dallas. They were waiting for their food to be served before they began full-scale conversations, so the staff didn't overhear too much.

Jorrie had stepped out to use the lady's room and had been gone for some time. Bridget was just starting to get concerned when she came back. Jorrie looked thoughtful when she walked in but quickly put on a smile and skipped to her chair next to Bridget.

"What's up?" Bridget asked her friend.

Jorrie smiled, "Nothing, just trying to remember if I asked that cute waiter for red or white wine."

Bridget looked at her, not quite believing her but too distracted to dig into it. She shifted in her chair again. She was a little sore from her time in the bedroom earlier that day. The man was gifted, for sure. *Sex God,* she sent him and smirked when she heard him cough into his glass behind her.

Behave, young lady, or I'll have to spank you again, he rumbled back to her.

You like it, she replied before shifting around again and smiling at Jorrie.

Her friend studied her with a knowing smile, asking with studied innocence. "Everything okay? You seem a little antsy."

It was finally time to make their plan. Everyone was all in to wipe out the Shadow Claw. They discussed the whereabouts of the Shadow King, having narrowed it down to a heavily guarded compound in Hawaii on the island of Maui. It was a large windowless base with escape tunnels, its own utilities, and lots of patrols.

They'd discovered this because Baltrus was a traitor. He had been secretly siding with the Shadow King for years. His treason was uncovered, and information extracted before he was put to death by the remaining members of the Council. He was complicit in the plot that had resulted in Brian's murder. Bridget's only complaint was she hadn't been there to witness the execution.

"Great," huffed Jack.

Bridget gave him a questioning glance.

"This guy's living it up in paradise while we are slogging halfway around the world trying to find him and end him. Doesn't seem very fair. I'm stuck in rush hour traffic every morning and he's relaxing on a tropical island sipping Mai Tais."

She tried not to laugh; it wasn't time for jokes, but it was pretty funny.

Jorrie held no such compunction and burst out with her usual bright laughter.

Bridget noticed several male heads turned towards Jorrie in appreciation, including Shepard, who grinned at her.

Liam noticed, too, and she heard a faint growl coming from him. She needed to give him some advice before some of the other dragons moved in on what he clearly wanted.

Davis did not need any encouragement and had his hand on Jack's knee.

Bridget heard some whispers about Mai Tais, and they were smiling at each other. She shook her head; she knew they'd started sharing a room. She laughed at their obvious delight in each other, it was adorable. Vaughn absently laid a hand on her leg, and she blushed, remembering her own activities earlier.

"Okay so that covers most of it. We know where, and we know our approach." Vaughn recapped for everyone. He looked around and saw nods of agreement. "We need a large squad to infiltrate and subdue the guards. My team back in Dallas has been running drills for this type of scenario, and I'm confident they can handle it if any of you want to join that group. As soon as we adjourn, I will update Marco and have them begin preparations immediately. We just need to finalize how we will actually take out the King. The prisoner we interrogated seems to feel his King has no weaknesses and believe me, he has told us everything he can, but I disagree. He's not immortal."

Bridget nodded vigorously; she wanted revenge and justice as well.

Hilde spoke up, "This is all good and well, my friend."

Bridget glared at her for daring to call him friend.

Hilde continued, "But it doesn't answer how the prophecy will be put into motion."

Circe giggled, and Hilde shot her a look full of daggers.

"Oh, dear sister," Circe trilled in a singsong voice and stood. She began to spin around in slow circles, dancing about the room. She hauled Shepard up from his chair and spun around with him, dropping him next to Jorrie, where they grinned at each other. She continued to dance and spin, picking someone up, dancing them around and dropping them in different chairs. She moved Gabe next to a lady with blue hair and several rings in her nose. They laughed at each other before she was spun off and then deposited in Jorrie's chair, while Jorrie was deposited in Liam's lap, where Circe stopped spinning.

"You see, dear sister, the prophecy is already in motion, bringing all of these fine people together. The circles brought our Drake and his Bridget together. Then it brought Ivan to Drake and Drake to us. It brought Jack and Davis to us, and it brought these two together." She motioned at Jorrie and Liam, who were staring into each other's eyes.

They really need that pep talk, Bridget thought, turning her attention back to Circe.

"The circles create ripples, which create more circles, which make waves, waves become larger and large waves can topple buildings.

Buildings fall and topple empires until *boom!*" she clapped, making everyone jump. "The circles start anew."

There was absolute silence in the private room, only the quiet hum of conversation and clinking forks from diners in the outer areas of the restaurant filtered through. Hilde stood, walking to Circe where she was swaying, petting Liam like some small animal.

He looked very confused and was making faces at Jorrie, who had decided now was a good time to find a chair of her own.

Hilde sighed, "Sister, as usual, you speak in riddles and insanity, but I understand." She looked at Vaughn, "You know how to take down Azrael don't you."

Everyone in the room gasped as she used the Shadow King's name. Bridget looked at her friends, who were as confused as she was. *Is using his name like some taboo thing, like He Who Must Not Be Named,* she sent to Vaughn.

He snorted and tried to cover it up by drinking wine. *The old ones believe names have power, so in a way I guess you are right. They fear that saying his name anywhere there are shadows can draw his attention to the speaker. Many avoid saying it. I don't care. I want the bastard dead.*

Bridget held his hand under the table.

Vaughn realized everyone was staring at him, waiting for his answer. He squeezed Bridget's hand and stood up, pulling her with him. "I do," he said.

Murmurs went around the room reminding her of when he'd spoken to the group in Dallas. That seemed so long ago, although it was only a few weeks. Bridget just hoped there were no surprise guests this time. Vaughn refused to speak about his father's betrayal. No one had seen or heard from Ivan since.

Vaughn continued, "It was my dear brother Jack here who gave me the insight I needed." He nodded at Jack, who waved jauntily around the table.

What? When did that happen? Bridget thought. Obviously, Vaughn hadn't told her everything he and Jack had talked about.

"We need to get as close as possible to him, obviously, and we will need to keep him in solid form without him being able to escape into shadows. That's the hardest part. We need a diversion. Davis, Shepard, and Jack have been working on that plan. They assure me it's a good one, but will be hard to pull off. They will need a green wielder to go with them."

No one was surprised when Siobhan volunteered. Vaughn shook his head, "Shi, I appreciate it, but you will be needed at base; we have another task for you."

She frowned; she clearly wanted to be on the front lines but deferred to Vaughn's leadership.

Another hand rose. It was a wielder from Greece who was quite powerful. He and Shepard had been hanging out and quickly became friends. Many nods indicated this was a good choice.

"Thank you, Dio," Vaughn said, then turned and faced her. "My darling Bridget, you know I promised to keep you safe always. I promised I would never hurt you."

She nodded, nervous about where this was going.

"You know you are the key to the success of our efforts. Only with your powers can we stop the Shadow Claw."

She shrugged and nodded again.

"This has to be your choice, my dear. I cannot protect you from harm during this mission. It will be my number one priority, but I cannot guarantee it. Some of us may not make it out, but we are all going into this with years of knowledge of what the Shadows can do. Prophecy or not, this is your decision."

Hilde started to protest, but Circe slapped a hand over her mouth and sighed happily. "I love a happy ending," she whispered. Hilde looked at her like she was insane. Bridget figured she might be, just a little bit.

Everyone was waiting for her answer. She stood tall, "Of course, I'm in. These shadows have caused my family too much pain. I can't let them do it to anyone else when I have the ability to stop it." The group cheered, toasting each other.

After a round of drinks were passed out, Vaughn nodded at Jack who smiled and came around behind him. Vaughn tapped a spoon on a glass to quiet the room. He stood, looking extremely uncomfortable.

Bridget looked at Jorrie, who looked back at her and shrugged; she didn't know what was going on either.

Jack waved at Gabe, who bolted from his chair and ran to stand next to them. He was bouncing on his toes and grinning.

Bridget tried to link Vaughn to ask him what was going on, but Drake was humming and not responding. Something was up.

"As we are here, surrounded by our closest friends and family, I have one more thing to do before we launch this mission. I have been warned and threatened that I am, under no circumstances, to leave this child." Here he wrapped Gabe in a playful headlock, then let him go.

"What was it? Ah, yes, a poor motherless child. So, to that end, I need to get some insurance. It's something that I never thought I would be able to do, so I'm not the best at this. In fact, I'm probably doing a terrible job. But you know when something is right, you must move on it. You must move quickly before life throws changes your way. I had this wonderful speech all prepared, but I can't remember a word of it." Vaughn paused and blushed.

Everyone was looking at him in shock. He was babbling. Vaughn Drake did not babble. And he did not blush.

Jack leaned forward and stage whispered, "Just get on with it."

Vaughn pulled Bridget to her feet. As she stood, he dropped to one knee. A loud cry went around the table as they realized what was happening. He held out a hand to Jack, who passed him a velvet box.

Bridget's eyes were fixed on Vaughn's face.

"Bridget, I know we haven't been together long, but we are bonded mates, and that is a bond that transcends a lifetime. I'm usually more eloquent, but all I can think to say is I love you beyond reason and everything else in this world. You are my world and my reason for living. Please, do me the honor of becoming my wife."

A tear rolled down her face as he slipped a large black diamond on her finger. The band was gold, with two sweeping pieces cradling the diamond, reminding her of his beautiful wings. It was stunning. She looked at him and nodded. "Yes, of course, Vaughn Drake, I will marry you."

He stood and wrapped her in his arms, delivering a passionate kiss that made most of the ladies and some of the men fan themselves.

Cheers resounded around the room, and everyone clamored to congratulate the couple.

Gabe tugged on Vaughn's arm and whispered in his ear. Vaughn held his hand up for silence. He motioned Jorrie over. She stepped warily to the growing group. "Earlier, I mentioned this was also an insurance policy. Now, Jack and Gabe have already given their blessing. Obviously, I love Bridget and want to marry her as soon as possible, but I have been advised that if we were to get married without giving Jorrie the opportunity to participate, she will—"

He turned to Gabe, who announced, "Rip your balls off and feed them to you." The room was suddenly full of choking sounds as people tried to cover their laughter.

Jorrie covered her face with one hand and shook it.

Vaughn continued, "So to ensure that Jorrie does *not* get her hands on my balls," more laughter, "We will hold the wedding after we defeat the Shadow King to make absolutely sure Jorrie gets her chance."

Applause broke out, and Jorrie decided to accept it and bowed deeply.

Jack popped the first of many bottles of champagne. "We expect you all at the wedding, but for now, drink up everyone! Tomorrow, we fly."

Jorrie ran around Vaughn to Bridget and grabbed her friend's hand. She looked at the ring and then up at Bridget's happy face. She squealed in that high-pitched shriek of hers that shouldn't be in the audible range of human hearing but somehow was. All of the dragons in the room with their super sensitive ears clapped their hands to the sides of their heads and stared at her wide-eyed.

"Hey Bridget," called Liam, "If you don't defeat the Shadow King, maybe Jorrie can do that and liquefy his brain!"

Jorrie pointed at Liam, motioned like she was cutting a throat and pointed at him again. The grin fell from his face, and the guys around him slapped him on the back, laughing. Jorrie turned back to Bridget. "Girl, my teeth hurt from all this sappy sweetness." she smiled, then faltered. She whispered, "Can we go somewhere and talk? In private?"

Bridget looked at her friend in concern, Jorrie wouldn't ask if it wasn't important. She sent Vaughn, *be right back!* She saw him nod while he was having his ear talked off by Gabe and Bunny. She took Jorrie's arm, and they left the banquet room, going outside under the guise of getting fresh air.

There was a lovely bench outside under some hanging bougainvillea, so they sat and breathed in the warm night. Jorrie was sitting with her hands on the edge, leaning slightly forward over her knees. She was tapping her left foot at a fast tattoo.

Bridget became concerned. This was very unlike her friend. She waited for her to speak, but she continued to sit there, tapping her toes. Finally, she couldn't take it and grabbed her friend's hand. "Jorrie. Talk to me. Now," she ordered.

Jorrie looked at her. "I need to tell you something, but I don't know how. I don't even know if I believe it, but I promised I would tell you." She took a deep breath. "I need a minute. Talk about something else." She waved a hand at her.

Bridget sat back and thought, then smiled and said, "Okay, something else? You're on, sister! So, tell me when you are going to jump the lovely, masculine, and oh-so-yummy Liam. Hmm? Don't you want to? What was it you told me, oh yes, climb him like a tree? I recall that's what you told me to do with Vaughn, and here I am, bonded and engaged?"

Jorrie stared wild-eyed at her friend.

She laughed and had mercy. "I'm not saying you need to do all that, but come on, Jorr. The sexual tension wafting off you two is enough to get ten virgins pregnant. He wants you so bad, he's ready to roast any man who comes near you. You don't have to marry him, but you need to have sex and find out if you're compatible. It's exhausting watching you circle each other."

The blonde woman nodded, her curls bouncing furiously. "I know, it's frustrating because he doesn't want to overstep, with you being my best friend and mated to his boss, and he's sorta old fashioned. He wants to 'court' me. I just don't know." She looked at Bridget for guidance. "It doesn't seem this is the time to start something, with this battle on the horizon."

Bridget gazed softly at her best friend. She put her arm around her and leaned their heads together. "Jorrie, that's why this is the best time. You never know what tomorrow will bring. It's not guaranteed. Also, let me tell you, girl, it will be the best sex of your life. Two words: magic healing."

Jorrie laughed and gave her a thumbs up. "Sold! Okay, Bridge, here's the rest."

CHAPTER 41

THE FOLLOWING AFTERNOON, EVERYONE gathered in the field at Bunny's parents' farm. It had been a hectic morning, and Bridget hadn't seen Jorrie. When she finally spotted her, she positively sparkled. She smiled and snuck up behind her. "So, how was it?"

Jorrie jumped and turned around. "Bridge." Her friend smiled. "I. LOVE. YOU!"

She hugged her. "Told ya."

Liam strolled by just then, glancing over.

Bridget grinned at him, giving him a thumbs up.

He blushed at first, then came over and dipped her over his arm, giving her a big, noisy kiss. Both ladies laughed themselves silly.

Vaughn appeared. "Excuse me, Liam? May I ask why you are kissing my future wife?" Fortunately, he was smiling, knowing they were playing.

Liam turned, smiling back at him. "Because your mate is the reason I can do this!" He grabbed Jorrie, threw her over his arm in a similar dip and kissed her deeply. Cheers and wolf whistles echoed across the field. He slowly brought her back upright, but they continued with their kiss.

Bridget thought she was going to have to remind them to come up for air when they finally broke apart.

They stared into each other's eyes for a moment, and he pulled on one of her curls before strutting away, whistling. Jorrie sighed with deep satisfaction and wandered the other way, humming lightly.

Your work, I assume? Vaughn asked Bridget.

She grinned. *They were already heading that way. I just gave them a nudge so we could avoid the huge cloud of pheromones when we walk past them.*

Vaughn laughed, *so who's next on your matchmaking radar?* Just then, Gabe and Bunny strolled past, hand in hand. Vaughn wiggled his eyebrows suggestively.

Oh, HELL no! Bridget replied. She looked around and saw Siobhan leaning against a tree, looking sad and a little lonely. She smiled.

Vaughn put his hands on her shoulders. "I wish you luck with that." He sauntered away, laughing, to coordinate the take-off of a large contingent of dragons in the middle of the day. It wasn't going to be easy, but she knew he could handle it.

Bridget ambled casually over to Siobhan and leaned against the tree with her.

Siobhan sighed. "Don't."

"Don't what?"

"Don't come over here and do whatever it is you were going to do. Don't be cheerful, don't ask my opinion about my brother and your friend, don't try to set me up with anyone, and don't try to give me any sympathy." She crossed her arms.

Bridget continued to lean against the tree quietly. "Hmm. That's a lot to unload. I can't help but be cheerful, but I'll do my best to be a downer around you. I don't want your opinion about your brother and my friend. They're happy, and that's all that matters. I'm not going to set you up with anyone because you are too grumpy for me to offer up to anyone I care about, and I'm not giving you an ounce of sympathy, you ungrateful brat." She stood in silence for a moment. "I just wanted to know if you'd read any good books lately." Out of the corner of her eye, Bridget saw Siobhan slowly turn towards her in shock.

She heard a strange noise and realized Siobhan was giggling. She turned to face the girl, who began to belly laugh so hard that others dropped what they were doing to stare. It transformed her face, and she was stunning. Bridget mentally checked a point for herself on her internal scoreboard. "I'm waiting."

The squads were ready to take off, and Bridget not only had a list of surprisingly interesting books to read, but Siobhan had loaned her a thriller she had just finished and recommended. She wondered if she could read while flying. Did one get carsick on the back of a dragon? Or would that be airsick? Dragon sick? She'd have to ask Vaughn. Speak of the devil, he strode over to her, his black hair gleaming in the Italian sun.

She was struck all at once; this amazing, gorgeous, and kind man was her soon-to-be husband. This man she'd lusted after, fantasized about, wanted for months; he loved her, and he was hers. He started to tell her something, but she grabbed him and kissed him soundly.

He smiled and brushed her hair from her face. "Not that I'm complaining, my love, but what was that for?"

She shrugged, "I just love you. I have a question, though. Do people get carsick on dragon back? Like, would that be air sick or?" Her questions continued until it was time to fly.

They were able to transform in groups this time as they had much more space to spread out. Since everyone knew what to expect, it went much faster than their previous group flight. Before you could say Holy Dragon Shimmer, they were off.

Vaughn's group took the lead flight as they had the vehicles parked near the rendezvous point. They were going to secure and ward the site, then get more vehicles for the remainder of the force coming back with them. Bridget learned that Vaughn had been counting on bringing back a team, so had already made arrangements. The man was a wonder.

This time, they were one dragon short of the original squad, as Ivan was long gone. Bridget noticed that Vaughn looked towards the spot where his father should have been, then turned away, a cold look in his eyes. The strange but kind Circe had offered to fill that spot instead and carry the baggage. Bridget learned that Circe was a silver dragon, which was why she looked like Killian to an extent. The silvery hair was a common trait.

Once they landed, the men went to get the additional vehicles, while the women and Gabriel stayed to direct the remaining groups in and set up wards. The next squad to land consisted of Hilde in the lead, with Bunny's parents, and Bunny herself. Her mother was a dragon, a brown like her daughter, her father a wielder.

There were also two red dragons from the island. Their names were Lorenzo and Tomi. They were very serious about their duties and didn't speak much. Bridget hoped she could keep their names straight.

The first round of SUVs began to pull up, and gear was being loaded as the next few squads flew in. This continued for several waves until she spied Wu, a green dragon, and another group of reds that Bridget had met just that morning. She waved them in and counted. That should be everyone. Combined with their team in Dallas, they now had a significant fighting force. Soon, everything would be loaded, and they could go.

Bridget stood halfway down the point looking out at the ocean as a sudden cold wind whipped in and churned the waves. She heard someone calling her name and figured it must be time to leave. But she was drawn to the sea. It seemed that's where the voice was coming from. She walked to the end of the point and leaned over the railing. She couldn't see anything below but gray water as the waves got rougher and began to crash against the rocks, sending a chilly spray in the air.

The wind picked up, whipping into a frenzy and her hair was blown all around. It seemed time slowed down, and everything stopped. She was waiting for someone or something but couldn't explain it. She heard Vaughn screaming her name and turned slowly as if she were stuck in syrup or glue. He looked like he was running, reaching out to her, but he was barely moving. It was strange; she felt disconnected, and she couldn't explain it. She heard laughter behind her and turned again.

Rising from the depths was a large menacing shadow, growing quickly in size and reaching for her. A man stepped out and stood on the waves with his hand outstretched.

"Come to me, Bridget," she heard, "Come and see what I can show you in the shadows."

Bridget shook her head. The shadows? She didn't want to go there. She studied the man in front of her. He was incredibly handsome, with rich brown hair hanging in waves to his collar and piercing emerald-green eyes, but they were hard and cold. Colder than the water deep below him. He had beautiful, full lips that should have been enticing, but they were instead set in a cruel sneer. His face was angular and sharp, not warm and welcoming.

She heard Vaughn behind her, still yelling her name. It was muffled as if he were far away. The man smiled again and reached towards her. A cold wind wrapped around her ankles and flowed up her body until it cleared her head. She shook away the greasy fog clouding her mind and turned, "Vaughn!" She screamed as the cold hand grabbed her left wrist and pulled her towards the looming shadow with the Angel of Death waiting within. She saw it in his eyes. Vaughn was terrified. She inhaled to scream again when the shadow wrapped itself around her throat and squeezed. She couldn't draw a breath! The shadow squeezed harder and began to climb upward to her mouth and nose. It was going to cut off her air completely. She began to panic.

Fight.

She heard it. That same whisper she'd heard in the dark. And those quiet moments in her dreams.

Fight it!

Bridget nodded as best she could and pulled on her magic. Her hair began to lift and snap. Blue arcs sizzled between the fingers on her right hand. She reached over and clamped it down on the wrist that was gripping her own. Electricity zinged up the arm of her captor, causing him to spasm and release her. She threw herself away from him as he yelled, grabbing his arm.

"You bitch!" he roared. He retreated into the shadow, and Bridget shuddered in relief.

Gasping for air, she turned towards Vaughn and smiled. It was short-lived when she saw his eyes widen in fear. She turned back to see the shadow looming over her, ready to crash down like a wave on the shore. She closed her eyes and tried to scream, but no sound came out. The cold wind came again as it rushed over her, a second before she was snatched up by a large golden claw.

She heard a roar of frustration and looked back at the shadow. It was sinking back into the ocean. Thank goodness Vaughn had grabbed her just in time.

"BRIDGET!" He screamed her name.

Wait, how could that be? He couldn't speak in dragon form. She looked up beyond the golden claw and realized it wasn't Vaughn who had her. She panicked and began to squirm when a whisper came to her mind.

Shh, my daughter. You are safe now. The huge white dragon above her circled the point, decreasing his altitude before lining up to land.

Bridget's mouth gaped open. The dragon had spoken in her mind! And it was white. She didn't remember Vaughn mentioning anything about white dragons.

How can you speak in my mind? She asked.

She heard a laugh, then a whisper, *it's a secret, tell no one.*

Bridget nodded silently, and the dragon laid her gently in Vaughn's outstretched arms before landing smoothly in the plaza.

After checking her over multiple times, Vaughn finally let her stand on her own feet. The white dragon, which strangely now looked gray, was still standing nearby. He seemed in no hurry to change.

"Who is that?" demanded Vaughn, but she had no answer for him.

She slowly walked to the dragon and stood in front of him. He lowered his massive head and looked her in the eyes. She could swear he looked white again. He slowly blinked one eye.

He winked at me, she realized. She glanced over her shoulder, but no one else seemed to have noticed. Okay, so they had a secret for now. She had an awful lot of those lately. "I," she croaked. She swallowed and had to try again, her throat was still sore from the shadow attack. "I want to thank you for saving my life. I don't know how you managed to be there in time, but I'm glad you were. If there's anything, well, I don't know what I could offer you, but if I can ever do anything for you, please let me know." She spread her hands to show that she was not sure what she could really do.

He nodded at her.

She glanced around again and saw that Vaughn was talking to Wu, who had hobbled over. *You do want something,* she thought to him.

He nodded again. The whisper came to her: *Fight.*

Bridget's mouth dropped. This was the same voice she'd been hearing. This strange dragon, who kept shifting from white to gray, was the one pushing her to be strong and keep going.

Wu walked up to them. "Bridget, my dear, thank goodness you are safe. I do hope you have suffered no ill effects from your experience?" He seemed relieved when she shook her head no. She was in pain, but it wasn't permanent. He turned to the large dragon sitting there, who suddenly lifted a hind leg and scratched his ear like a dog.

Bridget slapped her hands over her mouth to stifle the laugh that almost came bursting out. Not only would it have hurt her throat, she didn't want to offend the white dragon.

The dragon winked at her again before focusing on Wu.

"Okay Tar'n. Enough showing off. If I'd known you were coming with us, I would have waited for you."

The dragon shimmered and suddenly, the tall, robed man from the Council hearing was there, hood and all.

How did he do that, she wondered.

Tell no one, he reminded her.

Bridget nodded slowly.

Vaughn stepped up and grabbed his hand. "Tar'n, please, accept my thanks and gratitude for saving my mate from the Shadow King. We never thought he'd dare show his face here, but I cannot ever repay you for the gift you have given me. I owe you a life debt."

Tar'n's hood studied Vaughn. "And I believe you would honor such a debt, young Master Drake. But your life is destined for other things. It was a pleasure to save your lovely mate. That is all the thanks I need."

He walked away with Wu tottering next to him, looking so much like Yoda and Obi Wan, Bridget began to laugh, but it hurt too much and turned to sobs, just as painful.

Vaughn gathered her close and held her until her shaking subsided. He brushed her hair away from her face in a familiar gesture and kissed her forehead before picking her up and carrying her to the car.

Back in Rome, they were gathered at the restaurant of the kind family that had hosted them weeks earlier. It was a lifetime ago to Bridget. She was exhausted and somewhat queasy from her ordeal. Jorrie sat next to her, rubbing her back in small circles, while Gabe sat on the other side, holding her hand and refusing to let anyone else near her. The conversations were a mix of voices at different levels and tones, and it was giving her a headache. She rubbed her temples and couldn't wait until they were on the plane so she could lie down in the back. Vaughn had told her it had a bedroom, and she could take a nap.

Vaughn picked up on her distress and signaled to get everyone's attention. The lessening of the noise had a significant impact on her well-being, and she began to feel somewhat better.

"You all saw what happened on the point to an extent, but here's what you don't know. The shadows now have confirmation that Bridget is the Wielder of Prophecy. They tried to grab her right in front of us and saw her wield. This tells me they are desperate. Also, the one who made the attempt was none other than the Shadow King himself." Gasps went around the room.

Bridget reeled. She'd heard Vaughn say that earlier but didn't quite connect the dots. Now, she was stunned. She jumped to her feet and was dizzy for a moment. She steadied herself on the back of a chair and straightened. She looked around and thought no one had noticed until she saw Jack's face.

He was studying her seriously. He tilted his head at her.

She begged him with her eyes not to mention it.

He gave an almost imperceptible nod.

She inserted her still raspy voice into the conversation, which gained everyone's attention. "Thank you all for your kind concern today. I'm fine. I just need a little rest. Before we head to the airport, there are things you need to know. One, the Shadow King definitely knows what we are doing, and he is going to be prepared for us. We need to adjust our tactics; no simple diversion will work. Two, he is pissed about what I did to him and wants me dead. Three, I know for certain now, we can kill him."

CHAPTER 42

B RIDGET LEANED HER HEAD against the cool glass of the window and looked out at the bustling city of Rome. She hoped they could come back someday, on vacation and see more of the sights. She glanced over and saw Gabe sitting with Bunny. They were playing Cloud Warrior on his handheld. Jorrie had her hand in Liam's they were staring into each other's eyes. Davis and Shepard were whispering together with their new friend, Dio, about the diversion plan they had devised.

Many of the others were on the second plane that Vaughn had sent to accommodate the large group now traveling to the US.

They were getting ready for take-off, just waiting for Jack, who'd had some errand he needed to run before he got on the plane. He leapt on board, and the attendant sealed the door behind him.

He came and flopped down in the seat next to hers and looked at her. "Babe," he said softly, "You know I love you, right?"

She looked at him startled. "Of course, I do!" she rasped.

He smiled and replied, "Good, because I mean this in the most loving way possible. But you look like shit. I got you something." He handed her a brown paper sack.

She shook it, "What is it?"

"Medicine for your headache and your poor throat," he told her. "Now be a good girl and buckle your seat belt; we're leaving."

After the plane reached cruising altitude and it was safe to move, Jack shooed Bridget to the bathroom to wash her face, take the medicine, and go to bed.

In the bathroom, she looked in the mirror and had to admit he was right. She did look pretty peaked, and her throat had ugly bruising. Great, she was going to need to wear a scarf in summer until that healed. Her head was pounding again. She opened the bag and saw it wasn't just Tylenol in there. She stared down at the contents and thought, *God bless you Jack.*

After downing the pills and getting some bottled water from the attendant, she went and laid down on the bed. It was surprisingly soft and perfect for her to stretch out. She lay there, reading the book Siobhan had loaned her and eating gummy bears.

Vaughn walked in and sat down next to her. He glanced at her snack and said, "Where did those come from?"

She winked and saluted him with a red bear before she bit its head off. "Jack. He got me some Tylenol and my favorite candy to help me feel better."

Vaughn sat silently and then kissed her forehead. "I'm sorry, my love; I should have thought of that myself."

She waved off his apology. "It's okay, you've been so busy coordinating this rabble. It's fine. Jack could tell I had a headache, and he knew I needed some sugar to combat the after-adrenaline crash. He's known me for years. He just picked up on it quicker because he wasn't trying to save the world." She smiled to let him know he was off the hook.

"How are you now, my love?" he asked her softly.

"Much better, but you know what would really help?"

He gestured for her to go on.

"If you would lie here with me and hold me for a while?"

He laid back on the bed and pulled her over to him.

She snuggled in and sighed. They lay there for a moment, and he closed his eyes, breathing her in.

Shortly, he realized she was shaking and crying. "Bridget," he said, knowing she had been putting on a brave face. "Shh. My sweet Bridget, it's okay, you're safe now. He will never touch you again."

"You don't know that!" she wailed.

He gripped her tightly. "You're right, I can't guarantee it. But I swear to you, if he does touch you, it will be because I'm dead. Because that's the only way he would get you."

She cried harder, and Vaughn cursed himself. Apparently, that had not been the right thing to say.

"My love! I'm sorry! I didn't mean to make it worse. I just wanted you to know that I would rather die than ever let him touch you. And I have no plans of dying; dragons are very long-lived." He kissed her temple.

Her tears slowed, and she gripped his shirt tightly. "That's the other problem," she said softly, her voice shaking.

He pondered a moment, "I'm so sorry, I don't understand. What is the other problem?" She was silent for so long that he became nervous. "Bridget?" he prompted, his voice thick with emotion.

"You're so long-lived. You're already over two hundred years old, I'm thirty-seven, you have centuries, I have forty, fifty years at most. I'll be an old, wrinkled mess, and you'll still look like that," she said, waving at his face. "Why would you shackle yourself to that? And when I die from being an old woman? Will you lose your magic? I don't want you to die!" She was nearing hysteria.

Vaughn couldn't help it; he burst out laughing.

Bridget was so shocked she stopped crying and stared at him incredulously.

He sat up and leaned over her, covering her lips with his, kissing her fiercely.

She responded with a desperation that scared her.

"I'm so sorry! I don't mean to laugh. I'm not laughing at you; I'm laughing at my own stupidity. I shouldn't have assumed you knew." He shook his head.

"Knew what?" she sniffed, suspicious.

"Bridget, Wielders already age very slowly. They are very long-lived as well. Killian is almost a century old. When a dragon mates with a Wielder, that Wielder receives part of the dragon's magic and longevity. That's why there is a ritual for the mating bond. It transferred some of my life force to you. You will age at the same rate I do."

She stared at him, not quite believing what she was hearing. "But, but," she stammered.

He smiled gently, "I *am* sorry, my dear. Why else would dragons willingly tie their lives to humans if that wasn't a perk? No dragon ever wants to outlive their mate. You and I will be together for a long time. A *very*, long time. I hope you don't get tired of me."

She sniffled a few more times, whispering, "Thank you, my love. Sorry, I flipped out like that. I guess a near-death experience left me off balance."

He kissed her forehead and laid back down, pulling her to him again.

She snuggled right back like a puzzle piece locking in.

"Don't ever apologize for having normal feelings. You went through an awful situation. Quite frankly it surprises me you didn't fall apart before now. You're one tough lady." He closed his eyes.

"Vaughn?" she said softly.

He opened his eyes and saw a green bear dancing in his face.

"Gummy bear?"

"Bridget," Vaughn whispered sometime later.

"Mmm," she mumbled back.

"Bridget," he said a little louder and shook her gently.

"Five more minutes," she grumbled into the pillow. She heard a deep, rumbly laugh.

"My darling, you know I would give you all of the time in the world, but we are landing soon, so you have to go back to the main cabin."

Bridget opened one eye and saw Vaughn smiling at her. "It's a good thing you're cute," she grumped. The medicine had helped her headache, but she was still out of sorts. Almost being kidnapped and strangled by a shadow creature, dangling from a dragon's claws, and having an emotional breakdown could do that, she supposed. She stretched, her arms up over her head, arching her back and pointing her toes. She looked at Vaughn and saw him staring at her with hunger in his eyes as her shirt rode up, exposing her stomach.

Caught staring, he smiled at her wolfishly, reaching for her.

She laughed, smacked his hand, and rolled away. She got out of bed and straightened her clothing. She let out an "oomph" as Vaughn wrapped her in his arms.

"Are you feeling better now?" he inquired softly.

"Mmm, much better," she replied, laying her head on his chest. They stayed that way for a few minutes until a knock sounded on the door, followed by the attendant's voice reminding them they needed to return to their seats.

"Be right there!" Vaughn called out. He was sure they had time enough for one more kiss.

Safely buckled in her seat, feeling much more alert, she caught Jack's eye and nodded. She mouthed thanks to him for his thoughtfulness earlier. He smiled in return. He really was everything she would have wanted in a brother of her own. She glanced around and saw the rest of the group was engaged in various activities, a slight tension in the air.

Jorrie was still sitting with Liam, holding hands, their heads bent low over what looked like some sort of diagram. As if sensing she was being observed, she glanced up at Bridget and gave her a wink. Seemed things were going well in that department.

She looked for Gabe and finally located him at the far end of the cabin. He appeared to be asleep in his seat, Bunny next to him, asleep as well, with her head on his shoulder. Bridget pursed her lips. She was not looking forward to the moodiness she would have to endure when Bunny eventually went back to Italy and Gabriel stayed in Dallas for school.

Vaughn appeared next to her, bringing her a ginger ale and sitting down. She thanked him and took a few sips, appreciating the cold bubbles on her throat.

"Figured you needed to settle your stomach; you were a little green earlier," he told her.

The plane made its descent into Dallas and touched down smoothly at the private airport. She wasn't sure how he managed all of this, the money, the international rules they were probably breaking, but she figured there must be some magic involved to grease those wheels.

She glanced at Vaughn, but he was busy organizing the squads and arranging transport to the various hotels, so she decided not to bother him. She realized everyone was busy talking to someone or doing something useful. Feeling a bit out of sorts, she found a folding chair and plopped down in it. She propped her chin in her hands and observed the scurrying back and forth.

Siobhan walked over and gestured at her throat. "I could maybe help with that," the girl said shyly. "Sorry, I should have thought of it earlier, but I was on the other plane."

Bridget smiled; it seemed their talk earlier had broken down some more walls. "That would be lovely if you think you can. I was thinking I'd have to wear a scarf for a while, and it's too hot for that."

Siobhan nodded emphatically, understanding exactly what she meant. She held her hands near Bridget's throat and sent gentle green waves over it.

"Oh wow!" Bridget said, stretching her neck. "That feels amazing! I'm so impressed with how you've managed to tweak your talents into something more. You should be proud of yourself too; I hope you'll be willing to teach me more about my own powers. I could learn a lot from you!"

Siobhan straightened and beamed. She was like a flower blossoming in the warm sunshine.

Bridget figured it must have been hard growing up in a dragon family, in Liam's shadow, knowing she would never have wings of her own. She smiled, "I'm so appreciative of all you've done. Thank you so much."

"It was most impressive, Wielder. I am never seeing someone master skills outside of their own spectrum before." A rich male voice came from behind the girl.

Siobhan whirled to face the man who had spoken. It was one of the very handsome red dragons from Italy. Lorenzo or Tomi, Bridget couldn't remember which.

She spoke up, "Our Siobhan is very talented, isn't she? She's got an impressive amount of control over her magic. She taught me how to perform basic things without frying my brain in one day!" She saw Siobhan blush and try to deny it.

He nodded. "That is fascinating. I desire to learn more about you, Wielder. Would you walk with me?" He held out his arm for Siobhan.

She looked at Bridget, who nodded and made shooing motions.

"I'll be damned!" she heard from behind her. Vaughn was standing there watching Siobhan walk off arm in arm with the red dragon. She was smiling, a faint blush on her cheeks. He shook his head. "You really have a way with people, you know?"

She grinned at him. "Nothing a little positivity couldn't have handled."

"In that case, how about some positive thoughts for a safe trip home?" he grinned.

"Way ahead of you babe!"

CHAPTER 43

ONE WEEK LATER

Vaughn watched as Bridget wandered into the living room after spending some time with her cats. There were dragons and wielders everywhere. Almost every room in the large home was full of people. Some were their local force, and some were the Italian team. After their return home, dragons and wielders from all over the world had begun showing up. They came from Australia, China, Mexico, and Nigeria, to name a few. According to the rumors he'd heard, all the local hotels were full for some convention. Bridget was smiling; she'd told him she was fascinated with so many accents and dialects.

He continued to watch her flitting from group to group, smiling and talking to people. She certainly seemed to feel better. He'd worried about her after the attack. She hadn't bounced back quite as quickly as he'd hoped, seeming restless. He sensed there was something she wasn't telling him, but he didn't want to push her. Regardless, she seemed herself again and for that, he was grateful. He reasoned being back home and in familiar surroundings had done wonders. Home. The word made his smile falter.

They'd come back to a gazillion waiting messages: police and arson inspectors wanted to speak to her about her house. They'd also received messages from the insurance company needing statements. They still needed to replace many of the things she'd lost. He looked at some of the rooms and imagined what they'd look like with her touch on them. He smiled, realizing he was looking forward to it.

"Drake," he heard the hesitant voice from the doorway of the dining room where he'd set up his war room. He saw Marco standing there, tablet in hand, no doubt the data he'd sent him to obtain waiting for review. It had already been a week since they arrived back in Dallas, and everyone was getting antsy. He waved him inside, and they sat down to review the information with the appointed leaders of the different squads.

The plan hadn't changed too much. There was really only one way to approach, and they still needed to take out the guards. The plan to have the Shadow King isolated and unable to shift into the shadows was solid, if a little unorthodox. They would have to trust they had sufficient lure to get him outside of his base.

Vaughn wasn't so sure about that part. Once he was out, he hated that Bridget had to get near him to use her power on him. He'd been agonizing over it for weeks. He sensed eyes upon him and looked up at the hood of Tar'n. He saw the hood dip slightly and frowned. He sometimes thought the ancient dragon could see into his mind.

The hood dipped again.

He sat back, floored. Okay, this was a little unnerving. It seemed like Tar'n could read his thoughts and agreed with him their plan to lure the Shadow King out was shaky.

Once again, the hood dipped, and he heard a low chuckle come from that direction.

"We need better bait," Vaughn said suddenly. Everyone in the room stopped and looked at him. "The plan, it's solid; it will work, but we need to provide him with a better reason to be outside at that time. He's not stupid. We need something that he can't resist. What is it he wants most in the world that would draw him out? Get him to lose sight of the significance of the day?" He looked around the room, seeing frowns of concentration. They agreed with him, he could see that, but it seemed no one could think of the one thing the Shadow King wanted, besides more power.

Vaughn sat there, his brow furrowed, chin in his hands, thinking. They needed to get this figured out, and soon or, they would miss their chance and have to wait two more months. He didn't think they could fend off the attacks that much longer. Reports were coming in from all over the world. Shadows were attacking wielders, ambushing dragons, stealing precious artifacts and generally wreaking havoc. They were getting bolder by the day. He slammed his hand on the table, making everyone jump. "Think!" Vaughn commanded, "What does a King who can just take anything really want? What is the one thing he doesn't have?"

The answer came from a small, soft voice at the doorway. "Me," Bridget whispered.

"*Absolutely not!*" Vaughn roared as he paced the length of his bedroom. His steps were quick and forceful.

Bridget stared at the carpet in detached interest. "Vaughn," she began.

"NO!" he whirled, smoke pouring from him like a chimney.

He watched her turn on the bathroom exhaust fan, in an effort to clear up the room a bit. He sat on the bed, with his hands clenched in his hair. Quietly, she sat next to him, her hands in her lap, and waited.

He grabbed her and crushed her to him, "I can't lose you," he whispered. "It would kill me."

She heard the note of panic in his voice and began to run her fingers through his hair. "Vaughn," she tried again, and this time he was silent. "We both know he wants me. I'm the prophecy. I'm the one foretold to destroy him. How else can I do that if you don't let me get close to him?" She heard him heave a big sigh. "Think, my love, he tried to grab me in Italy. He's been trying to have his shadows grab me for weeks now. I'm the one thing he can't have, and you know I'm right."

He growled, "That part is right. He. Can't. Have. You." He bit out each word like it had a terrible taste.

She smiled, "My fierce warrior. That's why I'm willing to do this. Because I know you won't let him have me. I know you will protect me and bring me home. We have a wedding to plan, remember?" She kissed his burning brow, jumping back before her lips were scorched. His flames were close to the surface.

He looked at her, defeated. "I can't save you though, can I?"

She looked at him, his eyes full of misery.

"I couldn't save you at the point. He almost had you because I wasn't fast enough." He dropped his head again.

"Vaughn," she whispered, "That wasn't your fault. I shouldn't have wandered away from the group. He found me alone and isolated. He surprised us because we never thought he would come himself. This is different. This time, we are bringing the fight to him, and you will be by my side the whole time."

Vaughn looked at her. He knew she was right. He knew this was the way it had to be, but the thought of setting her out as bait in a trap, like a carrot dangling on a stick, he couldn't stomach it. The thought of losing her or her being harmed gave him a cold sweat. He'd barely slept at all since she was attacked. When she slept on the plane, he lay awake the whole time, watching the scene over and over in his head. The Shadow King grabbing her, wrapping his tendrils around her throat. He wanted to kill the bastard for touching his mate, but to think he'd almost taken her away forever, he wanted to go full scorched earth. He stood and pulled her up to him.

Grab a blanket, meet me on the roof in ten, he told her. The smile on her face lit up the room and told him she knew exactly what he was doing. It settled his heart. Vaughn strode into the dining room and told the group the plan was going ahead with Bridget as bait. He left them to finish out the small details after advising he was going to be out of pocket the rest of the night.

There was some protest, but he growled and said, "If my mate is going to risk her life for you all, then I get to spend a night with her away from all of this." He went to the kitchen and packed a small cooler with water and a light dinner. He'd already grabbed a couple of towels and a brush for her, knowing she hated how messy her hair could get. He smiled at the strawberries and whipped cream in the fridge, thinking he could have some fun with those, when he sensed someone behind him.

He turned and saw Jack standing there with his arms crossed, looking concerned. Vaughn stood there, waiting for the man to say what was on his mind.

"I heard you're making Bridget the bait to lure the Shadow Douche from his hidey hole."

Vaughn smiled quickly at the nickname and nodded. Not trusting himself to say more.

"I don't like it!" Jack burst out, throwing his hands out in an explosive gesture. "It's not safe, she's not safe, how can you do that to her?" he demanded.

Vaughn understood Jack's feelings. He'd been there himself not too long before. "Jack, my brother, I know. But this was her idea, not mine. I tried to talk her out of it, but she's determined. She's the Wielder of Prophecy, and as she pointed out, how can she fulfill her role if we keep her coddled behind the line of fire? You've known her a long time. Have you ever talked her out of something when she has her mind set on it?"

Jack studied Vaughn's face. His shoulders sagged as he sighed. "Take care of her."

Chapter 44

BRIDGET THREW HER ARMS out to embrace the night air. It was glorious as the heat of the day had burned off, and the cooling effect from a rain shower earlier made the sky feel like silk on her skin. She leaned over Drake's neck as they flew north, patting the scales and enjoying the strong feeling of them. She didn't know if she'd ever get tired of flying with him this way. For a brief moment, she thought of telling him to keep flying and not to stop until they were far away from it all. But she knew she couldn't do that. She had her son and her family to think about. Quite a few things to think about, really. She sat up and watched the world pass by below them, the traffic and homes thinning out as they left the bigger cities behind and closed in on the lake.

Soon, Drake's wings flared up to slow them as they descended to his island.

As they settled into the sand, she spread the blankets out while he changed. She was bent over, looking for his clothes, when his arms went around her waist. She straightened and spun around into his arms. He kissed her with desperate passion, and she knew dinner would be delayed. They laid down on the blankets and made love as if they never would again. When they were both spent, he lit a small fire to keep her warm.

They sat by the fire, eating and talking about anything and everything except the coming battle. He was almost able to forget it was looming. After dinner, they lay wrapped up in each other, staring up at the stars, just enjoying the quiet and being together. He was right; the whipped cream was worth it.

As the morning sun filtered through the gaps between Drake's wing and body, Bridget woke, more rested than she'd been in a long time. This was exactly what she'd needed. No other people, no planning, no discussions of prophecy or magic, just being with the man she loved. She looked up at the giant scaly head next to her. Dragon, she loved, she smiled. Drake was still sleeping so she settled back into his body and dozed. She knew he hadn't been sleeping well lately, although he tried to hide it. He deserved the extra rest.

She was not going to admit it to Vaughn, but she was terrified. The risk was enormous, but the reward was too. She wrapped her arms around herself and listened to his breathing, warm and safe. She felt his side twitch slightly and knew he was rousing. She got to her knees and blew gently on one of his ears. It wiggled, and she gave a soft laugh. She started scratching the soft spot behind it, and a rumble came from him, as he tilted his head and leaned into it more. She giggled, and one eye opened, then winked at her.

As they were flying back, Bridget leaned forward and kissed Drake on top of his head. He chuffed to let her know he was aware. *Thank you for bringing me a brush and a bandana for my hair. Now, when we land, I won't look like I just lived through a tornado!*

A rumble sounded, and she knew that was all she was getting from him. He'd been strangely silent for most of the morning. She knew he was anxious about the days to come. She decided to just enjoy the flight and the gorgeous morning.

As they got closer to home, she glanced down at the traffic backing up for miles; it was rush hour. *Ha! So glad I'm not stuck in that. This is the only way to commute. You're like the DART, Dragon Area Rapid Transit!*

Drake turned his head back to look at her best he could and rolled his eyes.

She laughed so hard she had to tighten her grip so she didn't fall off.

After they landed back on the roof, Bridget sat in one of the chairs and studied the buildings around her while Vaughn changed to his human form and dressed.

He quietly sat beside her and took her hand. They sat together for a while before he sighed and stood, indicating it was time to go in. He held the door open for her, such a gentleman. SMACK! He whacked her on her butt.

She whirled, her mouth hanging open in surprise.

He was grinning.

"What was that for?" she demanded.

"That last joke, I'm not a metro transit service," he replied with a wink.

She stared at him in mock fury until she couldn't hold it together and laughed. She turned around and started down the stairs. She was almost to the bottom when she heard him laugh under his breath.

"DART."

They walked in the front door, and as expected, there were people everywhere. Bridget made a beeline for the kitchen; she smelled bacon, and she was suddenly starving.

Liam was cooking breakfast for an army, literally.

"Hey, Bridget!" he called and waved her over. He handed her a plate full of eggs, bacon, and some tortillas with salsa.

She tried to tell him she could wait; others were already in line, but he told her the Wielder of Prophecy didn't wait for breakfast in her own home. She blinked at him. She hadn't thought about it much, but she guessed this was her home now. She felt a wave of sadness wash over her at the thought of her house and the memories that had been reduced to ashes. Her shoulders drooped a little, but she reminded herself the most important thing was she, Gabe, and the cats were safe. She chewed a piece of bacon as she walked to the table to sit.

Jack and Jorrie came over with plates as well and sat with her. Jack pointed at his plate and said, "Brother of Wielder of Prophecy privileges."

Jorrie rolled her eyes and kicked him. "I helped cook so I grabbed us both plates," she confided. She studied Bridget's face. "I'm glad you two were able to escape last night; you look positively radiant today. You're glowing!"

Bridget thought about it, "I *feel* radiant today. I just have a really good feeling about this. We are going to pull this off, get rid of the Shadow threat, and then you two have a very important task."

They looked at each other and back at her.

"You have to help me plan my wedding!"

Jack leaned forward, "Okay, but which one of us is going to be your maid of honor?"

Jorrie kicked him again.

It was almost go time. Bridget took a deep, steadying breath. She ran through her mental checklist one last time. She practiced some of the hand movements Siobhan had taught her. She rechecked her gear for the tenth time. Finally, she had to admit everything was ready. She walked back to the room Liam and Gabe were sharing. Liam wasn't there, but Gabe was.

He was lying on the bed, throwing a tennis ball at the wall and catching it. His expression was thunderous.

She sighed; she knew he was upset that he wasn't going with them this time. "Gabe," she said softly.

Thump. Thump. Thump went the tennis ball.

"Gabe, baby, please."

Thump. Thump. Thump.

"Gabriel Ridgeway, you sit up and talk to me right now."

He sighed and set the ball down, sitting up. He didn't look at her, though.

"Honey, I know you are upset, I know how much you want, maybe even feel you need to come, but it's just not safe. I can't do what I need to do if I know you are there somewhere, unable to defend yourself."

Gabe turned hurt eyes full of angry tears on her. "I can take care of myself!" he declared.

Bridget shook her head, the mantra of all teens. "I know in a regular situation you could, you're super smart and very fast. But Gabe, this isn't a video game. These are real weapons, real teeth and claws, deadly magic, and real shadows. I need you here, where I know nothing will take you away from me. I couldn't stand to lose you too," she said softly but firmly so he knew she was serious.

He stood and clenched his fists. "I know that!" he yelled at her.

She was taken aback, he'd never even so much as raised his voice to her before.

"What if something happens to you? What happens to me then? Do you have a plan for that? Don't leave me, Mom. Don't leave." Suddenly, he threw his arms around her, sobbing into her shoulder.

She wrapped her boy in the tightest hug she could and held on.

Vaughn stood in the doorway, watching the heartbreaking scene in front of him. He couldn't imagine what the boy was going through. He'd lost his father, and now his mother was going off to do something extremely dangerous with no guarantee she would return. He knew that pain as well, having seen his own mother cut down in front of him. His father, well, that was a whole can of feelings he was not going to open just now. He walked in silently and wrapped his arms around them both.

He tousled Gabe's hair, like he'd seen Bridget do, and began speaking softly. "Gabriel, I swear, I will do everything within my power to get your mother back to you. Even at the cost of my own life."

Both mother and son looked at him, protesting. Gabe grabbed Vaughn in a hug, saying, "No! Don't you dare. I need you, too."

Vaughn stood there, with his emotions at war as he struggled not to breakdown with how much that moved him. He hugged him back. "You got it, Gabe. We will both come back to you."

Jorrie walked in and added herself to the hug, Jack right behind her. Jorrie added, "You better bring Jack back, too. I don't want to lose my Margarita buddy."

They all laughed, which broke the tension.

Jorrie would be staying behind with Gabe and Bunny. She wasn't super happy either but recognized that she was safer here as she had no magic, or claws. She didn't have fighting skills like Jack, either. Before they walked out, Jorrie grabbed Vaughn's sleeve and indicated he should stay. As the other voices faded down the hall, he looked at her quizzically.

She looked down for a moment and then spoke quietly. "While we are making requests, I was wondering if I could ask that you please bring Liam back to me as well."

Vaughn kissed Jorrie tenderly on the forehead and nodded. "I know, I love him too."

In the dining room, Vaughn paced the floor. He'd been waiting on a few people to show up that were uncharacteristically late. He was uneasy. With the attacks from the Shadows getting stronger by the day, he'd sent a small team to shore up the warding at Cloud Warrior headquarters. He glanced at his watch again and pulled out his phone to call Killian. As if he'd summoned him with his thoughts, the phone lit up with Killian's name. Vaughn sighed in relief and answered impatiently, "What the hell is…" He trailed off, hearing sirens in the background.

He listened then in stunned silence as Killian shared terrible news with him. Tears streamed down his face unchecked, and he whispered, "No." From the corner of his eye, he saw Bridget enter the room with concern on her face. She'd sensed his distress. He hung up with Killian after softly instructing him to hurry back.

He filled Bridget in through their mind link, the actual words being too painful to say out loud. "I have to tell them. I don't know if I can do this." He saw her eyes fill with tears as well; he knew she would also feel this loss deeply.

She cupped his cheek and kissed him gently. "Just do it. They deserve to know before someone else finds out and they hear it that way."

He nodded, "Let's go find them."

In the living room, only their closest friends and family were assembled. Liam looked up at them and grinned, "Hey, Drake, where've you been? We were…" He trailed off, seeing the grief plain on his Godfather's face. He leapt over the chair and slowly made his way over to stand in front of Vaughn.

"Drake? Vaughn, what happened?" His face looked much younger as fear traced across his features. He held out his hand and felt his sister take it, her grip hard and clammy.

"Vaughn?" The normally prickly woman whimpered as she looked at her brother for reassurance.

"I'm so sorry Liam, Siobhan. Brady and Joanna were with Eric, shoring up the warding at Cloud Warrior. They were ambushed, and, well, Eric was the only survivor. I'm so sorry."

Liam broke the stunned silence that followed, roaring loudly, his voice full of pain. As the others looked on, he and Siobhan dropped to the floor, holding each other, openly sobbing.

Bridget walked over to Siobhan and Liam. There were waves of green radiating around them, their grief visible to all. She looked back and saw the rest of the family following her to surround the siblings in love and comfort.

Liam gave Bridget a pain-filled stare, at a loss for what to do. He clearly wanted to put on a brave face to support his sister, but he didn't know how. Bridget had been that person for Gabe when Brian had died. Now, she could be there for Liam and Siobhan. She hoped anyway.

She settled a hand on Siobhan's shoulder and whispered, "I'm so incredibly sorry. Your parents were very brave. I know it doesn't seem like it now, but we will get through this. All of us, together."

Siobhan was full of rage and needed someone to explode at. "Yeah, you're so sorry, aren't you? We lost our parents. *Our parents!*" she yelled. "Our parents are dead. Do you understand that? Dead because of you!" She stood nose to nose with Bridget, her chest heaving, her fists clenched.

Bridget nodded slowly. "I do understand, Siobhan. I appreciate their sacrifice. I know what it's like to lose someone you love that much. My husband was killed by the shadows eight years ago, and there's not a day that goes by that I don't think about him and feel his loss. My parents died when I was young, too. Gabe and Jack are the only family I have left. I just want you to know that your other family is here for you when you need us." She stepped back then and turned to Liam.

He came to her and hugged her tightly, burying his face in her hair, sobbing.

She could hear Siobhan's rapid breathing behind her. Suddenly, Liam's arms were ripped away, and she was shoved back.

"Don't touch her!" Siobhan screamed at Liam.

He looked shocked. "Shi," he said tenderly.

"No!" she shouted, whirling on Bridget again. "She's the reason Mom and Dad are dead. Oh, she talks a big game; she lost her husband. I bet she doesn't think about him at all when she's fucking Drake. They're after her. It's her fault!" Siobhan was gathering herself to leap at Bridget when a deafening roar shook the room, followed by a burst of flame that narrowly missed her face.

"*Enough!*" Vaughn bellowed, standing next to Bridget, flames in his eyes. He looked terrifying. "Do not speak to my mate like that," he ordered in a ringing voice.

The girl jerked back like she'd been shot, then shuddered. "I'm sorry, I'm so sorry, Bridget, I know you didn't kill my parents. I know it wasn't your fault. I'm just so angry and I took it out on you when you were just trying to help. Please forgive me," she sobbed, covering her face.

Bridget smiled softly. "Honey, all is forgiven. I know that anger, come here."

Siobhan nodded and wrapped her arms tightly around Bridget before they sank to the floor.

Liam sat down and added himself to the hug, needing comfort, too.

Gabe, who had been sitting quietly throughout the situation, crawled under his mother's arms and hugged his friends, whispering his understanding to them as well. Soon everyone had joined them on the floor, and the group comforted the siblings late into the night.

CHAPTER 45

BRIDGET STRETCHED IN HER seat; she was glad she wasn't on a commercial flight like most of those going to Hawaii. There were just too many of them to all fit on the private plane. She'd met so many people lately, she didn't want to be cramped in with any more of them than necessary.

Shortly into the flight, Bridget caught Vaughn studying her face. She guessed he was wondering yet again if they were doing the right thing. She smiled to reassure him there wouldn't be any changing her mind.

She closed the book she'd been reading and took his hand. "You know, Jack and Jorrie are fighting over which of them gets to be my maid of honor."

He laughed, "If you chose Jack, would he wear a dress?"

She snorted, "No, Jack wouldn't wear a dress, he can't walk in heels and wouldn't be caught dead in flats. But, have you thought about who your best man will be? Liam or Killian?"

He shook his head, "No, I already have someone in mind. When we get back, and I show him his mother is fine, I'll ask him."

She sucked in a breath, and her eyes were damp. "Gabe?" she whispered.

He nodded, "I want him to know without a doubt that he's part of the benefits of being your husband."

She smiled, "Maybe Jack can be the flower girl."

He laughed, "Good choice and Liam can be the ring bearer. I'd want Killian up there with me."

"Tell me more about him. He's so quiet, but he seems to be a good friend of yours."

He told her more about the silver Wielder, how they'd met, about his family and then they talked about wedding plans, dates, locations, and other details.

She fell silent and saw he was watching Liam and Siobhan as they sat quietly together, holding hands and grieving their parents. She knew they were doing what they could to contain their grief so they could focus on the battle. Vaughn had offered for them to stay behind, but they'd wanted the battle to help them get justice for their family. She just hoped they didn't let their pain make them reckless.

Hours later, they were at their rendezvous spot, making final preparations. There were a few things they needed that they couldn't bring on the planes, so they were sourcing them locally. For the moment, they were just waiting on those they'd sent out to reconnoiter to return.

Marco came running into the large conference room at the hotel. "Drake, Drake!" he shouted, looking frantic.

Vaughn stood and waved him over.

Marco dashed to him, shoving a paper in his hands. "Sir, reports have been coming in from all over. Shadows are increasing attacks on wielder and dragon families alike, multiple times in each place, but only in these places. We can't account for it. It doesn't make any sense as a pattern. They started in Italy and moved to Ireland, then Russia, Spain, Japan, and finally to the US. They've attacked multiple cities. What do you think it means?"

A low growling filled the room, and conversation died down. The growling grew louder, and everyone turned to stare at Vaughn. A snarl left his lips, and suddenly, the paper was ashes on the floor. A small curl of smoke rose from the remaining fragments.

Bridget placed a hand on his arm, and he whipped his head towards her, flames flickering in his eyes. "Darling, what's wrong?" she said gently, smoothing a lock of hair away from his face.

"The list!" he spat out, staring down at the ashes again.

She nodded for him to continue.

"The list is about me. It started where I was born, where my mother was killed. Then, to the island where the Council imprisoned me. When I finally gained my freedom, do you remember I said I traveled for a while before settling in the US and finally Dallas?"

She nodded again, "I remember."

"These are all the places I stayed during my travels. At each of these places I made contact with wielders or other dragons. He's attacking the places and people that are important to me. It's a message that he's willing to destroy everything I love. To get you." He stared at her, anger and pain warring on his face.

She heard the intake of gasps around the room as the others gained the significance of what he was saying. She took his face in her hands, "Then let's go kill the bastard."

The flight to the island didn't take long enough, in Bridget's opinion, but the sun was already rising. The island was waking up, and they needed to set up their shields so no humans would see the battle or get caught up in it.

The green dragons and wielders set out for their stations, positioned evenly in a radius around the Shadow King's base. Their role was to erect and maintain a barrier around the base to deter bystanders and keep the Shadows inside. Liam flew off to manage his team on the north side of the complex.

The browns were burrowing underground, cutting off all utilities, and collapsing the tunnels under the compound. They were systematically destroying all methods of escape to keep the battle as contained as possible. The blues and silvers would play their part in providing distractions and traps, and the reds would siege the windowless base, taking out key areas and strafing anyone who tried to restore any services. Bridget knew it was more complicated than that, but she was focusing on her part instead.

She was going to channel Drake and use her EMP-type wave to knock out all power and energy sources, including backups, to the facility so they would have no light. They'd tested it, and even the batteries didn't work when she zapped them. Not even a basic flashlight would give them a shadow to use if she did it right. Being reliant on shadows, they would have to come outside to escape where they could be picked off quickly.

Bridget looked at Drake as he waited for the signal from the brown team. She could tell he had received it when he looked sharply at the blue and silver team leaders and nodded. They were off. It was beginning.

She made her way over to Jack, who was strapping a few more knives to his vest and getting ready to leave with Davis, Shepard, and Dio. They had a special mission, a diversion they hoped would leave the Shadow King off balance. She threw herself at him, and he held her tightly.

"You know he's going to be pissed when he finds out. He already doesn't understand why I'm going," he whispered to her.

She only nodded.

"Bridget, you should really think—"

"Shh," she cautioned. "I know what I'm doing. It has to be this way. He would never agree otherwise."

Jack looked at her and kissed her forehead. "I love you, baby sister. You live through this, you hear me? Or I swear to God I will find some crazy hooker voodoo Queen to raise your pain in the ass self from the dead just so I can yell at you. Understand me?"

"I love you too, Jack." They hugged then she turned to the blue dragons stretching their wings. "Hey, Davis!" she called. He turned to look at her. She pointed and said, "You bring him back to me, or I'm sending Jorrie after your balls."

The dragon's eyes widened, and he nodded emphatically. His brother was chuffing in a way that sounded suspiciously like laughter. Dio winced and looked busy.

She made her way back to Vaughn but was stopped in her tracks when Tar'n suddenly stepped in front of her.

You've done well so far, my daughter, he whispered in her mind.

She studied his hood, trying to discern any facial features at all. She could just make out a small smile on full lips.

Your hardest challenge is still to come. Are you willing to do what is needed?

She stared nervously at him, unsure what he meant.

When the time comes, you will need to reach deep inside. Will you be able to do that?

Bridget shook her head slowly, *I don't know.*

The cold wind suddenly wrapped around her ankles; she heard rustling leaves and one word. *Fight.*

She blinked, and Tar'n was gone.

Vaughn took her elbow. "Bridget? My love?"

She shook her head and focused on him. She'd been staring at the spot where the mysterious Tar'n had been standing before. She smiled at Vaughn and moved with him to the place where they were going to launch the next part of the attack. She heard the rumbles as the brown teams collapsed tunnels. She saw the blues and silvers preparing for their launch.

"Were you talking to Tar'n?" Vaughn asked her.

She wondered how much she could tell him. She was tired of keeping so many secrets, tired of the deception. She wanted to confide in him but knew it wasn't time yet. "He just wished us luck," she said, tasting the bitter, acrid tang of lies on her tongue.

Vaughn studied her; he knew something wasn't right. "Please, what's going on?"

She smiled at him, "Just nervous, it's almost time. I keep thinking, what if this goes wrong? What if we miss the window? What if Jack gets hurt, or Liam, or Marco, or anyone else we love? I'm trying to keep my mind off of it, but I'm doing a terrible job." That was better, as it was true.

He squeezed her shoulder, knowing he couldn't promise her otherwise.

CHAPTER 46

I T HADN'T BEEN LONG since the blues and silvers had left on their mission. They'd seen a few people try to escape. They were sucked down into the earth by the browns lurking there before they could get their bearings enough to escape into shadow. So far, the plan was going well. She'd seen Jack and the others leave on their side mission. She closed her eyes and prayed for them that all would go well.

Vaughn stood nearby, coordinating with the red's commander. It was almost time for their main attack. They finished speaking, and Vaughn shook hands with the fierce-looking man before he walked off to his squadron to brief them.

She heard a fluttering motion and noticed a large red dragon flying in behind them. *Who is that?* She wondered. The dragon landed, and she heard a snarl rip from Vaughn's throat. *Oh shit,* she had a second to think before he launched himself at the red.

It was Ivan.

His father transformed into human form just in time for Vaughn to barrel into him, already in his half-shifted form. He dug his talons into his father's shoulders. "Why are you here?" he demanded through his fangs. "You have no business here. This is not a mission for cowards and traitors."

"Son, listen," Ivan began.

"I'm *not* your son!" Vaughn shouted, "My father died over two hundred years ago, a hero in battle. He would never have walked away from me."

Bridget heard the pain in Vaughn's voice, and she wanted to tell him.

She heard a whisper in her mind, *not yet.*

She was angry, *then when?* She demanded in return.

Soon.

Several dragons had barely managed to restrain Vaughn and pull him from his father. One red lay on the ground, gasping for air for his efforts.

She turned to face him, knowing it was dangerous but trusting he wouldn't hurt her. "Vaughn!" she grabbed his arms.

He wrapped his talons around her wrists and snarled at her. Then he looked into her eyes and dropped her like she'd burned him. His fangs and claws retracted, and his eyes held shame. His wings dropped at his side.

"Bridget!" he whispered, horrified at what he'd almost done.

"Vaughn, I'm fine. You didn't hurt me. I knew you wouldn't. Listen to me, dammit, I'm fine, and we don't have time for this. Remember, we are here to kill the Shadow King. If he wants to help, let him. You don't have to speak to him."

She guided Vaughn away, returning him to his post. She turned her head to look back at Ivan, giving him an almost imperceptible nod that he returned.

Good girl, she heard.

The reds had launched their mission and now it was time for her to do the first part of her task. This one she knew she could do, the rest, she would see when the time came. Drake flew with her, about halfway from their post to the compound.

Siobhan was behind her, shielding them from view and would drop the shield at the last minute so it wouldn't block her blast. She rolled her shoulders and cracked her neck. She was ready.

She opened herself and began to draw in the energy. It was much easier than the first time. Now, it entered like a welcome friend; like it was water, and she was a desert begging for rain. Again, she could feel the hairs on her body standing tall, her hair floating, and Siobhan nudged her when her eyes went black. She could hear the arcing and crackling all over her as it gained more strength.

Remember, my love, you have to control the channel. Give it a finite lane, or it will drown you, came the reminder from Drake.

Bridget could only squeeze his neck with her legs to acknowledge. She needed to concentrate on her aim, so she didn't accidentally knock out power to the entire chain of islands. She was waiting for the signal that all of their side were clear. Suddenly, they heard the explosions that signaled Jack's team had started their diversion and Siobhan dropped their shield. Bridget grinned and then unleashed hell on the Shadow compound.

A huge wave slammed into the building and blew the front of the structure into pieces. Lightning came from the ground and surrounded the building in a blue haze, crackling and popping. The compound shimmied and shook, the sound of screaming filled the air. Then everything went quiet.

Bridget dropped her arms and closed the channel. It had been difficult; she wasn't sure she would be able to stop as the very air seemed to want more and began pulling it from her. She wrestled it under control. Breathing heavily, she shakily patted Drake on the neck, letting him know it was time to return.

He turned and began making the descent to the command post. His flight was jagged, though, and she could tell he was having trouble.

Drake? she asked, concerned.

I'm fine, he replied, *just a little drained. I need to get down and conserve my energy.* They landed roughly, and she jumped to the ground, followed by Siobhan. Vaughn shimmered into human and lay there on the ground, breathing hard.

She lifted his head to her lap and covered him as she whispered to him comfortingly.

Siobhan quickly examined him and said a few spells. She smiled at Bridget shakily and said, "He's okay, just magic drained. I can boost his recharge, and he will be better in about ten minutes or so."

Bridget breathed a sigh of relief and gestured for her to go on. She checked her watch. It would be cutting it close, but they were still doing okay on time. She sat with him while he absorbed energy and recharged his magical batteries.

He told her contact with the earth helped, so he stayed on the ground as they listened to the sounds of the battle continuing in front of them. Some of the Shadows were trying to shoot down the red dragons and were being bitten and slashed for their wasted efforts.

Many were opting to surrender to the silvers who were standing guard nearby.

Bridget heard a commotion and looked up. Jack, Davis, and Shepard were returning, and they had someone with them, but it wasn't Dio. It was a woman. She was very dirty and frail looking.

It's time, Bridget heard in her mind.

"Vaughn!" she said urgently.

His eyes snapped open, and he sat up, looking at her.

"Listen, we don't have a lot of time, so I need to tell you something quickly, and I need you to listen and not interrupt. Promise me!" she said.

"Of course, Bridget, what—"

She shushed him and began speaking rapidly.

"Your father didn't abandon us. He was ordered by Baltrus, the traitor, to leave, or he would kill you. He didn't want to risk it; he was torn about it. Baltrus bound him so he couldn't tell us. You remember, in Italy, after you proposed, and Jorrie and I went outside?"

He nodded, bewildered.

"Okay, well, she told me about it. See he couldn't tell you, he couldn't tell me, but he didn't say anything about Jorrie. She told me and swore me to secrecy. I know you may not believe it at first, I didn't either, but it is true. And here's the really hard part. Okay, whew. Vaughn, please forgive me. I didn't tell you any of this because I couldn't. If you knew, you'd never have waited and would have gone off angry, and this wouldn't have succeeded. It's been killing me not to tell you. But Vaughn..." She heard the thump as the diversion team landed behind him. She needed to talk faster.

"Vaughn, there's a reason your father isn't dead. It's because the bond was never broken. The Shadow King didn't kill your mother. It was an enchantment, a decoy. He's had her this whole time, suppressing her magic. The Council found out someone was dirty and helping him. That's why they kept your father prisoner, and that's why I couldn't tell you."

Vaughn stared at her, pain filling his eyes. "Why would you say these things to me?" he whispered.

"Because it's true, my love. Jack and the others found her for you. Look." She pointed behind him.

He turned his head and saw Jack limping towards him. He was ashen and covered in blood, but he held Mirra in his arms, who Bridget thought looked very much like Vaughn.

Vaughn tried to stand but dropped to his knees again. He shook his head, "No, it's not possible."

Mirra weakly turned her head as Jack dropped next to Vaughn and set her down gently. She stared at Vaughn and raised a hand to caress his face. "My son," she whispered and closed her eyes.

A broken roar echoed across the battlefield.

Bridget sat with Jack as Siobhan tended to his wounds. He winced as the deep gash on his side knitted together.

"Hold still you baby!" Siobhan told him.

He glared at her, "Ma'am, your bedside manner is atrocious."

She rolled her eyes and slapped his leg. "All better, now get out of here so I can tend to your boyfriend," she ordered.

Jack gave her a sarcastic salute and walked away with Bridget on his arm. "She's as prickly as a cactus," he told her.

Bridget laughed; relieved Jack wasn't too gravely injured. Then sobered.

He had quite a few cuts and bruises, and he'd been stabbed in his side, hence all the blood, but assured her the other guy looked worse. Davis had taken on a few cuts and bruises as well, but Shepard had been gravely injured.

A jagged tear in one wing and a broken leg in his dragon form had meant a broken arm and a massive knife wound from his shoulder down his side. In human form it would reach his waist. He'd lost a lot of blood, and it was a miracle he'd made it back at all. Siobhan had tended him first and now he was stabilized while Davis looked on, refusing to leave his brother's side. They would be sending him to the hospital shortly.

Dio had not returned. He had taken a knife to the heart meant for Jack.

Shepard had tried to bring the fallen wielder back, but he couldn't. Jack couldn't either, it was carry Dio or carry Mirra.

She pulled Jack to a stop and held him. "Thank you, brother, for taking that on. I know Vaughn appreciates it. Eventually, he will forgive us for keeping this from him and thank you himself."

Jack hugged her back and said, "Anything for you, sister, but you know you owe me in Dio's honor." He closed his eyes in pain from what he'd seen and whispered, "Dio."

Bridget and Circe stood together, ready to enact the next part of their plan. Circe was going to enhance Bridget's voice so it could be heard throughout the compound. Many more of the lower-level Shadow Claw had come out, surrendering, begging for refuge. They all claimed the King was still inside, and they'd only acted on his orders because he tortured those who defied him.

Mirra confirmed much of this as well. Her jailers were kind to her over the years unless they were caught by the King when he came down to taunt her. He'd taken her those years ago because he'd been struck by her beauty and wanted her for himself. She refused him, she had a mate and a son. She could never love someone as cruel as him. He wasn't a take no for an answer kind of guy.

Bridget smiled softly as she watched Ivan and Mirra reunite after so many years. Tears fell all around when they pulled Vaughn into their embrace. She hated Azrael even more now, but she couldn't afford to let that emotion distract her.

Chapter 47

"I CALL UPON THE Shadow King Azrael. I implore you to come out and end this violence. Meet with me. You have stolen something from us, but we have taken it back. We are tired of the bloodshed, the violence, and the killing. We offer you a trade. In exchange for you stopping your attacks upon the Wielders and Dragon kind, I will come with you willingly. I am the Wielder of Prophecy. I am the one you want, and I have something else you want as well. Come now and meet with me. You have five minutes to appear, or I will trigger the volcano beneath you and demolish this place." She motioned to the brown team who pushed energy into it, making it rumble in warning.

Bridget nodded at Circe; she was done. She hoped her appeal worked, and he took the bait. She knew what he wanted; she'd seen it in his mind when he grabbed her. She shuddered at the thought of him getting his hands on her. She waited there, Circe drifting back to the others, leaving her alone.

Bridget, Vaughn called to her, *what was that part about having something else he wanted? What do you mean?*

She was quiet for a moment and finally said, *because I do.* She heard growling behind her, and then he appeared next to her.

"What does that mean?" he demanded softly, taking her hand.

"It means we have an extra bargaining chip. I have something else he wants. How's your mother?" she asked.

"She's weak, but she will be okay. Bridget, I know you are trying to change the subject, but I do thank you for bringing her back to me. We need to have a little talk about secrets, but I can't tell you what it means. I love you so very much. Thank you." He kissed her.

"Well, isn't this a touching scene," she heard Azrael say with a sneer in his voice. Bridget and Vaughn turned to face him.

"Azrael, I welcome you, King of the Shadows," she said.

"Hmm, somehow I doubt I'm very welcome, but I'll take it for now," he drawled. He walked around Bridget and Vaughn, circling, appraising them. "My, my, how the little Drake has grown. I see you found mommy dearest and dear old dad, too. What a sweet reunion that must have been. But now, you have something much better. A yummier prize for me to take, isn't that right, Bridget dear."

Vaughn growled.

"Oh, come now, Drake, do be a good sport. After all, you took my trophy. I can't see a reason why I shouldn't take yours."

"Why?" Vaughn gritted through his clenched teeth. "Why are you so intent on killing us? We would have left you alone, we could have lived in peace. Why would you lead your own people to slaughter? What do you get out of it?"

Azrael laughed, a slightly unhinged sound. "Oh, silly dragon. Why not? Why be content with second place when you can rule the world?

Be Lord of all, making the silly regular humans worship me. You'd never let that happen. The Wielders and the Dragons, favorites of the gods. And for what? Just to wipe us all out like some experiment gone wrong? Never again. I won't be second or even third to you animals again. Animals, that's what you are. And the wielders who prostitute themselves to you just to enhance their elemental magic. It's disgusting. But not her." He looked Bridget up and down. "This one has pure power, light and energy, so much more than the rest of them. I'm willing to overlook the fact that you've been with this animal, and I can take his most precious possessions."

A shadow snaked up towards Bridget's throat. She flinched, and he pulled back.

"Oh yes, we mustn't damage the goods now, should we? After all, it needs a little more time to be done and I don't want you to shock me again. That hurt," he snapped at her. Then he resumed his drawling tone that set her teeth on edge. "So, tell me, dear Bridget, will you truly give both of your lives to me if I promise to leave little Drake and his friends alone?"

She nodded, unable to speak. She saw Vaughn looking at her from the corner of her eye, confusion clearly on his face.

Azrael noticed it as well. "Oh, this is just too delicious. He doesn't even know what he's giving up, does he? I cannot wait to tell him. No, better, Bridget dear, you tell him. So it hurts him more when I take it." He turned her to face Vaughn, then clapped like a child at the circus.

Bridget took a deep breath, looked up at the sky and counted down. *30, 29, 28.* She smiled at him. "Vaughn, I love you with all of my heart.

I can't wait to spend the rest of our lives together." She turned back to Azrael.

"No!" he yelled, "That's not what you are supposed to say!"

She stepped closer to him. *15,14,13.*

"Azrael, have I told you what a stupid name that is, like really, Angel of Death? Giant ego much? And seriously, why do bad guys always have to monologue? It's so cliché. It always happens. They start talking and don't realize they're wasting time. Although I guess it does serve its purpose. Allowing us time to set things up."

She watched the shadows getting rapidly smaller and turned back to Vaughn, *5,4,3,* "Before I end him, would you like to at least get in one good punch?" *2,1.*

He saw the shadows around the man disappear completely and broke into a feral grin, "With pleasure." He advanced on the Shadow King.

Azrael laughed. "Nice try, but you can't touch me. I'll just do this." He stood there. Nothing happened.

Bridget clapped slowly. "Nice job, really, standing like a statue? Great likeness, but you talk too much. Vaughn?"

Vaughn threw all of his weight into smashing Azrael's face with his fist. The Shadow King dropped like a sack of wet oatmeal. Vaughn smiled at Bridget, "Yeah, that felt really good."

"Be a dear and get him back on his feet for me. I need him standing," she told him.

Vaughn dragged Azrael to his feet, where he stood, wobbling under the sun directly overhead. Bridget turned her face up to the sky and inhaled deeply, feeling the light filling her up. She looked back at Azrael who was staring at her warily.

"What have you done?" he asked.

"Who me? Nothing yet. It's what I'm *about* to do. Because you can't run from me anymore. It's called Lahaina Noon, Angel of Death." She waited until the information clicked.

Lahaina Noon. The celestial event that took place around the summer solstice in a few sites on Earth when the sun's path took it directly over the planet. For a few minutes, the sun's rays beat straight down instead of their usual forty-five-degree angle. During this time, there were no shadows. A neat science trick for the kids, but for the Dragons and Wielders it was a perfect opportunity to render a shadow harmless.

"And now, you asshole, it's time for your reign to end." Bridget reached for him as he tried to run, but Vaughn grabbed him and stopped him in his tracks.

"You can zap me all you want," Azrael screamed, spittle flying. He was enraged at being played so easily, "But your sparky act won't kill me!"

She merely laughed and put her hand on his forehead, "I'm not going to zap you, but you know what does kill shadows?" She leaned in closely. "Light." Bridget focused on the darkness in him and let the light of her magic flow from her body to his.

He stared at her for a moment, not understanding, but then sensed it in his feet, his legs.

She was filling him with light and burning him up from within. Scorching and scarring every surface so he could no longer reach his dark magic.

He screamed and cried out, begging her to stop, straining against Vaughn's grip.

She did not stop. The light quickly reached his stomach and his chest, and then it faltered. His heart was so black it resisted her efforts. She closed her eyes and concentrated, pouring more light into him. She shook and trembled with the enormous effort.

It will be alright, my daughter, I promise. She felt the cold wind and heard the rustling of dry leaves.

Bridget groaned with the strain and kept pushing the light deeper into the Shadow King's core. Sweat poured from her. A small stream of magic rose within and enhanced her efforts. She placed a hand quickly over her stomach to acknowledge it, then back on his chest. She pushed the light past his heart and into his neck. She began to weaken, then rebounded as hands rested on her back. It was Vaughn, then Jack, Siobhan, and Liam. They had all come to her as well. Her family. She opened as their energy flowed into her. She made them more. She looked around then and saw they were surrounded by all of the warriors who had come to fight that day and smiled as their will and magic flowed into her.

She shouted a warrior's cry, shoving the last bit of her will into Azrael's body, and fulfilling a promise to her family, ground through her teeth, "This is for Brian, Brady, Joanna, and everyone else you've harmed." Finally, her arms dropped, and she smiled before collapsing to her knees. She put her hands on the ground in front of her, breathing heavily. She heard Azrael screaming.

Lahaina Noon had passed. He had a shadow again, but he could no longer use it.

He lunged at her, but Vaughn caught him by the throat and lifted him from the ground. He laughed and said, "I've been waiting a long time for this." He threw Azrael into the air using his dragon strength, shouting, "Jack!" a second before he transformed into a dragon and launched himself at the man.

Jack pulled Bridget's face to his chest so she wouldn't see, but she heard the loud screech and crunch as Vaughn ripped his body to shreds the way he'd vowed all those years ago.

She shuddered in relief and promptly passed out.

CHAPTER 48

BRIDGET WOKE TO THE gentle sounds of the ocean lapping at the sand outside the window, the breeze blowing across her face. "Ugh," she moaned. "What is it with me passing out and waking up in strange beds?"

She heard Vaughn chuckle. He leaned over her before saying, "I don't know, but you should stop doing that, especially the strange beds part."

She smiled, pulling him down for a kiss. "Is it done?" she whispered. "Is it truly over?"

He nodded and brushed her hair from her forehead. "Yes, my love, it's over. And now, is there anything else you need to tell me? Any more secrets?"

She flinched, and his eyes narrowed, "Bridget!" A warning note in his voice.

It's okay, my daughter, now. She heard the whisper.

She sighed, *thank you, but someday soon you're going to explain this my daughter thing to me, because you are not my father.* She heard a chuckle as it faded away.

"Bridget?" came Vaughn's worried voice.

She gestured that she wanted to sit up. He helped her and then sat next to her. She took his hands in hers. "Vaughn, I couldn't tell you sooner because of the same reasons we didn't tell you about your mother. I knew you would never have let me do what needed to be done." She eyed him warily and took a deep, fortifying breath, then let it out.

"Vaughn, how could you not have figured it out already?" She shook her head sighing. "I mean, good grief, there were so many clues and signs. I thought for sure, any minute now, he's going to figure it out. Jack figured it out."

Vaughn frowned at her in confusion.

She laughed, cupping his face. "My love, you silly man, I'm pregnant." She watched his eyes glaze over and was scared he was the one about to pass out.

Vaughn was sure he was dreaming. He thought Bridget had just said she was pregnant. And now he was sure she was getting worried because he wasn't saying anything. He reached out a shaking hand, placed it on her stomach and closed his eyes. He searched with his mind and found it, faintly, a little pulse of magic and fire.

He opened his eyes, "Bridget, our baby is going to be so fierce. We're going to have to teach her not to set things on fire." His eyes filled with tears as he pulled her to him. "Our baby."

They held each other that way for a long time and watched the shadows play in the trees outside, no longer afraid of what might be in them.

Their arrival home was much celebrated. Some had gone home to heal their wounds and, mourn their losses, start rebuilding. Many came back to Dallas to revel in the sense of freedom from the end of the Shadow rule. In total, they had lost Dio, one brown dragon from Germany, and two red wielders from Russia.

The Shadows lost many more.

The remaining Shadows had all surrendered and begged for asylum. Many had asked to have their power removed as well to prove their sincerity. Bridget wasn't able to do any more currently, being so drained, and she knew Vaughn would never agree to it while she was carrying his child.

It was agreed that they would keep their powers, but they were placed under a magical restraint that Siobhan had worked out with Lorenzo, the red dragon from Italy, to ensure they didn't use their powers for evil. Many wanted to learn to work with the dragons and wielders, to use their powers to right some of the wrongs done by their King.

The ones who refused and sought to continue the work of the previous regime? They were handled.

Bridget hated the idea of more death but remembered the pain they had caused her family and knew they couldn't be allowed to do that to others. The dragon world was sometimes a brutal one. But as she watched Vaughn laughing with his friends, she knew she didn't ever want to leave it.

Vaughn caught her eye and joined her on the couch where she had been safely ensconced with her feet propped up the second they walked in the door. A table full of snacks and drinks was within easy reach. A pile of books at her elbow. He sat gingerly like he was scared to break her.

She laughed, "You know, I'm pregnant, not sick."

He smiled and touched her stomach tenderly. "I'm not taking any chances with the two most precious things in my hoard."

Jack flopped down in a chair across from them, still wincing a little from his injuries. "Oh, so Papa Drake knows now, does he? Good, that was a helluva secret Bridge, you know I hate that."

Vaughn's gaze narrowed on him, "Yes, Jack, how is it that you knew?"

Jack rolled his eyes. "I was there when she was pregnant with Gabriel. I know her tells."

Bridget laughed, "Yeah, that bag Jack gave me on the plane? It wasn't just medicine. It was also gummy bears and a pregnancy test. I didn't want to believe it at first, but I took it anyway to prove him wrong. He wasn't. I craved gummy bears like crazy when I was pregnant with Gabe." She looked around, "Speaking of."

Vaughn looked panicked and started patting his pockets for his keys, ready to run out and buy a whole store's worth if she wanted.

Jack laughed and said, "I got you covered." He threw a bag to Bridget, who immediately tore into it. Just then, Jorrie walked into the room and stopped dead in her tracks.

"Bridget, are you okay?"

Her friend nodded, "Yeah, just a little worn out from all of the traveling."

Jack waved his hand, "Hello! Injured over here, how about a little sympathy for me?"

Jorrie laughed and sat on Jack's lap, kissing his cheek, "My handsome hero!" She looked over at Bridget, digging through the bag of candy and narrowed her eyes. "Damn, Bridge, I haven't seen you tear into gummy bears like that since—"

Jack shouted, "Cover your ears!" just in time for Jorrie to jump up and squeal her signature eardrum-shattering shriek.

"*Bridge!*" her friend shouted. "No fucking way!" and wrapped her friend in a tight hug before jumping up and down and dancing.

Vaughn watched her in amusement and said, "Hey, watch your mouth. There are children present."

They were still laughing when Gabe walked in, "Jeez, Aunt Jorrie, what the hell?"

They all smiled at him, and Bridget told him, "Well, baby, how do you feel about being a big brother."

Gabe froze and looked at her, then Vaughn, who nodded and stood. Gabriel walked over and shook his hand, then wrapped him in a hug. "I'm going to be the best damn brother ever," he whispered.

Later in the evening, Bridget smiled as she saw Jorrie and Liam sitting in the corner, making out like a couple of teenagers. Apparently, they were way past the scratching the itch phase.

Vaughn and Killian were making plans to help the families that had lost loved ones and set up services for them. They would need to get back in and find Dio and the other fallen fighters.

Siobhan and Lorenzo were sitting in another corner, laughing and talking in a way that made Bridget think there was a spark there. She looked for Marco and saw him leaning against a wall, watching Siobhan, sadness on his face. Well, not everyone got a happy ending, she thought.

She rubbed her stomach, amazed she was getting another chance at a larger family. She and Brian had tried and tried after Gabriel, but it seemed they were only destined for one. Then she'd lost Brian. She'd been so devastated she didn't realize she was also mourning the loss of any future children.

Bridget eased out the front door and went up to the roof. She made it to the terrace area and sat in one of the chairs, watching the sun setting. Golden rays pierced the soft clouds drifting lazily across the horizon.

She heard the rustle of leaves and felt a cold breeze again, the same when she heard the call to come up here. She smiled, "Okay, Tar'n, I'm here. What do you want?"

He chuckled and sat across from her, his hood shaking with amusement. "Well done, my daughter, you succeeded where others would have failed. I am pleased with you."

She sighed, "Cut the crap. Who are you really, and why do you keep calling me your daughter?"

He roared out a laugh and dropped his hood back from his face. Across from her was a startlingly young, handsome man with long golden hair and fair skin. He had bright blue eyes that sparkled, actually sparkled. Gone was the whispery, mysterious air, replaced by an impish grin and an air of power.

She stared. "What the fuck?"

He shook with laughter, "Shh!" he cautioned, "Your young lady is listening."

She clasped her hands protectively over her stomach. "It *is* a girl?" she asked breathlessly. "Vaughn said that, but I wasn't sure. It's still so early."

He nodded, "She is special, and she will be feisty like her parents. She will wield magic of pure light and will bring about a new era of dragon-kind."

Bridget nodded, "Okay. I need to fireproof my home, don't I?"

He winked at her and stood, strolling to the open area.

"Wait!" she called and ran to him, "What about this 'my daughter' stuff? Is that some creepy father of the species thing, or what is that?"

He smiled and brushed her hair from her face. "You are not my actual daughter, no, but you are descended of my followers from long ago. I'm so proud of you and all of them. My children are especially gifted. But I think it's time I go back home now. I've been on this plane too long."

Bridget stared, "You're Taranis, aren't you, God of Light and Thunder."

He tapped her on the nose and smiled.

"Bridget?" she heard and turned to see Vaughn coming up behind her. "There you are. What are you doing up..."

He trailed off, seeing the man standing there with her. "Tar'n?" he asked uncertainly, startled by the man's youthful appearance and the fact that no one in living memory had ever seen his face.

Taranis smiled again and winked. "You two are my favorites of all my children, you really are. I'll be watching you."

He turned and walked to the center of the clearing, swirled around, transforming instantly into the large white and gold dragon. There'd been no shimmer or building of power. It was like a finger snap. His scales shifted to gray, then a light blue, then back to white as he preened a long golden talon. He bowed his massive head, then took off, flying straight towards the last rays of the setting sun. Suddenly, he was gone.

Vaughn looked at Bridget. "Okay, please explain that."

She kissed him and drew him to a chair, then took a deep breath and told him about Taranis, his role in everything and how he'd guided her hand in so many things.

He sighed, "Well, he seems to like you, so maybe we can call on him some day and ask him for help to finish tracking down the last of the Shadows."

She looked up at him. "There's still some out there?"

He nodded, "The ones who weren't at the compound. A few high-ranking lieutenants, some minor muscle based on what those who have surrendered have shared. But we will get them all, my love. They won't hurt us anymore."

She sighed, "You have to go back to that awful place, don't you?"

Vaughn gently placed his palm on her cheek. "We need to find our fallen warriors so we can take them home to their families. And gather any intelligence they had— there may be worse things out there waiting to step in, Bridget. Nature abhors a vacuum, and with Azrael gone, someone else may get ambitious."

She placed a protective hand over her daughter. "Make it safe for her, Vaughn."

He leaned down and kissed her still flat stomach, "What are we going to name our little sunbeam?"

They leaned their heads together and watched until the last bit of light dropped below the horizon.

Thank you for reading Lahaina Noon.

(I hope you enjoyed reading it as much as I loved writing it.)

Every review matters, and it matters a *lot!*
Head over to Amazon or wherever you purchased this book to leave a
review for me.
The Dragons and I thank you endlessly.

Read More!

If you're like me, you get invested in characters and want to know what happens after the last page. Head over to my website to subscribe to my newsletter to be the first to know when the next book in the series will be released. Who knows, I may give you a sneak peek at it!

www.tristaricketts.com
Book 1: Lahaina Noon
Book 2: Circles in the Sand